SHARPEST
Sting

AN ELEMENTAL ASSASSIN BOOK

JENNIFER ESTEP

Sharpest Sting

This is a work of fiction. Names, characters, places, brands, media, and incidents are either the product of the author's imagination or are used fictitiously. Any resemblance to actual or fictional characters or actual or fictional events, locales, business establishments, or persons, living or dead, is entirely coincidental. The fictional characters, events, locales, business establishments, or persons in this story have no relation to any other fictional characters, events, locales, business establishments, or persons, except those in works by this author.

Print book ISBN: 978-1-950076-02-4
eBook ISBN: 978-1-950076-01-7

Interior Formatting by Author E.M.S.

Fonts: *CCAltogether Ooky* and *CCAltogether Ooky Capitals* by Active Images, used under Standard License; *Times New Roman* by Monotype Typography, used under Desktop License; *Trajan Pro* by Carol Twombly/Adobe Systems Inc., used under EULA.

Published in the United States of America

THE ELEMENTAL ASSASSIN SERIES

FEATURING GIN BLANCO

Books

Spider's Bite

Web of Lies

Venom

Tangled Threads

Spider's Revenge

By a Thread

Widow's Web

Deadly Sting

Heart of Venom

The Spider

Poison Promise

Black Widow

Spider's Trap

Bitter Bite

Unraveled

Snared

Venom in the Veins

Sharpest Sting

E-novellas

Thread of Death

Parlor Tricks (from the Carniepunk anthology)

Kiss of Venom

Unwanted

Nice Guys Bite

Winter's Web

Sharpest Sting

AN ELEMENTAL ASSASSIN BOOK

JENNIFER ESTEP

To all the fans of the Elemental Assassin series who wanted more stories, this one is for you.

To my mom and my grandma—for everything.

✲ 1 ✲

"I didn't think our date night would end up *here*."

I looked over at Owen Grayson, my significant other. "I thought you were looking forward to our quiet time," I said. "You, me, together in the dark, having a nice romantic interlude."

"Oh, you and me together in the dark is one of my favorite things." Owen's voice took on a low, husky note that sent chills racing down my spine, and a sexy grin slowly curved his lips.

The moonlight streaming in through the windshield frosted the tips of Owen's black hair, bringing out the blue sheen in the thick locks, and added a soft, silvery tint to his face, as though he was made of polished marble instead of flesh and blood. Violet eyes, a slightly crooked nose, a white scar that cut across his chin. The small imperfections gave Owen a rough, rugged vibe that only made him that much more handsome to me.

Even better, his minor flaws, both physical and otherwise, fit together perfectly with my own many sins and much deeper faults. Sometimes I thought we were like two pieces of a jigsaw puzzle that had snapped together, despite the small odds of us ever finding each other.

"Oh, yeah. You and me together in the dark is always great." His grin slowly faded away. "It's the location that concerns me."

Several minutes ago, Owen had pulled his car over to the side of the twisty mountain road. In the distance, a large sign gleamed in the moonlight, the letters spelling out a familiar name: *Blue Ridge Cemetery.*

"Don't get me wrong. I always love spending time with you, Gin."

I arched an eyebrow. "But?"

"But when you suggested a date night, I was hoping for something warm and cozy. You, me, a roaring fire, some good food, maybe a nice bottle of wine."

"We already had some good food," I said. "Or have you forgotten about the rehearsal dinner already?"

We had spent the last three hours at the Five Oaks Country Club. Our friends Mallory Parker and Stuart Mosley were getting married in a few days, and Owen was a groomsman, while I was a bridesmaid. After running through the ceremony, Mallory and Stuart had treated the wedding party to a private dinner at the club.

Grilled chicken kebabs served with a warm fig dipping sauce. Filet mignon sliders slathered with tangy blue-cheese mayonnaise. Crispy spring rolls filled with sweet-and-sour carrots, cabbage, and other veggies. And those had just been the appetizers. The main course had been roasted, apricot-glazed turkey with apple-sage dressing and mashed potatoes. For dessert, we had enjoyed a decadent pear bread pudding drizzled with warm caramel sauce and topped with vanilla-bean ice cream. The food had been absolutely delicious, and the company of our friends even better.

"The rehearsal dinner was great." Another sly grin curved Owen's lips. "But I was looking forward to having a nightcap at your place."

I rolled my eyes. "You've been hanging around Finn too long. That cheesy line sounds like something he would say."

Finnegan Lane was my foster brother and had been a shameless flirt until he'd gotten involved with Detective Bria Coolidge, my baby sister. Finn still liked to flirt, but everyone knew his heart belonged to Bria.

"You can't blame a guy for trying," Owen replied. "Either way, I was hoping for something a little less…"

"Dark, dirty, and dangerous?"

"Yeah."

I didn't begrudge Owen his dreams of a more typical date night. I would much rather have been curled up somewhere warm and cozy with him, instead of sitting in his car, slowly freezing in the dark.

But I was Gin Blanco, the supposed queen of the Ashland underworld, and this was my life, like it or not.

"What do you think?" Owen asked, looking through the windshield. "Are we clear?"

I checked the time on my phone. Ten minutes had passed since we'd stopped and Owen had stuck a plastic bag in the driver's-side window, as though we were having engine trouble. Owen and I had been waiting to see if we were being followed, but not a single vehicle had zoomed by. Most people didn't like visiting cemeteries in the daylight, much less on a cold winter's night.

I peered into the woods that flanked both sides of the road, but nothing moved in the shadows, and I didn't see any human-size shapes lurking farther back in the trees. "We're clear."

We got out of the car. Owen popped the trunk, and we

each grabbed a thin black vest, along with a pair of heavy-duty black coveralls. Owen put his vest and coveralls on over his navy suit. I ditched my heels, zipped my vest and then the coveralls up over my royal-blue pantsuit, and shoved my feet into a pair of socks and then boots. We both pulled black toboggans down over our hair, completing our transformation from normal folks out for a night on the town to a couple of cat burglars up to no good.

Then again, as the assassin the Spider, I was almost always up to no good.

"You ready?" Owen also grabbed two shovels out of the trunk.

"Yeah. But why are you suddenly so eager to get on with our mission?"

Owen grinned, his eyes glimmering like amethysts in the moonlight. "Because I still have hopes for that fire, food, and wine tonight."

I snorted. "I'm starting to think *fire, food, and wine* is code for *sexy times*."

"*Sexy times*? Now you sound like Eva." His grin widened. "Although my sister does have a way with words."

I crinkled my nose. "You are totally ruining your attempt at suave, seductive charm by bringing up your baby sister."

"Well, then, I'll have to try harder and make it up to you later."

"Promise?" I teased.

"Promise." His low, husky voice sent more chills down my spine.

Owen reached out, grabbed my hand, and pressed a kiss to my knuckles. The heat of his skin soaked into mine, and those chills pleasantly zipping through my body settled in my stomach and spread out, turning into warm waves of anticipation.

Owen released my hand and straightened. “After all,” he murmured, another mischievous grin spreading across his face, “this humble blacksmith does so love to please his pirate queen assassin.”

I groaned. “Don’t remind me about the renaissance faire.”

A couple of weeks ago, Owen and I had attended the Winter’s Web Renaissance Faire in Riverfront Park. What had started as a fun, innocent event had quickly spiraled into a dangerous confrontation, with Owen getting kidnapped and both of us almost dying at the hands of Darrell Kline, a greedy, disgruntled accountant who had wanted to steal everything from Owen.

“Look on the bright side,” he rumbled. “At least we won’t run into any costumed characters with swords tonight.”

“No, but we might run into Hugh Tucker and some Circle goons instead.”

The muttered words slipped out before I could stop them. Owen’s grin vanished, and a troubled look filled his face.

I grimaced. *Way to kill the mood, Gin.*

Hugh Tucker was my personal nemesis, a smart, cunning vampire who worked for the Circle, a secret society responsible for much of the crime and corruption in Ashland. For the last few months, I had been investigating and slowly killing my way through the Circle ranks, trying to find the group’s leader, the person who had sent Fire elemental Mab Monroe to murder my mother and my older sister. A few weeks ago, I’d finally found that leader, the head of the monstrous hydra, as it were.

My uncle Mason.

The revelation had come as an absolute *shock*, like lightning striking my head, a knife plunging into my back, and a bomb exploding underneath my feet all at once. I'd known that my mother, Eira Snow, had been a member of the Circle, but I hadn't realized that my father, Tristan, had also been part of the group. My father had supposedly died in a car accident when I was a kid, so I didn't remember much about him, and I knew nothing about his family.

I had certainly never *dreamed* that his brother, my uncle, was the root cause of so much pain, misery, and suffering in my life. But now that I'd found out about Uncle Mason, I was determined to kill him.

"Gin? Are you okay?"

Owen kept staring at me, that troubled look still on his face, so I forced myself to smile as though nothing was wrong.

"You're right. We won't run into any costumed characters tonight, which is a definite plus after what happened at the ren faire. So let's go."

"Why the sudden hurry?" he asked.

I leaned over and kissed his cheek. I breathed in his rich, metallic scent, then drew back. "You're not the only one looking forward to *fire, food, and wine* tonight. The sooner we leave here, the sooner we can get there."

"Work first, nightcap later?" Owen teased me again. "That could be your new motto as the Spider."

"When it comes to you and me?" This time, my smile was completely genuine. "Definitely."

I shut the trunk, while Owen hefted the two shovels up onto his shoulder. Together, we left the car and headed into the trees.

I took the lead, slipping through the shadows and scanning the surrounding woods, with Owen creeping along behind me. It was just after nine o'clock on this clear February night, and the luminous full moon and pinprick stars brightened the landscape, as did the crusty patches of snow and ice that still dappled the ground from the most recent winter storm. The woods were utterly still and quiet, and not so much as a breeze rattled the tree branches.

The silence should have reassured me, but a frosty finger of unease slid down my spine, even colder than the night air, and I palmed one of the knives hidden up my sleeves. The mark stamped in the silverstone hilt pressed into the larger, matching scar embedded in my palm—each of them a small circle surrounded by eight thin rays. A spider rune, the symbol for patience.

A pendant shaped like a spider rune hung from a chain around my neck, and the symbol was also stamped into the ring on my right index finger. My Ice magic rippled through both pieces of silverstone jewelry.

Normally, the cool touch of the jewelry on my skin and the solid strength of my knife in my hand would have comforted me but not right now. Or perhaps my continued unease was caused by our destination, along with our mission. I scanned the landscape again, but I only saw the same trees, ice, and shadows as before. The woods seemed to be completely empty, and even the owls, squirrels, and other animals had vanished for the night.

A few minutes later, we reached the edge of the woods. Owen stopped beside me, and we peered out at the area before us.

Blue Ridge Cemetery.

The moon- and starlight clearly illuminated the cemetery, which spread out for acres. An uneven carpet of dull brown winter grass rose and fell with the hills and ridges that creased the land like wrinkles grooved into an elderly dwarf's face. Tombstones of all shapes and sizes dotted the ground, from square slabs to Celtic crosses to tall, elegant spires topped with wings and other symbols. A few trees rose up here and there, their bare branches hanging over and casting long, bony, fingerlike shadows onto the tombstones below. The shadows filled in many of the names and dates carved into the markers, making the old weathered letters and numbers look like they had just been stamped on the stones in thick, wet black ink.

Most people would have been creeped out to be in the cemetery at night, but I had an extra reason to be uncomfortable: I could hear the tombstones' wails.

Love, hate, anger, grief, rage, despair. Over time, people's feelings sink into whatever stone is around them, and few places conjured up more deep, wild, varying emotions than a cemetery. As a Stone elemental, my magic let me hear the soft sobs and bitter, plaintive wails of everyone who had grieved for loved ones, as well as the sly, smug murmurs of happiness from those who had been delighted to see the deceased go into the ground. The sorrow and the satisfaction made for an odd, disturbing, disparate chorus, and the incessant screeching between the two factions caused a dull headache to bloom in the back of my skull.

"Gin?" Owen asked. "Are you okay?"

I blocked out the stones' cries as best I could and scanned the grounds again, but I didn't see anyone lurking behind a tree or crouched beside a tombstone. "Yeah. Let's go."

We left the woods and went over to a gray stone path that curled through the grass like a dull, tattered ribbon.

Owen and I followed the winding walkway for about three hundred feet before stepping off the path and climbing up one of the hills. We stopped atop a ridge that featured a massive maple looming over five graves, each one marked with its own separate tombstone. Another, much larger stone statue shaped like a snowflake was set into the ground above and behind the tombstones, denoting this as a family plot.

The tombstones represented the five members of the Snow family—my mother, Eira; my older sister, Annabella; my younger sister, Bria; and myself, Genevieve Snow. Of course, Bria and I were still alive, although, sadly, the rest of our family was very much dead, thanks to Mab Monroe and Uncle Mason.

Owen rested his hand on my shoulder, letting me know he was there if I wanted to talk. I flashed him a grateful smile and squeezed his hand. Then I moved over to the fifth and final marker—the one for my father, Tristan.

His tombstone was the oldest and most weather-worn, and I crouched down and yanked off the dead kudzu vines that had snaked across the stone. It didn't take me long to get rid of the frozen, brittle tendrils and reveal the writing underneath.

Tristan. Beloved Husband and Father.

The words flowed across the stone in a simple script, along with the dates of his birth, June 2, and death, March 24, and the corresponding years. I pulled my phone out of my pocket and snapped some photos of the tombstone, zooming in and focusing on the dates. Then I texted the photos to Bria, and also to Silvio Sanchez, my personal assistant.

My sister had left the rehearsal dinner early to work a shift at the police station, so she didn't respond, although my phone chimed with a new text from my trusty assistant less than a minute later.

Got them. Starting work right now! ☺

"Silvio?" Owen asked in an amused voice.

I tucked my phone back into my pocket. "Yep. There is something seriously wrong with that man. No one should be that eager to work, especially not this late."

Silvio had also been at the rehearsal dinner, and I had told him where Owen and I were coming afterward. My vampire assistant had an annoying habit of tracking my phone and car, so it was just easier to tell him what I was up to rather than trying to keep it a secret. Silvio had made me promise to send him what was on Tristan's tombstone so he could start digging up info on my father and see if he could find any clues that would lead me to Mason.

My mother had claimed that my father died in a car accident, although I doubted that was true. No, I had a sneaking suspicion the Circle was behind Tristan's death, just as the group had been behind my mother's and Annabella's murders.

Perhaps Tristan hadn't liked being under his brother's thumb and the two of them had some falling-out that led to Mason eliminating my father. Then, later on, Mason had ordered my mother to be killed when he learned that she was planning to expose the Circle. At least, that was what I thought Eira had been planning. So much of this was still just hunches and guesswork on my part.

I'd come here hoping to get some answers, but the information on Tristan's tombstone didn't tell me anything new. Frustration flooded my stomach, curdling the fine dinner I'd eaten earlier. Owen was wrong. My motto as the Spider should be *More Questions*, because that was all I ever seemed to get regarding my parents and Mason.

Owen slung the shovels off his shoulder and crouched down beside me. "I never realized it until right now, but you've never told me your father's last name."

"That's because I don't know what it is."

He frowned. "Why not?"

"My father died when I was five, so I barely remember him. Ever since we discovered that Mason is the head of the Circle, I've been thinking back, trying to remember every little thing I can about my father. But Tristan is just this vague, hazy image in my mind—a nice smile, a warm laugh, a pair of gray eyes like mine." I shook my head. "I don't know if that image is real or simply what I want him to be."

"And Mason?"

I shook my head again. "Nothing. I draw a total blank when it comes to him. I don't remember anything about my father's family. I always assumed Tristan didn't have any family, but of course, now I know that's not the case. But no matter how hard I try, I haven't been able to remember anything helpful about Tristan, not even his last name."

Owen pointed to my mother's marker. "But Snow is your mother's last name, and yours too. Not your father's."

"I was hoping Tristan's last name would be on his tombstone, but it's not."

"Maybe your father decided to use your mother's last name," Owen said. "Maybe he didn't want anything to do with Mason, not even something as simple as sharing the same surname."

"That's what I think too. That Tristan was so disgusted with Mason and the Circle that he disowned himself from their family."

At least, that was what I hoped. I didn't want to contemplate the idea that my father might have been just as evil and horrible as Mason was.

"Well, Silvio is working on it now, and if anyone can figure out my father's last name and where Mason is hiding, then it's him. But we have another mission."

Owen lifted the shovels and tapped them point-first against the ground. "Are you sure you want to do this? We don't have to. I know how hard this is."

"I appreciate that, but we need more information about the Circle, and this is the only place I can think of where Fletcher might have hidden it. Even Silvio hasn't been able to crack all the codes in that Circle ledger, and we're running out of time to decrypt the info before Mason and Tucker target us again."

A few weeks ago, during an auction of items from Mab Monroe's estate, I had stumbled across what seemed to be a blue book of Circle secrets. Hugh Tucker had been after the ledger, as had Alanna Eaton, a vampire cannibal. That book had turned out to be a decoy, but I had still ended up with the genuine item. Fletcher Lane, Finn's dad and my assassin mentor, had given the real ledger to Stuart Mosley for safekeeping years ago, but Fletcher had never gotten a chance to tell Mosley what to do with the tome.

But perhaps the most surprising thing was the fact that my mother had written the book.

I had recognized her handwriting immediately, and Silvio and I had been working to decode the contents ever since. My mother had been some sort of accountant or bookkeeper for the Circle, and the blue ledger chronicled assassinations, kidnappings, and other crimes the group had committed, orchestrated, and profited from, as well as bribes and payments they had doled out to various people.

Silvio was still trying to crack the last few bits of code, but the ledger hadn't been quite the smoking gun I was hoping for. Sure, it cataloged some of the Circle's dirty deeds, but most of the crimes were more than twenty years old, and many of the people associated with them were long dead. I wanted—*needed*—more information about the Circle's past plots, as well as what its members had been up to in recent years, so I'd come to the cemetery to try to get it.

"Do you really think Fletcher knew how Tristan was connected to the Circle?" Owen asked. "And that Fletcher left something here for you to find? Buried in your father's grave?"

I shrugged. "If anyone knew about Tristan and Mason, then it was Fletcher. Besides, the old man seemed to know everything else about the Circle."

Owen tapped the shovels against the ground again, still unsure. I didn't blame him. I didn't want to dig up my father's grave, but Fletcher had left me information in this cemetery before, and it was the only place I hadn't checked yet.

Owen shifted his stance, and a bit of moonlight slid past his body and hit the tombstone, illuminating a small dark spot in the lower right-hand corner. I scooted forward and leaned down to get a better look at it.

"Find something?" he asked.

"I'm not sure."

The spot was right above the grass, and I wouldn't have noticed it if I hadn't cleared away the dead vines. I yanked up a tuft of grass and tossed it aside, then leaned down lower so that I could get an even better look. It wasn't a spot at all but rather a rune that had been carved into the tombstone.

And not just any rune—a small circle surrounded by thin rays. My spider rune.

"Fletcher," I whispered.

I traced my fingers over the rune. Unlike the name and dates on the tombstone, which were neat and smooth and had obviously been done by a carver with professional equipment, this symbol looked thin and jagged, as though it had been crudely scratched into the stone with a blade meant for something else—like an assassin's knife.

I stared at the knife in my hand, then dug the point into the stone and drew a short line with the blade. My gaze snapped back and forth between my mark and the rune already on the tombstone. They matched exactly.

"Fletcher," I whispered again. "You sly fox."

The old man had once again left me a clue from beyond the grave. My heart lifted, excitement zipped through me, and I surged to my feet and turned to grab one of the shovels from Owen. To my surprise, he was also on his feet, frowning and looking off into the distance.

"Something wrong?"

He stabbed his finger toward the bottom of the hill. "There's a freshly dug grave down there."

"So what? This is a cemetery."

Owen shook his head. "So there are no flowers on it. And look where that grave is. I know that spot, Gin, and so do you."

I peered in that direction. A grave had been recently dug at the bottom of the hill not too far away from where we were. No flowers were strewn across the turned earth, and no funeral wreaths were propped up on metal stands. But what made my heart sink was the grave's location. Owen was right. I knew that spot all too well.

"That's Fletcher's grave." Shock blasted through me, but it was quickly drowned out by sick understanding. "Someone dug up Fletcher's grave."

"Who would do that?" Owen asked. "And why?"

It took me a moment to force the words out past the hard knot of emotion clogging my throat. "Because they were looking for clues, just like we were. They must have thought there was something in Fletcher's grave—or his casket—worth stealing."

Owen's eyes narrowed in understanding. "Like a blue ledger full of Circle secrets?"

"Yeah."

I kept staring at the grave, not wanting to believe that someone had been so cruel as to disturb Fletcher's final resting place, even though I was here to do the same thing to my father.

Then my assassin training kicked in, and I realized how much danger we were in. Not only had the grave been freshly dug, but a couple of shovels were propped up against Fletcher's tombstone.

"We need to get out of here," I told Owen. "Right now. Before whoever dug up that grave comes back—"

It was as if my whispered words made the very worst possible thing happen. Footsteps crunched on the frosty grass, and two giants rounded a tree and stepped into view at the bottom of the hill, heading straight for Fletcher's grave.

✲ 2 ✲

Owen and I both froze like two deer caught in the harsh glare of unexpected headlights on a dark, deserted country road.

Then I grabbed his arm and yanked him back, tugging him behind the large snowflake statue that marked my family's graves. The sharp motion pulled Owen off-balance, and he lost his grip on the two shovels, which *thump-thumped* to the ground.

I grimaced at the unwanted noise, but I hunkered down behind the statue with Owen beside me. The seconds ticked by, and I strained to listen, but I couldn't hear anything above the pounding roar of my heart and Owen's quick breaths rasping in my ear. Maybe, just maybe, the giants hadn't heard the shovels hit the ground, and they would go on about their business without realizing that we were here—

"Hey, Wynn. Did you hear that?" one of the giants called out.

"Yeah. I think it came from the top of the hill," the second man responded. "C'mon, Vance. Let's check it out."

So not only had the giants and I picked the exact same time to dig up graves, but now they were coming to investigate the noise Owen had made. I bit back a curse. Lady Luck was really screwing me over tonight. But I couldn't track what I couldn't see, so I scooted forward and peered around the side of the statue.

The two giants were climbing the hill. Both were around seven feet tall, with thick, wide, strong bodies and guns clutched in their hands. Each man had brown hair and tan skin, but what really caught my attention was their clothes. The giants were wearing long black coats over black suits, and their black wing tips were as shiny as glass, despite the fact that they'd been digging up a grave. They looked like they'd showered and shaved just a few minutes ago, and I got a whiff of spicy sandalwood cologne wafting off one of them.

The giants weren't mere grave robbers—they were Circle enforcers.

Once again, I bit back the curse dangling on the tip of my tongue. I had been so worried about someone following Owen and me from the rehearsal dinner to the cemetery that it hadn't occurred to me that Mason might dispatch his own men here.

It seemed Uncle Mason and I were on the same wavelength, at least when it came to where Fletcher might have hidden Circle secrets. The fact that I might have *anything* in common with Mason made my skin crawl, but I shoved the disgusting thought aside and focused on the two problems at hand.

"Stay still and quiet," I whispered to Owen. "Maybe the giants will think it was the wind and leave. I don't want to fight them unless we absolutely have to."

Owen nodded, and the two of us held our position

behind the snowflake statue. I peered around the side of the stone again and watched the giants climb the hill.

They took their time, not hurrying but not dawdling either, and their heads swiveled back and forth as they scanned the grounds. Both men had their guns up, ready to shoot anything that crossed their path. They seemed well organized and well trained, which made them even more dangerous.

I looked past the giants, examining the rest of the cemetery, but the area was empty, and the two men appeared to be alone. Well, at least there wasn't a whole squad of them. Maybe Lady Luck hadn't screwed me over as badly as I'd thought.

The giants stopped about twenty feet away from Owen and me and turned around in a circle, once again scanning their surroundings. They must have seen the same emptiness that I did, because they relaxed and lowered their guns.

My heart lifted. Maybe the giants would return to Fletcher's grave. The second their backs were turned, Owen and I could grab the fallen shovels, creep down the opposite side of the hill, and disappear into the woods beyond. Normally, retreating was a last resort for me, as was leaving bad guys alive to fight another day, but I didn't want Mason to realize that I'd been here searching for clues.

The giants shrugged at each other, as if they didn't know what had made the mysterious noise.

Go on, I thought. *Leave. You don't want to stand around with the cold wind whipping in your faces. Go down the hill, down the hill, down the hill...*

I kept chanting the words over and over again in my mind. Maybe if I thought them long and hard enough, I could actually make them happen.

One of the giants moved as if to head down the hill, but

then he stopped, and his gaze locked onto the two shovels Owen had dropped.

I let out a soft, resigned sigh. Nope, not going to happen. I should have known better than to hope for something as capricious as luck to fall in my favor. This would only play out one way now. Of course. This was how my late-night trips to the cemetery almost always ended.

"Hey, Wynn," one of the giants said. "Did you bring some extra shovels up here?"

"Nope, Vance. Those aren't mine. I thought you brought them?"

Wynn shook his head. The two giants exchanged a look and raised their guns.

I let out another soft, resigned sigh and tucked my knife back up my sleeve.

"What are you doing?" Owen whispered.

"I don't want to kill them with my knives or my Ice magic unless I have no other choice," I whispered back. "Stay hidden while I distract them, then follow my lead. Try to grab one of their guns and shoot them, if you can."

Owen frowned in confusion, but he nodded. He always had my back, which was one of the many things I loved about him.

I loudly cleared my throat, got to my feet, and lifted my arms.

"Hey, fellas." I stepped out from behind the snowflake statue where they could see me. "Funny running into you guys here. I didn't realize the cemetery was such a popular late-night hangout."

The two giants whirled around and aimed their guns at my chest.

"Shit!" Wynn muttered. "That's Gin Blanco. That's the Spider."

He shuffled back a few feet, as if he didn't want to be within arm's reach of me. Smart man. It was good to know my reputation preceded me, even among Mason's minions.

Vance gave his friend a short, sharp nod, although he never took his gaze off me. "Yep. She'll want to know about this. You call her. I'll keep an eye on Blanco."

I took a step forward. "*She*? Who are you going to call?"

"You'll find out soon enough," Vance said. "But trust me, you won't like the surprise."

So the giants were reporting to someone other than Mason. Interesting. Maybe I could get them to scream out exactly who it was before the end.

I took another step forward, my arms still raised. "You're right. I *hate* surprises. So why don't you go ahead and tell me? It's so much easier to talk when you're not choking on your own blood."

Vance's dark brown eyes narrowed, and he aimed his gun a little more carefully at my chest. "You take one more step, and I will shoot you where you stand, orders or not."

Orders? What kind of orders? And who had given them? Mason? Hugh Tucker? The mysterious she?

Wynn stared at me, his pale blue eyes wide in surprise and fear, but Vance jerked his head at the other man.

"Quit gaping like an idiot, and make the call," Vance growled. "Tell her that we've captured Blanco."

I couldn't help myself. I laughed.

Wynn yanked his phone out of his coat pocket, but instead of calling for reinforcements, he kept staring at me. "What's so funny?"

I let my chuckles trail off and spread my arms out even wider. "You think this is me being *captured*? Really? Oh, fellas. You are in for a very rude awakening."

Wynn wet his lips and shifted on his feet. He was clutching his gun in one hand and his phone in the other, not sure what to do. Vance didn't have that problem. He kept his gun trained on my chest and his gaze locked on my face.

"Wynn," he snapped. "Make the call. Right *now*."

"Yes, Wynn," I drawled. "Make the call. Let's invite some more people to our graveyard soiree. I'll kill them just like I'm going to kill the two of you."

Wynn's eyes bulged even wider, and he sucked in a ragged breath and shuffled back another couple of feet. He looked at Vance again and opened his mouth to say something, but Vance turned his head and stared down the other man.

"I told you. Make the call—"

The second Vance focused on Wynn, I charged at the giant. But Vance was expecting the attack, and he immediately snapped back to me. A second before I would have tackled him, Vance pulled the trigger and shot me.

The bullet punched against my chest with brutal force, but it didn't actually slam into my body and blast my heart to pieces the way Vance had intended. My coveralls were just heavy-duty fabric, but the vest I was wearing underneath was lined with silverstone, and the magical metal stopped and kept the bullet from killing me. Still, I let out a loud scream and toppled to the ground, as though Vance had murdered me on the spot.

And then I waited, just waited, for the giant to come close enough for me to strike. I knew he would. They always did.

But Vance was smarter and more careful than most. Five seconds passed, then ten, then twenty. Finally, after about thirty long, silent seconds, I heard his wing tips scuff through the grass, and his shadow fell over me, blotting out the moonlight. I reached for my Stone magic and flexed my fingers.

"Is she dead?" Wynn asked in a high, nervous, breathless voice. "No one is going to like it if she's dead."

I frowned into the grass. Someone wanted me alive? Who? Why?

"Better her than us," Vance growled. "Let me check and make sure she's dead before you call it in."

The giant crept even closer, and his shadow engulfed me like a black cloak. I curled my fingers into a fist and kept waiting.

"Hey," Vance muttered. "I don't see any blood—"

Before he could finish his thought or shoot me again, I surged up and onto my feet and cracked my Stone-hardened fist against his chin.

Vance yelped and staggered back. I darted forward, reached out, and grabbed hold of the barrel of his gun. I curled my Stone-hardened fingers around the weapon, getting a firm, concrete grip on it, then yanked the gun away from him.

"Wynn!" Vance yelled. "Shoot her! Shoot her, you idiot!"

Wynn dropped his phone and snapped up his gun, but before he could shoot me, Owen charged out from behind the other side of the statue, lowered his shoulder, and plowed into the giant. The two of them went down in a heap on the grass, rolling, rolling, rolling all the way down the hill to Fletcher's grave. Owen landed on top of Wynn, knocked the giant's gun out of his hand, and started punching him in the face.

I would have raced down the hill to help Owen, but I had my own giant to battle. Before I could flip the stolen gun around and fire it, Vance growled and charged forward. He wrapped me up in a bear hug, lifted me off my feet, and then threw me down. I barely had time to grab hold of my Stone magic and harden my skin into an impenetrable shell before my body slammed onto the cold, frozen ground.

THUD!

I landed hard on my back side. The blow rattled me from head to toe, but thanks to my Stone magic, the damage was minimal, and it didn't do much more than bruise my ass and my ego. Vance threw himself down and forward and reached out, trying to wrest his gun away from me. I fumbled with the weapon. Somehow I managed to flip the gun around so that it was pointing at him. Then I pulled the trigger—

Crack!

Vance yelped again and dropped on top of me like a tree felled by an ax. His heavy weight punched the air out of my lungs, as well as bruising a little more of my ass and my ego. I tensed, expecting the giant to try to punch or strangle me, but Vance remained limp and still.

I sucked down a breath and grabbed his shoulder. It took me a few seconds, but I managed to shove him off me and over onto his back. Vance's arms and legs flopped out to his sides, but his face didn't so much as twitch. Blood had already covered his shirt from the wound in his chest, and he stared up at the night sky, his eyes fixed and frozen in death.

One giant down, one to go.

Still clutching Vance's gun, I scrambled to my feet and started down the hill. I'd only taken a few steps when my boots slipped on a patch of grass, and I fell on my ass. My hand slammed into the ground, and I lost my grip on the giant's gun, which tumbled away. Rather than waste time chasing after the wayward weapon, I surged to my feet and raced down the rest of the incline to where Owen and Wynn were still fighting.

Wynn had gotten to his feet and was reaching for one of the shovels propped up against Fletcher's tombstone, although Owen had latched onto his leg and was trying to pull the giant back down to the ground with him.

I scanned the grass around them, searching for Wynn's gun, since I still needed a weapon to shoot the giant. Where was it? Where was it?

There.

I darted forward and snatched up the weapon. Wynn finally broke free of Owen's grip, stumbled forward, and grabbed one of the shovels. The giant snarled, whirled around, and lifted the tool high, intent on bringing it down on top of Owen's head.

I moved forward, snapped up the giant's gun, and shot him in the chest.

Wynn screamed and pitched to the ground, still clutching the shovel. He moaned a few times, but he quickly went quiet and still and bled out just like Vance had.

When I was sure the giant was dead, I lowered the gun to my side and looked over at Owen. "You okay?"

He got to his feet and dusted some of the dirt and grass off his coveralls. "Yeah. You?"

"Fine."

Owen stared down at Wynn's body, then peered up at Vance's, which was still at the top of the hill. "Why did you kill the giants with their own guns? Why not use your knives? Or your Ice magic?"

"Because the giants have to be working for Mason. Otherwise, why would they dig up Fletcher's grave?"

Understanding flashed in Owen's eyes. "You don't want Mason to know that we were here, that *you* killed the giants."

"Yeah. Right now, my only advantage is that I know who he is. I need to hold on to that for as long as possible. Once Mason realizes that I know he's the leader of the Circle, he won't have a reason to hide anymore. Then all bets are off, and there's no telling what he might do in order to get what he wants."

Owen focused on Fletcher's grave. "What *do* you think Mason wants? What do you think the giants were looking for?"

I shook my head. "I don't know, but whatever it is, they didn't find it. Even Fletcher couldn't cheat death long enough to bury something in his own grave, which means we still have a chance to find this mystery item before Mason does."

Owen gestured at the dead giants. "What are we going to do about them? Call Sophia?"

Sophia Deveraux was the head cook at the Pork Pit, my barbecue restaurant in downtown Ashland. In addition to making delicious sourdough rolls, Sophia was also the best body disposer in the city. She could make a corpse vanish into thin air, and I'd used her services more than once as the Spider.

I shook my head again. "No. If the giants disappear, then Mason and Tucker will suspect that I was involved, and Mason will start wondering what I was doing here. I'm not ready to face him. Not yet. So we need to make it look like the giants killed each other."

More understanding flashed in Owen's eyes. "That's why you wanted to shoot them with their own guns."

"Yeah, but it's not that simple. We need to set the scene—fast. The giants were probably supposed to report to someone about what they found here."

Owen and I trudged up the hill and grabbed Vance, along with his gun and Wynn's phone. Vance was heavy, but we managed to pick him up and haul him down to where Wynn was lying close to Fletcher's grave. From there, it was just a matter of wiping off my fingerprints and putting the guns in the giants' hands to make sure the ballistics matched. I also used the giants' hands to fire two more shots into the air so their skin would be covered in gunshot residue. Mason might have such a test—or others—performed to find out how his men had died.

The only problem was that I had killed Vance and Wynn with their own guns, instead of the other way around. I couldn't fix that mistake, so I just had to hope no one else would notice that minor detail.

Once the giants' bodies were arranged, I patted down their pockets and pulled out their wallets. Vance and Wynn were both carrying driver's licenses and credit cards, but I didn't recognize their names. The giants were just hired muscle.

I also looked at the giants' phones, but the devices were locked with pass codes, so I slid them back into the giants' pockets. If I took anything, even the loose change from their wallets, it would be a sign that someone else had killed the giants, instead of them offing each other. And that was something I couldn't afford.

Not yet. Not until I'd put my own plan in place to deal with this unexpected, unwanted complication.

Once we were done arranging the bodies and the guns, Owen and I walked back up the hill to my family's graves and smoothed down the scuffs and divots in the grass from the fight. I also grabbed the brittle vines and draped them across my father's tombstone, hiding Tristan's name from sight again.

Oh, I doubted my crude gardening job would fool anyone for more than a few seconds, and the wind could always blow off the vines, but I hoped the tendrils would keep anyone from looking too closely at the tombstone—or wonder what secrets might be buried in my father's grave.

Owen picked up our two shovels and hoisted them onto his shoulder. "Are you sure you don't want to dig up Tristan's grave?"

My gaze dropped to the spot where my spider rune was carved into my father's tombstone. I had covered the rune with vines just like the rest of the marker. As much as I wanted to see what secrets Fletcher might have left behind, I couldn't risk it. Not tonight. Digging up Tristan's grave would be a sure sign that I had been here and killed the Circle giants.

"No. We'll come back and do it another night. We've already been here way too long—"

A phone rang, cutting me off. It wasn't my phone, and Owen shrugged, indicating that it wasn't his either. I palmed a knife and whirled around, thinking someone else was in the cemetery, but no one was lurking among the trees, shadows, and tombstones. I cocked my head to the side, listening. The ringing was coming from...Wynn.

I tucked my knife back up my sleeve, hurried down the hill, and fished the device out of the giant's pocket. I expected the phone to cut off, but it kept ringing and ringing. Whoever was on the other end definitely wanted to be answered. I flipped the phone over so I could see the screen. And that person was...

Hugh Tucker.

The vampire's name and number filled the screen. I yanked my own phone out of my pocket and snapped a photo of the screen so that I would have Tucker's digits. Then I showed the device to Owen. His face tightened with worry, and he started scanning the cemetery.

The ringing finally cut off, the sudden silence seeming even louder and more ominous than the phone's cheerful chimes.

I slid the device back into Wynn's pocket, then stood up. "Time to go."

We hurried away from Fletcher's grave and quickly reached the woods on the edge of the property. Owen stepped into the trees, but I stopped and looked back over my shoulder, staring at the giants' bodies in the distance, still lying where Owen and I had arranged them.

I might have sold Owen on the idea that everyone would believe the two giants had shot each other, but Mason and Tucker were both smarter than that. I had made a grave error tonight, and I couldn't help but wonder when Mason would realize my mistake—and retaliate.

✲ 3 ✲

Owen and I made it back to his car with no problems. Twenty minutes later, he steered the vehicle up a long, bumpy gravel driveway. The car crested the top of the hill, and a sprawling, ramshackle structure came into view.

Fletcher's house—my house now—was a mishmash of styles and adorned with everything from white clapboard to brown brick to dull, gray, weathered tin. Owen parked in the driveway in front of the house and threw the car into gear, but he left the engine running.

I scanned the front yard, along with the surrounding woods and the steep ridge that dropped away on the other side of the house, but I didn't see anyone skulking through the trees or hiding among the rocks. I also reached out with my Stone magic. The driveway gravels chirped of the churn of tires across them, the rocks in the woods grumbled about the icy leaves piled on top of them, and the bricks in the house murmured sleepily about the cold night air that had crept into their cracks and crevices.

"We're clear," I said.

Owen killed the engine, and we got out of the car and went inside the house. I locked the front door behind us, then toed off my boots and stripped off my coveralls and silverstone vest, revealing my pantsuit underneath. Beside me, Owen did the same.

"I need to get cleaned up." He showed me his dirt- and grass-stained hands. "Then maybe we can have that fire, food, and wine?"

"Why wait?" I murmured.

I gave him a wicked grin, then grabbed his hand and tugged him along behind me. We ended up in one of the downstairs bathrooms. I shut the door behind us, then turned the shower on a warm, slow trickle so I could wash my hands and bring a bit of heat to the chilly tile room. Owen rinsed and dried off his hands as well.

We faced each other. He stared at me, and I looked right back at him. Then, with one thought, we both surged forward and came together.

I pressed my lips to Owen's, even as I unbuttoned his suit jacket. He kissed me back just as fiercely, even as he unbuttoned my own jacket. Our lips and tongues dueled, darted, and stroked together time and time again, but it wasn't *enough*. I wanted to feel, touch, taste more of him. Steam rose up from the running water, but it was nothing compared to the liquid desire scorching through my veins.

Once our jackets were out of the way, we went to work on our shirts, undoing the buttons and peeling them off each other as fast as we could. I stepped into Owen's arms, and he cupped my face in his hands and gently stroked his thumbs over my cheeks. I splayed my fingers across his bare chest, feeling the *thump-thump-thump* of his heart, beating hard and fast, just like mine was.

Owen leaned forward and pressed soft butterfly kisses to

my eyelids, nose, and cheeks. I drew in a breath, drinking in his rich, metallic scent, which was somehow made even more intense by the hazy steam slowly filling the bathroom.

"I don't say this nearly enough, but you mean everything to me, Gin," he whispered in a low, husky voice between kisses. "Whatever happens with Mason and Tucker and the Circle, we'll face it together. You and me."

His words, his certainty, his devotion filled my heart with even more love, and I reached up and curled my arms around his neck, drawing him closer still. "You and me," I promised, staring into his violet eyes.

I leaned forward and kissed him again. I licked at his lips, and Owen opened his mouth, his tongue darting out to meet mine. I trailed my hands over his broad shoulders, then down his chest, enjoying the flex and quiver of his strong, hard muscles under my searching fingertips. My heart beat faster, and that liquid desire burned even hotter as it trickled down into my stomach and pooled between my thighs.

Owen nuzzled my neck, and his hands snaked around behind my back and unhooked my bra. My hands darted lower, and I undid his belt. Still nuzzling my neck, Owen slid my bra down my arms and tossed it aside. I did the same thing to his belt, then unbuttoned and unzipped his pants. He reached around, grabbed his wallet from his back pocket, and drew out a condom. I took my little white pills, but we always used extra protection.

Owen stepped out of his pants, socks, and black silk boxers, then covered himself with the condom. I peeled off my own pants and socks, along with my underwear.

"Now," I whispered in a breathless voice. "I want you inside me right *now*."

Owen grabbed me and picked me up. Our mouths crashed together again, and he set me down on the edge of the bathroom counter. I hissed at the feel of the cool tile against my ass, but then Owen moved forward and thrust inside me, and I forgot about everything else.

We both moaned. I kissed him again, raking my nails down his back, even as he surged inside me again.

"You feel so good," Owen murmured against my lips. "You always feel so good, Gin."

I would have told him that he felt the same, but I was too busy kissing him and gasping for breath every time he slid inside me.

We plunged into a quick rhythm, and the sensations crashed over me one after another. Owen's breath rasping in my ear. His scent filling my nose. His warm, strong hands locked on my hips as we moved together. So wonderful, familiar, and overwhelming all at once. My head fell back, and my hands left streaks in the steam on the bottom of the mirror behind me.

The pressure and the pleasure inside me built and built, and it wasn't long before I was leaning forward and digging my nails into Owen's back as the orgasm ripped through me. He surged forward again and cried out, finding his own release. We stayed like that, locked together, every single part of us tangled up, and both of us riding the waves of pleasure cascading through our bodies.

Sometime later, Owen shuddered out a breath and drew back.

"What do you say, Grayson?" I asked. "Was that *fire, food, and wine* worth the wait?"

He pressed a kiss to the top of my bare shoulder. "It's always worth the wait with you, Gin."

Owen got rid of the condom, then reached down and dug another out of his wallet.

I arched an eyebrow. "What are you up to, Grayson?"

He picked me up off the counter, and I looped my arms around his neck and locked my legs against his waist.

With one hand, Owen held me tight against his body. With the other, he opened the glass shower door. "Showing you that I'm worth the wait too."

He grinned and carried me into the shower. I laughed and kissed him again, even as the warm water cascaded down on our intertwined bodies, and more steam rose up all around us.

After a very nice interlude in the shower, Owen and I actually did light a fire in the den and have some food and wine before going to bed.

Owen quickly drifted off to sleep, but I stared up at the ceiling, replaying the events in the cemetery over and over again in my mind. I came to the same worrisome conclusions as before, so I slipped out of bed, put on some clothes, grabbed my knives and phone, and went downstairs to Fletcher's office—my office now.

I flipped on the lights, walked past the metal filing cabinets and the bookcases along the wall, and sat down behind the old, battered desk in the back of the room. Instead of the usual office clutter, only a few things were perched on the surface—a bottle of gin, a couple of glasses, a framed photo of Fletcher, and a single manila folder.

I poured myself a glass of gin and used it to make a toast to the old man's smiling face. Then I opened the folder and started reading through the information inside.

I had already reviewed the file a dozen times, and the documents said the exact same things as before. Fletcher had kept tabs on all the major criminals in Ashland, as well as anyone else he thought might be a threat to us, given his past as the assassin the Tin Man and my activities as the Spider.

A couple of weeks ago, I'd gotten an idea about one of the folks in the Ashland underworld, and I'd dug out the old man's file on that individual. I had also conducted my own discreet investigation into the person in question, but Fletcher's information and observations had been spot-on, and I had agreed with his conclusions. Now it was up to me whether to go through with my crazy plan.

Decision time.

I grabbed my phone and pulled up a message I'd saved in the drafts folder a few days ago. My thumb hovered over the button, and I thought of the dead giants lying in the cemetery, just waiting for Hugh Tucker to come find them. Death was the one thing nobody could undo, not even me, and my decision had been made the second I killed those two men.

I hit the send button.

Less than five minutes later, my phone chimed with a new message. ***On my way.***

Short and sweet, just how I liked things. Good. Maybe this would go better than I thought.

I grabbed the bottle of gin, the other glass, and the folder and left the office. I stopped long enough to shrug into a coat from one of the downstairs closets and carried everything out onto the front porch to wait for my guest. I'd already had my date night with Owen, and now it was time for my final nightcap.

From Fletcher's file and my own investigation, I knew that he lived nearby, and it didn't take him long to arrive. Fifteen minutes later, the crunch of gravel sounded, a pair of headlights popped into view, and a baby-blue sports car crested the hill and stopped in the driveway.

I was sitting in a rocking chair, with the bottle of gin, the glasses, and the folder on a table beside me. I took another sip of my drink and watched while a man climbed out of the car, smoothed down his long navy overcoat, and headed in my direction.

He was alone, although I was betting he had at least one gun tucked away in his coat. I would have been armed to the teeth if I'd been called to a mysterious late-night meeting with the Spider. But one of the perks of being the supposed queen of the underworld was that I could summon anyone anytime, day or night.

The man stepped onto the porch, and the boards *creaked* ominously under his weight. I didn't know where he'd been or what he'd been doing before this, but the man was dressed as though this was just another business meeting. His stylish navy overcoat topped an equally snazzy navy suit, and his black wing tips were spotless, despite his walk across the icy gravel driveway. His dark brown hair, blue eyes, and tan skin gleamed under the golden glows cast out by the porch lights. He was tall and muscled and quite handsome, although his good looks weren't the reason I had asked him here.

Liam Carter glanced around. A wary expression filled his face, as though he was expecting someone to run around the far side of the porch and start shooting at him. This would have been an excellent place for an ambush, but I wasn't planning to kill him.

He had far too much potential value for that.

My plan to protect not only myself but especially my loved ones from Mason, Tucker, and the Circle wouldn't work without his help. Like it or not, my friends' survival hinged on Liam agreeing to my scheme. He was my last resort, my last line of defense, in case everything went wrong. And knowing my luck, things would most definitely go wrong sooner or later. Oh, yes, I desperately needed Liam Carter—even if I wasn't sure I could trust him.

He waited several seconds. When it became clear that no one was going to try to murder him, and I was content to sit in my rocking chair and sip my gin, he cleared his throat. "Ms. Blanco."

"Mr. Carter. Thank you for coming so late. And on such short notice."

He respectfully tipped his head to me. "When the queen calls, I come running."

I grimaced. Like all the other underworld bosses, Liam Carter wrongly assumed that *I* was the one who ruled over the city's crime. I was about to dissuade him of that notion, though, along with a great many others.

He glanced around again. "Is your handsome assistant here?"

Liam had been steadfastly flirting with Silvio at the Pork Pit for the last several weeks, trying to persuade the vampire to go on a coffee date. So far, Silvio had resisted Liam's advances, although I thought my assistant was far more interested in the other man than he let on.

"No, Silvio's not here. This meeting is just between you and me, and everything we say tonight stays strictly between the two of us. No confiding in one of your associates, no notes on your phone or computer, no paper trail. Is that understood?"

He tipped his head again, accepting my terms. Not that he had much choice in the matter. Liam Carter might be formidable, but I could palm a knife, cross the porch, and kill him before he drew whatever guns he might be carrying.

I lifted my glass to my lips and tossed back the rest of my gin before setting the empty container aside. No sense beating around the bush. It was too cold, and I was too desperate for such nonsense.

"I want to hire you."

Liam's eyebrows shot up into his forehead in obvious surprise. "Hire me? To do what?"

"What you do best—protect people."

Liam Carter was a bit of an odd fish among the criminals swimming in the Ashland underworld. Instead of running guns or drugs, he offered protection services and shielded criminals from other criminals who wanted them dead. Turf wars, internal power struggles, assassination attempts. You name it, and Liam Carter could probably get you through it—alive.

And he didn't limit his services to the city's criminals. Liam and his company, Carter Corp., were legit enough to protect rich businesspeople, government officials who'd received death threats, and even police witnesses. He employed a variety of giants, dwarves, vampires, and elementals whom he could mix and match together depending on his client's needs, who wanted them dead, and how badly.

Then there was Liam himself. He was a crack shot who was rumored to have a mix of dwarven and giant blood that made him incredibly tough and strong, and he had taken several bullets and blasts of magic meant for his clients. Best of all, Liam offered his clients a guarantee: once you hired him, he was yours until the job was done. He wouldn't sell you out to your enemies, and he would do everything in his power to keep you safe.

His sterling reputation and code of honor were among the reasons I'd decided to approach him. I just hoped I was trusting the right person. But if things went the way I expected, then time was running out, and I had no choice but to take a leap of faith and hope that Liam Carter would do right by me and mine.

"Let me get this straight. *You* want *me* to protect *you*?" He pointed back and forth between the two of us.

"Yes. *I* want to hire *you*." I made the same back-and-forth motions with my index finger.

Liam gave me an incredulous look. "Is this a joke? You're an *assassin*. And not just any assassin, but *the Spider*. One of the very best. You killed Mab Monroe. And Madeline Monroe. And lots of other underworld bosses. Why would you ever need anyone's protection?"

"I made a mistake tonight."

He eyed me. "What kind of mistake?"

"I killed a couple of people I shouldn't have."

He snorted. "Strange thing for an assassin to say, especially the Spider. You're the queen of the Ashland underworld. That means you can pretty much kill whomever you like."

I let out a harsh, bitter laugh. "I'm not the *queen* of anything, except maybe lies. And someone wants me dead. Or at least out of the way. Someone far more dangerous and powerful than the underworld bosses. That's where you come in."

Liam crossed his arms over his chest, clearly wanting answers. Even though I had summoned him here to dole out those answers, I still hesitated. Because once I uncorked this particular genie, there was no shoving it back into the bottle.

I had been thinking about hiring Liam for a few weeks, ever since I'd discovered that Mason was the head of the Circle. But now that the moment was finally here, I was wondering how much I could trust Liam. Then again, I wondered that about practically everyone.

The mere *idea* of putting my faith in someone new and risking his betrayal made me feel as though my stomach was a tank filled with hungry sharks just waiting to break through the thin, fragile glass and tear me to pieces. Perhaps even worse than that watery tank of worry was this steady, phantom *tick-tick-ticking* in my ears, almost as if there was a clock inside my mind counting down the seconds until Mason came after me. But like it or not, it was time to take a chance and jump into the water.

I drew in a breath, then slowly let it out. "Have you ever heard of the Circle?"

His eyebrows drew together in confusion. "What's that? Some weird assassin coven?"

Liam was closer to the truth than he realized, but I shook my head.

"No. The Circle is a secret society. Its members are the ones with the *real* power in Ashland, especially in the underworld. I'm just a reluctant figurehead of sorts."

He still looked skeptical, so I told him everything I knew about the Circle and all the horrible things that had happened over the past few months. Hugh Tucker trying to recruit me. Finding out that my mother had been a Circle member. Learning that my uncle Mason was the one pulling everyone's strings, including mine.

By the time I finished, Liam Carter was leaning back against the porch railing, his arms still crossed over his chest, a thoughtful look on his face. He stayed silent for the better part of a minute, digesting my words, then let out a low whistle.

"If what you're telling me is the truth..." He shook his head. "Then *nothing* is the way I thought it was in Ashland. Not when it comes to how things really work, the other crime bosses, you, nothing. Down is up, and up is fucking *sideways*."

"Unfortunately, it's the sad, inescapable truth. As is the fact that I need your help."

"Why me?" he asked. "Why *me* out of all the people in Ashland you could reach out to? There are lots of folks who would be willing to do the Spider a favor."

I shrugged. "Because you're the only one I can trust."

Or at least *hope* to trust. I didn't say the words, but I still felt the weight of them, like a couple of those hungry sharks had bumped into the sides of the watery tank of worry, fear, and misgivings that was still sloshing around in my stomach.

A smile creased Liam's face, and an amused chuckle escaped his lips. "Trust? You think *you* can trust *me*? Oh, that's *funny*. Because we both know I'm a mercenary at heart. Besides, I don't work for free. Not even for the Spider."

I opened the file folder on the table and pulled out the check I'd written a few days ago. Then I got to my feet, crossed the porch, and held it out to him. "I never expected you to work for free."

Liam eyed the check like it was a lit stick of dynamite that would explode the second he touched it. He was right to be wary. Because if my plan didn't work, then no amount of money would fix things, and I doubted either one of us would live much longer.

Several seconds ticked by. I thought he wasn't going to take it, and I started to drop my hand, but his curiosity must have gotten the better of him, because he plucked the check out of my fingertips.

Liam leaned back against the porch railing. He made sure that it wasn't some trick and that I was going to stay put before glancing down at the piece of paper. He blinked. "Well, that is certainly…generous. But the question remains. Why *me*?"

"Because you're not nearly as mercenary as you claim to be."

He shrugged. "I don't know what you're talking about."

"I thought you might say that."

I crossed the porch, sat back down in my rocking chair, and gestured at the sheets of paper inside the open folder. I'd memorized the contents days ago.

"Liam Alexander Carter. Age forty-five. Born and raised in Ashland by a single mother. You grew up in Southtown but managed to claw your way out of a bad neighborhood. Worked several jobs, some legal, some not, to put yourself through college, then got your master's degree in business. You saw an opportunity to offer protection and other bodyguard services to both criminals and legit business-people and started your own security firm more than twenty years ago. Now, Carter Corp. is the premier protection service in Ashland. Impressive. Truly."

A muscle ticked in his jaw, and he tapped his right foot in a quick, annoyed rhythm. He didn't like my condensing his life down to the bare bones. "You did your homework."

I shook my head. "Not me. My assassin mentor. He kept files on everyone who was anyone in Ashland, especially those folks on the shady side of the law."

"Should I be flattered?" Liam drawled.

"Absolutely. Fletcher, my mentor, wrote several complimentary things about you in his notes. He didn't do that for many people."

Hardly anyone, although I wouldn't tell Liam that, not while we were still feeling each other out.

He glanced at the check in his hand again. I'd put enough zeroes on it to get and keep his attention. Good. I just hoped the information in Fletcher's file would help seal the deal.

"What, exactly, do you want me to do? Tell me the truth—the whole, unvarnished, absolute *truth*," Liam said. "That is my one and only rule with my clients. I don't care what you've done or how many people you've hurt and killed. But if you lie to me, I can't properly protect you, and neither can the folks who work for me. I won't have my people risk their lives over a stupid fucking *lie*. The second I find out you haven't been completely, one hundred percent honest, I'm gone, and nothing you do or say or offer or threaten will convince me to come back."

I nodded. "That seems fair."

He gave me a suspicious look, but I told him *exactly* what I wanted.

I laid it all out for him, full disclosure. All the horrible things I thought might happen and how I wanted him to handle them. Liam was right. He and his people were going to risk their lives, and it would be insulting to lie—even if I wasn't sure I could trust him.

At first, Liam looked wary, then shocked, then incredulous. By the time I finished laying out my plan, he was shaking his head *no-no-no*, as if he couldn't believe what I was proposing.

"*You* want *me* to take on this Circle secret society?" he asked, still shaking his head *no-no-no*. "That's the craziest thing I've ever heard."

"Why?" I countered. "Everyone knows you run the best protection service in Ashland. Why, you've almost thwarted me a time or two."

"*Almost* thwarted you?" Liam's blue eyes narrowed in

thought, as though he was flipping through a mental list of his clients—the ones he hadn't been able to protect. "Wait a second. *You* were the one who killed Lennie Wilson?"

I grinned and gave him a not-so-modest shrug.

"I worked for *weeks* setting up a safe house for Wilson. And you came along and killed him, just like that." He snapped his fingers and gave me a harsh, accusing glare.

I shrugged again. "And you did an excellent job. It took me almost a week to find Lennie in that penthouse apartment and three more days to figure out how to climb to the top floor."

"You *climbed* up the side of the building?" Liam blanched. "It was ten floors!"

"Don't you know? Spiders like to climb."

Liam glared at me again, but his anger quickly melted into more of a speculative look. "How did you do it? I've always wondered. I could never quite figure it out."

I gestured at the rocking chair across from mine. "Sit down, and I'll tell you all about it."

Liam thought about it for a few seconds, but he stepped forward and settled himself in the chair. He also laid the check on top of the file on the table between us. He still wasn't ready to take my money or agree to my proposal. Smart. I liked him already.

I poured him some gin, along with another for myself, and told him how I'd assassinated his client all those years ago.

"Fletcher, my mentor, occasionally delivered food from the Pork Pit, and he decided to gift your men with several boxes of barbecue they hadn't ordered. The old man drew you and the rest of the guards to the front of the penthouse while I slipped in through one of the windows, killed Lennie Wilson, and slipped back out."

"I *knew* there was something fishy about that guy," Liam muttered. "But he really did work for the Pork Pit, and I could never prove anything against him."

"Fletcher was sly and sneaky, and he excelled at getting other people to do exactly what he wanted them to," I replied. "The old man called that move his *Reverse Trojan Horse*. Only instead of getting someone to bring something inside, like a bomb or poisoned food, he would get the person to come outside to him. And then he would do whatever he needed to, depending on the job. In your case, it was distracting you and your men long enough for me to kill Lennie Wilson."

Liam gave me another speculative look. "Is that where you got the idea to hire me?"

"More or less."

"What you're asking…" He shook his head. "It's not what I normally do."

"I know. And that's exactly why I want you to do it."

He leaned back in his chair and looked at me over the rim of his glass. "But you don't *know* me. Despite whatever information is in that file, you don't know me. Not really. Not well enough to put your trust in me for something this dangerous."

"So?"

"So what makes you think I'm the person for the job? And don't tell me it's because your assassin mentor gave me a glowing review way back when. He probably thought I was a complete idiot after he hoodwinked me."

"Fletcher didn't think you were an idiot. He was the smartest person I've ever known, and he could beat anyone at their own game. I can't even tell you how many times he mock-killed me over the years, even after I was fully trained and working as the Spider."

Liam kept staring at me, suspicion filling his eyes.

I drained the rest of my gin and waited until that sweet, slow burn ignited in the pit of my stomach before I set my glass aside. I didn't often need liquid courage, but the night was cold and dark, and so was what I was about to say.

"I want to hire you because of Fletcher's file, but there are other reasons." I paused. "Mainly, what happened to your sister."

Liam had been about to take another sip of his own gin, and he froze, his glass poised in midair. That muscle in his jaw ticked again, and he slammed his drink down on the table hard enough to make a loud *clank* ring out. Gin sloshed over the side of the glass and dripped onto my file. His fingers clenched around the container, and I got the impression he'd like to smash it into my face.

"What do you know about my sister?" he growled.

"Her name was Leila," I said, my voice as quiet as his was harsh. "She was five years younger than you. Smart, kind, pretty. One of her girlfriends started hanging out with the wrong people, including a guy who became obsessed with Leila. And not just any guy, but a crooked cop."

Liam abruptly released his glass, leaned forward, clasped his hands together, and dropped his head. The porch lights added a golden halo to his dark brown hair, even as they cast his face in shadow.

"This cop, Dwayne Nelson, wouldn't take no for an answer, and he started stalking Leila. Eventually, your sister came to you for help."

A low, harsh, bitter laugh tumbled out of Liam's lips and splattered onto the floorboards. "But I didn't help her."

"Yes, you did," I replied in a firm voice. "You hid your sister in a safe house for *weeks*. It wasn't your fault Nelson eventually found her. It was just bad luck."

"Sometimes I think that's the only kind of fucking luck I have," Liam growled again.

I could certainly sympathize with that sentiment.

He jerked his head at the file folder. "I assume you have the police report. And photos of what that bastard did. How he killed the men guarding my sister, then beat and strangled her."

Beat and *strangled* were bland, technical words for the brutal trauma and torture that Leila had suffered.

"Yes. I'm sorry."

And I truly was. I didn't like using Fletcher's information this way. Emotional blackmail and manipulation were a new low, even for me. But I didn't want to see my loved ones end up like Leila Carter—or worse. And if that meant being selfish and inflicting some pain on Liam, then so be it. Fletcher wasn't the only one who knew how to get people to do what he wanted.

"I'm also assuming you know that Nelson skated on a technicality," Liam muttered. "His cop buddies didn't properly read Nelson his rights. Or so his scumbag lawyer claimed."

"Yes."

I also knew the cop's lawyer had been Jonah McAllister, one of my old enemies, although I didn't mention it. Thanks to me, McAllister was stewing in his Northtown mansion, awaiting trial on multiple counts of murder, among other things.

Liam shook his head, as if pushing away bad memories, then sat up and violently rocked back in his chair, making it *screech* in protest. His gaze locked onto the folder sitting on the table, although I got the impression he wasn't really seeing it.

"Ever since your sister's murder, you've been quietly doing pro bono work on the side," I continued. "You help women and men get out of abusive relationships, deal with stalkers, things like that. Sometimes you help people navigate their problems through the legal system. And sometimes, if there isn't a legal solution, you help them disappear. You give them new names, new jobs, new lives far from the people who want to hurt them. Your own sort of witness-protection service."

"Running and hiding is the only option for some folks," he said in a dull, defeated tone. "Some people just don't know when to leave someone else alone. They would rather see their wives or girlfriends or husbands or boyfriends dead than let them leave."

"Sadly, I know all about the twisted things people do to each other because of money or jealousy or what they think is love."

We both lapsed into silence. Liam slowly rocked back and forth in his chair, staring out into the dark night, while I poured myself another glass of gin and topped off his. Liam roused himself out of his memories, grabbed his drink, and threw back the alcohol.

"After Leila was murdered, I looked for Dwayne Nelson for *days*." He eyed me over the rim of his glass again. "Strange thing, though. I never could find him."

I leaned back in my chair and took a sip of my own gin.

"But the really strange thing was that Nelson turned up dead about two weeks later. His throat was cut, and he'd been stabbed through the heart for good measure." Liam kept eyeing me. "His crooked cop buddies found Nelson's body stuffed in an old, empty oil drum outside a Southtown bar where they hung out. The cops initially thought I had killed Nelson, but I was protecting a client at a corporate event and had a rock-solid alibi for the night he went missing."

"Lucky you had an alibi," I murmured.

"Luck?" He snorted. "We both know it wasn't luck."

I took another sip of my drink.

"You know what else is strange?" He didn't wait for me to respond. "Lennie Wilson, my client, was killed the exact same way as Nelson. Throat cut, stabbed through the heart. When the cops showed me the photos of Nelson's body, I had this weird flashback to Lennie Wilson, and I had this crazy thought that someone was trying to send me a message."

We both knew it wasn't crazy at all.

"Why did you do it?" Liam asked. "Why did you kill Nelson?"

"It wasn't me. That was all Fletcher," I replied. "As for why he did it, well, the old man never enjoyed seeing innocent people get hurt. But when people did get hurt, he liked to give their loved ones what justice and closure he could."

"He robbed me of getting my own revenge," Liam growled.

"That's one way to look at it."

He threw his hand up. "How else am I supposed to look at it?"

I stared him down. "Fletcher kept you from getting caught. After your sister was murdered, you weren't exactly subtle about your desire to kill that corrupt cop. So Fletcher waited until there was a night he was sure you would have an alibi before he took out Nelson. The old man had a code, and he didn't want you to go to prison for a crime you didn't commit on top of losing your sister."

Liam's fingers clenched around his glass, and I once

again got the impression he wanted to smash it into my face. Couldn't blame him for that. His jaw clenched, and emotions flashed like lightning strikes in his eyes. Grief. Rage. Sorrow. And finally, the thing I had been hoping to see all along: a bit of grudging respect.

"It's too bad your mentor is dead. I would have liked to meet him." Liam snorted. "Although I'm not sure whether I would shake his hand or punch him in the mouth. Maybe both."

A familiar, sharp sting of guilt throbbed in my heart at the fact that I hadn't been able to save Fletcher from being tortured and murdered inside the Pork Pit, but I pushed the pain aside. Now was not the time to wallow in my own regrets.

Liam waved his hand over the check and the file still on the table. "So this is why you picked me. You thought you could summon me here, give me a big, fat check, drop these revelations, and recruit me over to your side. That is stone-cold, even for an assassin."

I shrugged. "I'm sorry to dredge up bad memories, but I didn't have time to wine and dine and woo you. Not after the mistake I made at the cemetery tonight. Besides, you wanted the truth, so I gave it to you."

He grimaced, but he couldn't argue. Instead, he leaned back in his chair again, and a far more speculative look filled his eyes. "Say that I actually agree to this madness, to help you. What's to keep me from betraying you? And not just to Mason. There are plenty of people in Ashland who want you dead."

He tapped his finger on the check. "I could easily double, triple, quadruple this, just by making a couple of phone calls when the time is right."

"Well, I can think of three things right off the top of my

head. The most obvious is that I don't take too kindly to betrayal, sugar."

Despite my threat, Liam kept staring at me, not backing down. His courage and tenacity made me like him even more.

"The second thing is that I've killed a whole lot of powerful people, many of whom mistakenly thought they were stronger and smarter than me." I gestured at the file. "Lennie Wilson is proof of that. I got the better of you back then. If you were to *ever* betray me, I would be *far* more motivated to kill you than I was with Wilson or any of your other clients I've offed over the years. Only I wouldn't be so quick and kind as to cut your throat and stab you. Betrayal makes me want to take my time and use my knives and elemental magic to their fullest extent."

He blanched a little, but he kept his gaze steady on mine. "And the third thing?"

"Betrayal's not in your nature, Liam. When you give someone your word, then you do your best to keep it, no matter what."

He barked out a laugh. "That's it? That's your big justification for trusting me? I'm a *criminal*, Gin. Just like you are. I take money from bad people to do bad things. That makes me a sinner, not a saint."

"I'm not interested in hiring a saint," I snapped back. "I need a sinner who's just as bad as I am to make sure my friends survive this. You lost your sister, and I lost Fletcher. We both know the sharp stings of their losses will never completely vanish. I can't *stand* to lose anyone else. I don't care what happens to me, but I *will* protect my family. And if that means trusting you, then so be it."

Liam kept staring at me. For once, I lowered my guard and let the worry seep into my features. Several seconds ticked by in silence.

Finally, Liam dropped his gaze and reached inside his coat. I tensed, thinking that maybe I had pushed him too far too fast, and he was going to yank out a gun and try to shoot me. Instead, he drew out a dollar, along with a black marker. Then he uncapped the marker and scribbled a few words on the bill.

When he was finished, he capped the marker and slid it back inside his coat. Then he handed the dollar to me. He'd written our names on the bill, along with today's date.

"I give one of these to all my clients as proof of contract. As of this moment, I'm officially yours. I'll help you implement your plan and protect your friends as best I can from Mason and anyone who works for him."

"Thank you."

He shook his head. "Don't thank me until it's over."

I nodded and slid my check across the table. Liam took the paper and slipped it inside his coat.

I grabbed my glass of gin and held it up. Liam sighed, but he grabbed his own glass and *clinked* it against mine. And with that soft, solitary note, we both took a drink, sealing our dangerous bargain.

✡ 4 ✡

Despite my worries about Mason striking out at me, the next few days passed by quietly. Just after ten o'clock on Wednesday, three mornings after the cemetery fight, I was standing behind the long counter in the back of the Pork Pit, getting ready for another day of catering to my customers' cravings for barbecue.

"I still can't believe you hired *him*," a low voice muttered.

I looked up from the tomatoes I was slicing for the day's sandwiches and focused on the fifty-something man sitting on a stool across the counter from me. He looked quite dapper and distinguished in his sleek gray suit, which brought out his gray eyes and hair, along with his bronze skin. A small silverstone pin shaped like my spider rune glinted in the middle of his gray striped tie.

Silvio Sanchez, my personal assistant, was *tap-tap-tapping* his finger against his tablet screen and glancing over at the booth in the far back corner. Liam Carter must have heard the vampire's words, because he cheerfully toasted Silvio with his coffee mug. Liam turned his attention back to his newspaper, although a wry, knowing smile curved the corners of his lips.

"Come on," Silvio muttered again. "The man still reads in print. Barbarian."

I hid a smile. "Just because Liam prefers to peruse old-fashioned paper over the latest, greatest electronic gizmo doesn't mean he's not good at his job."

Silvio ignored me, still staring at the other man. "Just *look* at him. Sitting over there drinking coffee, reading the newspaper, and being smug. I still don't understand why you felt the need to hire him to protect the restaurant. You're an assassin, Gin. By now, most people know better than to mess with you."

"Most people, but sadly not all. I'm tired of random punks trying to kill me whenever I take out the trash to the back alley. One of the reasons I hired Liam was to put an end to that. Thanks to the giant guard he has stationed in the alley, no one's tried to murder me there so far this week."

Silvio swiveled back around to me. "And the *other* reasons you hired him? The ones you're not telling me about?"

I bit back a curse. The vampire knew me far too well, which was one of the many things that made him such a good assistant and a great friend.

"You know all the other reasons," I said in a light, breezy tone. "Mason and Tucker are out there somewhere, not to mention the underworld bosses, most of whom would be delighted by my death. I figured it wouldn't hurt to have Liam review my security procedures and give the restaurant an added layer of protection. At least until the situation with the Circle is resolved. Then we can go back to dealing with our regularly scheduled bad guys on our own."

"Right," Silvio drawled in a disbelieving tone. "Because you're not *nearly* careful and paranoid enough already. Tell me, after you parked your car this morning, how many times did you check and make sure you weren't being followed before coming to the restaurant?"

"Three, and Liam said that I should have made it four. See? He's earning his keep already."

Silvio's gray eyes narrowed. And he thought I was paranoid. Please. He definitely took the gold medal in that sport.

I didn't want him to keep asking questions about what Liam was really doing here, so I changed the subject. "Just because you have a little crush on Liam is no reason not to trust him."

Silvio sniffed. "And I would argue that is *precisely* the reason I shouldn't trust him. I don't have a great track record when it comes to picking men, and my last coffee date was an unmitigated *disaster*."

His face darkened, and a disgusted scowl twisted his lips the way it always did whenever he mentioned his holiday date. Something bad had happened then, although Silvio had never told me about it. I'd get the truth out of him sooner or later, though.

Still, I understood his suspicion and hesitation. It was hard for me to trust people too. I thought I'd gotten past the worst of it, but the recent revelations about my parents being Circle members had brought all my old fears bubbling back up to the surface again.

If you couldn't trust that your parents were good people, then how could you ever put your faith in anyone else? That question haunted me, especially given how open, honest, and vulnerable I'd made myself with Liam and how much I was relying on his help to deal with Mason. If I was wrong about Liam Carter, well, my death probably wouldn't be the worst thing that happened.

But I also didn't want Silvio to make the same mistakes that I had, to isolate himself the way that I had for so long and potentially miss out on something great. So I put down my knife, reached over, and grabbed the vampire's hand, making him stop his incessant *tap-tap-tapping*.

"I showed you Fletcher's file. Liam Carter is a good guy."

"*Mostly* a good guy," Silvio muttered again. "He might protect people, but he's still a criminal, Gin."

"And so are we," I pointed out. "Look at it this way. I'm trusting Liam—for now. But the second he breaks that trust, then I will slice him up just as quickly as I did these tomatoes. I've made it abundantly clear to Liam *exactly* what will happen if he even *thinks* about betraying me. Does that make you feel better?"

Silvio eyed the serrated tomato knife lying on the counter. "If I say yes, does that make me a horrible person?"

"No more horrible than me."

He nodded, then cleared his throat and picked up his tablet. "Well, trust or not, it's time for the morning briefing. Unfortunately, I haven't been able to find out much about those giants you killed in the cemetery. No criminal records, no bad habits, nothing like that. As far as I can tell, they were just hired muscle, and I haven't found anything in their personal lives or social-media accounts that will lead us to Mason or Tucker."

I hadn't expected Silvio to find anything, but at least he'd tried. My assistant was rather tenacious that way.

He swiped through a couple of screens. "As to why the giants dug up Fletcher's grave, well, that's anybody's guess.

You're absolutely sure Fletcher didn't hide something in his own casket?"

I shook my head. "No. Finn and I picked out that casket after Fletcher died. The old man didn't have anything to do with it. Fletcher didn't take any secrets with him into the ground. He just buried them in other people's graves."

Silvio chuckled at my black humor and focused on his tablet again. "Well, several other things need your attention this morning..."

He continued the briefing, informing me about the shenanigans of the various underworld bosses and those who wanted me to settle their petty disputes before they turned even more violent.

Silvio had just wrapped up his report when a key scraped in the lock, and a woman opened the front door and stepped inside the restaurant. She was a dwarf, a little more than five feet tall, with a thick, muscled body. She shrugged out of her black trench coat, revealing a neon-blue sweater with a grinning skull done in silver sequins, along with black jeans and boots. The tips of her shoulder-length black hair were dyed the same neon-blue as her sweater. Her lips were also painted blue, and silvery shadow and liner made her black eyes pop in her pale face.

Sophia Deveraux hung her coat on the rack by the front door, then looked out over the restaurant. I tracked her gaze, also scanning the familiar furnishings. Blue and pink vinyl booths lining the storefront windows. Tables and chairs squatting in the middle of the restaurant. Blue and pink pig tracks crisscrossing the floor.

Sophia nodded, as if satisfied that everything was as it should be, and glanced over at Liam Carter, who was still sitting in the back corner booth. She waved at him, and he returned the gesture.

Sophia crossed the storefront and stepped around the counter to where I was now slicing up green and purple cabbages for the day's coleslaw. She grabbed a black apron patterned with blue skulls from a hook on the back wall and tied it on over her clothes.

"Bodyguard here again?" Sophia rasped in her eerie, broken voice.

"Yep. He stays until I say otherwise."

She nodded again, then headed over to the stoves to start cooking.

"See?" I told Silvio. "Sophia doesn't have a problem with Liam being here."

He snorted. "That's because she could crush his smug skull with her bare hands."

"Absolutely." The Goth dwarf winked at the vampire. "I take requests too."

Silvio glanced at Liam again. "Maybe later," he muttered.

I laughed and helped Sophia whip up a pot of baked beans, which she put on the stovetop to simmer away in Fletcher's secret barbecue sauce with its sweet brown-sugar notes and spicy cumin kick. While we worked, the rest of the waitstaff showed up, including Catalina Vasquez, Silvio's niece, and I opened the restaurant at eleven o'clock on the dot.

For the next few hours, I lost myself in the familiar rhythms of cooking, cleaning, and cashing out customers. By the time the lunch rush slowed down, I was feeling much calmer and more optimistic. Working in the restaurant always soothed me. Sometimes I almost thought I could see Fletcher perched on the stool behind the old-fashioned cash register, smiling and softly whispering ghostly advice whenever I walked by.

Only a few folks were eating, the waitstaff was taking a break, and I was fixing my own lunch when the bell over the front door chimed, and two people strolled into the restaurant.

The man was my age, early thirties, and wearing a gray overcoat on top of a dark green suit that brought out his green eyes, tan skin, and walnut-brown hair. The woman was in her mid-twenties, about five years younger than me, with shaggy blond hair, blue eyes, and rosy cheeks. She was sporting a short navy peacoat over a navy sweater and dark jeans and boots. A gun was clipped to her belt, right next to a shiny gold police badge.

Finnegan Lane, my foster brother, and Detective Bria Coolidge, my baby sister, walked over to the counter and slid onto the stools beside Silvio.

"Hey," I said. "What are you guys doing here?"

An amused smile creased Bria's face. "Don't tell me you forgot."

"Forgot what?"

Her smile widened. "The final fitting for our bridesmaid dresses."

I groaned. I had totally forgotten. Ever since I'd killed the giants in the cemetery, I had been focused on when and how Mason and Tucker might come at me, not the events that Mallory Parker and Stuart Mosley had planned leading up to their Saturday wedding.

I looked at Silvio. "Why didn't you remind me the final fitting was today?"

He waggled his tablet. "I *did* remind you during the morning briefing. Right at the fifteen-minute mark when you usually start tuning me out. Perhaps if you had paid attention during the *entire* briefing, you wouldn't be so surprised."

I rolled my eyes at his chiding, but I couldn't argue. I did tend to tune him out after a while, especially these days, when I was so preoccupied with the Circle.

"Aw, don't look so glum, Gin," Finn chirped in a bright voice. "I had the final fitting for my new Fiona Fine tuxedo yesterday."

Stuart Mosley was Finn's boss at First Trust bank, and the two of them had a very close mentor-mentee relationship. My brother was in the wedding as Mosley's best man.

"Yes, but you actually *enjoy* that sort of thing," I muttered.

"Absolutely. I never pass up an opportunity to wear a tuxedo and show off my handsomeness to its fullest, most devastating potential." Finn preened and straightened his tie, which was already perfectly in place. Then he nudged Bria with his elbow. "Tell her where the fitting is."

She grinned again. "The Posh boutique."

I let out another, louder groan. The Posh boutique was the scene of another one of my many crimes. Last summer, Finn had dragged me out dress shopping there, and I'd stopped a would-be robber from holding up the joint. However, the salesclerks hadn't been too thrilled about the blood I'd gotten on their fancy designer gowns in the process.

"Wait. What happened to the bridal shop where we got the dresses?" I asked.

"The seamstress started working at Posh instead," Bria replied.

"You have got to be kidding me."

My sister's grin widened. "Nope. We're supposed to meet Mallory and Lorelei there in thirty minutes."

I sighed, but there was no getting out of it, so I stripped off my blue work apron and told Sophia where I was going.

She grunted and kept stirring another pot of baked beans simmering on the stovetop.

Liam Carter watched me grab my black fleece jacket from the coatrack beside the cash register. He raised his eyebrows in a silent question, but I shook my head, telling him to stay put.

"You're not taking *him* with you?" Silvio asked in a snide voice.

"Nope. Bria and I will be fine. Besides, the restaurant is a much bigger, more obvious target. So you get Liam all to yourself for the next few hours."

Silvio shot me a sour look, then glanced over at Liam, who had finished with his newspaper and was now reading an epic fantasy book. I heartily approved of his literary choice.

"You should go sit with him," Finn chimed in. "Liam looks a little lonely."

My assistant turned his sour look to my brother. "I don't see how that's any of *your* business."

Finn threw his arm around Silvio's shoulder. "Aw, come on, man. Let me help you with this. We all know I'm the lady-killer of our group, with my handsome good looks, witty banter, and devilish charm."

"Oh, really?" Bria drawled, crossing her arms over her chest. "And what ladies have you killed lately?"

Most men would have wilted under her cool, steady gaze, but not Finnegan Lane. Instead, he flashed her a wide, dazzling smile and threw in a saucy wink for good measure. "Only you, baby," he purred. "Only you."

Bria huffed. "And you'd better keep it that way, pal."

Finn batted his eyelashes at her and drew a big, dramatic *X* over his chest. "Cross my heart and hope to die in your arms."

The two of them stared into each other's eyes, their faces soft and their mutual love clear for everyone to see. Finn winked at Bria again, then turned his attention back to Silvio.

"As I said, I'm the most accomplished lady-killer of our group." He paused. "Although I suppose we could change my title to *man-killer* for this particular operation. Either way, I'm the best chance you have of getting your guy."

Silvio's head drew back, his lips curled with disgust, and he actually shuddered, but his obvious reluctance didn't deter Finn. Few things did. My brother clapped the vampire on the shoulder, leaned forward, and started talking in a low voice. A few of his whispered words drifted over to me. *Optics, first date, new suit.*

Silvio looked at me and mouthed a distinct phrase: *Help me.*

I laughed and shrugged into my jacket, leaving my assistant and his burgeoning love life in the trusty man-killing hands of Finnegan Lane.

Bria and I left the Pork Pit, got into her sedan, and drove over to Northtown, the ritzy, glitzy part of Ashland, where those with money, power, and magic lived, dined, shopped, and schemed. I watched the mirrors while Bria drove, but no one followed us, and she pulled into the parking lot in front of the Posh boutique about twenty minutes later.

Bria cut the engine. "Silvio's love life aside, I find it highly interesting that Liam Carter is still hanging around the restaurant."

"I told you before. I figured it wouldn't hurt to have

Liam analyze my security protocols and station a couple of his giant guards around the Pork Pit in case Mason, Tucker, and their goons come calling. The last thing I need is a shootout or an elemental fight in the restaurant."

"Yes, but why are you suddenly so worried about that? Why *now*? We've been investigating the Circle for months, and you've never hired bodyguards before."

I bit back another curse. Like Silvio, Bria knew me far too well, and she realized that I wasn't telling her everything. She waited a few seconds, but when I remained silent, she let out an aggravated sigh.

"Fine. Don't tell me," she muttered. "But I can't help if you won't let me in, Gin."

"I know, but I don't want you to worry. This is *my* mistake, *my* mess, so *I* should be the one to suffer the consequences. Not you or anyone else."

"*We* will suffer the consequences *together*," Bria said in a fierce, determined voice. "You, me, Finn, Owen, and everyone else. We're all behind you, one hundred percent, no matter what happens."

She paused, but when I still didn't confess, she gave me a more speculative look. "This should go without saying, but you do realize that none of this is your fault, right? Not our parents being part of the Circle, not Mason killing them, not Tucker trying to recruit you to become a member. None of that is on *you*, Gin."

I let out a tense breath and thumped my head back against the car seat. "I know that. In theory, at least."

Bria's eyes narrowed. "But?"

I let out another breath. "But part of me feels like if I hadn't been so determined to expose Deirdre Shaw as a fraud, then none of this would have happened. I wouldn't know about the Circle, and you and I would still be blissfully ignorant about our parents being involved with the group."

Deirdre Shaw was Finn's mother and another member of the Circle. She'd come to town a few months ago and weaseled her way back into my brother's life so she could try to rob First Trust bank. She had tortured Finn with her Ice magic, although he had eventually ended up killing her in order to save me, which was something else I felt guilty about.

"If you hadn't exposed Deirdre for the snake she was, then Finn would be dead," Bria pointed out. "You had no way of knowing she was involved in the Circle."

I shrugged, not wanting to argue. We could go 'round and 'round about it, but part of me would always think it was my fault we'd ever heard of the Circle. Bria might not blame me, but *I* was the one who'd set us on this dark road of discovery, and I wouldn't be able to live with myself if my sister was murdered like our parents had been.

Bria hesitated, then reached down, pulled a manila file folder out from between her seat and the center console, and held it out to me.

I took the folder and set it on my lap. "What's this?"

She hesitated again before answering. "It's the police report of the car crash that supposedly killed our father."

The folder suddenly felt as heavy as a cement block crushing my legs. "What does it say?"

"Nothing good, which was pretty much what I expected," Bria replied. "The police might have said that Tristan died in the crash, but I had Ryan review the info."

Dr. Ryan Colson was the coroner and another one of our friends. He often helped Bria with her cases, and he'd also done me a few favors.

"What did Ryan say?" I asked, dreading but still wanting to know the answer.

Bria chewed on her lower lip. "That our father was tortured to death, given the injuries he sustained."

The folder got a little heavier on my legs. "Is his name listed in here?"

"No. The car was reported stolen, and Tristan was never officially identified. He's listed as a John Doe. No last name." Regret rippled through Bria's voice. She'd been a baby when our father died, so she didn't have any memories of him.

I frowned. "But if he was listed as a John Doe, then how did you find the file? And how do you know this is our father?"

"Because the victim looks just like the photo of Tristan that you bought during the auction at the Eaton Estate a couple of weeks ago. His face is intact. It's the rest of him that was...damaged." Bria cleared her throat, as if the last word had somehow choked her.

"As for how I found the file, well, it wasn't easy. I've been searching for it for weeks, going through the accident reports from around the time we thought he died. When you sent me the actual date of death from his tombstone a couple of days ago, I was finally able to narrow down my search. The file wasn't where it was supposed to be, but I kept looking, and I eventually found it in the cold-case storage room. Here's the interesting thing. Tristan supposedly died in a single-car accident, so there was no reason for the report to be in the cold-case room, unless..."

"Unless someone deliberately misfiled it." I finished her thought. "But why do that? Why not just steal the file and destroy it?"

Bria shook her head. "I don't know. Maybe the person who moved the file was interrupted before they could get rid of it, or maybe they forgot about it. Either way, I found it, although part of me wishes that I hadn't."

"So there's no concrete info in here about our father? Nothing that would help us track down Mason?"

She shook her head again. "No. Like I said before, Tristan was listed as a John Doe. Even weirder is the fact that I can't figure out what happened to his body. There's no record of Mom or anyone else claiming his remains and no mention of him being cremated. It's like Tristan's body vanished into thin air. *Poof!* He's gone."

Bria stopped and cleared her throat again, as if she was having trouble getting out her next words. "There are pictures in the file, if you want to see them."

My whole body involuntarily jerked back, trying to get away from the folder, even though I couldn't go anywhere in the car seat. I drew in a deep breath, slowly let it out, and forced myself to relax, although several seconds passed before I mustered enough courage to open the folder and peer at the photos inside.

They were *awful*.

The pictures had been taken more than twenty-five years ago, so they were in black-and-white, but the lack of color made the images seem even bleaker, starker, and more depressing, as though the life had been drained out of them the same way it had been drained out of my father. The first few photos had been taken from a distance and showed my father sitting in a crushed car, his body tilted forward, his head resting on the steering wheel. Tristan wasn't wearing a seat belt, although, strangely enough, the car was crumpled up like a sheet of paper around him, and he was perfectly untouched in the center of the destruction.

I moved on. Other photos showed different angles of the car, as well as the crash site. According to the police report, Tristan's car had skidded on a snowy road, plowed through a guardrail, and careened two hundred feet down a mountainside until the vehicle hit the trees and rocks at the bottom.

Lies, all of it.

No churned snow or skid marks streaked across the road indicating that he had tried to stop, and the guardrail looked like it had been cleanly sliced apart instead of being smashed to pieces. The crash site had obviously been staged to cover up his murder.

Finally, I reached the photos in the very back of the file. The first few shots showed my father stretched out on a metal autopsy table, with a white sheet draped over his torso. Bria was right. Tristan's face had been left untouched, and he looked the same as in the photo I'd bought at the Eaton Estate. Dark brown hair, straight nose, strong jaw, although his gray eyes were closed in death.

I traced my fingers over his face, then moved on to the other photos, the ones that showed close-up views of his injuries.

My father was a *mess*.

The blood had been washed away, but cuts and bruises covered his body from neck to toe. Some of the bruises were thick, solid, circular masses about the size of a fist, while others were long and thin, as though he'd been whipped. All put together, the marks looked like fat black spiders suspended in the center of the blue webs that had been etched into my father's skin.

The bruises were only the beginning. According to the coroner's notes, most of Tristan's major bones had either been crushed or snapped in multiple places, and the shattered ends stuck up at odd, impossible angles, like needles trying to poke through his skin. Every single one of his fingers had been dislocated and broken, and the swollen digits resembled purple sausages that were barely clinging to his hands. His toes had been given the same treatment, and several of them were missing altogether, as though they had been chopped off with a sharp blade.

My father had been completely, utterly *broken.*

As an assassin, I had done a lot of horrible things, hacked and slashed and hurt and killed people in cold, vicious, ruthless ways, and I had been injured myself in equal, severe fashion many, many times. All that violence haunted me, no matter how much someone might have deserved to die. But what had been done to Tristan, to my father… Well, it was a whole new disturbing level of brutality done for one reason only: to torture him to the fullest extent possible before his death.

A choked sob rose in my throat, and I had to clamp my hand over my mouth to keep from screaming. I managed to swallow down the sob, but I couldn't stop the tears from leaking out of the corners of my eyes. The drops dripped off my chin and landed on the photos, slowly oozing across the black-and-white images.

Bria reached over and grabbed my other hand with both of hers, squeezing tight. I threaded my fingers through hers, clutching her hand as strongly as she was clutching mine. We sat there in silence for a few minutes, drawing what strength and comfort we could from each other.

"You okay?" Bria whispered.

I wasn't, but I had to pretend like I was. Otherwise, I'd break down completely, and I couldn't do that. Not in front of my baby sister. Not when she was hurting just as much as I was.

So I gently tugged my hand out of hers and wiped away my tears. "Yeah. Tell me the rest of it."

"Ryan thinks an elemental caused those injuries." She paused. "A Stone elemental."

I could hear what she wasn't saying. Not just any Stone elemental—*Mason.*

A loud, vicious curse spewed out of my lips. My fingers clenched around the edges of the open folder, and a sudden urge filled me to rip it to shreds, along with the papers and photos inside. But destroying them wouldn't change what had happened to my father. Nothing would *ever* change that, and the awful images were now permanently burned into my brain, as though each picture was a red-hot brand sizzling inside my mind.

Bria wet her lips. "You're a Stone elemental too. How…how would you do something like that, Gin?"

I closed my eyes. I didn't want to answer her question, didn't want to think about this a moment longer. But she needed to know what we were up against, so I forced myself to open my eyes and study the photos again. Not as a daughter and not even as an assassin. What had been done to my father went beyond mere *killing.* This action had sprung from a deep well of hatred, a sharp sting of rage unlike any I had ever encountered before.

"Gin?" Bria asked in a low, strained voice. "How would you do it?"

I held up my hand and slowly curled my fingers into a tight fist. "I would coat my hand with my Stone magic to make my skin, my fist, as hard as a cement block. Then, when I had a good grip on my power, I would start hitting the other person. Over and over again. Their skin would bruise first, but I would keep going, using more magic, more power, more force, until I broke their bones."

Bria shuddered out a ragged breath at my cold, clinical tone. "And then?"

"And then, when their bones were broken, I would coat both of my hands with my Stone magic, so that I had a strong, unbreakable grip. Then I would dig my fingers deep into their skin, grab hold of their arms and legs and fingers and toes, and wrench their bruised muscles and broken bones even farther apart. Twisting and twisting, again and again. Until you got *this*."

I couldn't stand to look at the photos anymore, so I shoved them and the folder off my lap and down to the floorboard. They landed with soft whispers, although the faint scraping sounds seemed as loud as my father's phantom bones breaking in my mind. I flinched, and another sob rose in my throat. This time, I couldn't swallow it down, and the small, strangled, anguished cry escaped my lips.

Bria grabbed my hand again, her fingers shockingly warm as they wrapped around my cold fist. Even though I wasn't using my Ice or Stone magic, wasn't reaching for my power at all, my body still felt frozen and stiff.

"It's okay, Gin. It's okay," Bria murmured. "We're going to find Mason. We're going to get the bastard. For Dad, for Mom, for Annabella. He's *never* going to hurt anyone else like he's hurt us."

She squeezed my hand again, then rubbed it between her own two, trying to bring some warmth to my skin and get me to unclench my fist. I sat there and dully watched her work.

Bria kept murmuring words of revenge and encouragement. She probably thought I was upset about what had happened to Tristan. That was part of it, but our father was dead. Mason couldn't hurt him anymore.

No, what coated my heart with icy dread was the agonizing worry and paralyzing fear that I wasn't strong enough to stop Mason and that my murderous uncle would torture and kill Bria and everyone else I loved the same way he had killed my father.

✲ 5 ✲

It took me a few minutes to push away my dread, worry, and fear, but I forced myself to lean forward, pick up the papers and photos, and shove them back into the folder. I laid the file on the center console between Bria and me, then scooted away from it. I didn't even want to *look* at it right now, much less think about the ugly things it contained.

Bria's phone chirped. She fished it out of her pocket and read the message. "Lorelei says they're waiting for us inside."

"Then we should go," I said in a dull, tired tone.

"I didn't mean to upset you, Gin. I just thought you would want to know. That you would want to see the photos…no matter how horrific they were."

I forced myself to nod as though everything was okay. "You're right. I did want to know. I'm glad you showed them to me."

If nothing else, the photos had made me even more determined to protect my sister and everyone else. The thing that concerned me was that I didn't know *how* to actually do it.

Bria and I left the folder in her car, crossed the parking lot, and stepped into the Posh boutique.

The boutique had been remodeled and had expanded into a neighboring storefront since the last time I'd been here. Designer dresses lined the walls, while free-standing racks of even fancier frocks took up the center of the store. Cocktail, evening, bridal, prom. The boutique featured a gown, pantsuit, and catsuit for every occasion, along with counters brimming with makeup, shoes, and purses. A glass case full of sparkling sapphire bracelets, gleaming ruby rings, and other expensive jewelry ran along the back wall, in case you wanted to add some serious bling to your ensemble.

I was so busy looking at the dresses, shoes, and jewelry that it took me a few seconds to realize that the boutique itself had been decked out for today's occasion.

Enormous white paper wedding bells and hearts swooped down from the ceiling, along with royal-blue ribbons with *Mallory + Stuey* printed on them in shiny silver letters. More white, blue, and silver ribbons curled along the tops of the dress racks and display counters, while a large silver banner bearing the happy couple's names in blue sequins glittered on the back wall above the jewelry counter. Crystal vases filled with white, blue, and purple orchids sat on tables throughout the boutique, along with platters of chocolate, strawberry, and vanilla petit fours. Several bottles of champagne were chilling in ice buckets beside the tables.

"What's going on?" I whispered. "I thought we were just doing a final fitting for our bridesmaid dresses."

"I have no idea," Bria whispered back.

"Gin! Bria! There you are!" a light feminine voice called out.

A woman stepped out from behind a rack of dresses and walked over to us. Her short black hair framed her face, and her mint-green pantsuit highlighted her lovely toffee eyes and skin, along with her gorgeous curves. A square emerald dangled from the silver chain around her neck, and a matching ring sparkled on her finger. She looked like a model who had stepped out of the pages of some high-fashion magazine.

"Roslyn?" I asked. "What are you doing here? Are you in the wedding too?"

Roslyn Phillips, another one of our friends, laughed. "In a manner of speaking. The wedding planner came down with the flu, so Mallory asked me to help with a few last-minute details for your fitting, along with some of the other events leading up to the big day."

Roslyn ran Northern Aggression, the hottest nightclub in Ashland, so she was used to showing people a good time. Helping Mallory navigate through the rest of her wedding week would probably be a piece of cake compared to dealing with everyone who crammed into Roslyn's club on a nightly basis.

"Gin! Bria! I'm so happy you're here!" another voice called out, although this one was older and rougher and had far more of a hillbilly twang than Roslyn's soft, dulcet tones.

Two other women stepped into view. The first was my age, early thirties, with blue eyes, pale skin, and black hair pulled back into a pretty French braid. She was wearing a dark blue pantsuit, and a diamond, rose-and-thorn ring glinted on her finger, a symbol for how deadly beauty could be.

"Hey, guys." Lorelei Parker smiled at Bria and me. "And here is the blushing bride-to-be."

She gestured at the other woman, a much older dwarf who was around five feet tall. The dwarf was also wearing a pantsuit, but hers was a cool off-white that was just a shade darker than her teased cloud of hair.

Mallory Parker waved her hand, dismissing her granddaughter's words. The motion caused the many carats in her diamond engagement ring to flash and sparkle.

"Blushing? Hardly. I've been around the block too many times for that." Mallory's face softened, and a smile curved her lips, warming her blue eyes and adding a few more wrinkles to her tan skin. "But I'm so happy to be marrying my Stuey."

I grinned. I would never get used to her nickname for Mosley. "And where is the groom-to-be?"

Mallory snorted. "Oh, he was here earlier, picking up his tux, but he skedaddled when Roslyn broke out the decorations. You would have thought the ribbons and bells were snakes and spiders the way Stuey hightailed it out of here."

We all laughed, and Mallory stepped forward and threaded her arms through mine and Bria's. "Come on, ladies. I'm getting married in a few days, so we need to get this show on the road." She winked at us. "Besides, all these desserts and bottles of champagne aren't going to eat and drink themselves."

She pulled us deeper into the boutique, still quite strong, despite her three-hundred-plus years.

Roslyn had reserved the entire store for our fitting, and a large area had been cleared next to the dressing rooms. Several white velvet chairs had been arranged around three round, raised daises that reminded me of oversize mushrooms. Two salesclerks were standing by, along with Willa, the seamstress.

Mallory released Bria and me and gestured at a couple of racks of dresses. "I thought we could start with these. As you know, I've decided on a cool color palette. Lots of silvers and blues. None of that tacky pink and red you always see this time of year."

Mallory and Mosley were getting married on Saturday, Valentine's Day, but during the rehearsal dinner, she had announced that she'd opted for a winter-themed wedding instead of the more traditional white gown and red roses extravaganza. The dwarf started flipping through the dresses, muttering to herself about royal versus sapphire blue and satin versus silk.

"What about the dresses she picked out for us at the bridal shop last week?" I whispered to Lorelei. "The ones we came here to try on for our final fitting?"

Lorelei glowered at Willa, the seamstress, who winced and ducked her head. "I left Grandma alone for ten minutes while Roslyn and I hung the bells and the banner, and Willa and the salesclerks started talking about a new shipment of bridesmaid dresses they got in yesterday. Grandma insisted on seeing them."

"And now we have to try them on?" Bria asked.

"Yes. Apparently, I have a bridezilla on my hands." Lorelei sighed and gestured at one of the tables. "But at least we have dessert. And champagne. *Lots* of champagne. I insisted on that."

"Smart woman," Bria said.

"Very smart woman," Roslyn chimed in.

Mallory gestured at me. "Gin! Come here! This color would look *amazing* on you!"

I might be the Spider, but bridezilla definitely trumped assassin, so I shrugged out of my jacket and tossed it onto a nearby chair. "Pour me a glass of champagne, and keep 'em coming," I muttered as I walked past Lorelei.

She saluted me, then grabbed the closest bottle.

An hour later, I had drunk two glasses of champagne, eaten a platter of petit fours, and tried on a dozen dresses. Now I was standing on one of the daises, while Bria was on a second one and Lorelei was on the third.

We were all wearing the same thing: a royal-blue gown with short sleeves, a high neckline, and a skirt dotted with small silver sequins. More silver sequins glinted on the sleeves and the bodice, making us look as though we had draped ourselves in a gorgeous night sky, complete with sparkling stars.

Mallory clapped her hands together. "That's it! That's the one! I love the color, and it looks gorgeous on all three of you. It's *so* much better than that other cheap rag I picked out last week."

The other dress had hardly been cheap or a rag, but she was right. This gown looked stunning on Bria and Lorelei and pretty good on me too. Plus, it had a long skirt to hide my knives. I might be attending a wedding, but I was still going to be armed.

Mallory waved her hand at the two clerks. "Ladies, ring up those dresses, and put them on my account. Willa, do whatever is needed for the alterations. I want my gals to look perfect."

The clerks scurried away, while the seamstress grabbed a plastic box filled with pins, measuring tape, and other sewing supplies.

"I thought bridesmaids were supposed to pay for their own dresses," Bria said. "I'm happy to do that."

Mallory waved her hand again. "Nonsense, darling. It's my shotgun wedding, so to speak, so I'm paying for everything, including the dresses."

Bria opened her mouth to protest. I did too, but Mallory stared us down over the rim of her champagne glass.

"I won't hear another word about it," she said in a stern voice. "You're doing me a huge favor being in the wedding on such short notice. Paying for your dresses is the least I can do."

My sister looked at me for help, but I shrugged back. Bridezilla also trumped detective.

"Yes, ma'am," Bria and I said in unison.

Now that Mallory had finally decided on our dresses, the seamstress got to work, pinning up Bria's skirt, taking in my bodice, and adjusting Lorelei's neckline just a bit.

Roslyn picked up a tablet from a table and swiped through a few screens. "Now that we've taken care of the two bridesmaids and the maid of honor, we need to find you a dress, Mallory."

The dwarf nodded, got up, and started flipping through another rack of dresses.

A few minutes later, the seamstress finished with my bodice. I stripped off the gown in one of the dressing rooms and put on my long-sleeve dark blue T-shirt and black jeans, along with my five knives—two tucked up my sleeves, one nestled in the small of my back, and two hidden in the sides of my black boots.

Bria and Lorelei also shimmied back into their normal clothes, and then it was our turn to sit while Mallory tried on dress after dress after dress.

"Too poofy." Lorelei dismissed the first choice.

"Too many sequins." Bria doomed the second.

"Too much tulle." Roslyn rejected the third.

"Too many feathers." I nixed the fourth.

Finally, nine (ten?) gowns later, Mallory emerged from the dressing room and stepped up onto the dais.

"*Ahhh,*" Lorelei, Bria, Roslyn, and I sighed in unison.

"That's the one," Lorelei declared.

"Yep," Bria agreed.

"Definitely," Roslyn replied.

"Absolutely," I chimed in.

Mallory was wearing a simple sheath dress with cap sleeves. The color was somewhere between silver and blue, and the cool tone brought out the dwarf's blue eyes and the pink in her cheeks. A thin band of silver sequins circled the waist, adding a bit of sparkle to the garment.

"You're right. This is the one. I won't find a prettier dress." She beamed at us, and we started clapping, as did the seamstress and the salesclerks.

Mallory gave us an elegant curtsy, then held her arms out to her sides so that Willa could flutter around and mark down some minor alterations. Once the seamstress was finished, Mallory disappeared into a dressing room to put on her regular clothes, while Lorelei, Bria, Roslyn, and I relaxed and noshed on more desserts.

Mallory was still changing when Bria's phone chirped. She pulled it out of her pocket and made a face.

"Something wrong?" I asked.

"Duty calls," Bria replied. "Although I have no idea why Sykes would be texting me."

"Who's Sykes?" I asked.

Roslyn rolled her eyes. "He's this awful cop that Bria and Xavier work with. Sykes is totally lazy and can't be bothered to do much of anything, other than drink coffee, eat doughnuts, and take bribes. He's a total cliché, even for Ashland."

Xavier was Roslyn's significant other and Bria's partner on the force.

Bria snorted out a laugh and started texting. "Coffee, doughnuts, and bribes. Yeah, that's Sykes in a nutshell. But he says there has been a robbery in one of the nearby shopping centers. I need to respond to the scene. Gin, can you catch a ride back to the Pork Pit with someone else?"

"I can drop her off," Roslyn volunteered. "I'd love to get some barbecue for dinner."

"Thanks," I replied. "That would be great."

Roslyn smiled and went back to her tablet. Lorelei pulled out her phone to check her own messages, while Mallory came out of the dressing room and started talking to Willa and the clerks. Bria kept texting, and a frown flickered across her face.

"Something wrong?" I asked again.

She shook her head and got to her feet. "Apparently, Xavier hasn't heard about the robbery. I texted and told him I was on my way, and he wanted to know the address."

That was weird. Xavier was usually right on top of things like that.

"Anyway, I've got to go," Bria said. "I'll swing by your house tonight, and we can talk more about that…file. Okay?"

She meant the folder of information on our father's murder. I put down the chocolate petit four I'd been about to eat. My appetite had vanished.

"Yeah. Sounds like a plan."

Bria left the boutique. My sister was a tough-as-nails cop, with a gun on her belt and Ice magic flowing through her veins, and she could definitely take care of herself. It wasn't unusual for her to be called to a crime scene, but this summons seemed more abrupt than most, so I got to my feet, went to the front of the boutique, and peered through the window.

Bria hurried across the pavement, still looking at her phone. I scanned the parking lot, but I didn't see anyone lurking among the rows of luxury vehicles. Still, the closer Bria got to her car, the more unease filled me.

"Gin?" Lorelei walked over to me. "Is something wrong?"

I shook my head. I couldn't explain the worry suddenly swirling through my body—

Wait a second. I tilted my head to the side and listened, *really* listened. The whole time we'd been in the boutique, the brick storefront had been crowing about the pretty dresses, shoes, and jewelry inside, but those smug whispers had transformed into harsh mutters brimming with dark, deadly intent.

Suddenly, I knew the text Bria had gotten from that corrupt cop was bogus, a ruse to draw her outside the store where she would be more vulnerable.

"Bria's in trouble!" I yelled.

"Gin! Wait!" Lorelei hissed.

But there was no time to wait or explain, so I rushed over, yanked open the door, and raced out into the parking lot.

My sister was almost to her car, her gaze still focused on her phone. At the far end of the lot, an engine roared to life, and a black SUV zipped out of a parking space, heading straight for her.

"Bria!" I screamed. "Behind you!"

Her head snapped up, and she glanced at me, clearly startled. I stabbed my finger, telling Bria to look behind her, and she finally got the message. She whirled around, her free hand dropping to the gun holstered to her belt, but it was already too late.

The black SUV screeched to a stop in front of her, and three giants poured out of the vehicle and trained their guns on her. Bria hesitated, as if she was thinking about fighting back, but she did the smart thing, took her hand off her weapon, and raised her arms.

"Get her in the car! Now!" A voice bellowed from inside the vehicle.

Maybe it was my imagination, but I could have sworn I'd heard that voice before. I'd find out exactly who it belonged to once I killed the giants who were trying to kidnap my sister.

Two of the men latched onto Bria's arms, yanked her forward, and forced her into the SUV. The third giant piled in after the other two and yanked the door shut behind them. Then the vehicle started rolling forward.

Despite the fact that I'd been running this whole time, I was still on the far side of Bria's sedan. Rather than waste time going around the car, I put on an extra burst of speed, leaped up, and slid across the hood like a hero in an action movie.

I managed to slow down just enough so that I didn't fall when my boots hit the ground on the other side. The second I regained my balance, I darted forward and planted myself on the pavement in front of the SUV.

The driver slammed on the brakes, and the vehicle jerked to a stop ten feet away from me. The windshield was tinted, so I couldn't see who was driving or how many more giants might be inside. My hands curled into fists. Didn't much matter. I'd kill everyone in that vehicle to save Bria.

I took a step forward and reached for my magic. I'd shoot out the tires with a spray of Ice daggers, then shatter the windshield with my cold projectiles—

The driver stomped on the gas. I tensed, thinking they were going to zoom forward and try to flatten me into a bloody pancake, but they threw the SUV into reverse and zipped backward instead. I let out a vicious curse and sprinted forward, chasing after the vehicle.

"Gin! Gin!" Shouts rose up behind me, and I heard

Lorelei's voice, along with Roslyn's, but I tuned them out and kept running. I couldn't let the giants escape with Bria.

I pumped my arms and legs and moved even faster. The driver was running out of pavement, and they'd have to veer to one side or the other, stop, and throw the SUV into gear to leave the parking lot. The second the vehicle slowed down, I would put on a final burst of speed, flatten the tires with some Ice daggers, throw myself onto the hood, shatter the windshield, and attack whoever was inside—

The driver slammed on the brakes again, right before the SUV would have careened back into a light pole. I put on that extra burst of speed, still sprinting toward the vehicle. What was the driver doing? Why weren't they throwing the SUV into gear and cranking the wheel to the right to leave?

The driver shoved the vehicle into gear, but instead of steering away, they stomped on the gas and came straight at me. The bad guys hadn't been retreating. No, they'd wanted some distance to build up as much speed and force as possible for when they tried to mow me down.

I threw myself to the side. The SUV raced by me and slammed into a silver sports car. The smaller vehicle crumpled up like a paper napkin at the brutal impact, although it didn't seem to do much damage to the SUV.

I had dived toward an empty parking space, but I misjudged the distance, and my shoulder clipped the passenger's-side mirror on a parked sedan. The impact tossed me to the side, and the pavement rushed up to meet me. I grabbed hold of my Stone magic and hardened my skin a split second before I hit the ground. Even then, I still slammed into the asphalt with breathtaking force.

Pain spiked through my left shoulder, arm, hip, and leg. A low groan escaped my lips, but I forced myself to stagger back up and onto my feet.

"Gin!" Lorelei rushed over to me. "Are you okay?"

Behind her, the SUV backed up, zoomed away from the crumpled car, and turned in our direction.

"Watch out!" I yelled.

I surged forward, grabbed Lorelei, and spun us around so that my back was facing the SUV. Then I churned my legs, trying to get us out of the path of the charging vehicle. I also reached for my Stone magic again, hardening my body into an impenetrable shell.

Once again, I misjudged the distance, and the SUV's passenger's-side mirror clipped my shoulder, making me stagger forward and lose my balance. I still had my arms wrapped around Lorelei, and she shrieked in surprise as I took her down with me. Somehow I managed to twist my body around so that I hit the pavement first, with her landing on top of me.

Her body slammed into mine, punching the breath out of my lungs and making my head snap back against the unyielding pavement. Despite the protective shell of my Stone magic, white stars still exploded in eyes, and my brain sloshed around inside my skull like it was made of warm gelatin.

Lorelei lifted her head and looked at me, concern creasing her face. "Gin! Are you okay—"

Hands grabbed Lorelei's shoulders and yanked her away. My brain was still sloshing back and forth, but I managed to sit up. A shadow fell over me, blocking out the afternoon sun.

A female giant around seven feet tall loomed over me. My dazed gaze focused on her black ballet flats, then traveled up her gray pantsuit and matching shirt to her face. The giant had hazel eyes, milky skin dotted with faint freckles, and a sleek bob of golden hair that curled under at the ends.

Shock smacked into me just as hard as I had hit the pavement. I blinked several times, wondering if she was really here, but I wasn't imagining her familiar features.

Emery Slater, one of my many enemies.

I hadn't seen Emery since the night she'd fled from the Monroe family mansion after I had killed Madeline Monroe, Emery's boss at the time. That had been several months ago, and there had been no sign of the giant anywhere in Ashland since then.

She? Who are you going to call? My own voice floated through my mind, along with the answer from Vance, one of the giants I'd killed at the cemetery a few days ago. *You'll find out soon enough. But trust me, you won't like the surprise.*

He had been right. I most definitely did not like the surprise. Emery Slater showing up here only meant one thing: she was working for the Circle.

"Hello, Blanco," Emery purred. "I've been looking forward to seeing you again."

She gave me an evil gin, then drew back her fist. I raised my hand and reached for my Stone magic again, but my brain was still sloshing around, and I couldn't quite get a grip on my power.

Emery Slater slammed her fist into my face, and the world went black.

✲ 6 ✲

"Gin! Gin!" a voice hissed, penetrating the darkness cloaking my mind. "Are you okay?"

I jerked my head to the side, away from the demanding voice, and immediately wished that I hadn't, since an intense ache exploded in my left cheekbone and spread out through the rest of my face. In an instant, my entire head felt like it was wrapped in hot, stinging vines that were twisting tighter around my skull and pounding through it at the same time.

"What's going on?" I said, my words slurring.

"You'll find out soon enough," another voice drawled.

I blinked and blinked and drew in several deep breaths. Slowly, I pushed the pain down to a more manageable level and focused on my surroundings.

I was propped up in the SUV's middle seat, sandwiched between Bria and Lorelei. A male giant was driving, and Emery Slater was sitting in the front passenger's seat, pointing a gun at me. Three more male giants were sitting in the seat behind Bria, Lorelei, and me, also pointing their guns at us.

I glanced down, but Bria's gun was still on her belt. The giants hadn't bothered to take away my weapons either, and I was still wearing all five of my knives in their usual spots. Then again, the giants' guns trumped my knives in this situation, and they could easily shoot us before I could palm a blade and stab any of them.

Still, if it had just been me in the SUV, I would have hardened my skin with my Stone magic, grabbed Emery's gun, and shoved the weapon through her teeth before attacking the driver and the other giants. But Bria and Lorelei couldn't protect themselves the same way, and I couldn't risk them getting shot in the crossfire. Something Emery realized, judging from her smug smirk.

"When did you slither back into Ashland?" I asked.

"Oh, I've been negotiating terms with my new employer for a few weeks," Emery replied. "But this is my first official day on the job. So far, I'm enjoying it very much. I do so love flattening little Spiders."

She laughed at her lame joke, as did the other giants.

I ignored her cackles and glanced at Bria, then Lorelei. They both looked pale and worried, but they were still in one piece. Good. Now I just had to figure out how to get us away from the giants without one of my friends getting shot.

But I didn't get the chance to come up with an escape plan. I didn't know how long I'd been unconscious or how far we'd driven, but a few minutes later, the driver steered off the road and stopped at a wrought-iron gate with the letters *AHA* running through the black metal. I eyed the fancy cursive symbol. *AHA*? I'd seen those letters before, although I couldn't remember when or where, thanks to the continued pounding in my face and skull.

The two halves of the gate split apart and rolled back,

and the driver steered the SUV through the opening and up a long, steep paved driveway lined with pear trees on both sides. About half a mile later, the driver crested the top of the hill, and the trees fell away, revealing an enormous mansion.

I peered through the windshield. The wide, massive structure was five stories of white stone supported by thick columns that stretched from the ground all the way up to the top level. Porches wrapped around each story, although no one was lounging in the white wicker chairs, given the February chill. White stone planters full of primroses, jasmine, and other hardy flowers added splashes of color here and there, and the surrounding lawn was perfectly landscaped, despite its carpet of brown winter grass. Even among the Eaton Estate and many other Northtown mansions, this one was truly impressive, and I suddenly realized where we were.

The Ashland Historical Association.

This mansion served as headquarters for the preservation group and was filled with antique furniture, old photos, and vintage tools that showed the progression of life in Ashland through the years. The mansion was open for tours much of the year, and historical reenactors staged battles and festivals on the grounds during the summer months. I had been here more than once, first as a schoolkid learning about ye olden days and later on as the Spider, getting close to targets at the association's various fund-raising events.

I had expected the giants to take us to some deserted warehouse. What were we doing here?

The driver parked in front of the mansion, and Emery gestured with her gun.

"Get out," she growled. "And don't cause any trouble, or my men will start shooting."

Lorelei crawled out of the SUV first, followed by me, then Bria. The driver and the three giants in the back also got out and flanked us. They kept their guns trained on us, although Emery put her weapon away. Then again, she didn't really need a gun, since she could easily beat us to death with her fists and her massive strength.

I peered at the mansion again and reached out with my magic. All the other times I'd been here, the stones had sleepily murmured about the comings and goings of the association members and historical reenactors, along with long-suffering sighs from the bored schoolkids who'd shuffled through the hallways. Those quiet murmurs had vanished, and the stones now purred with pure, raw power, as though they'd been struck by lightning and jolted awake.

A shiver rippled down my spine. I'd only sensed that sort of brute strength once before, and I knew exactly who Emery had brought us here to see, as if it hadn't already been obvious enough.

My friends shot me uneasy looks. Bria was an Ice elemental, and Lorelei was gifted in both Ice and metal magic. They couldn't hear the stones' purrs like I could, but their magic let them sense the elemental power that permeated the mansion.

The double doors on the front opened, and two more giant guards appeared, with a third man who was shorter and leaner trailing along behind them.

He was wearing a dark gray suit, along with a matching shirt and tie, and his black wing tips were polished to a high gloss. His black hair gleamed in the afternoon sunlight, as did his black eyes and the neat, trimmed goatee that clung to his chin. He had one of those tan, ageless faces that would make him look handsome, strong, and vital no matter how old he got, although I knew he was in his fifties, roughly the same age my parents would have been if they had lived, if this man hadn't stood by and let them be murdered.

Hugh Tucker walked down the steps and stopped beside Emery. The vampire looked at Bria, then Lorelei, before his gaze settled on me. He frowned. At first, I wondered what he was staring at, but then I realized that I probably had an enormous bruise from where Emery had punched me. I gingerly touched my cheek. More pain rippled through my face. Yep, definitely bruised.

The vampire's gaze flicked back to Lorelei, who was also bruised, dirty, and disheveled, thanks to our hitting the pavement together.

Tucker turned to Emery. "You were only supposed to bring Bria. Unharmed. Not bang up and kidnap the whole bridal entourage."

The giant shrugged. "It couldn't be helped. Blanco tried to save her sister, and then Parker joined in the fun too. Besides, what does it matter? The mansion is closed for the winter, so no one knows we're here. Even if someone did try to rescue them, I have more than enough men to handle Finnegan Lane and Owen Grayson."

She obviously didn't know my friends as well as she thought. Finn and Owen would move heaven and earth to rescue Bria and me, and Mallory would do the same for Lorelei. Still, I kept quiet. The more Emery underestimated my friends, the better chance we had of Finn and Owen finding us.

Mallory and Roslyn would have called the guys, along with Xavier, the second they realized we'd been kidnapped. Silvio was probably already tracking my phone, which was stuffed in the back pocket of my jeans. I just hoped the device was still working and hadn't been broken by my hard falls.

"What if someone decides to ping Blanco's phone? Or Bria's to try to locate them?" Tucker asked.

"And that's precisely why I installed those cell-phone and other signal jammers on the grounds last week, along with the surveillance cameras in and around the mansion," Emery replied. "No one is going to track them. We are completely secure here."

Well, there went my hope that Silvio could pinpoint our exact location, but maybe he could at least get close enough to stumble across the mansion. Either way, I couldn't wait for him or anyone else to show up. I was going to rescue myself, the way I so often did, and Bria and Lorelei too.

"In my experience, no place is completely *secure* when Blanco and her friends are involved," Tucker murmured.

Well, at least he wasn't underestimating us. Then again, my friends and I had thwarted the vampire's plans too many times for him to dismiss our skills.

"Maybe they weren't secure when *you* were running things, but I won't make the same mistakes you have," Emery replied, a sneering note creeping into her voice.

She looked down her nose at Tucker, but his face remained blank. Bria and Lorelei glanced back and forth between the two of them, as did the six giant guards, some of whom shifted on their feet, as if they weren't sure whom to support in this war of words.

From the sound of things, Mason had brought Emery Slater in to be his new head of security over Hugh Tucker. Interesting. Very interesting.

I wondered what Tucker had done to make Mason so unhappy. Or perhaps the vampire's continued failure to kill me had finally led to his demotion. Either way, Tucker kept staring at Emery, that same blank expression on his face. To most people, he would have seemed as calm as a statue, but the faint pucker of his lips and the slight narrowing of his black eyes indicated that he wasn't happy with Emery and this new status quo.

The giant should watch her back. Hugh Tucker had an uncanny habit of surviving the infighting that went on among Circle members. He'd already outlasted Deirdre Shaw, Damian Rivera, Bruce Porter, and Alanna Eaton, and I had a feeling he would outlive Emery Slater too.

Especially since I planned to kill her the second I got the chance.

The giant hated me because she thought I'd murdered her uncle, Elliot Slater, who had worked for Mab Monroe. Roslyn had actually killed Elliot, who had been stalking and harassing her, but I had taken credit for his death in order to protect my friend. If Emery knew the truth, she'd try to kill Roslyn, and I needed to eliminate the giant before that happened.

Or perhaps Hugh Tucker would finally snap and do it for me right here and now.

I held my breath, hoping that the giant would foolishly keep insulting him, but Emery must have realized that she'd pushed Tucker far enough, because she crossed her arms over her chest and gave him a wary look.

"Well, if *you* think we're secure, then I'll take your word for it," Tucker said in a smooth voice.

My breath escaped in a soft, disappointed sigh. I should have known better. My luck could never, ever be that good.

Emery's face crinkled with suspicion, but Tucker gave her another bland look in return. She huffed, then waved her hand at her men. "Get them inside."

A couple of the giants kept their guns out, while the

others holstered their weapons and stepped forward. One reached for Lorelei, but she jerked her arm away from him.

"If you touch me, I will break your face," Lorelei snarled.

The giant's nostrils flared with anger, and he drew back his fist, as though he was going to punch her. I started forward to put myself between Lorelei and the giant, but I didn't have to protect her.

Hugh Tucker did it for me.

Quick as a blink, Tucker glided forward and caught the giant's fist in his hand. Even though the giant was a foot taller and at least a hundred pounds heavier than Tucker, the giant was the one who abruptly stopped, as though he'd run into a cement wall, while the vampire didn't so much as rock back on his heels.

I'd known that Tucker was amazingly fast, but that was an impressive show of strength. He was even more dangerous than I'd realized.

"That won't be necessary, Nate," Tucker said in a cool voice. "I'm sure Ms. Parker knows how tenuous her situation is. There's no need to manhandle her as well."

Nate, the giant in question, glanced over at Emery, who jerked her head, telling him to let it go.

The giant started to pull his hand away, but Tucker dug his fingers into Nate's fist. Tucker barely seemed to be touching the giant, but the other man's face contorted in pain, and his knuckles *crack-crack-cracked* one after another from the bone-crushing pressure Tucker was exerting on them.

The vampire was letting everyone know he was not to be ignored, despite the fact that Emery was in charge—for now.

The rest of the giants exchanged uneasy glances and shifted on their feet again. Tucker must have been satisfied he'd made his point, because he released the giant's fist. Nate staggered back and cradled his red, puffy hand to his chest, trying to massage away the lingering sting of Tucker's iron grip.

"Wow," Lorelei drawled in a sarcastic, mocking voice, breaking the tense silence. "And people say that chivalry is dead. My hero."

I grimaced, as did Bria. Lorelei should have known better than to antagonize the vampire, especially given what he'd just done to that giant.

Tucker paused, as if he wasn't sure he'd heard her right, then smoothly spun around on his wing tips to face her. Lorelei stared right back at him. Tucker's head tilted to the side, and his eyes narrowed, as if he was truly seeing her for the very first time. Lorelei kept right on staring at him, her blue gaze rock-steady on his black one.

Tucker's eyes narrowed a bit more, but he didn't appear to be angry. Perhaps it was my imagination, but the vampire almost seemed...*intrigued.*

Lorelei stepped closer to Tucker. The giants tensed, as did Emery, but the vampire held up his hand, telling them to stand down.

"Let's get one thing straight," Lorelei said in a cold voice. "I don't need you or anyone else to protect me. Are we clear?"

Tucker didn't respond. Lorelei drew back her fist as though she was going to punch him. Once again, I started forward to do something, and once again, I didn't have to intervene.

Lorelei whipped around, stepped up, and punched Nate, the giant who'd tried to grab her. She slammed her fist right into his windpipe, making him cough, choke, and stagger back. Nate glared at her, anger filling his now beet-red face, but Lorelei gave him an icy glare before turning back to Tucker.

"Are we clear?" she asked, a sharp note in her voice.

An amused smile quirked Tucker's lips before his features smoothed out into their usual bland mask. "Crystal."

Then the vampire respectfully tipped his head and held out his arm, as though he was a suave Southern gentleman about to escort a beautiful lady into a grand manor house.

Lorelei blinked, clearly surprised by the gesture. She hesitated, but this had turned into a battle of wills, and my friend wasn't one to back down. She stepped forward and threaded her arm through Tucker's, once again staring into his eyes and not showing the faintest flicker of fear.

"If you two are finished, perhaps we can get on with things," Emery snapped in an impatient tone.

Tucker swept his free arm out to the side in a grand, dramatic gesture. "After you, Ms. Slater."

Emery huffed again, then brushed past him and strode through the open doors. Tucker gestured with his free hand again, and he and Lorelei headed in that direction, the two of them still weirdly arm in arm.

The rest of the giants clustered around Bria and me, and we had no choice but to follow them.

The inside of the mansion was just as I remembered from my childhood and other visits.

Enormous foyers with hardwood floors. Tall, wide staircases lined with white-plaster banisters featuring flowers and vines. Alcoves brimming with quilts, looms, and old-fashioned sewing machines. Walls covered with gold-framed paintings showcasing Ashland landmarks, along with smaller tintypes and black-and-white portraits of citizens dressed in their Sunday best. Dining rooms filled with antique mahogany tables set with fine silver and delicate china. Old-timey hobnail lamps in the corners of those dining rooms, with crystal chandeliers dangling from the ceilings. And all of it labeled with identification cards and larger plaques explaining each item's historical significance.

The architecture and furnishings were as grand and fine as any in Ashland, but everything was much older here, and many of the paintings, quilts, and lamps were priceless heirlooms that had been passed down through the generations. A hushed sense of history filled the mansion, and the people in the portraits and tintypes seemed to turn their heads and glare at me, the modern, uncouth intruder who'd dared to disturb their peace and quiet. I shivered. Creepy.

But the worst part was the stones. Now that I was inside the mansion, the rumbling purrs of pure, raw power were louder than ever, and the smug continued chorus grated on my nerves. The person we were going to see thought they had so much magic they were untouchable.

I was worried they might be right.

We walked through the first floor to the back of the mansion, where we climbed a grand staircase to the third level. Eventually, we wound up in front of some closed double doors at the end of a hallway. The stones' purrs were much stronger here, indicating that the person who had caused the emotional vibrations was on the other side of the thick wood.

Another shiver swept down my spine. I was about to come face-to-face with the dangerous lion in the center of this den.

"Cheer up, Gin," Tucker said, noticing my apprehension. "You're finally getting your wish to meet the real power behind the Circle."

"Well, it's about time," I drawled, as if his snide tone didn't bother me. "I've been looking forward to the family reunion for weeks now."

It took a moment for my words to sink in, but once they did, Tucker blinked in surprise, and realization dawned in his eyes. He looked at me, then at Bria, who gave him a hate-filled glare.

Lorelei stared at the three of us, a frown on her face, clearly wondering what was going on, as were Emery and the other giants. Seemed as though Emery and her men didn't know about my familial connection to the Circle.

"Don't say I didn't warn you," Tucker murmured.

"Oh, I can't say that, because you certainly did." I didn't even bother trying to keep the bitterness out of my voice.

He gestured at one of the giants to open the doors. I held my breath, expecting our captor to be standing right behind the doors, but he wasn't there, and all I could see of the room beyond were a couple of large bookcases.

Tucker slid his arm out of Lorelei's. She started to step back, but he grabbed her hand, bent down, and pressed a light, gallant kiss to her knuckles. Lorelei froze.

The vampire straightened and dropped her hand. "Thank you for allowing me to escort you, Ms. Parker."

Lorelei's hand curled into a fist, as though she was thinking about sucker-punching Tucker the same way she had done to that giant earlier. Instead, she relaxed her hand

and gave him a wide, toothy smile. "Why, I was absolutely *delighted*, Mr. Tucker."

"Is it just me, or are the two of them doing some really weird passive-aggressive flirting?" Bria whispered in a voice only I could hear.

I shook my head. I had no idea what was going on between the two of them. Part of me didn't want to know. I had enough problems already without worrying about Tucker and Lorelei.

Emery flapped her hand in an impatient wave. "Inside. Now."

I looked at Bria. Her face was pale and tight with worry, and I could feel my features twisting into a similarly grim expression. After all these months of looking for the person behind the Circle, now that I was finally going to face *him*, I didn't know what to do or especially how to feel.

"Move or die," Emery growled.

A couple of the giants aimed their guns at me, Bria, and Lorelei again, and I had no choice but to swallow my feelings and walk forward.

The doors opened up into a small antechamber. We moved through that, made a right-hand turn, and stepped into an enormous study that easily took up half of this level.

The walls were made of glossy golden hardwood, as was the floor, which was covered with thick rugs done in varying shades of black, gray, and forest green. A white stone fireplace took up most of the right wall, while floor-to-ceiling bookcases adorned the left one. A large antique desk was positioned in front of three glass doors set into the back wall that opened up onto a wraparound porch.

Dark green leather chairs and couches were scattered throughout the study, along with low tables, and a glass liquor cabinet was nestled in the back corner between the fireplace and the porch doors. The bottles of brandy, whiskey, and gin inside the cabinet gleamed in the glow cast out by the crystal chandelier hanging down from the white-plaster-lined ceiling.

The room looked like an old-timey gentleman's study except for one thing: all the stones on display.

Sapphire paperweights squatting on the desk. Smooth, flat ovals of rose quartz lining the bookshelves. Chunks of common limestone perching on the end tables. Emeralds, opals, rubies, agate, pyrite, gypsum. Those stones and dozens more glittered, gleamed, and glinted in various nooks and crannies throughout the room, as though I had stepped into a museum and was looking at some prize rock collection. All the stones were interesting shapes and sizes, but the most troubling thing was that they all pulsed with elemental magic.

The cold, hard power emanating off the rocks was almost exactly the same as my own Stone magic. Normally, the feel of another Stone elemental's magic wouldn't bother me, not the way the pricking pins-and-needles of Air power or the hot, burning sparks of Fire magic would have. But knowing who this magic belonged to and all the horrible things he'd done with it made me grind my teeth, and I had to swallow down a snarl rising in my throat.

Bria shuddered and wrapped her arms around herself, while Lorelei's lips pressed into a tight, thin line. They couldn't hear the rocks' smug, proud murmurs, but they could easily sense the elemental power radiating off the baubles.

Radiating off *him*.

A man was lounging in a dark green leather chair behind the antique desk, reading through some documents as though this was his private study. Maybe it was. The Circle had people everywhere, and it wouldn't surprise me to learn they had infiltrated the historical association too.

The man didn't look up as we approached the desk, and neither Tucker nor Emery nor any of the giants called out to him. None of them made so much as a squeak of sound, as though they were afraid to breathe wrong and interrupt his task, whatever it was.

After another thirty seconds of study, the man finished reading through the documents and set the last piece of paper aside. Then he finally deigned to look up at us.

He was in his mid-fifties and quite handsome, with high cheekbones, a straight nose, and a strong jaw. His wavy dark brown hair was perfectly cut and styled and peppered with silver, and his eyes were the same gray as mine. Wrinkles fanned out from the corners of his eyes and grooved into his tan skin, as did a few lines around his mouth, but he looked fit, muscled, and strong. His navy suit jacket stretched across his broad shoulders, as did his light blue shirt, and a large silverstone pin shaped like a ring of swords pointing outward glinted in the center of his silver tie.

I wondered if the ring of swords was his own personal rune or one he'd created for the Circle. Maybe I would ask before I killed him.

If I could kill him.

The man glanced at Lorelei first. He studied Bria a little bit more closely, then focused on me. He looked me over from head to toe before his gaze locked onto my face. I wondered if he saw something of Tristan, my father, his brother, in my features. I wondered if the sight haunted him the way it had haunted me ever since I found that photo of my father at the Eaton Estate. Probably not. I doubted anything bothered this man.

After about a minute of silent contemplation, the man pushed his chair back from the desk, got to his feet, and buttoned his suit jacket. Then he looked at me again, a smile stretching across his handsome face.

"Hello, ladies," he said, in a rich, deep baritone that was as smooth and polished as the stones that filled the study. "My name is Mason Mitchell. Welcome to my home."

✲ 7 ✲

M*ason Mitchell.*

The words echoed in my mind in time to the ache still pounding in my skull. So that was his name, which meant that my father's full name was Tristan Mitchell.

Tristan Mitchell. Tristan Mitchell. Tristan Mitchell.

I silently repeated my father's name, waiting for it to ring a bell or stir up some vague memory, but nothing happened. It could have been a stranger's name for as little as it resonated with me.

But the longer I stared at Mason, the more *his* name echoed in my mind over and over again, like a record that was skipping and stuck on the worst part of the chorus. *Mason Mitchell... Mason Mitchell...*

Mason fucking Mitchell.

Fletcher's voice sounded in my mind, as loud and clear as that proverbial bell I'd been waiting for, making me jerk back in surprise. Maybe it was the continued pounding in my skull, but for a moment, I could have sworn that the old man was actually in the study, that he'd said those words aloud, and I had to resist the urge to check and see if he was hiding behind the furniture.

But Fletcher was dead, and Mason Mitchell was not, and I struggled to focus on the enemy in front of me, instead of the ghostly specter of the old man's voice rattling around in my brain.

Mason tipped his head to Lorelei. "Ms. Parker. How lovely to finally meet you. Your reputation as one of Ashland's premier smugglers precedes you. Please. Have a seat."

He gestured at one of the chairs in front of the desk. Lorelei glanced at me, but we all knew it wasn't a request. Lorelei moved forward, sat down, and perched stiffly on the edge of the chair.

Mason turned his toothy shark's smile to Bria. "Detective Coolidge. Another woman whose tough, honest reputation precedes her. Please. Sit."

Bria reached out and squeezed my hand, her fingers cold and clammy against my own, but she kept her face calm and her chin held high as she marched forward and took a seat.

And then there was one. Mason's sharp gray gaze traced over my face again. "Ms. Blanco. The famed assassin the Spider. The purported queen of the Ashland underworld and the person who's been giving my associates so much trouble over the past few months."

I didn't respond, and he waved his hand, graciously indicating that I should take the final seat between Lorelei and Bria, the one that was directly across from his own chair behind the desk.

I too didn't have a choice, so I moved forward and dropped into the chair. Unlike Lorelei and Bria, I settled myself back against the cushions, as though this was a friendly visit and not a forced introduction. Mason wasn't going to immediately kill us. No, he wanted something from one or more of us, most likely me. That was the only reason we were still breathing.

For now.

Mason sat back down in his own chair. Tucker went over to the liquor cabinet, opened it, and grabbed a glass, along with a bottle of Scotch. He poured Mason a drink, then set it and the bottle on the desk, but Mason didn't even glance at the objects. Instead, he focused on me again.

"I would offer you ladies a beverage, but I'm afraid you might do something silly, like break a glass and try to use it as a weapon against me." His smile dropped away, and his gray eyes were suddenly as cold as a winter blizzard. "That would be a very foolish thing to do."

He put a little bit of bite—and magic—into his last few words, and several soft, ominous *rattle-rattles* sounded. The sapphire paperweights on the desk violently vibrated, as though they were seconds away from shattering. The rest of the stones scattered throughout the study did the same thing, like they were bombs about to explode and tear us to pieces with their sharp, splintered shrapnel.

Neither Lorelei, Bria, nor I said anything, although Lorelei curled her hands around her chair arms, while Bria fisted her fingers in her lap. They'd seen and felt that elemental display just like I had.

I might be an assassin with considerable Ice and Stone magic, but Mason had more pure, raw power than anyone I'd ever faced before, including Mab Monroe. No wonder Emery and her men hadn't bothered to confiscate Bria's gun or my knives. They knew Mason could simply wave his hand and bludgeon us to death with the stones in the study.

This was a fight I couldn't win, not here, not now. Fletcher had taught me that sometimes the key to an ultimate victory was surviving the smaller battles you shouldn't survive along the way, and this was one of those crucial moments. As long as Lorelei, Bria, and I escaped with our lives, then I would consider this a grand success.

Tucker moved to stand on Mason's left, while Emery went around the desk to his other side, becoming his literal right-hand woman. The other giants lowered their guns and took up positions along both walls, still flanking Lorelei, Bria, and me.

Mason rocked back in his chair, making it *creak*, and picked up his Scotch. He took a large swallow of the amber liquid before letting out an appreciative sigh and setting the glass aside. Then he leaned his elbows on the desk, steepled his hands together, and looked at me over the tops of his fingers.

"You're probably wondering why I invited your sister here and why my people brought you and Ms. Parker along for the ride." He kept staring at me. "It's because of you, Gin."

I'd figured as much. Snatching Bria—and Lorelei too—was a great way to get leverage over me. Mason had to know that I would do anything to protect them. Oh, yes. He definitely wanted something. I just wondered how much it would cost me in the end.

Everything, most likely.

Mason stared at me, clearly expecting an answer. I settled back a little deeper in my chair, as though I wasn't intimidated by him—or by the invisible waves of magic pouring off his body with every breath he took.

"And what did I do to finally merit your personal attention?" I asked.

"You killed two of my men in Blue Ridge Cemetery. Clever, shooting them with their own guns instead of stabbing them with your knives like usual. But you made one mistake: you switched their weapons. I'm very thorough, Gin. You should have realized I would check something like that to find out what really happened."

Oh, I had definitely thought about that, which was one of the reasons I'd hired Liam Carter to protect the Pork Pit, among other things. But here I was anyway, a fly struggling to escape the web—the noose—Mason was slowly tightening around my heart.

"What were you doing at the cemetery, Gin?" he asked.

No way was I admitting that I'd been there to dig up my father's grave to look for clues from Fletcher. I needed to change the conversation, so I decided to drop the biggest bombshell I had on him.

"Oh, Owen and I were just out for a casual, romantic, late-night stroll…Uncle Mason," I drawled in a light, easy voice.

Mason *tap-tap-tapped* his fingertips together, and annoyance flickered across his face. He didn't like me calling him that. Too damn bad. I didn't like the fact that he was my uncle, that we were related, that we shared the same blood.

He glanced up at Tucker, a silent question in his eyes, but Tucker shook his head.

"Oh, don't blame Tuck," I said. "I figured out you were the leader of the Circle all on my own."

"How did you do that?" Mason asked.

I shrugged. "After I drowned Alanna Eaton in her own lake, I turned the security cameras back on at the Eaton Estate. I figured when Alanna didn't check in with Tucker, he would come to the estate to see what was wrong.

Imagine my surprise and delight when the big boss man himself showed up."

Tucker stared at me. He was probably wondering why I hadn't told Mason the whole truth—that Tucker had let me kill Alanna before saving me from freezing to death. Maybe I should have revealed that tidbit. Maybe I should have clued Mason in on the fact that his enforcer wasn't quite as trustworthy as he pretended to be. But I had precious few advantages right now, and Tucker's questionable loyalty was one of them. I was going to keep that card tucked up my sleeve until the time was right to play it.

"And how did you know who I was?" Mason asked. "Your father died when you were young. I doubt you remember much about him."

I shrugged again. "You're right. I didn't really remember Tristan, but I didn't have to. Remember that auction of Mab Monroe's things at the Eaton Estate a few weeks ago? Well, she had a photo of my parents. That was the first time I'd seen Tristan's face since the night Mab killed Eira and Annabella and burned our mansion to the ground. I'm sure you remember that, since you were the one who gave Mab her marching orders."

Mason didn't respond.

"Although I have to admit I was surprised when you showed up at the Eaton Estate. For a few seconds there, I actually thought *you* were my father. Believe me when I say that was a bit…unsettling."

Sickening was more like it, but I wasn't about to confess that.

"But then I compared the photos I took of you at the estate to the one I had of Tristan, and I realized that while the two of you look almost identical, you weren't *him*. I'm ashamed I ever thought you were. I don't remember much about my father, but I know he loved me and my sisters and my mother. He would *never* order someone to murder his family. But you don't have such basic decency."

An amused smile curved the corners of Mason's mouth. In that moment, he looked so much like my father that my heart stumbled inside my chest and plummeted down into my stomach. Beside me, Bria tensed, tears gleaming in her eyes. She'd never known our father, and I imagined it was even harder for her to see this twisted imitation of him than it was for me.

"*Decency*?" Mason purred in his smooth, silky voice. "What a quaint little word. Who needs decency when you have power?"

He casually waved his hand. An invisible gust of magic rippled out of his fingertips, making the polished gems and chunks of rock in the study rattle and vibrate again. Each soft *shimmy-shimmy* of the stones scraping across the tabletops was a clear, ominous warning. I felt like I was sitting in a room full of grenades, just waiting for them to explode and rip me to shreds.

Mason waited until his magic faded away and the stones stopped rattling before he spoke again. "But you're right about one thing. I'm not your father. Tristan was my brother, my twin, actually. I was born first, and he came into the world three minutes later."

Twins? Well, that explained his uncanny resemblance to Tristan. Although the knowledge made this even more bizarre, as though I was peering into a carnival fun-house mirror at the most distorted version of my father imaginable. Every word Mason said, every look, every small tilt of his head and sly flick of his fingers blotted out my hazy memories of my father and replaced them with this horror show of a man who had caused so much death and destruction in my life.

"And you took him out of this world," Bria accused in a harsh voice. "I found the police report of Tristan's supposed car accident. I saw what you did to him. How could you do that to *anyone*? Especially your own *brother*? Your *twin*?"

Mason raised his eyebrows. "You're assuming Tristan and I had some warm, loving, close relationship. We did not. We might have been brothers, but we were as different as night and day. Rather like you and Gin."

Bria's cheeks flushed with anger. "Gin is *nothing* like you."

Mason's low, mocking laugh made more than a little guilt, shame, and embarrassment flare up in my chest. "Really? Think about it. How many people has Gin killed? Probably far more than me. I rarely get involved in such menial tasks these days. But Gin? She's been killing people right and left for *years*, and nothing you do or say will ever change that fact, sweet, naive Bria."

My sister opened her mouth, probably to keep defending me, but I shook my head. There was no use arguing with Mason, not when he was right.

And he *was* right.

I had killed a lot of people, both as Genevieve Snow back when I was trying to survive on the mean streets of Ashland and especially later on, after Fletcher had taken me in and started training me to be the Spider. My hands were drenched in just as much blood as Mason's, maybe even more.

"Why did you send your men to kidnap Bria? Why did you bring us here?" I snapped. "What do you *want*?"

More annoyance flickered across Mason's face. He didn't like my demanding answers, but he leaned forward and picked up a book lying on the corner of the desk. The black cover featured a single symbol done in raised silver foil—the Circle's ring-of-swords rune.

Surprise rippled through me, along with a good amount of wariness. The black book was the same size and shape as the blue ledger my mother had used to record Circle secrets, the one Silvio was still trying to decode.

Maybe this was all about the blue ledger. Maybe Mason had finally realized that I had the tome, and he wanted it back. Although if that were the case, why not show me a blue ledger instead of this black one?

Beside me, Bria tensed, as did Lorelei. They too must have noticed how similar this black book was to the blue ledger.

"What's that?" I asked, playing dumb.

Mason waggled the book back and forth. "This? It's a ledger, of sorts."

Another ledger? An odd, unwelcome sense of déjà vu washed over me, and I bit back a groan. Alanna Eaton had almost killed me because she'd been searching for the blue ledger, and now here I was, faced with another one of the cursed books.

My gaze flicked over to the bookcases along the wall. No black or blue ledgers there, just old, thick tomes on Ashland's history. Mason's little black book hadn't come from those shelves.

How many ledgers did the Circle have? What did the different colors mean? And where were the volumes kept? Whoever was responsible for the ledgers must not do a very good job of watching over them, given how many of the books seemed to be floating around Ashland.

"I'm a bit old-fashioned," Mason continued. "Especially when it comes to Circle business. Computers are too easily hacked, information too easily downloaded onto discs and drives."

"So you write everything down in books. How quaint," I quipped. "Do you use feather pens too? Pots of ink? Wax seals? Or have the folks who work for the historical association taught you how to use carrier pigeons?"

He ignored my sarcasm. "Some years ago, one of these black ledgers was stolen from my personal archives at another location. You're going to find it, Gin."

I frowned in genuine confusion. "Why would I know where your ledger is? Especially if it's been missing for years? I only learned about the Circle a few months ago."

Mason set the ledger on the desk and tapped his index finger on the cover. "Because it was stolen by Fletcher Lane."

And just like that, everything made sense, including why those two giants had dug up Fletcher's final resting place the other night. They thought the old man had literally taken the ledger with him to his grave.

Fletcher had left me several clues about the Circle, including some safety-deposit boxes filled with documents and photos at First Trust bank, but I'd never *dreamed* he'd stolen something directly from Mason. Still, Fletcher was nothing if not persistent. If he'd known that Mason was the leader of the Circle, then he would have done everything in his power to get an advantage over the other man. Stealing a ledger of Circle secrets might have taken him a while, but Fletcher would have eventually figured out how to do it. He was tenacious that way.

So what was in the missing black ledger? The information must be extremely important for Mason to still be searching for it.

"If Fletcher hid that book years ago, what makes you

think I can find it now?" I asked, genuinely curious to know what his reasoning would be.

Mason gave me another amused look, then casually flicked his fingers. An invisible wave of magic surged off him, and two of the sapphire paperweights on the desk exploded.

I didn't have time to move, react, or reach for my own magic to block his attack. One moment, the paperweights were whole and intact. The next, razor-sharp pieces were hurtling toward Bria and Lorelei. I didn't even have time to scream, and even though I was sitting right between them, I couldn't protect either one of them.

The jeweled shards abruptly stopped—an inch away from Bria's and Lorelei's throats.

They both froze, their eyes wide, their mouths gaping in fear and surprise, as they stared at the long, pointed bits of shrapnel hovering in midair. I froze too, my hands curled around my chair arms. All Mason had to do was wave his hand, and the shards would shoot into their necks like arrows, killing them.

Hot, sweaty panic knifed through my heart, and my gaze darted back and forth between Bria and Lorelei. I might—*might*—be able to save one of them, but in doing so, I would doom the other to a sudden, gruesome death. It was an impossible choice and one I didn't think I could make.

My uncle flicked his fingers again, and the sapphire shards zipped across the study and embedded themselves in an old-fashioned dartboard hanging on the wall. Bria and Lorelei both sucked in ragged breaths and slumped back in their chairs. I did too.

"Why do I think you can find my ledger, Gin? The proper motivation, of course," Mason drawled, finally answering my question.

More hot, sweaty panic filled me at his obvious threat, but I forced myself to try to reason with him. "All the *motivation* in the world doesn't matter in this case. Fletcher never said anything about stealing a ledger from you."

"I find that very hard to believe," Mason said, an angry note creeping into his voice. "Especially given all the trouble you've caused over the past few months."

His anger sparked my own, and I latched onto the emotion with both hands. Anger was always better than panic, and *anything* was better than the paralyzing fear still crashing through my body in hot, clammy waves.

"If you didn't want me to know about the Circle, then you shouldn't have sent Deirdre Shaw to worm her way into Finn's life. And you definitely shouldn't have told Tucker to try to blackmail me into joining your little group," I growled. "The way I see it, *you're* the reason I've caused you so much trouble, Uncle Mason."

He shook his head. "I knew it was a mistake to let Fletcher walk away all those years ago."

Confusion filled me. "Fletcher? Walk away? What are you talking about?"

Mason tilted his head to the side, studying me. "You really don't know, do you? What any of this is truly about? What Fletcher did?"

My hands gripped the chair arms even tighter, and my entire body tensed. "What do you know about Fletcher?"

Mason kept staring at me, an amused smile crawling across his face. Emery eyed her boss with open curiosity. She wanted to know the answers to my questions too, as did the giants still flanking us.

The only person who already seemed to know the answers was Hugh Tucker. The vampire sighed ever so softly and gave me a resigned, regretful look, almost as if he was sorry for what was going to happen next.

"What do you know about Fletcher?" I repeated, my voice dropping to a low, strained whisper.

"Isn't it obvious?" Mason leaned forward and stared me in the eyes. "Fletcher Lane worked for the Circle."

Fletcher Lane worked for the Circle.

Fletcher worked for...

Fletcher....

Mason's words kept ringing in my mind, booming louder and louder, until all I could hear was his snide tone, and all I could feel was the ugly truth of those simple syllables stabbing into my heart over and over again.

"*No*," I choked out. "You're lying. Fletcher didn't—*wouldn't*—do that. Not for the Circle. Not for *you*."

"Oh, yes, he *did*," Mason purred. "Why, the Tin Man was the Circle's go-to assassin for years, and Fletcher was a close personal friend of mine."

I stared at him, desperately searching for any sign of a lie, but no trace of deception flickered across his face, his gaze stayed rock-steady on mine, and his voice pealed with smug certainty. Mason was telling the truth, and he knew exactly how devastating it was.

Fletcher had worked for the Circle.

My mind spun around, my heart clenched tight, and my breath stuttered in my lungs, but the rest of my body felt stiff, numb, and frozen, as though someone had suddenly encased me in elemental Ice from head to toe. I couldn't move, couldn't speak, couldn't protest. All I could do was sit there and stare at Mason, dumbstruck, while sick shock flooded my veins. In an instant, the cold, inescapable tidal wave had drowned all my warm love for and unshakable trust in the old man.

Bria reached over and grabbed my hand, tears gleaming in her eyes. Lorelei grabbed my other hand, squeezing it tight. My sister and my friend were trying to help, support, comfort me, but they seemed distant and far away, even though they were sitting right beside me, and the heat of their fingers didn't even come close to penetrating the chills that kept crashing through my body.

"I thought you might have a little trouble accepting the truth," Mason continued, "so I had Tucker go through my personal archives and dig out some things."

He snapped his fingers, and Tucker grabbed a manila file folder from one of the bookshelves, stepped around the desk, and held it out to me. I stared dully at the folder. Whatever was inside would only wound me more, just like the info Bria had shown me on our father's murder. But even now, when faced with this awful, awful truth, my curiosity won out the way it always did, and I took the folder from Tucker.

The thin file seemed as heavy as an anvil, and it slipped through my numb fingers and dropped to my lap. With shaking hands, I slowly cracked it open. Bria and Lorelei leaned forward, and we all peered at the information inside.

The first thing in the file was a photo of Fletcher and Mason.

My heart clenched tight again, but I picked up the picture. The color photo had yellowed with age, but it clearly showed Fletcher leaning against the counter inside the Pork

Pit and grinning at Mason, who was sitting on the stool closest to the cash register and eating a plate of barbecue.

Part of me didn't want to believe it, and I thought about throwing the photo down and screaming that it was a fake—but it wasn't. In the background, I could see several old menus, along with some ancient napkin holders that had been inside the restaurant for years. Things no one would know about, except for me, Finn, and Sophia, and things you wouldn't be able to find today, much less drop into a doctored photo.

This picture was very, very real.

That first image was only the beginning of this twisted trip down memory lane. I flipped through photo after photo, all of Fletcher and Mason. Eating in the Pork Pit, drinking lemonade and relaxing in lawn chairs in someone's backyard, even fishing in a mountain stream. No matter the locale, one thing remained the same in every single shot: the two men grinning at each other as though they were the best of friends.

With each new image, each warm smile and cozy scene, my heart splintered into smaller and smaller pieces. By the time I finished with the photos, my heart was thoroughly *crushed*, although each small, serrated shard of shrapnel kept grinding itself deeper and deeper into my body, slowly, surely, thoroughly shredding everything I thought I knew about Fletcher.

Besides the photos, there was one more thing in the folder: a handwritten note on a sheet of yellowed paper.

Mason,

I appreciate the opportunity you've given me to join your group. Together I think we can do great things as the Circle grows even stronger...

I couldn't read the rest of the note. Hot, sour bile clogged my throat, and it took every ounce of my self-control to keep from vomiting all over the note and the photos.

"Gin?" Bria asked in a low, strained voice.

"That's Fletcher's handwriting. It's true. It's all true," I said in a dull, defeated voice. "The old man really did work for you. He really was a Circle assassin."

Mason rocked back in his chair and gave me another smug smile. "Oh, the Tin Man was one of the best. Elemental, vampire, dwarf, giant. There was no one he couldn't find and eliminate. We had quite a productive partnership."

"Why?" Lorelei asked in a suspicious voice. "Why would Fletcher ever work for you?"

Mason shrugged. "After Deirdre left Ashland, Fletcher was desperate to find and kill her for tricking him into murdering her parents and threatening sweet baby Finn. One thing led to another, and Fletcher eventually found his way to me. He stormed into this very study one night and demanded I tell him where Deirdre was."

"So he knew that you and Deirdre belonged to the Circle?" I asked, still confused.

Mason shook his head. "Of course not. He'd never even heard of the Circle at that point. All Fletcher knew was that I had done business with Deirdre's parents, and he thought I might know where she had gone. Fletcher didn't realize that Deirdre had already asked me to hide her from him."

"That was when Deirdre started working for the Circle," I said, filling in the gaps in his story. "You kept her safe from Fletcher, and in exchange, she started all those fake charities to launder the Circle's money."

"Now you're catching on, Gin," Mason replied. "Most people would have eliminated Fletcher right then and there, but I knew his reputation as the Tin Man, and I saw a way to turn the situation to my advantage."

"You manipulated Fletcher," Bria accused. "You told him some story and got him to work for the Circle."

Mason shot his thumb and forefinger at her, making the remaining sapphire paperweights on the desk rattle again. Bria tensed. So did I, along with Lorelei.

He dropped his hand, and the stones stilled. Bria, Lorelei, and I let out a collective relieved breath.

"Exactly," he said. "I told Fletcher that I would help him find Deirdre—if he did a few jobs for me."

"You tricked him," Lorelei said in a flat voice.

Mason let out a low, throaty laugh. "Oh, my dear. I did no such thing. Fletcher went into our arrangement with his eyes wide open—and he *enjoyed* it."

"What do you mean?" I asked.

"After he discovered how thoroughly Deirdre had used, betrayed, and fooled him, Fletcher was brimming with bitterness. I helped him channel that bitterness, and he happily took his rage at Deirdre out on my enemies. He was exceptionally good at his job, and we got along quite well for several years."

I seized onto his words, desperate to focus on something—*anything*—besides the turbulent emotions rolling through me. "What happened between the two of you? Why did Fletcher leave the Circle?"

"Eventually, the sting of Deirdre's betrayal wore off, and Fletcher started asking awkward questions about who we were and what we were doing. At first, I thought he was taking a deeper interest in Circle business, but then I realized he'd figured out that the group wasn't nearly as noble as I'd made us out to be."

Mason paused, and his gray gaze dropped to the photos

on my lap, as though he was thinking back to those happier, simpler times. Then his nostrils flared with anger, and his mouth flattened out into a hard, thin, unforgiving line. "Tristan didn't help matters."

I blinked at the unexpected change in topic. "What did Tristan have to do with you and Fletcher?"

"Everything."

I waited for him to elaborate, but Mason stared into the amber depths of the bottle of Scotch and *tap-tap-tapped* his fingers on top of the black ledger. Several seconds passed before his fingers stilled. Mason roused himself out of his thoughts, pushed back from the desk, and got to his feet.

I studied the positions of Tucker, Emery, and the six giants, wondering how we could kill our enemies. I could handle Emery, and Bria and Lorelei could take out the giants, but that still left Tucker to deal with and, of course, Mason, who could just wave his hand, explode all the stones in here, and drive the chunks into our bodies. Hard fists of worry and dread punched into my chest. It was still a fight we couldn't win, and I didn't know if we could even escape.

Mason gestured out at the study. "I doubt your father ever mentioned it to you, Gin, but this mansion was built by our Mitchell ancestors. Our family lived in it for generations, and Tristan and I grew up here."

No, I hadn't known that, but it didn't surprise me, given how at home he seemed and how the structure's stones reacted to his presence.

Mason glanced around the room a few more seconds. "Let's take a walk."

He headed toward the back of the study. Emery scuttled in front of him and opened one of the glass doors. Mason stepped outside and disappeared from view, but Emery stopped and jerked her head at the other giants.

"Bring them," she ordered.

The giants stepped forward and lifted their guns, and Bria, Lorelei, and I had no choice but to get up, skirt around the desk, and head for the open door. Our path took us right by Hugh Tucker, who was still standing beside the desk like a dog waiting for a summons from its master.

"I tried to warn you, Gin," he murmured. "You should have listened to me."

The undeniable truth of his words slapped me across the face, and the file of photos that I was still clutching felt as heavy as an old-fashioned ball and chain weighing me down. Tucker was right. I really should have listened to him, but my arrogance, stubbornness, and curiosity had gotten the better of me, and now I was stuck in Mason's web—one that would probably end up strangling us all.

We stepped out onto the porch that wrapped around this level of the mansion. Emery led the way, with Bria, Lorelei, and me behind her and the giants clustered behind us. Tucker brought up the rear and closed the glass door behind him.

We plodded down the stairs to the ground level. Emery strode across the stone terrace that jutted out from the back of the mansion, through the grassy yard, and over to a path that curled past a garden filled with whitewashed trellises and a pretty gazebo. We followed the path into the neighboring woods.

About a quarter mile later, the trees receded, revealing a large clearing in the woods. Despite its distance from the mansion, the grass here was smooth and even, and the ground was free of dead leaves, indicating that the area was regularly landscaped, even during the winter. Several crosses jutted up from the grass, along with square stones and other markers, all of which had been worn smooth by the wind, weather, and passage of time.

It was a cemetery.

Mason was waiting at the edge of the grass, and he held his arms out wide like a carnival barker showing off a wondrous attraction. "Welcome to Ashland Memorial Cemetery."

He moved deeper into the cemetery, and we followed him. I eyed the tombstones we passed, reading the names carved into the markers. Monroe, Shaw, Tucker, Rivera, Porter, Snow, Mitchell. Various symbols were also carved into the markers, including the sunburst rune that had belonged to Mab Monroe. Mab herself was buried at Blue Ridge Cemetery, just like Fletcher was, but I spotted a tombstone with her name on it, and it seemed as though several members of her family had been laid to rest here.

No matter the family names, the tombstones all had one thing in common: they all prominently featured the Circle's ring-of-swords rune.

Mason stopped and turned to face us. "Several years ago, when my business started taking me away from Ashland for extended periods of time, I leased the mansion to the historical association. The members take care of the house and the heirlooms, but no one ever comes back here except for me and a few hard-core history and genealogy buffs."

"What's so special about this place?" Lorelei asked. "It's just an old cemetery. There are dozens of them in Ashland."

He smiled at her. "You're right, Ms. Parker. There are dozens of old, forgotten cemeteries in the surrounding mountains, but this was the very first cemetery ever built in Ashland. Our founding fathers and mothers are resting in this hallowed ground."

Bria frowned. "Wait a second. You're saying that the people who founded Ashland also created the Circle?"

"Exactly! They were one and the same." Mason gestured at the markers. "The Mitchells, Monroes, Snows, and other families banded together to decide how to run their new city. Eventually, that first large group winnowed down, as certain members' fortunes rose and fell, and there came a clear divide among some of the families, an inner circle, if you will."

I'd always wondered how the group had gotten its name. A bit cliché, if you asked me.

"And somewhere along the way, the Circle families decided that it would be better to slip into the shadows and rule from behind the scenes," Lorelei said. "Smart."

Mason shrugged. "That was my grandfather Merle's idea. He was a politician, but he realized that the more he was in the public eye, the more he had to answer to the common people and the less he could do the things he truly wanted. Merle decided he would rather run things discreetly than have to listen to the riffraff. If people don't know you exist, then they can't demand favors, blame you, or hold you accountable for things."

He looked at me. "Take Gin, for example. For years, you thought Mab acted alone and killed your mother because of some old family feud between the Monroes and the Snows. You were right, and you were wrong."

Before I could come up with some snarky retort, he walked on, heading deeper into the cemetery. Mason pointed out various tombstones and markers and shared interesting tidbits about the people buried here, as though he was some genteel tour guide showing us a historic attraction instead of just a sick, sadistic son of a bitch.

Mason finished sharing his latest bon mot, and we stopped in front of a stone pavilion in the heart of the cemetery. Light gray marble columns rose up to support the A-line roof, also made of marble, but the rectangular structure was open on all four sides. Tall wrought-iron torches stood at all four corners of the pavilion, and flames flickered inside the glass globes, despite the afternoon sunlight. Wide, shallow steps led up to the front of the pavilion, and the name *Mitchell* was engraved in fancy cursive letters in the wide band of stone that topped the entrance. I held back a derisive snort. Of course, Mason would erect a monument to *his* family.

I peered inside the structure. A single gray marble tomb was standing in the center, although it was much plainer than the other markers and didn't feature the ring-of-swords rune.

Mason gestured at the tomb. "I thought you girls might like to see where your father is really buried."

I jerked back in surprise, as did Bria beside me.

"What do you mean?" she whispered.

Mason gestured at the tomb again. "Tristan is buried here, not in Blue Ridge Cemetery next to your mother."

Suddenly, I saw the pavilion with new eyes. It wasn't a monument to the Mitchell family. No, it was a fucking *shrine* to Mason and his power and how he had killed Tristan with it. Why else display your dead brother's tomb in such garish, ghoulish fashion?

Anger spiked through me, but I pushed it away. Right now, I needed answers, and I couldn't afford to foolishly give in to my rage and disgust. Not if I wanted to escape with Bria and Lorelei.

"Why did you kill Tristan?" I asked. "Why did you order Mab to murder our mother and Annabella?"

Mason casually leaned a shoulder against one of the columns. "Tristan never liked being part of the Circle. Neither did Eira. They both kept whining and crying about some of our bloodier, more illegal activities. Tristan wanted us to turn over a new leaf and use Circle resources to help the city, rather than hinder it. His words, not mine. Once Fletcher started asking questions, Tristan thought he had finally found a way to wrest control of the group away from me."

"How?" Lorelei asked.

Mason ignored her and stared at me. "Tristan told Fletcher the truth, that I had been hiding Deirdre all along. My brother begged Fletcher to kill me, and the Tin Man was stupid enough to take the assignment."

My heart clenched. I knew what was coming next. These sorts of stories always ended the same way—with death.

"I suspected that Tristan was plotting against me, so I had him followed. As soon as he started secretly meeting with Fletcher, I knew what he was up to." Mason paused. "And I punished him for it."

Lorelei grimaced, while Bria clamped her hand over her mouth, as though she was trying not to be sick. I just stood there, still clutching that folder of photos of Fletcher and Mason. Every word my uncle said made the thin file get a little heavier and harder to hold.

"Tristan thought he could eliminate me, but I gathered up the Circle members who were loyal to me, and we killed the ones who weren't." Mason gestured at the tomb for a third time. "Fletcher managed to escape, but I had Tristan brought here, along with Eira. And then I killed him right in front of her."

Hot tears stung my eyes, and try as I might, I couldn't stop the salty drops from streaking down my face. A couple of them splattered onto the folder in my hand, forming dark, wet spots on the manila.

"Eira begged me to stop, but she had also betrayed me, so I made her watch while I dealt with Tristan. And then, once he was dead, I told her that if she *ever* betrayed me again, I would do the exact same thing to her and her three lovely daughters."

Mason told the story of my father's torture and murder calmly, casually, as if it was of very little importance in the grand scheme of things. Lorelei stared at him with a horrified expression, while Bria dropped her head, her hand still clamped over her mouth.

A faint buzzing sounded in my ears. It took me a few seconds to realize it was coming from the marble slabs of my father's tomb. Unlike the sapphire paperweights and other knickknacks in the mansion study that had vibrated with delight at the feel of Mason's magic, the stones here shuddered with revulsion at the low timbre of his voice.

No! Please! Don't! Stop!

The buzzing sharpened, and I almost thought I could hear the stones crying out with distinct words—the ones my mother had screamed as she watched her husband being brutalized by his own brother. Somehow I resisted the urge to slap my hands over my ears to block out the phantom screams.

Mason shook his head. "But Eira didn't listen to me. Oh, she played it cool at first. For a long time, actually. Doing her job, keeping Circle records, and waiting for her girls to grow up. But one of my sources in the police department told me that Eira was plotting to expose the Circle to the cops, the media, and anyone else who would listen. I couldn't have that, so I told Mab to kill Eira, along with her daughters."

By this point, Bria was openly weeping, and Lorelei slung her arm around my sister's shoulder, trying to comfort her. I should have done it, but I felt rooted in place, stuck in the ground as firmly as the tombstones around us, although tears continued to roll down my face.

"After I killed Tristan, Fletcher fell back in line, and he kept working for the Circle, even though I could tell how much he hated me. But I enjoyed having the infamous Tin Man under my thumb, so I let him live. Mab didn't know about Fletcher's history with me or the Circle, and I found it highly amusing and ironic when she tried to hire him to kill your mother. Even though Fletcher refused, I still let him live. It only made him more miserable to know he had failed Eira and her daughters the same way he had failed Tristan."

"You bastard!" I hissed. "You kept Fletcher around to torture him."

An evil grin creased Mason's face, and his gray eyes glittered with a cold, vindictive light. "Yes, I did. And it was *extremely* satisfying."

Mason fucking Mitchell.

Once again, Fletcher's voice snarled in my mind, even louder and clearer than it had in the study, although I still couldn't remember when or where I'd heard him say my uncle's name.

"So what happened?" Lorelei asked. "How did Fletcher finally get away from you?"

"After a while, I grew tired of his petulance, and I started using him on fewer and fewer jobs," Mason replied. "I was happy enough knowing that he was simmering in his own sauce inside the Pork Pit. But Fletcher, well, he just couldn't be satisfied with our arrangement."

"What did he do?" I asked.

Mason stared at me. "He broke into my personal archives and stole a ledger. But Fletcher was much smarter about using the information than your mother was. He didn't go to the police or the media and try to expose me. Instead, he used the ledger as blackmail. He said as long as I left him alone, he would do the same to me, so we reached our little détente."

"And what about Bria and me?" I asked. "Did you know that we survived Mab? That Fletcher had saved us?"

After the attack, the old man had found Bria wandering around the woods near our home and made arrangements for her to be adopted by a loving family. Then, later on, I had stumbled into the alley behind the Pork Pit, and he had taken me in.

Mason glanced at Bria, then focused on me again. "No. I thought you were both dead. Fletcher hid the two of you very well. It was only after Detective Bria Coolidge returned to Ashland that I realized the Spider and Genevieve Snow were one and the same."

Bria let out a soft, strangled cry and shot me a guilty look, but I shook my head. None of this was her fault.

"Of course, I tried to break my stalemate with Fletcher many times over the years, but he always managed to escape my traps," Mason said. "Eventually, he became less of a concern, and I moved on to more important matters."

He shrugged again, as though it was ancient history, but it wasn't. Not to him—and certainly not to *me*.

More and more anger pounded through my body, but I ignored the sensation and thought about this coldly, critically, the way Fletcher would have, the way he had taught me to think as the Spider. The old man had been dead for more than a year. If Mason had been truly desperate to get his hands on the missing ledger, he would have come for it as soon as he got word Fletcher was gone. Instead, he'd let months go by without revealing himself.

So what had changed in Mason's world? What had made him want—*need*—the ledger now?

Something else was going on, something Mason didn't want me to know about. But I was going to find out what my dear uncle was hiding, and then I was going to put the bastard in this cemetery, right alongside the other Circle members.

Emery cleared her throat, drawing Mason's attention, and tapped her finger on her silver watch. He nodded at her, then looked at me again.

"I have another appointment, but it's been so nice to finally meet you all in person and reminisce about our dead loved ones," Mason said.

I didn't respond, and neither did Bria or Lorelei. Nothing had been *nice* about this, especially not the ugly truths Mason had revealed about Fletcher and my parents.

"But back to the business at hand." Mason pushed away from the column, straightened up to his full height, and peered down his nose at me. "You will find the ledger Fletcher stole."

I shook my head. "I know you won't believe me, but I'll tell you again anyway. Fletcher never told me anything about you or the Circle, and he never mentioned any ledger. I have no idea where he might have hidden it."

"Then figure it out," he snapped. "You *will* find the ledger and deliver it to me by midnight Saturday."

"Or else?" I asked, even though I already knew the answer.

Mason stepped forward, leaned down, and stared me in the eyes, his gray gaze colder than the bitterest blizzard. He reached for his magic, and his Stone power rippled off him, making my father's tomb and the rest of the pavilion quake, as well as the surrounding tombstones. He didn't shatter any of the markers, though. He didn't have to. He'd already shown me exactly what he was capable of.

"Or else I will kill every single person you love, Gin. Starting with Bria."

His threat delivered, Mason released his grip on his magic, moved past me, and strode away. All I could do was stand in the middle of the cemetery and watch him go, his poison promise ringing in my ears.

9

Mason vanished into the woods, heading back toward the mansion, but Emery, Tucker, and the giants remained behind.

Emery looked at Tucker. "Take care of them. I need to go with Mason."

She didn't wait for a response before she spun around and hurried after my uncle. Two giants went with her, but the other four stayed with Tucker, their guns still trained on Bria, Lorelei, and me.

Tucker stared at Mason's twisted shrine to the brother he had murdered. The corners of the vampire's lips curled with disgust. "Come on," he said, his voice surprisingly gentle. "Let's get out of here."

Tucker and the four giants shepherded us out of the cemetery, through the woods, and back to the mansion. Tucker skirted around the house and led us to the front driveway, where the black SUV was still sitting. He gestured for us to get inside. Three of the giants climbed in after us, their guns still out, while the fourth man got behind the wheel. Tucker slid into the front passenger seat.

No one said a word as the driver cranked the engine, coasted down the driveway, steered through the open gate, and pulled out onto the main road. Fifteen minutes later, the SUV stopped in the parking lot in front of the Posh boutique.

I glanced over at the storefront. People were moving around inside, although I couldn't tell if any of my friends were there.

Tucker turned around in the passenger seat. He glanced at Lorelei and Bria before focusing on me. "Maybe now you'll finally take my warnings to heart," he said. "Do what Mason says. Find the ledger, Gin. Or Bria and everyone else you love will suffer the consequences."

I was too tired and heartsick to muster up a snappy comeback or pithy threat, so I ignored him and climbed out of the SUV. I was still clutching the file Mason had given me, and the manila folder felt heavier than ever, as though it contained an anchor instead of a few photos.

Bria and Lorelei also climbed out of the vehicle. One of the giants yanked the door shut, and the driver hit the gas. The SUV peeled away from the curb and headed toward the parking lot exit. A few seconds later, the driver steered out onto the main road, and the vehicle zoomed away.

"Gin! Bria! Lorelei!"

Several muffled voices sounded, the boutique door flew open, and a giant rushed outside. He was around seven feet tall, with a strong, muscled body, and was wearing a black leather jacket, jeans, and boots. His head was shaved, and the afternoon sunlight glinted off his ebony skin, as well as the black aviator sunglasses hooked into the top of his dark green sweater.

Xavier, Bria's partner on the force, skidded to a stop in front of us. His dark gaze snapped from Bria to Lorelei to me and back again, and he visibly relaxed when he realized we were okay.

The boutique door flew open again, and Roslyn hurried outside, followed by Mallory, who was moving just a bit slower, given her age. Roslyn rushed forward and hugged Bria, while Mallory did the same to Lorelei.

"Pumpkin!" Mallory cried out in a choked voice. "I thought I'd lost you!"

Lorelei rubbed her grandmother's back. "Never." She hugged Mallory again, although she stared at me, worry filling her face.

Roslyn let go of Bria. My friend started to hug me but stopped short when she caught sight of my face. "Gin! Are you okay?"

I reached up and gingerly probed my cheek. With everything that had happened, I'd almost forgotten that Emery had plowed her fist into my face. The bruise pulsed and throbbed like a rotten tooth underneath my cold fingers, but it was a small sting compared to the crushed, serrated shards of my heart still scraping together.

"I'm fine. It looks worse than it is."

"I don't think that's possible, since it looks like an eggplant exploded all over your face," Xavier rumbled. "What happened? Roslyn called me and said that you guys had been kidnapped. But your kidnappers brought you back?"

"I—"

My phone rang, cutting me off. I pulled the device out of the back pocket of my jeans. To my surprise, it had survived all my hard falls intact, and the screen said Silvio was calling. Of course he was. My assistant had probably been trying my phone every minute on the minute since I'd been gone. Now that I was away from the signal jammers at the mansion, he could finally get through.

I answered the call. "Hey. It's me. I'm fine."

"Gin!" Silvio's voice filled my ear. "Where are you?"

"At the Posh boutique. Hugh Tucker just dropped off me, Bria, and Lorelei. We're all okay. Where are you?"

"I'm with Finn. The two of us left the Pork Pit as soon as Xavier called and told us what was going on. We've been driving around ever since, searching for you. So has Owen."

Out of the corner of my eye, I spotted Willa the seamstress and the Posh salesclerks lurking by the storefront windows. They were clearly wondering what was going on, as were the shoppers from the surrounding stores, many of whom were gathered around the ruined car that the giants' SUV had smashed into when they'd been trying to run me down. A uniformed cop was also standing by the car, taking photos of the damage.

Time to go. The Circle had spies everywhere, and I wouldn't put it past Mason to have planted some people at the shopping center to see how my friends and I reacted to his ultimatum. The thought of him hurting—*killing*—Bria and the rest of my loved ones made me want to scream with rage, but I forced myself to push down my anger, fear, and dread.

"Gin?" Silvio asked. "Are you still there? What do you want me to do?"

"Call Jo-Jo and ask her to shut down the salon for the rest of the day. Tell Owen to meet us there. Stuart Mosley too. We all need to get someplace safe where we can regroup. Also, call Sophia and Catalina and tell them to close down the Pork Pit early. I'll text Liam Carter and fill him in."

"Catalina has a study date this evening with Eva Grayson and Violet Fox at Country Daze," Silvio replied. "I'll ask Sophia to drive them up there."

The Country Daze store belonged to Warren T. Fox, Violet's grandfather. Warren was an ornery old coot who had been Fletcher's best friend growing up. He would protect Violet with his life, and Eva and Catalina too.

"Good idea," I replied. "Tell Warren what's going on, and ask him to let the girls spend the night there. He'll keep them safe."

"Gin?" Silvio asked. "Are you okay? You sound... strange."

Strange? I supposed that was his polite way of saying *shattered*, but I didn't correct him. "See you soon."

I hung up and focused on my friends. Xavier had his arm around Roslyn's shoulders, while Mallory was clutching Lorelei's hand like she never wanted to let it go. And Bria, well, Bria looked as tired, defeated, and heartsick as I still felt.

"Let's get out of here," I said.

Bria and I got into her sedan, which had survived the kidnapping unscathed, and she cranked the engine and steered out of the parking lot. Xavier, Roslyn, and Lorelei and Mallory followed us in their own vehicles. I texted Liam Carter and asked him to meet us at the salon.

Bria and I didn't talk on the ride. Neither one of us knew what to say.

What *could* you say when confronted with an evil like Mason Mitchell? When you shared the same blood? When your own uncle had tortured and murdered his twin brother, your father? I had tangled with a lot of bad, bad people over the years, everyone from Harley and Hazel Grimes to Beauregard Benson to Raymond Pike, but Uncle Mason put them all to shame.

Mason's lack of remorse was absolutely chilling, but what truly worried me was his Stone magic. I was a strong elemental, something I'd proven to myself and my enemies time and time again, but Mason had far more raw magic than I did. He could use his Stone magic to utterly *crush* me the same way he had crushed my father, and I wouldn't be able to do a damn thing to stop him.

Just like I wouldn't be able to stop him from hurting everyone I loved.

That stark truth sliced through me as cleanly as one of my silverstone knives, cutting away my self-confidence and carving up every frantic, half-assed plan that sprang to my mind about how to kill Mason. Try as I might, I just couldn't think of a way to do it. I was an assassin, I was *the Spider*, and I couldn't think of a way to kill my murderous uncle when it mattered most.

I had never felt like more of a *failure*.

I was still dreaming up and discarding plans when Bria steered her sedan into a subdivision, climbed up a hill, and stopped in a driveway in front of a white plantation house. Xavier, Roslyn, and Lorelei parked their own vehicles nearby.

Silvio had spread the word, and several other cars were already clustered in the driveway. Silvio, Finn, Owen, and Liam Carter were waiting on the front porch, along with a dwarf who was around five feet tall with wavy silver hair, hazel eyes, and a hooked nose. Stuart Mosley, Finn's boss at First Trust bank, and Mallory's fiancé.

Bria and I got out of her sedan. Finn rushed over to her, while Owen did the same to me. Mosley hurried over to Mallory and Lorelei, but Silvio and Liam hung back on the porch.

Owen wrapped me up in a fierce, tight hug, and I buried

my face in his neck, drinking in his rich, metallic scent and trying to pretend the last two hours had never happened. That I hadn't finally learned the horrible truth I had been so desperately seeking.

Owen must have sensed how much I needed him right now because he pulled me closer, stroked his hand down my back over and over again, and whispered in my ear, telling me how much he loved me, how everything was going to be okay, and how we were going to get through this together.

I held on to Owen, hiding in his warm, strong embrace, until I felt steady enough to let go. I pulled back, and Owen cupped my face in his hands, careful not to touch my bruised cheek.

His violet gaze searched my gray one. "Are you okay?"

The love and concern in his tone almost broke me again, but I swallowed the hard knot of emotion in my throat. "I'm okay. Come on. We have a lot to talk about."

Owen nodded and hugged me again. Then we trooped inside with everyone else.

We went to the back of the house, which opened up into an old-fashioned beauty salon filled with cherry-red chairs. Style, fashion, and gossip magazines were stacked on tables throughout the room, while scissors, combs, curlers, hair dryers, and other tools covered the long counter that ran along one wall. The air smelled of perms, hair dyes, and other chemicals, along with a sweet, soft note of vanilla.

The salon was empty except for a middle-aged dwarf who was adding water to a metal dog bowl and a black-and-brown basset hound standing next to her. The dwarf's white-blond hair was perfectly curled and styled, and her subtle makeup highlighted her pale skin and clear, almost colorless eyes. She was wearing a string of white pearls over a white dress patterned with tiny pink roses, although her feet were bare, despite the February cold outside.

Jolene "Jo-Jo" Deveraux added the last of the water to the bowl, then patted the dog's side. "There you go, Rosco," she crooned to her beloved hound.

Rosco licked her hand and slurped down some water before curling up in his wicker basket in the corner.

Jo-Jo straightened and caught sight of me lurking in the doorway. Her eyes widened. "Darling! Your face!"

She stepped toward me, but I waved her off. "You can fix it later. Right now, we need to talk."

We all crammed into the salon. Me, Owen, Bria, Finn, Silvio, Roslyn, Xavier, Lorelei, Mallory, Mosley, Jo-Jo, Liam. It was a tight fit, but we managed it.

Jo-Jo washed her hands, then fluttered around, offering her unexpected guests everything from water and chicory coffee to sandwiches and cookies, but no one took her up on it.

I ended up standing in the corner, next to Rosco. The basset hound whined, clearly upset by the tension in the air, and curled up into an even tighter ball in his basket. I crouched down and rubbed his long, floppy ears. Rosco whined again, but he licked my hand, as if he knew how much I was hurting and was trying to comfort me.

I patted him again, then got to my feet and stared out over the salon. The longer I looked at the familiar furnishings, the more I thought about Fletcher. The old man had brought me here countless times so that Jo-Jo could use her Air elemental magic to heal whatever injuries I'd received on my latest job as the Spider.

Fletcher, who had worked for the Circle, who had once been Mason's right-hand man.

The shock had finally worn off, although equal parts

anger and disgust had taken its place, but I once again forced down my emotions. I couldn't give in to my feelings. Not now, when everyone was depending on me to tell them what to do and how we could protect ourselves from this deadly new threat.

I drew in a deep breath and slowly let it out. Then I stepped forward and faced my friends. "Here's what happened."

I calmly, quietly, ruthlessly told them everything that had transpired. Emery Slater and her giants kidnapping Bria, Lorelei, and me and taking us to the historical association mansion. Meeting Mason and hearing his horrible revelations about Fletcher and my parents. Trekking out to the Circle family cemetery and seeing my uncle's twisted shrine. I also told my friends about the black ledger Mason wanted me to find—and what would happen to us all if I failed.

Silence dropped over the salon, and no one moved or spoke. Finally, Finn shook his head.

"*No*," he said in a low, raspy voice. "It has to be a lie. Dad would never work for someone like Mason. *Never*."

My fingers tightened around the manila folder still in my hand. I hadn't put it down for a second, not even while I'd been petting Rosco. Part of me wanted to rip it to pieces, but I couldn't keep this from Finn, no matter how much it would hurt him. So I shuffled across the salon and handed the file to my brother, who was sitting on a couch with Bria.

Finn took the folder, set it down on his lap, and opened it. As soon as he saw the first photo of Fletcher and Mason in the Pork Pit, he knew it was true, just as I had. In an instant, all the fight leaked out of him, and his whole body sagged.

Finn flipped through the pictures and studied the handwritten note. After several seconds of silent contemplation, he snapped the folder shut and tossed it down onto the table in front of him, as if he couldn't bear to look at the contents any longer.

Mason's folder hit the one on my father's death that Bria had laid on the table, and pictures slid out of both files—Fletcher and Mason smiling inside the Pork Pit and Tristan's broken body stretched out on an autopsy table. The two images couldn't be any more different, and it was still hard for me to believe they were connected.

My brother stared at the photos, hurt, anger, and disgust twisting his handsome features into a grim, horrified mask. A few tears slipped down his cheeks, but he angrily slapped them away. Bria put her arm around his shoulders. A muscle ticked in Finn's jaw, but he slowly leaned into her.

Jo-Jo delicately cleared her throat and looked at Finn, then at me. "I know you don't want to hear this right now, darlings, but don't judge Fletcher too harshly. Sometimes when we're faced with a tough choice, we don't always make the right decision."

Part of me wanted to scream that this was about far more than just making a bad choice and that Fletcher had betrayed everything I thought I knew about him. But once again, I shoved down my anger. My emotions didn't matter right now—only answers did.

"Did Fletcher ever tell you anything about Mason?" I asked. "About working for the Circle?"

Jo-Jo shook her head. "Not a word. I knew Fletcher had a regular client he did jobs for from time to time, but he never told Sophia or me anything about Mason or who he really was. If I'd known, I would have told you, Gin. Trust me on that."

A harsh, bitter laugh escaped from my lips. "That's the problem. I put my trust in Fletcher, and look how well that has worked out."

Jo-Jo gave me a sympathetic look, but she didn't defend Fletcher any more. She knew this had shattered my whole world, and Bria's and Finn's too.

"What are we going to do?" Bria asked. "Xavier and I could round up the other cops we trust. We could go to the mansion and arrest Mason."

"He's probably already left by now," Xavier pointed out. "Besides, you, Gin, and Lorelei aren't kidnapped anymore. Mason could have Tucker, Emery Slater, and those giants say that he was with them the whole time and that he didn't do anything wrong. It would be your word against his, and it seems like Mason has more than enough juice to win that fight."

Frustration filled Bria's face, but she jerked her head, ceding his point.

Even if Bria and Xavier could have arrested Mason, I wouldn't have wanted them to. No, I wanted Mason *dead*, even if I still didn't know how to make that happen.

"There is another option," a low voice said.

We all looked over at Liam Carter, who was leaning against the doorway, hovering on the fringes of our group. His shoulder was on the far side of the doorjamb, and his feet were planted behind the threshold, as though he didn't dare step into the salon, as though he didn't belong here, as though he wasn't truly one of us. Then again, he was largely a stranger, despite the fat check I'd given him. Money and promises didn't make true friends—actions did—and it remained to be seen what actions Liam would take, either to protect us or to hurt us.

"And what option is that?" Silvio snapped in an annoyed tone.

Liam shrugged. "You all leave town and never return. That would be the easiest, safest thing to do."

Mallory and Mosley immediately started shaking their heads. The two dwarves were sitting on a love seat, holding hands.

"No," Mosley growled. "No way. Ashland has been my home for decades. I'm not leaving it just because this Mason fella has made some threats."

"Not just threats," Lorelei said. "Mason pretty much promised to kill all of us. Every single person in this room. And he has enough elemental magic to do it. He could wave his hand and easily open up a sinkhole big enough to swallow this whole house."

She shivered and wrapped her arms around herself. Lorelei didn't scare easily, and seeing her dread only increased my own guilt. I was the reason we were in this mess.

Me and Fletcher fucking Lane.

"Forget about leaving," Jo-Jo said. "That's not a viable option. Not unless we want to go into hiding and look over our shoulders for the rest of our lives, and no one wants to do that."

Everyone nodded, agreeing with her. Ashland was our home, and we all had lives, jobs, friends, and families that we couldn't—*wouldn't*—leave behind.

"So what are our options?" Roslyn asked. "I can't leave, and I can't close my club either. My employees count on me for a steady paycheck, not to mention how it would impact my own finances."

Worry rippled through Roslyn's voice, and concern darkened her lovely features. The others murmured similar sentiments. Mosley and Finn couldn't shut down First Trust bank, I couldn't leave the Pork Pit, and Jo-Jo couldn't abandon her house and beauty salon. Not to mention Owen's and Lorelei's businesses and Xavier's and Bria's jobs as cops. Like it or not, we were all stuck in Mason's web, and I could see only one way out of it.

"We have to give Mason what he wants," I said.

Mallory frowned. "What do you mean?"

"We have to find the black ledger and return it to Mason. That's the only way any of us will stay safe."

Maybe not even then, since Mason could still kill us after he got the ledger, although I didn't voice that troubling thought. Right now, the best I could hope for was to buy myself enough time to figure out how to take him down.

Silence descended over the salon as everyone absorbed my words. I could almost see the wheels spinning in their minds, particularly Finn's, as my friends tried to think of another way out of this. But they all slowly realized that we didn't have another choice. I could tell by the way their eyes dimmed, their shoulders dropped, and their bodies slumped back into their chairs, as if they suddenly needed something to support them.

Finn stared at me, his green gaze full of the same turbulent emotions that were still painfully throbbing in my own heart. "Do you have any idea where Dad hid this ledger? I don't remember seeing him with any black book, and he certainly never mentioned it to me."

I shook my head. "No. I have no idea where he might have hidden it."

Bria looked at Mosley. "What about First Trust bank? Maybe Fletcher put the ledger in a safety-deposit box, like he did those photos of the Circle members that Gin and Finn found a few months ago."

Mosley tapped his right foot on the floor, thinking about it. After several seconds, his foot stilled. “No. I know who owns every single safety-deposit box. There’s no way Fletcher had another box I didn’t know about, even if he put it under a different name. I’ll double-check just to make sure, but I’m almost certain the ledger isn’t at the bank.”

I hadn’t thought it was there, but it was still good to have confirmation. Fletcher probably hadn’t wanted to risk Mason storming into the bank and murdering Mosley, Finn, and the other employees to try to find it. An arrow of disgust shot through my heart. The old man had protected those innocent people, even as he had betrayed me.

“If it’s not at the bank, then where is it?” Mallory asked. “Gin, do you think Fletcher hid it in his house?”

“That’s the most obvious spot. I’ll start searching for it tonight.”

I didn’t tell her that I doubted it was in Fletcher’s house. Ever since the old man had died, I had slowly been cleaning out the various rooms, nooks, and crannies and going through the furniture, knickknacks, and odds and ends he had accumulated. In all my months of cleaning, I hadn’t come across any ledger.

Everyone fell silent again, wondering where Fletcher might have hidden the book, but no one had any answers, not even Finn, who still looked pale, shocked, and sick to his stomach. Finding out the truth about his father had hit Finn just as hard as it had hit me.

“There’s something else we need to discuss.” I looked at Mallory and Mosley, who were still holding hands. “I hate to even suggest this, but I think you guys should consider canceling your wedding.”

That stunned silence dropped over the salon again. Mallory and Mosley stared at each other, having a silent conversation. Then, together, in unison, they both shook their heads.

"No," Mallory said.

"Absolutely not," Mosley chimed in.

I opened my mouth to argue, but Mallory stabbed her finger at me, making the diamond engagement ring on her hand flash like a firecracker. Perhaps it was my imagination, but the gemstone practically glowed, as if each and every one of its many facets was suddenly as angry as its owner was.

"*No*," Mallory repeated in a louder, stronger voice. "I am *not* canceling our wedding just because some arrogant jackass has threatened us. I was part of Ashland before Mason was even a twinkle in his granddaddy's eye, and I will be here long after he's gone. So, no, I am *not* canceling our wedding for Mason Mitchell or anyone else. Isn't that right, Stuey?"

Mosley smiled at his bride-to-be and patted her hand. "That's right, doll. We're getting married on Saturday no matter what."

Once again, I opened my mouth to protest, but Lorelei beat me to it.

"Gin's right," she said. "Going through with the wedding is a big risk. Mason knew about the dress fitting today, and I'm guessing he knows all about the wedding too, especially since you guys announced it in the newspaper last week. Mason could easily crash the event, along with Emery Slater and those giants."

Mallory and Mosley looked at each other again, then glanced around at everyone else. Mallory's gaze snagged on Liam Carter, who was still leaning in the doorway, not quite a part of our group but not completely separate from it either. Mallory's blue eyes narrowed, and I could almost see the proverbial light bulb click on over her head. Uh-oh.

"Mr. Carter," Mallory called out. "What are you doing on Saturday?"

"Nothing as of right now," he replied. "What did you have in mind?"

A sly smile creased Mallory's face. "Hiring you and your people to protect our wedding."

Liam stared at me and raised his eyebrows in a silent question. This was not what we had agreed to, and it certainly hadn't been part of my plan, but I shrugged back at him. I might have engaged his services, but I didn't have an exclusive right to them. Of course, I still had my doubts about whether I could actually trust Liam, but I didn't voice them. Now was not the time to second-guess myself or add to my friends' worries.

Besides, Mallory was right. Having Liam and his bodyguards watch over the wedding was a smart idea, and it might make Mason think twice about attacking us there.

"It makes sense," Mallory continued. "You're already looking out for Gin at the Pork Pit. You might as well come to our wedding too, especially since Gin is one of the bridesmaids. Think of it as an opportunity to double your money for roughly the same amount of work." She paused. "Perhaps triple your money, if everything goes smoothly."

Mallory didn't bother with the stick. She didn't need to when dangling such a juicy, lucrative carrot. Even I would have been tempted to say yes for triple the money, especially given how much I was already paying Liam.

Still, he'd given me his word, and Liam stared at me again, silently asking for permission. I shrugged for a second time. It was his ass and his people on the line, so the decision was ultimately his, although I hoped he would agree. We could use all the help we could get.

Liam nodded at Mallory. "All right, Ms. Parker. I will

provide protection services for your wedding at double my usual rate, triple if the ceremony and the reception go off without a hitch. Do we have a deal?"

He stepped into the salon, walked over, leaned down, and stuck out his hand. Mallory gave it a strong shake that made Liam wince.

"Deal," she said.

Liam started asking Mallory questions about the venue, the number of guests, and more. Mosley chimed in, as did Lorelei. While the four of them worked on securing the wedding, the rest of my friends started talking among themselves, throwing out ideas about how we could take precautions until this situation with Mason was resolved.

This wasn't our first rodeo when it came to being in danger, and everyone had good, solid ideas. My friends were all strong, capable individuals who could take care of themselves, but the longer they talked, the more concerned I became.

I couldn't help but feel that no matter what we did to protect ourselves, Mason was going to come for us anyway—and kill everyone I loved.

✲ 10 ✲

While my friends continued their plotting, Jo-Jo made me lie back in one of the salon chairs so she could heal my face, along with the other bumps and bruises I'd gotten while being kidnapped.

The dwarf raised her hand and reached for her magic. A milky-white glow coated her palm, while wispy clouds of power floated through her clear eyes. "Emery Slater busted up your face pretty good," Jo-Jo murmured. "This might hurt more than usual. Sorry, darling."

She leaned forward and moved her hand back and forth in front of my bruised cheek. As an Air elemental, Jo-Jo could grab hold of oxygen and all the other natural gases in the atmosphere and use them to fade out bruises, pull skin back together, and repair broken bones.

Unlike my own cold, hard Ice and Stone magic, Jo-Jo's Air power felt like hundreds of tiny electric needles pricking my skin, as though I was getting stitches and being static-shocked over and over again at the same time. The uncomfortable sensation usually made me want to snarl. Air was the opposite element of Stone, and Jo-Jo's magic almost always felt wrong to me, just like my own Ice magic would rub a Fire elemental the wrong way.

Not today.

No, today Jo-Jo's power didn't bother me at all, and I didn't so much as wince as she undid the damage that had been done to me. The electric pricking feel of her magic was nothing compared to the dull, relentless ache in my heart. My entire body felt like a popped balloon, flat, ragged, and devoid of the helium that had given it shape, structure, and purpose. Only it wasn't something as simple as air that Mason had squeezed out of me with his harsh truths—it was my faith in Fletcher.

Jo-Jo finished with me, then checked out Bria and Lorelei, but they were fine and didn't require any healing.

We stayed at the salon another hour, making plans. From now on, everyone was teaming up, and no one was going anywhere alone unless absolutely necessary. Bria decided to room with Finn in his apartment in the city, while Owen would stay with me at Fletcher's house. Mosley agreed to move in with Mallory and Lorelei at their mansion, while Xavier and Roslyn would stick together. And of course, Jo-Jo and Sophia already shared a home.

"You could bunk with me if you like," Liam murmured to Silvio as we were getting ready to go our separate ways.

Silvio sniffed at the other man's suggestive tone. "Now is not the time for flirting. In case you haven't noticed, we're in a bit of a crisis."

A teasing grin spread across Liam's face. "And I say that makes it an excellent time for flirting. Live for today and all that."

Silvio tried to give him a stern look, but the corners of his lips twitched up, and he had to hold back a smile.

"Come on," Liam said, a wheedling note creeping into his voice. "It'll be fun. A chance for us to really get to know each other."

"And what if I don't want to get to know you?" Silvio countered.

Liam shrugged. "Then that's your loss, because I am fantastic."

He obviously liked Silvio, and I could tell that my assistant liked him right back. Silvio studied the other man, considering the proposition, but my assistant was just as guarded with his heart as I was with mine, and he shook his head.

"I'll stay at Fletcher's house. That way, I can help search for the ledger. Is that okay with you, Gin?" Silvio asked, a silent plea flickering across his face. He wanted me to say yes so that he wouldn't have to make a decision about Liam.

I understood his hesitation to open up to someone, and I still had my own doubts about Liam, so I obliged my friend. "That would be great. Thank you, Silvio."

He turned back to Liam. "I'm afraid you'll have to bunk alone tonight."

Instead of responding, Liam leaned forward and plucked Silvio's phone out of his hand. Silvio started to protest, but Liam held up his index finger, and the vampire actually fell silent. Liam Carter was a brave, brave man. No one, not even me, touched Silvio's precious electronics without his permission.

Liam swiped through a couple of screens, then punched some buttons and held out the phone. "There. Now you have my number. Just in case you get lonely and want to talk."

Silvio eyed the phone warily, like it was a scorpion about to sting him, but he reached out and took it.

Everyone else was busy making a few final plans, so I jerked my head at Liam, and he followed me out of the salon. I opened the front door, and we stepped out onto the porch. I shut the door behind us so we could speak privately.

"Did you notice anything unusual at the Pork Pit earlier?" I asked. "Did it look like anyone was following Bria and me when we left?"

Liam shook his head. "Nope. My folks were posted on the side streets around the restaurant, but no one paid any attention to you and your sister. Emery Slater must have been planning to snatch Bria from the Posh boutique all along."

That was my thought too, especially since Bria had gotten a text from Sykes, that corrupt cop, luring her out of the store.

Lorelei was right. Given Mallory and Mosley's recent newspaper announcement, it would have been easy for Mason to get details about the dwarves' upcoming wedding, including the fact that Bria and I were in the ceremony.

Emery could have trailed Mallory and Lorelei to the boutique and then waited for Bria to show up. Or the giant could have bribed one of the Posh clerks to text her when we arrived.

Or Liam could have tipped her off.

I eyed my supposed partner in crime, but Liam's blue gaze remained steady on my gray one. He didn't look guilty, like a man who had betrayed me. Then again, neither had Fletcher.

Those hungry sharks swimming in the watery tank of my worry and paranoia bumped up against the sides of my stomach again, but I ignored the phantom jolts. No matter how she had received the information, Emery had gotten the drop on us, and I couldn't afford to let that happen again. Next time, Mason wouldn't want to just talk. No, next time, he would hurt my friends.

"Is this the part where we talk about the job you hired me to do?" Liam asked. "And how I pretty much failed at protecting your friends today?"

I shook my head. "No. I told you to stay at the restaurant and watch over Silvio, Sophia, Catalina, and everyone else there. That's on me. Even you can't be in two places at once."

"So I'm not fired?" he asked in a light voice, although his face was serious, and he wasn't really joking.

"No, you're not fired."

Some of the tension eased out of his shoulders. "What do you want me to do now?"

"Exactly what we discussed the other night—if you're still up for it. I would understand if you wanted out. Emery Slater is dangerous, and Mason Mitchell even more so. They're not the kind to take prisoners or show any mercy. You and your people could be seriously hurt—or worse."

Liam shoved his hands into his pants pockets and slowly rocked back and forth on his feet, making the wooden boards *creak-creak-creak.* He dropped his head, staring down at a white stone planter full of white, blue, and purple pansies sitting by the front porch steps. A grinning royal-blue skull had been painted in the center of the white stone, indicating that Sophia had planted the pretty flowers.

Liam crouched down, reached out, and stroked the petals on one of the white pansies, making it bob up and down, almost like it was greeting him. "Winter was my sister's favorite time of year. Most people like spring or summer, but Leila always loved the cold weather, especially the snow."

I didn't say anything. I didn't want to interrupt whatever happy memories he might be having of his sister, especially given all the dark ones I had dredged up a few nights ago.

Liam stroked the petals again, then got to his feet and faced me. "You've been honest with me, which I appreciate more than you know. I'll see the job through to the end. I gave you my word, and I'll honor it, no matter what happens or how dangerous things get. Trust me on that."

Trust him? No way. Not yet. Maybe not ever. But for now, I would choose to believe that he would keep his word. I had to, given the circumstances.

"All right. Go get some more details about Mallory and Mosley's wedding, and keep me posted about any security measures you decide to implement for the ceremony and the reception. I'll see you tomorrow morning at the Pork Pit."

Liam nodded and opened the front door. Jo-Jo was heading outside, and Liam held the door for her. Then he stepped inside and shut it behind him, leaving me and the dwarf alone on the porch.

"How are you holding up, darling?" Jo-Jo asked in a soft, sympathetic voice.

I scrubbed my hands over my face. "As well as can be expected. I knew Mason would figure out that I killed his men in the cemetery and come after me sooner or later."

"But you didn't expect him to kidnap Bria and Lorelei—or tell you all those awful things about Fletcher," Jo-Jo finished my thought.

"Yeah."

She fixed her clear, almost colorless eyes on my gray ones. "You can't blame Fletcher. Not for all of it. He was lost in the fog of Deirdre's betrayal, and Mason took advantage of his hurt, anger, and confusion."

Everything she said made sense, but it didn't lessen my own hurt, anger, and confusion. Those wounds were far too fresh and much too raw to be soothed away by words.

Still, it wasn't Jo-Jo's fault, so I forced myself to smile at her. "Maybe I can understand that, eventually. But not right now."

She nodded, and her gaze grew soft and dreamy. Milky-white clouds started wisping through her eyes, and her Air magic gusted around us, pricking my skin. Once again, the sensation didn't bother me. If anything, I wished that it was stronger, harder, sharper. Maybe then it would have drowned out some of my own pain.

"What are you seeing?" I whispered.

In addition to using her power to heal people, Jo-Jo could also listen to all the emotional vibrations in the air the same way I could hear the ones in the stone. My magic usually spoke of the past, but Jo-Jo's Air power often gave her glimpses of the future, of the things people might do, both good and bad.

After a few seconds, the pricking feel of her Air magic vanished, and her eyes cleared. "No glimpses of the future. Instead, I saw Fletcher. Standing on the porch. Right in this very spot. I don't often get visions of the past, but I could see him, just for a second, as clearly as I'm seeing you."

I glanced around, but we were standing at the top of the steps, and there was nothing of interest on the porch, except for the planter, a couple of rocking chairs, a table, and some other outdoor furniture.

"Do you know when it was? How did he look? Was he saying anything?" Despite my current disgust with Fletcher, my curiosity got the better of me, and the questions tumbled out of my lips.

"No, he wasn't saying anything, but he seemed…sad

and…regretful." Jo-Jo shook her head. "I don't know if it's a true vision or not. Sometimes my feelings and memories, as well as other people's emotions, can interfere with my magic and make me see things that didn't really happen. Sometimes, if the emotion is strong enough, I can get a glimpse of something that happened to someone else, some memory that's not my own."

She shook her head again, making her white-blond curls dance around her face. "And there is plenty of emotion in my salon right now. I'm sorry, darling."

I shrugged. "It's not your fault. This all falls on Fletcher and me. Sometimes I wish that Deirdre Shaw had never come to town and that Hugh Tucker had never told me about the Circle. I would have been a lot happier, and we all would have been a lot safer."

"You can't think like that. We might have been happier, but we wouldn't have been safer. Mason could have blindsided us then. He could have lashed out and killed us without anyone realizing what was happening or who our enemy truly was. At least now we have a chance to plan and fight back."

She was trying to make me feel better about dragging us into this mess. It didn't really work, but I forced myself to smile at her again anyway.

"You're right," I lied. "Thank you, Jo-Jo."

"Anytime, darling. Anytime."

She slid her arm around my waist and hugged me close. Together we left the porch and went back inside the house.

✲ 11 ✲

After promising to be vigilant and to keep in touch, everyone split up for the night. Owen and I followed Silvio over to the vampire's house, so he could grab some clothes and toiletries. Owen stopped by his mansion to do the same, and the three of us ended up at my house—Fletcher's house.

I reached out with my magic, but the brick of the house only murmured about the cold, and the rocks hidden in the woods did the same. No one had been near the structure since I'd left this morning, so we got out of our vehicles and trooped inside.

We stepped into the den, and I threw the folders Mason and Bria had given me down onto the coffee table. Owen and Silvio lowered their bags off their shoulders and set them on the floor.

"What do you want to do, Gin?" Owen asked. "Start looking for the ledger?"

Instead of answering him, I stalked over to the fireplace and stared at the framed drawings on the mantel. One was a snowflake, my mother Eira's rune for icy calm, while another sketch was an ivy vine, Annabella's rune and the symbol for elegance. Matching silverstone pendants were draped over their respective rune drawings.

I traced my fingers over the necklaces, then focused on another sketch of a pig holding a platter of food. The image matched the sign outside the Pork Pit and was my way to remember and honor Fletcher along with the rest of my dead family.

What a sad, cruel joke this had all turned out to be.

Suddenly, I couldn't stand to look at the drawing anymore or even think about the fact that Fletcher had worked for Mason. I spun around to Owen and Silvio.

"Fuck it," I snarled. "I'm taking a shower and going to bed."

And that was exactly what I did, even though it was barely after seven o'clock.

Thirty minutes later, I was curled up in bed, my hair still wet from my shower. Owen came in and lay down beside me, and I could hear Silvio unpacking his things and rustling around in a bedroom down the hallway. For a long time, I lay there, nestled in Owen's warm, strong arms, and glared at the wall in front of me.

Sometime later, Owen's soft, steady breaths lured me to sleep and into the land of dreams, memories, nightmares…

"Mason fucking Mitchell."

The low, angry snarl startled me, and I whirled around. For a second, I thought someone had slipped into the back of the Pork Pit, but the space was deserted, and it was just me and my clipboard. For the last fifteen minutes, I had been examining the metal shelves full of sugar, flour, cornmeal, and ketchup. Business had been slow on this chilly February afternoon, hence my doing inventory.

"Mason fucking Mitchell."

The low, angry snarl sounded again, and I realized that Fletcher was speaking. His voice was a bit muffled, since he was in the storefront, but he seemed upset, especially given his continued vicious cursing. Curious, I walked over and peered through one of the round windows in the double doors.

The restaurant storefront was empty, except for two people. Fletcher was wearing his usual blue work clothes and was perched on his stool behind the old-fashioned cash register. A copy of The Count of Monte Cristo *was lying on the counter, with one of the day's receipts marking his place in the book. A giant with brown eyes, a pale face full of freckles, and curly carrot-red hair was standing on the opposite side of the counter.*

The giant plucked a manila file folder out of the depths of his black overcoat and held it out. The man's face was calm, as though Fletcher hadn't spoken. I didn't like the look of the giant, especially the way he kept staring at the old man as if Fletcher was a servant being summoned by some rich, powerful master. I palmed one of my knives, ready to race into the storefront if the giant pulled a gun or some other weapon.

"Take the file," the giant said. "You know what will happen if you don't."

"I told him that I was done, *Billings," Fletcher growled. "He agreed that we were finally* done.*"*

The giant, Billings, shrugged. "And now he's decided otherwise. You can take the file and do the job quickly and cleanly. Or he'll get someone else to do it, only not so quickly and cleanly. You know what that means."

Fletcher's nostrils flared, and anger stained his tan cheeks. For a moment, I thought he was going to tell the giant to stuff that file where the sun didn't shine, but he reached across the counter and reluctantly took the folder. Billings raised his hand and snapped off a mocking salute, then spun around and left the restaurant.

Fletcher watched the giant go. The second the other man was out of sight of the storefront windows, Fletcher let out a long, weary sigh and dropped the folder onto the counter as though it weighed a hundred pounds and he couldn't hold it up a second longer.

"Mason fucking Mitchell," he said for a third time, although his voice was now a low, resigned mutter.

Fletcher sighed again, then opened the folder and started flipping through the contents. I tucked my knife back up my sleeve and pushed through the double doors. His green gaze was locked on the info, and he seemed deep in thought, so I tiptoed up beside him and peered over his shoulder.

Fletcher was staring at a photo of a dark-haired middle-aged man standing with what must have been his young daughter, given the resemblance between the two of them. I also spotted a sheet of paper with the man's name and address: Wade Brockton, 37 Bookman Way.

"Who's that guy?" I asked.

"Gin!" Fletcher yelped, jerking away. "You scared me!"

I frowned. He could hear a quarter hit the restaurant floor from thirty feet away during the loudest lunch rush. I never *got the drop on him, not even during our training sessions at the old Ashland Rock Quarry. What was wrong with him?*

I waited until Fletcher had relaxed on his stool again, then pointed at the photo. "Who's that guy?" I repeated. "Some new job you're tackling?"

"Something like that," he muttered.

"What did he do? Steal from someone?"

He frowned, as though my questions bothered him. "Why would you say that?"

I shrugged. "The sweater vest and glasses make him look like an accountant. Plus, it says right below his address that he works at Ashland Accounting Services."

Fletcher slid the photo and info sheet back into the folder, closed it, and tucked the whole thing under his arm.

"Well, you're right. He is an accountant. As for what he did..." His voice trailed off, and his face darkened. "He embezzled money from the wrong people, and now he's going to pay for it."

"Why do you sound so upset about that? We've gone after embezzlers before. Two months ago, we took out that woman who was stealing money from a cancer charity, funds that were supposed to help sick people in need."

Fletcher shook his head. "This guy is different. He didn't steal the money for himself, to spend on clothes and cars and vacations. He took it because his daughter was ill and needed an operation."

"Oh." I frowned again. "Then why are you targeting him? Usually in a case like this, the Tin Man would pay someone a visit and pointedly suggest they pay back the money and try to make amends with whomever they wronged."

He shook his head again. "Believe me, I wish I could do that. But this...client, well, he's not the forgiving type. Never has been, never will be."

"Who's the client?"

Fletcher shook his head for a third time. "No one you need to worry about."

He smiled, but the expression didn't warm or soften his eyes, which were as cold and hard as green glass. This job troubled him. I could understand why. Sure, the guy, Wade

Brockton, had stolen money, but, like Fletcher had said, he'd done it to help his daughter, not for selfish reasons.

Normally, Fletcher wouldn't even consider *this sort of job, but he'd taken the file from the giant without any bargaining or pushback. Why? Why did Fletcher feel he* had *to do this job, despite the fact that it went against everything he'd ever taught me about being an assassin?*

"I know you've been busy with school lately, so I'm going to handle this one myself, Gin. Give you the night off," he continued.

"I'm not that busy," I protested.

I had recently finished up my bachelor's degree in English at Ashland Community College, but I was still taking classes in anything and everything that caught my interest or that I might put toward a graduate degree later on. I was only twenty-two, so I had plenty of time to decide what I wanted to do with my life, although I couldn't imagine myself anywhere but here at the Pork Pit with Fletcher.

*"In fact, I finished reading the first book for my new literature class earlier tonight," I said, trying to persuade him to let me help. "*Where the Red Fern Grows*. One of your favorites."*

Fletcher smiled a little at that, but the expression quickly slipped off his face. "Thanks for the offer, but I'll be fine. Lock up the restaurant, then relax. I'll be home soon. Okay, Gin?"

"Sure. Sounds great. See you later."

Fletcher got to his feet and grabbed his blue jacket from the rack in the corner. Still holding the file, he crossed the storefront and opened the front door, making the bell there chime out a high, almost warning note. He glanced over his shoulder, smiled at me again, and left.

I waited until he was out of sight, then ran over, locked the door, flipped the sign over to Closed, *and slapped off the lights. I grabbed my own jacket and pushed through the double doors to lock up the back of the restaurant. If I hurried, I could catch up to Fletcher by the time he reached the accountant's house...*

I woke with a start, the loud, harsh echoes of the Pork Pit's front-door bell still chiming in my mind, almost like an alarm telling me to get up.

For several minutes, I lay still and quiet in bed, thinking back over my dream, my memory. Well, now I knew why I'd heard Fletcher's voice muttering in my mind when Mason had introduced himself at the mansion. Seeing my uncle up close and finally hearing his last name had jarred another nightmare loose from the muck of my mind. I just wished that I'd remembered this particular horror sooner. Maybe if I had, I wouldn't be in such a bind now.

Beside me, Owen jerked, almost as if he was sensing my turbulent thoughts. I held my breath, not wanting to disturb him. After a few seconds, Owen rolled away from me, although he was still sound asleep, given the deep, throaty snores rumbling out of his mouth. I couldn't go back to dreamland, not yet, so I slipped out of bed, threw on a flannel robe and some slippers, and left my bedroom.

I stepped into the hallway and paused outside Silvio's bedroom, but everything was quiet inside, and I didn't see the glow of his electronics through the crack under the door. My assistant must have gone to sleep early too.

I plodded down the steps to the first floor and roamed through the house, checking the doors and windows and peering at the yard and woods outside. Everything was secure, and no suspicious shadows haunted the dark winter landscape. Mason had delivered his ultimatum, and it didn't seem as though he, Emery Slater, or anyone else was going to come knocking on my door tonight. Good.

But my uncle's threat was still hanging over my head, so I went into the den and grabbed the file folders from the coffee table, along with a sapphire paperweight from the fireplace mantel, and took them to the office.

Fletcher's office.

I flipped on the lights and stared out over the furnishings. Metal filing cabinets. Wooden bookcases. The half-empty bottle of gin and two now-clean glasses sitting on the desk next to a framed photo of a smiling Fletcher hiking on Bone Mountain.

The furnishings looked the same as always, yet completely foreign at the same time, as though I had never been in this room before and everything in here belonged to a stranger.

Just like Fletcher had been a stranger to me.

All sorts of unwanted, unwelcome feelings bubbled up inside me, but I pushed them down just like I had done all afternoon long. I trudged over and sat down in the old man's chair, as though everything was normal, as though everything was *fine*. I laid the sapphire paperweight on the desk next to the bottle of gin, then opened the two folders and got to work.

Even though I'd already seen the information on my father's death, I studied the photos much more carefully this time. Bria had asked me how Stone magic could be used in such a violent, vicious manner, and now I had time to really think about it. How much force, how much power, how much raw magic and ugly determination it would take to break someone's bones and then crush and twist and yank them so far out of place.

The answer? Quite a lot of magic—and much, much more power than I had.

I also coldly, calmly, ruthlessly considered how much pain doing such things would cause the victim. Breaking a bone hurt plenty on its own, but then having those bones crushed and forcibly pulled even farther apart…it would be excruciating.

Tristan must have suffered *so much.*

My stomach roiled, but I poured myself some gin and quickly downed it. The lukewarm liquor slid down my throat and exploded into that sweet, slow burn in my stomach. The gin drowned out the worst of the nausea, so I kept going. Clinically analyzing the horrible ways Mason had tortured my father was definitely morbid and gruesome, but maybe if I knew exactly how Mason used his magic, then I could figure out a way to defeat him.

But nothing came to me. No answers, no ideas, no sparks, glimmers, or shimmers of hope. Nothing.

I had felt Mason's magic earlier, and he had so much pure, raw power that I knew I couldn't go toe to toe with him. Not elemental-to-elemental in a duel to the death, as people were so fond of doing in Ashland. Mason would crush me the same way he had crushed my father.

If I had any hope of beating him, killing him, then I had to be smarter than Mason, and not just when it came to my magic—I also had to outthink him.

I'd already taken a step in that direction by hiring Liam Carter. I still didn't know if Liam would hold up his end of our bargain, but at least I'd given myself a fighting chance, just like Jo-Jo had said earlier.

So I sat there, drank some more gin, and forced myself to think about how I could possibly survive a full-frontal assault by Mason if—*when*—it came down to that.

The first thing I did was pick up the sapphire paperweight. The gemstone had been in a box of Mab's things that I'd bought at the recent auction at the Eaton Estate. When I'd initially found the sapphire, I'd thought it odd that Mab would have something that emanated so much Stone magic, since the invisible waves of power would have been a constant annoyance to a Fire elemental like herself. Of course, now I realized that Mason had coated the sapphire with his magic and given it to Mab, probably as a warning about how much power he had and to stay in line—or else.

I played around with the sapphire for several minutes, seeing how the Stone magic already coating it reacted to my own. I'd thought Mason's power might mix badly with mine, but I should have known better. After all, my uncle and I were gifted in the same element and were from the same bloodline. The sapphire's color actually brightened at my probing it with my magic, as if it was eager to soak up my power and add it to Mason's.

The only thing the sapphire didn't like was when I switched gears and coated it with my Ice magic. The gemstone shrieked in protest as the cold crystals engulfed it, although the layer of elemental Ice muffled the sound. The Ice also seemed to blunt the feel of Mason's magic, just a bit. Interesting but not particularly helpful, so I set the gemstone aside.

I swallowed the rest of my gin and poured myself another glass. When I was properly fortified, I let out a breath and slowly cracked open the folder that chronicled Fletcher's relationship with Mason.

Once again, the first thing I saw was that photo of Fletcher and Mason grinning at each other inside the Pork Pit.

The sight turned my stomach, just as it had earlier, but I grabbed the photo, tilted it toward the light, and studied every little thing about it. There wasn't much to see. Fletcher and Mason smiling widely, as though they were best friends, inside the blurry confines of the restaurant.

I set that photo aside and flipped through the others, but it was more of the same. More images of the two men and no real clues in any of them—except for the last photo.

The final picture showed Fletcher and Mason standing in the woods, although I couldn't tell where it might have been taken. Still, this image was a bit different from the others. For one thing, Fletcher looked older than he had in the first photo. For another, he wasn't smiling. Hmm.

I opened the center desk drawer and rummaged around until I found Fletcher's old magnifying glass. Then I peered through the lens at the photo, studying every little line, crease, and wrinkle on his tan face. Nothing in his features was particularly noteworthy, but I did notice something strange about the photo.

Fletcher was wearing a suit.

Perhaps that was why he looked so uncomfortable. The only time I'd ever seen him wear a suit was for some somber or formal occasion, like a funeral or Finn's and my high school and college graduations. Fletcher had been far more comfortable in his old blue work clothes than anything else, but there he was, wearing a black suit jacket over a white shirt. Why?

I looked through the magnifying glass again. Not only was Fletcher wearing a suit, but he was also sporting a tie pin. A disgusted snort erupted out of my lips. Mason must have had far more influence over the old man than I'd realized. I had never seen Fletcher wear a tie pin, or any other adornments, not even to a funeral. Finn had bought the old man a pair of silver cuff links for Christmas one year, and he'd never put them on, not even once. Then again, Finn should have known better than to give his father something like that. Suits, tie pins, and cuff links might be Finn's style, but they definitely weren't Fletcher's.

So why was he wearing them in this photo?

I peered through the magnifying glass again. The tie pin was a small circle with several thin rays radiating out of it that made it look like…

A spider rune.

Surprise spiked through me. I almost dropped the photo, along with the magnifying glass, but I tightened my grip on both and looked at the image again. It was an old picture, taken well before the days of digital cameras, so the resolution wasn't great, and I didn't have a crystal-clear view. Fletcher's tie pin might have been a spider rune, or it could have been some other round symbol. No way to know for sure.

Still, the longer I stared at the photo, the more anger bubbled up inside me. Fletcher had set this whole thing up like a treasure hunt. First, I'd found a box of keepsakes he'd hidden in Deirdre Shaw's empty casket. That discovery had eventually led me to find a note and a key buried in my mother's grave. The key had pointed me to several safety-deposit boxes at First Trust bank that had contained information and photos of all the Circle members—except for Mason.

Over the past few months, I'd wondered why Fletcher hadn't included Mason's photo with the others. This whole time, I'd thought he had been trying to spare me from the sickening discovery that my uncle had killed my father and ordered Mab Monroe to execute my mother, my sisters, and me. Now I finally knew the whole dirty, unvarnished truth. Fletcher hadn't been trying to protect me.

He'd been trying to protect *himself.*

Fletcher Lane worked for the Circle...

Fletcher worked for...

Fletcher...

Mason's sly voice echoed in my mind over and over again. Each and every one of his words was like a sharp sting in my heart, but what hurt the most wasn't that Fletcher had worked for Mason and killed people for the Circle. No, I could forgive him for those sins, for being lost in the fog of his anger, grief, embarrassment, and confusion over Deirdre's dark nature, just as Jo-Jo had said earlier.

What I *couldn't* forgive was Fletcher keeping this information to himself. He'd hidden the truth about what had really happened to my parents, and he'd never told me about the very real threat that Mason posed to me and everyone I cared about. I'd trusted the old man with my life, with my love, respect, and devotion, and it was the cruelest irony that he hadn't done the same.

Fletcher hadn't trusted me with *anything*—and that was the sharpest sting of all.

The anger pounding through my body doubled, tripled in size and kept right on growing and growing, until my heart felt like it was about to explode right out of my chest. I glanced over at the framed photo of Fletcher sitting on the desk. I couldn't stand to look at his smiling face right now, so I slapped the frame away. It skidded sideways, toppled over, and landed facedown on the desk.

That one soft *thump* seemed to boom as loudly as a sledgehammer cracking against a concrete block, and the sound blasted through the icy dam I'd built around the turbulent emotions churning inside my heart.

Suddenly, I couldn't stand the sight of the two glasses and the bottle of gin on the desk, so I slapped them away too. They flew off the edge and hit the floor with three loud, distinct, satisfying *crack-crack-cracks*. The caustic scent of the gin filled the air, burning almost as hot as my rage.

Next, I slapped the two manila folders off the desk, and they both landed among the broken glass and spilled liquor.

One by one, I snatched up the autopsy report and other papers dealing with my father's murder, crumpled them into tight balls, and threw them aside as well.

Finally, I came to the photos. I shoved them off the side of the desk en masse and watched while they dropped on top of the rest of the mess on the floor. Naturally, the photo of Fletcher and Mason inside the Pork Pit landed faceup, their happy smiles mocking my own rage, grief, heartbreak, and misery—

"Gin?" a soft voice called out.

My head snapped up. Owen was standing in the office doorway, a concerned look on his face.

"Are you okay?" he asked.

No. Of course not. I didn't know if I would ever be okay again. But I couldn't let him know that. I couldn't let *anyone* know that. Not when we were in so much danger. Not when I needed to be strong for everyone.

I shot to my feet, sucked down a breath, and opened my mouth to lie and say that I was fine, but my gaze darted back down to that photo of Fletcher and Mason. Instead of a calm denial, a choked sob tumbled from my lips. I staggered around the desk, my knees shaking.

"Gin!"

Owen hurried forward. His arms closed around me, catching me, but I didn't have the strength to stand, and he lowered me to the floor and eased me back, so that I was leaning up against the front of Fletcher's desk.

Owen crouched down beside me and cupped my cheek in his hand, his thumb gently sliding across my skin. "Oh, Gin," he murmured. "I'm sorry. So sorry."

Once again, I tried to smile, lie, and say that I was fine, but all that came out of my mouth was another one of those damn sobs. This time, I couldn't hold the rest of them back.

Hot tears slid down my cheeks, and great big wrenching, heaving sobs ballooned in my chest, zipped up my throat, and spewed out of my lips.

Owen sat down on the floor, put his arms around me, and rocked me back and forth like I was a child he was trying to soothe. "It's okay, Gin. It's okay. I know how much it hurts. I'm right here with you. Just let it all out…"

He kept saying those same things over and over again as I cried and cried about how Fletcher had betrayed me.

✲ 12 ✲

I didn't cry for long, maybe five minutes.

Slowly, my sobs stopped, and my torrent of tears diminished to a salty trickle. I swiped the unwanted wetness off my face and focused on once again building an icy dam around the rest of my anger, grief, and heartache.

I didn't have time to cry—I had a ledger to find and an uncle to kill.

"Gin?" Owen asked again. "Are you okay?"

I pulled away from his warm, comforting embrace. "Yeah. I just needed to…let that out."

He gave me a sympathetic look. "Is there anything I can do to help?"

I shook my head. "You're already doing it, just by being here, just by believing I can get us out of this mess."

Unlike Fletcher, my treacherous inner voice whispered, but I squashed the snide sound. I didn't have time for it either.

Owen gently brushed a wayward tear off my cheek. "Of course I believe in you, Gin. You'll figure this out, just like you always do, and you'll make Mason regret every horrible thing he ever did to your family."

The certainty ringing in his voice and burning in his violet eyes touched me more than I could ever say, so I grabbed his hand and pressed a kiss to the center of his palm instead. Owen curled his fingers into mine, stroking his thumb over the back of my hand, still trying to comfort me.

Someone cleared his throat, and Silvio stepped into the office. I had never really seen my assistant after hours, out of his usual suit, and he was wearing a dark gray flannel robe over light gray silk pajamas. The only thing that ruined his man-of-leisure look was his slippers, which were neon pink and covered with sparkly black sequined hearts.

Silvio caught me eyeing his slippers and held out one of his feet. "A Christmas present from Sophia. They are surprisingly warm and comfortable."

He wandered over and pretended to examine the books on the shelves, while Owen and I got to our feet, and I finished pulling myself together.

"All right, boys," I said when I was calm again. "Time's a-wasting. Let's start looking for the ledger."

We began in the office. This was the most logical place for Fletcher to have hidden the book, and I had found sensitive files secreted in here before. Owen and Silvio examined the filing cabinets, while I took the bookcases and the desk. Together we checked the floor, the walls, even the ceiling.

We didn't find anything. No ledger, no hidden files, no secret compartments, not so much as a random doodle on a piece of scrap paper.

"I don't think it's in here," Silvio said, after we'd been searching for almost an hour.

I shoved one of the books back into its slot on the shelf. "I think you're right. Let's try the den."

We went to that part of the house. Owen and Silvio pulled the couch out from the wall and searched on that side of the room, while I put my hand on the fireplace, listening to the stones' murmurs. But there were no secret hiding spots in the fireplace that I didn't already know about, and the stones only whispered about the burning and smoke of the fires I had recently lit.

Frustration filled me, but we kept going and searched the rest of the house from top to bottom. Owen, Silvio, and I squeezed the couch cushions, rapped on the furniture, jumped up and down on the floorboards, and searched a dozen other different ways, but we didn't find anything. No ledger, no hidden files, no secret compartments, not so much as an old, misplaced grocery list.

Finally, around one in the morning, we gave up. The ledger wasn't in the house. No one said anything, but I could almost see the gears grinding in Owen's and Silvio's minds, and I knew they were thinking the same thing I was.

If Fletcher hadn't hidden the ledger in his own house, his sanctum, the place he felt the safest, then where was it?

We went back to bed, but I didn't sleep much the rest of the night. The next morning, Thursday, I got up, took a shower, and went to the Pork Pit like usual. Silvio and I rode in his car, and we followed Owen over to his downtown office building and made sure he got inside okay.

Once Owen was safe and secure, Silvio drove me over to the restaurant. He parked the car while I checked the front door for rune traps, bombs, and other nasty surprises an enemy might have left overnight. The storefront was clean, and I found myself staring up at the sign over the door, the pig holding a platter of food, the symbol that always reminded me of Fletcher.

Once again, the sharp sting of his betrayal throbbed in my heart like a red-hot poker, but I pushed it aside. I didn't have any more time to cry or wonder what Fletcher had been thinking when he agreed to work for Mason. All that mattered was finding the black ledger before my uncle's midnight Saturday deadline. So I unlocked the front door, went inside, and got busy wiping down the long counter in the back of the restaurant.

Sophia showed up a few minutes later, and Silvio told her about our failed attempt to find the ledger in Fletcher's house.

I looked at the Goth dwarf. "Do you have any idea where Fletcher would have stored it? In the past, he hid files in his office or at First Trust bank, but Finn texted me this morning. He and Mosley double-checked the safety-deposit boxes, and the ledger isn't there. I'm running out of places to look."

Sophia stirred a pot of baked beans and stared off into space, thinking. After several seconds, she shook her head. "Nope. No idea. Jo-Jo and I will check our house tonight, but he could have hidden it anywhere."

She didn't say anything else, but I could hear and see her unspoken words hanging in the air like a dark, ominous cloud. They were the same ones I was thinking.

And we might never find it.

I shoved that worry to the back of my mind, tied on my blue apron, and started on the day's cooking. Fifteen minutes before we opened, a loud knock sounded on the front door. Sophia and Silvio froze, while I palmed a knife and whirled around in that direction.

Liam Carter was standing outside, peering in through one of the windows.

I let out a tense breath, tucked my knife back up my sleeve, and unlocked the door.

Liam stripped off his navy overcoat and hung it on the rack by the front door. "You know, Gin, I can't exactly help if you won't even let me inside your restaurant," he said in a chiding voice.

"How did things go with Mallory and Mosley last night?" I asked, deliberately changing the subject.

Liam had followed the dwarven couple over to Lorelei's mansion so he could get cracking on his security plan for the wedding.

"Good," he replied. "They're having a relatively small wedding, at least according to Ashland society standards. Only about three hundred guests. We worked out most of the logistics last night, and I sent some of my people over to the country club this morning to check out things and inform the staff that we'll be taking point on security. Don't worry. The wedding will go off without any problems."

I couldn't tell if he truly believed that or was simply saying what I wanted to hear. Either way, I once again had no choice but to take him at his word. "All right. Have a seat. What do you want for lunch?"

Instead of heading to the back corner booth he'd sat in yesterday, Liam strolled over and plopped down on the stool next to Silvio. "Oh, I can think of a few things," he drawled.

Silvio snorted at the other man's obvious attempt to flirt, but he never took his eyes off his tablet. Not even Liam Carter held more charm and appeal than the vampire's electronics. At least, not right now, when Silvio was hot on the trail of the missing ledger.

At eleven o'clock, I unlocked the front door and flipped the sign over to *Open*, and hungry customers started streaming inside. I eyed everyone who came through the door, but no one seemed overtly shady, shifty, or suspicious, and no one seemed interested in anything other than getting a good, hearty meal.

I quickly lost myself in the hustle and bustle of the lunch rush, and I actually started to feel a little bit better. I still didn't understand why Fletcher had hidden the fact that he'd worked for Mason, but as Jo-Jo had said, the old man hadn't been perfect. I had certainly made my fair share of mistakes, both as Gin Blanco and as the Spider, and I was going to try not to begrudge Fletcher this whopper of a secret. That was the only way I was going to get through this. I could cry and scream and rant and rave later, after I found the ledger and figured out how to kill Mason.

So I focused on cooking and chopping, stirring and sautéing, and ringing up order after order on the cash register. The only thing that ruined the illusion that this was just another day was the sweet-and-spicy scent of Fletcher's barbecue sauce flavoring the air. Every time I breathed in the rich, deep aroma, I would think about the old man, which led my mind back to the missing ledger, Mason, and everything else. I'd shove those thoughts away and distract myself with work…until the next time I got a whiff of the bubbling sauce.

Still, I put on a calm, happy face for my normal customers and the underworld bosses and minions who came to the restaurant. Maybe if I pretended everything was fine long and hard enough, I could make it a reality.

Yeah, I didn't believe that either.

But the hours passed by pleasantly enough, and my phone chirped with texts from Owen, Finn, Bria, and everyone else. My friends were safe, and no one had seen any sign of Emery Slater or her giants. It seemed as though Mason was keeping his word. He wouldn't touch me or my friends—unless I failed to deliver the ledger by his midnight Saturday deadline.

After that, though, it would just be a matter of time before Mason came after us.

Even if we hid in a safe house, my uncle had enough men, money, and magic to eventually find us. He would most likely kill Bria first, then probably Owen and Finn, and then everyone else. Mason would want to punish me, to make me suffer for as long as possible, so he would probably murder me last.

Maybe it was morbid thinking about the death of everyone I loved, but Fletcher had trained me to be a realist. He had always said if you knew what was coming, then you could plan for it accordingly. I knew exactly what horrors were heading my way—I just didn't know how to stop them.

Even though I was still pissed at him, Fletcher's advice had gotten me out of more than one jam, and I embraced it again now. While I worked the lunch rush, I turned my many problems over in my mind. Every time I ladled baked beans into a bowl, scooped up mac and cheese, or piled smoked pulled chicken onto a plate, the situation became a little clearer.

I needed to do three things: Find the missing ledger. Protect my friends. Kill Mason.

Maybe it was being in the restaurant, in my safe place, or maybe it was Fletcher's ghostly presence lingering in the air right along with the scent of his barbecue sauce, but by the time the lunch rush slowed down, I felt calmer and more in control than I had since before I killed the two giants in the cemetery.

I decided my own fate, not Emery Slater, Hugh Tucker, Mason Mitchell, or anyone else. I would figure out how to defeat them. I'd worked too hard on my relationships, and I'd suffered through too much to just give up, lay down my knives, and die.

"You seem…better," Silvio remarked.

It was just after two o'clock. Only a few folks were dining in the restaurant, and the waitstaff was taking their usual break in the back.

I was taking a break too, sitting on my stool behind the cash register, and eating my own lunch—grilled chicken smothered with a spicy buffalo sauce and sprinkled with blue cheese crumbles, a new pineapple-and-carrot coleslaw I was thinking about adding to the menu, roasted sweet potatoes slathered with cinnamon butter, and some of Sophia's delicious sourdough rolls. For dessert, I was having a dark chocolate brownie covered with warm homemade cherry sauce and topped with a scoop of vanilla-bean ice cream.

I took a sip of my sweet blackberry tea. "That's because I *am* better."

"So you've come up with some more places to look for the ledger?"

"Nope."

Silvio frowned. "So then you've figured out a way to find Mason?"

"Nope."

His frown deepened. "So you at least know how to kill Mason when you see him again?"

"Nope."

He threw his hands up in the air. "Then why are you better?"

I gestured at the plates on the counter. "Because I am enjoying a good meal with good company. Everything else will work itself out. Trust me."

Silvio eyed me, clearly thinking I had lost my pickles. Maybe I had. But for now, I was going to enjoy my food and his company. My assistant gave me another wary look, but he returned to his tablet.

On the far side of the restaurant, Liam Carter's phone chirped. After Silvio had rebuffed his advances, Liam had retreated to the back corner booth. The vampire huffed and shot Liam a dirty look, as though the chiming device annoyed him, even though his own tablet let out far more burps and beeps. Liam saluted Silvio with his phone, and my assistant rolled his eyes.

I focused on my meal again. I hadn't finished all my food, but I was getting full, so I pushed my plates aside and dug my spoon into my dessert. The rich chocolate brownie melted on my tongue, combining with the sweet, tart cherry sauce and the cool, refreshing ice cream. So good. I quickly inhaled a second bite. I should have eaten dessert first.

The bell over the front door chimed. I scooped another bite of brownie, sauce, and ice cream into my mouth, then looked up, a smile on my face, ready to greet my next customer. My smile froze, then cracked and dropped from my lips like icicles snapping off a roof and plunging to the ground, as I realized exactly who was darkening my door.

Mason Mitchell.

✲ 13 ✲

I forgot all about my dessert. In an instant, I had dropped my hand down behind the counter, out of sight of everyone in the storefront, and palmed a knife. If Mason was here to make good on his threat to kill me and my friends, then I wasn't going down without a fight.

Instead of charging over to the counter, Mason unwrapped the navy scarf from around his neck, shrugged out of his navy overcoat, and hung them both on the rack by the front door. Then he turned and looked at me.

My uncle's gray gaze flicked from my face down to the counter, and a smug, knowing smirk lifted his lips. He knew I was clutching a knife, and it didn't bother him in the slightest. Then again, why would it? He had enough raw magic to reduce the Pork Pit to rubble with a mere flick of his fingers.

Even now, when he wasn't using his power in any active way, elemental magic still poured off him in cold, hard, continuous waves. The sensation made me feel as though I was trapped in a cement room, just waiting for the walls to snap together, crush every bone in my body, and grind my entire being to dust. Mason's power might be eerily similar to my own Ice and Stone magic, but it was hands down the most horrible thing I had ever felt.

Mason smirked at me a moment longer, then walked over and sat down in a booth next to the windows.

And he wasn't alone.

Emery Slater also strolled into the restaurant, along with two other giants. They left their coats on, but she and her men sat down at a table across from Mason's booth. Please. As if he needed their protection. He was more than capable of defending himself—and killing everyone in here.

Hugh Tucker also stepped inside the restaurant, bringing up the rear, slinking in like a copperhead in the grass. The vampire perched at a nearby table by himself, as if he didn't really belong with either Mason or the three giants.

Tucker might have been the Circle's top enforcer for years, but he was very clearly an underling, and Mason seemed to pay as little attention to the vampire as he did to the furniture. Oh, yes. Tucker was just a tool to be used and then forgotten about until the next time Mason needed him.

"Gin," Silvio said in a low, urgent voice. "What do you want to do?"

I focused on my assistant. Silvio's hands were curled around his tablet, as though he was going to whip up his precious device and bash someone over the head with it.

I glanced over at Sophia. The Goth dwarf had been chopping onions to add to the latest pot of baked beans, and she was still clutching a knife. She nodded at me, indicating that she was more than ready to charge forward and tangle with our unwanted customers.

And finally, I looked over at Liam Carter, who was clutching his phone and still sitting in the back corner booth. I thought of the chirp that had erupted from his device a minute ago. That must have been a text from one of his men stationed outside the restaurant saying Mason was on his way. Strange that Liam hadn't warned me. Perhaps he hadn't had time. Or maybe it had been a deliberate oversight on his part. No way to know for sure.

Even if he had given me a heads-up about my uncle's impending visit, there was nothing I could have done to stop it, especially since I'd told Liam to instruct his men not to engage Mason, Emery, or Tucker should they appear. Liam's people might be highly skilled bodyguards, but my uncle, the giant, and the vampire were all extremely dangerous, and they would kill whoever got in their way. My friends and I might be in the line of fire, but there was no use in Liam's people needlessly dying.

Liam raised his eyebrows, a clear question on his face, also wanting to know what I was going to do. But there was only one thing I could do: see what my dear uncle wanted.

If I had been alone, I would have considered going on the offensive and trying to end this here and now. But a few folks were still eating their barbecue sandwiches, fries, and onion rings, and I didn't want any innocent bystanders getting hurt because of my family feud.

So as much as it pained me, I tucked my knife back up my sleeve. Then I grabbed a menu, an order pad, and a pen off the counter and stalked over to the booth where Mason was relaxing.

I glanced over at Emery, who sneered at me, as did the two giants sitting with her. Over at his own table, Tucker gave me a blank look, his inscrutable expression neither mocking nor threatening. As usual, I couldn't tell what he was thinking, much less what he might be plotting.

I turned my back to Emery and the two giants and slapped the menu onto the table in front of Mason, who was studying the restaurant with a curious gaze. I wondered how long it had been since he'd set foot in here. Years, probably. I wished he wasn't here now, but I had wished for a whole host of things that had never come to pass. If wishes were horses, I'd have a dude ranch full of ponies by this point.

"What can I get you?" I asked in a bored voice, as though my long-lost uncle showing up at my gin joint didn't bother me.

Mason didn't even glance at the menu. "A barbecue pork sandwich. Baked beans. Onion rings. Sweet iced tea with lemon."

I wrote down his order, then jerked my thumb over my shoulder at Emery, the two giants, and Tucker. "And what will your charming entourage have?"

I half expected Mason to order for them too, since he seemed like such a control freak, but he let Emery and the giants choose their own food. How benevolent of him. Tucker didn't ask for anything, not even a glass of water.

I stalked back around behind the counter and handed the ticket off to Sophia. The two of us fixed their food in silence, and I carried the glasses and plates over to Emery and the two giants and then to Mason.

"Here you go," I chirped in a bright, sunny tone. "I hope you choke on it."

"Now, now, Gin," Mason replied in a chiding voice. "There's no need to be so hostile. Sit with me while I eat."

I started to tell him exactly where he could stuff his rebuke, along with his food, but magic flared in his eyes, making them gleam like gray moons, and the restaurant's brick walls quivered, as though they were suddenly cold. I was the only one who saw the brief, faint disturbance in the stones, although Sophia's head snapped around, and she gripped her chopping knife a little tighter. Sophia was an Air elemental, so she had felt the invisible wave of Mason's magic.

The message was clear. Mason was telling me to sit down—or else he would destroy my restaurant.

Emery and the giants were busy stuffing their faces with barbecue chicken sandwiches, so I glanced over at Tucker, who tilted his head, encouraging me to do as commanded.

I ground my teeth and plopped down in the booth across from my uncle. Not for the first time, I thought about installing a turnstile or some other barrier by the front door. I was tired of my enemies waltzing inside and eating my food while they threatened and insulted me, and I had no illusions that this little tête-à-tête would be any different. No, this one would be worse than most, given everything I now knew about Fletcher.

Mason scooted his plates around, arranging them just so, then leaned over and drew in a deep, appreciative breath. "Ahhh. The food looks and smells just like I remember. It's so nice you kept Fletcher's recipes, especially the barbecue sauce. I love the way the beans are simmered in it."

He dug his spoon into the beans and slid the utensil into his mouth. He chewed, swallowed, and let out another appreciative sigh. "Oh, yes. These are *exactly* as I remember. One of my biggest regrets with how things ended with Fletcher was that I couldn't eat here anymore. He really did make the best barbecue in Ashland."

Mason set his spoon down, shrugged out of his navy suit jacket, and laid it on his side of the booth. Next, he tugged up his light blue shirtsleeves as high as they would go so that he wouldn't get barbecue sauce on the ends. The motions made his silverstone cuff links wink at me. They were both shaped like the Circle's ring-of-swords rune.

For the first time, I realized what a gruesome symbol it was. All those swords pointed outward, as though each weapon was a person who would kill anyone who dared to threaten the Circle's power, money, magic, and status. Then again, from what I knew about Circle machinations, that was exactly what happened. The members eliminated anyone who stood between them and what they wanted. And the carnage wasn't limited to their enemies. Inside the Circle ranks, the stronger members killed off the weaker ones, then fought among themselves until only a few remained.

Unfortunately for me, Uncle Mason was the strongest of them all.

Mason picked up his sandwich and took a big bite, making his cuff links wink at me again. I studied them a little more carefully. One, two, three… The rune featured nine swords. I wondered if the number meant something, if perhaps each sword represented one of the main Circle families, but I'd be damned if I'd ask.

Still, the longer I stared at his cuff links, the more something about the two matching runes nagged at me. I'd seen that ring of swords, or something very similar to it, sometime over the last few days. I tried to remember when and where, but Mason let out yet another loud, appreciative sigh, interrupting my musings.

"Mmm-mmm-mmm! How I've missed this." He smacked his lips and sank his teeth into his sandwich again.

For the next fifteen minutes, I stewed in silence, watching Mason chew his food and slurp down his iced tea. Finally, when he was finished, my uncle crumpled up a dirty napkin and tossed it onto his empty plate. Then he sighed yet again and leaned back.

"Wonderful, Gin," Mason said. "Absolutely wonderful. Fletcher would be so proud of you."

My hands curled into tight fists on my lap, my nails digging into the silverstone spider-rune scars branded into my palms. Somehow I resisted the urge to upend what was left of Mason's iced tea over his head and then grab his empty plates and smash them into his smug face one after another.

"Yes, I'm sure Fletcher is proud of how I've kept the restaurant going since he died." I gave my uncle a razor-thin smile. "And I imagine he'll be even prouder when I finally put you in the ground."

Mason let out an amused chuckle. "Oh, dear little Genevieve. You are far too homicidal for your own good. Then again, the Tin Man was one of the best assassins around. I suppose it's only natural that Fletcher instilled all his worst traits in you, including his excessive, inflated ego about his own skills and his misplaced confidence that he could kill anyone, including me."

I ground my teeth again, trying not to let my anger show. I *despised* the sound of my real name on his lips. Mason Mitchell had killed Genevieve Snow years ago, and he had no right to invoke her spirit now. "Enough word games. What do you want?"

"Why, lunch, of course," he drawled in his smooth, silky voice. "And to check on my favorite niece."

I snorted in disbelief.

Mason shrugged. "I dropped several unexpected revelations on you yesterday. I wanted to see how you were processing things."

A low, harsh laugh bubbled up out of my lips. "You mean the fact that my assassin mentor worked for *you*, my uncle, the man who orchestrated the murders of my father, mother, and older sister? Yes, I suppose those were *unexpected revelations*."

Mason shrugged again. "Be bitter all you want. But at least I told you the truth, Genevieve. That's more than Fletcher ever did. He probably would have been quite happy if you had never found out about the Circle—especially his part in it. Fletcher and I did a lot of great things together. Why, he's the one who eliminated some of my more prominent, dangerous enemies and paved the way for me to finally, fully take control of the underworld. I'll always be grateful to him for that."

Every word he said made me want to kill him even more, and I had to dig my nails into my palms again to keep from reaching for my knives. For once, the feel of my spider-rune scars didn't calm, comfort, or steady me. No, sensing the symbols and thinking about all the death, violence, and destruction that went along with them made me angrier and angrier, until red-hot rage *thump-thump-thumped* through my veins in time with my heart.

As much as I hated to admit it, Mason was right. He had told me the truth, while Fletcher had done his best to bury it forever. And once again, I couldn't help but wonder *why*.

Had Fletcher been afraid that I wouldn't forgive him? That I wouldn't understand? That I would fly into a rage and try to kill him? I didn't know the answers to my questions, which only added to my anger, frustration, and confusion.

"What do you want?" I snapped again. "I have other things to do besides wait on you."

A thin smile tugged up Mason's lips. "So demanding. So arrogant. So self-righteous. You really are just like Fletcher."

I didn't respond. I *couldn't*, because the bastard was right about that too. A few days ago, pride would have filled me at being compared to Fletcher. Now disgust rolled through me instead.

Mason leaned forward, planted his elbows on the tabletop,

and steepled his hands together. "I assume by now you've torn Fletcher's house apart looking for the ledger. Any luck?"

"No," I muttered. "I searched the house from top to bottom last night, but Fletcher didn't hide it there."

"I didn't think he did. That would have been far too obvious. Besides, I sent some men to search his house a while back. They were quite thorough, and they didn't find the ledger or any clues to its location."

I frowned. I had been living in Fletcher's house for more than a year. No one had been inside without my knowing about it—

A vague memory popped into my mind. A couple of months before he died, Fletcher had told me that someone had broken into the house. He'd said that nothing had been taken and had dismissed it as drunk kids being stupid, but it must have been Mason's men.

"In case you were wondering, the ledger isn't here either." I gestured out at the restaurant. "Madeline Monroe burned the Pork Pit down to the brick walls last year. Emery was here. She stood right outside and watched it burn."

The giant shifted in her seat, and her hazel eyes glinted with anger. I couldn't tell if she was pissed at the reminder that I'd killed Madeline or because I'd suggested that it could partially be her fault that Mason didn't have his ledger.

"I considered the possibility that Fletcher might have hidden the ledger here," Mason replied. "My men also searched the restaurant, several times, as a matter of fact, but they never found it. And you're right. If it was secreted away in here, then it burned to ash when Madeline torched the restaurant."

Once again, I wondered exactly when his men had searched the Pork Pit, but I didn't ask. Besides, it didn't matter, since they hadn't found anything. Fletcher might have been arrogant, but he was also the smartest person I'd ever met. He would have anticipated Mason's men searching his house and restaurant, and he would have hidden the ledger someplace his enemies would never think to look.

I just hoped he hadn't hidden it someplace *I* would never think to look either.

Mason's gaze flicked past me and settled on Liam Carter, who had moved over to sit on a stool next to Silvio. Liam had his arms crossed over his muscled chest, watching my uncle, along with Emery, the giants, and Tucker.

"I see you've hired Mr. Carter for added protection," Mason said. "Smart. He has an outstanding reputation, and his clients almost always survive whatever trouble they're in. How much did you tell him about me?"

"Liam knows enough to do the job I'm paying him for," I replied, choosing my words carefully and being deliberately vague. The last thing I could afford was for my uncle to realize what I'd really hired Liam to do.

Mason nodded, accepting my ambiguous answer, then glanced at Silvio and Sophia. "And you're still employing Mr. Sanchez and Ms. Deveraux. Quite the motley crew you've assembled."

"They get the job done. I wouldn't be here without them."

It was true. Silvio and Sophia had saved me more times than I cared to remember, as had Owen, Finn, Bria, and the rest of our friends. I owed them all my life several times over, which was one of the reasons I was so determined to protect them from Mason.

"Fair enough. I prefer my employees to be a bit more deferential, but to each their own."

And that was one of the major differences between us. My friends were my *friends*, not my employees. Even though Silvio and Sophia technically worked for me, they were *family*, and I would take a bullet for both of them, along with everyone else.

Oh, it wasn't all sunshine and rainbows with my friends. Finn and I had fought like cats and dogs when we were kids, and I'd had serious arguments and disagreements with him, Bria, and Owen, but we always found a way to work things out and forgive each other.

But Mason didn't think that way, and he didn't seem like the forgiving type. He also didn't seem to have any true friends, not even Tucker, even though they'd grown up together. Then again, *forgiveness* and *friends* were probably alien concepts to a man who had tortured his own brother to death and ordered the murders of his sister-in-law and three nieces.

Mason's hands were still steepled together, and he considered me over the tops of his fingers. "After our meeting yesterday, it occurred to me that perhaps I should have used a different tactic with you," he said in a pleasant voice. "More carrot than stick."

I tensed. With people like Mason, there were no carrots, only sticks. Or stones, in his case. "What do you mean?" I asked, anticipating more threats.

"Come work for me, Gin."

Shock blasted through me. That was the very last thing I'd expected him to say.

"The Circle started out as a family business," Mason said. "I know we've had our differences, but you and I *are* family, Gin. Whether you like it or not."

Oh, I most definitely did *not* like being reminded of that ugly, inescapable fact.

"Somehow, despite all the obstacles and enemies that have come your way, you have thrived as the queen of the Ashland underworld," Mason continued. "Just think of what you could do—of what *we* could do—if you had my backing, resources, and approval."

I studied him, wondering if this was some cruel, sick joke, but he looked and sounded completely sincere. Nice smile, calm demeanor, smooth, silky voice, warm hypnotic stare. In that instant, Mason almost seemed...*charming*. Suddenly, I could understand how he'd snowballed Fletcher into thinking that he wanted to make Ashland a better place.

I glanced over at Emery and the two giants, but they were still eating. A muscle ticked in Tucker's jaw, but that was his only reaction.

I focused on Mason again. "You're actually serious." I didn't even try to keep the surprise out of my voice. "You really want me to work for you, for the Circle."

"Yes. Just like Fletcher did." The warmth in his eyes vanished, replaced by a cold, calculating light. "You must get tired of the underworld bosses sending their minions to try to kill you. How many times have you fought for your life in this restaurant? Or in the alley out back? Or at Fletcher's house?"

He was absolutely right. I *was* tired of the assassination attempts, as well as dealing with the bosses and their petty problems and disputes. Being the so-called queen of the underworld was nothing but an enormous, never-ending headache.

Mason took my silence for agreement and kept talking. "I could make all of that go away. No more people trying to kill you. No more bosses questioning your authority. No one causing problems for you and your friends. All your worries, troubles, and cares would vanish. Just like *that*." He snapped his fingers, and I couldn't help but flinch at the sharp sound.

Mason stared at me, expecting an answer, but I looked at the other people in the restaurant. Emery and the giants kept right on eating their food. They didn't care whether I agreed to my uncle's proposal. They knew the same thing I did—that *he* would always be the boss, no matter what sort of power or partnership he promised me.

Over at the counter, Silvio and Sophia were staring at me, concern creasing their faces, while Liam was eyeing me with curiosity.

And then there was Hugh Tucker. The vampire's face was as blank and impassive as before, but he quietly, subtly tapped his index finger on the tabletop. Once he was sure he had my attention, he deliberately slid his finger to the side in a clear *no*.

Why was he warning me away? Maybe the vampire didn't want his own standing within the Circle further diminished. Or maybe, just maybe, he didn't want me to get trapped in the same sticky web he was in.

Even without Tucker's warning, I knew a too-good-to-be-true offer when I heard one, and Mason was clearly serving up some bullshit, pie-in-the-sky hopes and dreams. Did he really think I was that stupid? Or gullible? That I would just forget the awful things he'd done to my family? But I decided to play along to see what he wanted—and what he really hoped to gain by coming here.

"And how would that work, exactly?" I asked. "Me being part of your organization? Becoming part of the Circle?"

A satisfied smile slowly stretched across Mason's face. He thought he'd hooked me, and now he wanted to reel me in. Fool.

"It would be simple," he replied. "You would be the figurehead and handle most of the day-to-day business with the bosses. Then, when needed, I would step in and supply men, weapons, information. Anything you needed to deal with whatever people or problems were threatening us."

It sounded like the same arrangement he'd had with Mab Monroe. Let me be the target so the other bosses would focus their time and energy on trying to kill me while Mason pulled the strings from behind the scenes. That hadn't worked out so well for Mab, since I'd killed her, and I had a feeling this arrangement wouldn't work out so well for me either.

As soon as Mason had the missing ledger, or accepted that its location had died with Fletcher, he would eliminate me and put someone else in my place. Someone he could control. Someone who didn't despise him and wasn't plotting to kill him.

"So I would do the hard, dirty work, and you would sit back and reap the rewards like you've been doing all along." I shook my head. "Sorry, Uncle. Hard pass. I'm nobody's *puppet*."

Mason sat back and crossed his arms over his chest. The motion made his ring-of-swords cuff links glint at me again, almost in warning. "You should reconsider my kind offer. Especially since it's the only one you'll ever get from me."

I barked out a harsh laugh. "Please. There's nothing *kind* about your offer. You want to use me, scare me, control me, just like you did Mab. Well, here's a news flash." I leaned forward, my gray eyes just as cold and hard as his were. "*I'm not Mab*. So you can take your magic and your men and your sick, twisted agenda and shove them up your ass. I will *never* work for the Circle. *I* will *never* work for *you*."

Emery and the two giants froze, while Tucker let out a soft, exasperated sigh. Over at the counter, Silvio tightened his grip on his tablet, and Sophia clutched her chopping knife, while Liam's hand drifted around to the gun holstered in the small of his back.

Mason's eyes narrowed, his lips puckered, and his head tilted to the side. His arms were still crossed over his chest, and he *tap-tap-tapped* his right index finger against his left elbow, considering how to respond to my insults. I grabbed hold of my Stone magic, ready to fight back if he decided to unleash his own power.

After several long, tense seconds, Mason's finger stilled, and he swept his hand out to the side. "Take a good long look around, Gin. Soak up this moment. Enjoy this day as much as you can, because your time is rapidly running out. And while you're doing that, here's something for you to consider." He leaned forward, his eyes utterly devoid of emotion. "I'm not Mab either, and you *will* regret this."

I gave him another razor-thin smile. "Maybe. But not nearly as much as you're going to regret threatening the people I love, sugar. Now, pay for your food, and get the fuck out of my restaurant."

My own threats delivered, I slid out of the booth and stalked away.

I went back over to the counter and started helping Sophia fix food as though everything was normal. As though everything was *fine*. The whole time, though, I kept an eye on Mason.

For several seconds, he sat in the booth, a blank look on his face, although a muscle kept *tick-tick-ticking* in his jaw, hinting at his anger. It had probably been a long, long time since someone had told him no, especially in such blunt fashion.

Mason slid out of the booth. I tensed, thinking he might unleash his Stone magic, but he only tugged down his shirtsleeves and slipped back into his suit jacket. Once that was done, he went over to the rack, shrugged into his overcoat, and wrapped his scarf around his neck.

I thought—hoped—he might finally leave, but to my consternation, he strolled over to the counter. I tensed again and palmed a knife in case he decided to attack me, Silvio, or Sophia, but Mason had a different target in mind.

Liam Carter.

He stopped in front of Liam, who was still sitting on a stool next to Silvio. Mason reached inside his overcoat, plucked out a business card, and laid it on the counter next to Liam.

"Mr. Carter, so nice to meet you," Mason said in a smooth tone. "I've heard wonderful things about your security firm. Call me. I have a proposal I'd love to discuss with you."

No doubt, that proposal was wooing Liam and his protection services away from me. My uncle was about as subtle as a brick upside the head.

"I'll take that under advisement," Liam said in a neutral tone, not looking at me.

Mason smiled at him, then turned and walked away. Liam watched him go, an unreadable expression on his own face.

So far, my supposed bodyguard hadn't lived up to his reputation. First, Bria, Lorelei, and I had gotten kidnapped from the Posh boutique, and now Mason and his minions had invaded the Pork Pit. Once again, worry trickled through me about Liam's true allegiance—or lack thereof—but I focused on my uncle again.

Mason opened the front door, making the bell chime, and strode outside. He moved past the storefront windows and vanished from sight.

I thought Emery and the two giants might hurry after him, but they got up slowly from their table. Emery dug a single dollar out of her coat pocket. She held it up where I could see it, then tossed it onto the table. So the bitch was a lousy tipper. No surprise there.

Emery smirked at me, then exited the restaurant, with the two giants trailing along behind her.

That left Hugh Tucker, still sitting alone at his table. He sighed again, as though he'd found this whole confrontation quite tiring, then climbed to his feet and walked over to the counter.

"How much do I owe you?" he asked in a low, polite voice.

I totaled up Mason's food on the cash register, along with what Emery and the two giants had eaten, and told him the amount.

Tucker pulled out his wallet and handed me a hundred-dollar bill. "Keep the change."

But I didn't want to be beholden to him, not for one lousy nickel, so I opened the register and counted out his change, down to the penny.

I shoved the money into his hand. "I don't want your damn change."

Tucker grimaced, but he tucked the cash into his wallet, then slid it and the coins into his coat pocket. "I'm sorry it's come to this," he said. "But you made a mistake killing those giants in Blue Ridge Cemetery. Mason figured out you were the reason they were dead, and he decided enough was enough. Plus, he thought you might have already found the ledger, and he just couldn't have that."

"So he arranges for Bria to be kidnapped, then threatens to kill everyone I love if I don't find his stupid book." I snorted. "You must be *thrilled* to work for such a kind, generous man."

Tucker's lips curled with disgust. "As I've told you before, I don't have a choice about working for Mason. No one in the Circle does. He killed your parents and took control of the group years ago, and no one has dared threaten him since." He paused. "Not that there are many members left to try to usurp him, thanks to you. Just Mason, me, and a few others."

"A member?" I clucked my tongue. "Oh, no, Tuck. You're nothing but a dog on a leash, waiting for your master to snap his fingers and summon you."

He shrugged off my insult. "We all belong somewhere and to something."

I would have found something and someone else to belong to a long time ago, but I kept my snarky thought to myself. Tucker had chosen this path, and he would most likely dutifully trudge along it until someone killed him. My bet was on Emery offing the vampire. The giant didn't seem to like sharing command, and she'd probably try to eliminate him sooner or later.

Tucker looked at me again. "I know you, Gin."

"So?"

"So I know you're already plotting some way you can trick Mason, or kill him."

"So?"

"So it won't *work*," Tucker snapped. "Mason is smart and strong and more ruthless than anyone you've ever faced. Tristan tried to find a way to undercut Mason for years, and he was brutally tortured for his efforts. I would hate for you to do something equally stupid and meet the same gruesome fate as your father."

My eyes narrowed. "Did you know what Mason was going to do to Tristan? Were you there when it happened?"

Tucker hesitated, debating whether to answer me, but he squared his shoulders and looked me in the eyes again. "Yes, I was there. We were all there. Me, Mab, Deirdre Shaw, Damian Rivera, Bruce Porter, Amelia Eaton, some members of the other families, your mother. Mason made everyone watch as a warning about what would happen if any of us ever thought about betraying him. A few folks ignored his message, and he did the same thing to them that he did to Tristan."

He paused and cleared his throat, as if he was having difficulty getting out his next words. "After that night, Mason managed to keep almost everyone in line, except for Eira, of course. But after Mab killed your mother, there was no one left to challenge him. Not in Ashland, anyway."

More anger exploded in my heart, even as my stomach churned with disgust. My parents had suffered so much because of Mason's ambition, greed, and need for control. I'd faced down a lot of bad folks over the years, but Tucker was right. Mason was smarter, stronger, and more ruthless than any enemy I'd ever encountered.

"I would hate to see you end up like your father," Tucker repeated. "And I would especially hate for Owen to grieve for you the way I have for your mother all these years."

His face remained blank and impassive, but his voice was low and strained, and emotion flickered in his eyes. It looked suspiciously like regret. Tucker had been in love with my mother from the time they were kids right up to her death, and part of him loved her still. Mason and I weren't the only ones snared by the past. Hugh Tucker was tangled up in the sharp, stinging web of it too.

He cleared his throat again, and the regret was snuffed out of his eyes, replaced by the usual emptiness. "Don't put Owen through that, Gin. Don't put Bria or any of your loved ones through that. Do what Mason wants. Find the ledger, and hand it over."

"And then what?" I asked.

He gave me a brief, humorless smile. "And then try to pretend you never found out about the Circle."

Tucker smoothly spun around on his heel and headed for the front door. He pulled it open gently, and the bell didn't even chime at his passing. He flipped up the collar of his gray coat, stuffed his hands into his pockets, and strode out of sight.

I stayed where I was behind the counter, staring at the spot where he had vanished, my mind churning. Tucker didn't realize it, but for once, I was actually going to take his advice to heart. In fact, I was going to follow it to the letter. He wanted me to find the missing ledger? Fine.

I would do exactly that, and then I would use whatever information was inside to destroy Mason.

✲ 14 ✲

The rest of the afternoon passed by quietly, with no more threats from Mason or anyone else. I closed the Pork Pit early. Liam went to check in with Mallory and Mosley about the security for their wedding, while Silvio and I headed to Fletcher's house.

Finn, Bria, and Owen were waiting for us in the den. Now that we'd ruled out Fletcher's house, the Pork Pit, and First Trust bank, my friends were brainstorming, trying to figure out where else Fletcher might have stashed the ledger. While they talked, I headed into the kitchen.

Even though I'd been working all day at the restaurant, we had a long night ahead, and we would need a warm, hearty meal to get through it. Besides, I always enjoyed cooking for my loved ones, and this might be one of the last chances I ever got to do it. So I was going to make the most of it, just as Mason had suggested.

Given the bitter cold outside, I wanted something that would stick to everyone's ribs, so I made one of my favorite meals: cube steak marinated in a zesty mesquite sauce, then baked low and slow in the oven until it was tender. I nestled some baby carrots in the same pan as the steak, so that they too would get coated with the mesquite sauce and absorb its delicious flavors. I added several generous pats of butter to give the dish a little extra richness, covered the pan with aluminum foil, and slid it into the oven to bake.

While the steak cooked, I peeled, sliced, and boiled a couple of pounds of potatoes. When the potatoes were fork-tender, I drained off the water, tossed in milk and butter, and mashed them. For an extra bit of tang and flavor, I added in some sour cream and horseradish. Then I scooped the potatoes into a bowl and sprinkled them with blue cheese crumbles, sliced green onions, and some chopped bacon. And, yes, a few more pats of butter. You couldn't have mashed potatoes without a little—okay, a *lot*—of butter.

For a lighter side, I threw together a green salad with cherry tomatoes, matchstick carrots, sliced cucumbers, and diced red onions topped with a tangy Italian vinaigrette. I also warmed a tray of Sophia's sourdough rolls in the oven and whipped up some blackberry iced tea. For dessert, there were brownies with cherry sauce and vanilla-bean ice cream, just like the one I'd eaten at the Pork Pit earlier.

When everything was ready, my friends and I trooped into the dining room, sat down, and ate. The smoky mesquite sauce was the perfect complement to the steak, while the horseradish potatoes had a great spicy kick that was offset by the tangy blue cheese. The salad added some cool, refreshing crunch, while the rich, dark chocolate brownies were the perfect, sweet treat to cap off the meal.

Finn scraped up the last of his brownie and ice cream, leaned back in his chair, and let out a loud, happy sigh. "Steak. Potatoes. More steak and potatoes. Brownies. Ice cream. This might be the perfect meal, Gin."

I rolled my eyes. “You say that about every meal.”

“Well, I agree,” Owen rumbled. “You really outdid yourself tonight.”

I nodded, accepting their praise and scooping up the rest of my own dessert. They were right. This perfect meal had definitely been the highlight of my not-so-perfect day.

But dinner was over, and it was time to get down to business, so I pushed aside my dessert bowl. I had roughly forty-eight hours left to find Fletcher’s ledger, and I needed someplace to start searching for it.

Everyone sensed the shift in my mood and moved their own plates aside. Silvio fired up his tablet, while Finn pulled a stack of papers out of his briefcase and set them on the table.

“Where are we at?” I asked.

Silvio started swiping through screens on his tablet. “Well, I’ve been trying to think of where else Fletcher might have hidden the ledger. According to what you and Finn have told me and some of the old family photos I’ve gone through, it seems like Fletcher spent the majority of his time at home, at the Pork Pit, or at Jo-Jo’s salon. But of course, we’ve already eliminated the house and the restaurant.”

“What about Jo-Jo’s salon?” Bria asked. “Do you think he could have hidden the ledger there?”

“Maybe,” I replied. “Sophia said that she and Jo-Jo would look through the salon and the rest of their house tonight.”

Finn shook his head. “I don’t know. I feel like Dad would have put the ledger someplace more secure, more remote. So many people come and go at Jo-Jo’s house every day. It would have been a risk hiding the ledger there, where anyone might have stumbled across it.”

He had a point. Fletcher had probably hidden the ledger somewhere else, somewhere you would have to exert a lot of time and effort in order to uncover it.

Owen looked at me. "What about your father's grave? The one in Blue Ridge Cemetery? Before all this started, you were planning to dig it up to see if Fletcher had left something there."

He was right. So much had happened the last two days that I'd forgotten about my previous plan to dig up Tristan's grave. And since none of us had any other bright ideas about where the ledger might be hidden, it was as good a place as any to start searching.

I grinned, leaned over, and bumped Owen with my shoulder. "You just want to have another date night in the cemetery. Admit it."

He groaned. "That's not what I meant. Not at all."

My grin widened. "It's too late to take it back now. Get your shovel, Grayson. We're going grave digging."

Owen, Silvio, and I quickly geared up. Bria had to go back to work, and Finn had some wedding-related stuff to take care of for Mosley, so the two of them left, although I made them promise to check in with me later. I still might have roughly two days left to find the ledger, but after my confrontation with Mason earlier, I wouldn't put it past him to try to kidnap Bria or another one of my friends in order to further *motivate* me.

Mason might not realize it, but he didn't have to threaten me again. I felt like there was a giant hourglass in my chest, nestled right next to my heart. Every grain of sand that dropped through that hourglass lessened my chances of finding the ledger and decreased my hope of saving my friends from Mason's impending wrath.

Owen drove Silvio and me over to the cemetery and pulled off the road, parking in the same spot as during our previous so-called date night. An eerie sense of déjà vu swept over me, but I pushed it aside. All that mattered was finding the ledger. Not the lingering ghosts of my past mistakes over the last few days.

We grabbed our supplies, left the car, and hiked through the woods, using the same route Owen and I had taken the other night. The three of us reached the edge of the trees and stopped, peering out at the landscape before us.

Hills and ridges. Towering trees and brown grass. Patches of ice and snow. Tombstones, crosses, and other grave markers glinting in the moonlight. The cemetery looked the same as before, and I didn't see anyone creeping through the shadows.

"All right, boys," I said. "Let's get to work."

We made our way up the hill to my father's grave. I stared at his tombstone, then over at my mother's marker. Now that I knew what had really happened to them, more waves of sorrow and bitterness washed over me than ever before. Mason had caused my parents so much pain and misery. And for what? To be the head of some outdated secret society with a dwindling membership? If Mason wasn't careful, he was going to be the king of nothing, with no subjects left to serve him.

"Gin?" Silvio asked. "Are you ready?"

I dragged my gaze away from the markers, slid my shovel off my shoulder, and stabbed the point into the ground. "Yeah. Let's do this."

Owen and I made quick work of digging up my father's grave, while Silvio kept watch. Truth be told, it wasn't a bad way to spend the evening. I liked the cold and the quiet, although I could still feel those precious sands sliding through the hourglass in my chest. Maybe I would get lucky and the ledger would be here—

Thunk.

Owen's shovel hit something. He tapped the point into the loose earth a few more times, and the same solid sound rang out again and again. "I think this is the casket."

Silvio maintained his watchful stance, while Owen and I scraped away the dirt, revealing the top of the casket.

I wasn't sure what I'd been expecting. Perhaps my spider rune, my mother's snowflake, or some other symbol carved into the wood, but the top of the casket was smooth and whole. Then again, if Fletcher had left a clue here, he had probably put it inside the container. At least I didn't have to worry about disturbing Tristan's bones, since they were actually entombed in the Circle family cemetery.

I wiped the sweat off my forehead, set my shovel aside, and crouched in the dirt next to the casket. Owen crouched down beside me, and we both reached out and took hold of the lid. Above us, Silvio clicked on a flashlight and shone it down into the hole.

"On three," I said. "One, two, three!"

Together Owen and I lifted the casket lid. Dirt and small rocks rained down around us, and I had to blink my eyes a few times to get rid of the grit. Eventually, the clouds of dust settled, and I peered into the casket.

Empty—it was completely, utterly *empty*.

Even when they were sitting in a funeral home, waiting to be used, most caskets contained some sort of cloth lining, perhaps even a small pillow to cushion the dearly departed's head. Not this one. It was just a plain casket, a wooden box, with no lining, pillows, decorations, or adornments of any kind.

"You see anything?" Owen asked.

I shook my head. "Nothing."

"Maybe there's a secret compartment?" Silvio suggested, slowly moving his flashlight back and forth across the length of the box.

Owen and I ran our hands over the casket lid and knocked on the sides and bottom, but all we got for our troubles were a few splinters stuck in our skin. No secret compartments and no symbols carved into the wood. It was a simple box and nothing more.

"Maybe Fletcher hid something *under* the casket?" Owen suggested, after seeing the disappointed look on my face.

"I doubt it," I muttered. "But we already dug the hole, so we might as well look."

Silvio helped me up out of the grave, and he got down into the hole with Owen. The two of them pried the casket out of the dirt and stood it upright, as though an old-fashioned, Dracula-type vampire was going to come along, crawl inside, and take a nap.

Once the container was out of the way, Owen and Silvio punched the shovels into the ground again, churning up more earth.

"Stop," I said, after a few minutes of digging. "Just stop. Nothing is down there. Fletcher didn't hide the ledger here."

"Well, if it's not here, then where is it?" Silvio asked. "You've already dug up your mother's grave and Deirdre Shaw's too."

Owen pointed at the other markers in the Snow family plot. "Maybe it's buried in Bria's grave or yours."

I shook my head. "I don't think so. Fletcher knew better than to try the same trick so many times. Besides, this is about my parents, not Bria and me. Plus, there are no emotional vibrations in those tombstones, and as far as I can tell, those two graves have never been disturbed. Fletcher must have hidden the ledger somewhere else."

Owen and Silvio grabbed my father's empty casket, lowered it back into the ground, and started filling the dirt in on top of it. I helped them. We smoothed out the dirt as best we could, but it was obvious what we'd done. Unlike last time, I didn't bother trying to cover our tracks. There was no point hiding our search now that Mason had given me his ultimatum.

After we finished, the three of us sat around the grave, getting our breath back. Digging up dirt was always a workout, even on a night as chilly as this one.

"You ready to go?" Owen asked.

"Give me a minute," I replied. "I want to sit here and see if I get any bright ideas about where else Fletcher might have hidden the ledger."

"We'll wait for you at the car," Silvio said.

The guys got to their feet, grabbed our shovels and other supplies, trudged down the hill, and headed for the woods.

I stayed seated on the cold ground and stared at my father's tombstone. The brittle, frozen kudzu vines I'd draped over the marker the last time I'd been here had fallen off and been blown away by the wind, giving me a clear look at Tristan's name and dates of birth and death. Another wave of sorrow and bitterness washed over me.

"I'm so sorry for what happened," I whispered. "For what Mason did to you."

But my father was long dead and wasn't even buried here, so he couldn't answer me. And neither could Fletcher.

I glanced down the hill, staring at the fresh dirt that marked his grave. Anger spurted through me that Mason's giants had disturbed his final resting place, although I supposed I couldn't throw stones about that. I'd dug up my fair share of graves here too.

But I'd come up empty tonight, and it was time to leave. I climbed to my feet and dusted some of the dirt and grime off my jeans. A slice of moonlight slipped around my body and bathed Tristan's tombstone in a ghostly glow. My gaze traced over his name, which now stood out in stark, ink-black relief, thanks to the shadows and the moon's silvery glimmer.

More sadness and anger welled up in my heart, and I had started to turn away from the marker when I noticed another ink-black spot in the lower right-hand corner. For a moment, I thought it was some dead bug frozen on the stone, but then I remembered the crude carving of my spider rune that I'd found on the marker when Owen and I had been here before.

I snorted with disgust. Some clue that had turned out to be, since my father's casket had been empty. Once again, I started to turn away from the marker, but something stopped me—probably my own sentimental foolishness—and I found myself moving forward, leaning down, and taking another look at the rune.

The moon wasn't quite as bright as it had been the other night, and Silvio had taken the flashlights, so I couldn't get a clear view of the symbol. Although I supposed it didn't really matter, since we'd already dug up my father's grave. For the third time, I started to turn away, but once again, that sentimental foolishness stopped me. I sighed, dug my phone out of my jeans pocket, and hit the flashlight app.

Yep, there it was, the symbol Fletcher had carved into the tombstone, a circle with nine thin rays radiating out of it—

Wait a second. My rune had eight rays, eight lines, for the eight legs on a spider. So why would this one have *nine*? Fletcher would never make such an obvious mistake.

Unless…it *wasn't* a mistake.

Unless…it *wasn't* a spider rune.

I bent down even closer to the marker, my chin hovering right above the ground, and slowly moved my phone back and forth, illuminating the rune. In addition to the extra leg, small arrows had also been carved at the end of each of the nine lines. The marks were so faint and thin that I'd missed them the other night.

I frowned. A circle with nine lines, each one with a sharp pointed end. It definitely wasn't my spider rune, but it reminded me of…

The Circle rune—that ring of swords pointing outward.

Surprise shot through me, and I blinked several times, wondering if I was so desperate for a clue that I was imagining things.

But I wasn't.

Now that I was *really* looking at the symbol, I could clearly see the circle and the nine lines capped with arrowlike points.

Fresh hope bloomed in my chest, and I used my phone to snap several close-up photos of the symbol. I should have done this the other night when Owen and I were here. Maybe I would have, if Mason's giants hadn't interrupted us. Either way, I knew what the symbol truly was now.

I finished taking photos, then placed my palm over the rune and reached out with my magic, listening to the murmurs in the tombstone, hoping to pick up another clue. Fletcher must have carved the symbol years ago, because I didn't sense any emotional vibrations that he or anyone else had left behind. The tombstone only sighed about the rush of wind, the patter of rain, and the fall of snow on it over the years.

Frustrated, I dropped my hand and leaned back on my heels. Fletcher might have left me a clue, but I had no idea what it *meant*. Was he trying to tell me the Circle had been involved in my father's death? Or did this have something to do with Mason's ledger? But how could the Circle rune possibly lead me to the hidden ledger?

I also couldn't discount the possibility that the symbol didn't mean anything. Maybe Fletcher had been angry or frustrated or bored and had carved the rune on a lark one day. No way to know for sure.

My phone beeped, and I read the message from Owen.

You coming? We could still have fire, food, and wine tonight. ☺

I snorted, but a smile lifted my lips, and I texted him back. ***On my way, Romeo.***

I got to my feet and slid my phone into my jeans pocket. My gaze darted back to the Circle rune, but this time, I finally did turn away from the tombstone. Fletcher might have left me a clue, but I wasn't going to figure out its meaning now, and Owen and Silvio were waiting.

So I trudged down the hill, crossed the lawn, and stepped into the woods, taking the familiar route back to Owen's car. I was so preoccupied with my thoughts about Fletcher, the Circle rune, and the missing ledger that it took me a while to notice the stones' mutters.

I jerked to a stop and looked around, but the trees, ice, frost, and shadows were the same as before. The wind wasn't blowing, and I didn't hear the *rustle-rustle* of some small animal scurrying through the underbrush. So what had upset the stones?

Still looking for signs of danger, I reached out with my

magic, listening. The stones were definitely muttering, each sound full of dark, deadly intent. I tilted my head to the side, listening even more carefully, and trying to pinpoint the exact location of the disturbance. The rocks buried in the leaves weren't the ones that were muttering. No, the sound was coming from…the stones that lined the road at the edge of the woods. The spot where we'd parked the car earlier.

The place where Owen and Silvio were right now.

In an instant, all thoughts of Fletcher and the missing ledger fled from my mind.

I started running.

✲ 15 ✲

I sprinted through the woods, my boots crashing through the ice, twigs, and leaves and *thump-thump-thump-thumping* against the ground, but I didn't care how much noise I was making. All that mattered was getting to Owen and Silvio before something bad happened.

And something bad *was* going to happen—the stones were screaming about it now.

I quickly reached the edge of the woods. Even though my heart was yelling at me to rush past the tree line and charge forward, I tamped down the frantic urge. Instead, I palmed a knife and slid behind a tree, listening to everything around me.

Nothing—I heard nothing but silence.

I waited for my heart to slow and the pounding roar of blood in my ears to fade. Then I listened again, but I heard the exact same nothing as before. My knife still in my hand, I crouched down and peered around the tree.

Owen's car was right where we had left it, pulled off in the hard-packed dirt on the side of the road with a white trash bag stuck in the driver's window, as though we'd had engine trouble.

But it wasn't the only vehicle here now. A black SUV was parked in front of Owen's car, its headlights on and its hood pointing toward the smaller vehicle.

Emery Slater was standing in the dirt beside Owen's car, cracking her knuckles. The two male giants who'd been at the Pork Pit earlier were flanking her, their guns pointed at Owen and Silvio, who were standing on the opposite side of Owen's car, next to the road.

"Where's Blanco?" Emery demanded, still cracking her knuckles. Each sharp *snap-snap-snap* of her bones sounded as loud as a gunshot.

"I told you already," Owen said, a sharp edge to his voice. "Gin isn't here."

Emery snorted in disbelief. "I find that hard to believe, since you're her little boy toy. She wouldn't send you two here by yourselves."

"That's exactly what she did," Silvio replied, trying to sell Owen's lie. "Gin sent us here to look for the ledger while she kept searching Fletcher's house."

Emery snorted again.

"The better question is what are *you* doing here?" Owen asked.

She shrugged. "Since Blanco killed Mason's men here the other night, I figured she wanted something in the cemetery and would come back for it sooner or later. So I had my guys set up a couple of security cameras and motion sensors around the perimeter. And what do you know? I got a text alert saying that some people were lurking around."

I bit back a curse. I'd been so busy looking for people stationed in the cemetery that it hadn't occurred to me that

Emery might be monitoring the area remotely. Smart of her, sloppy of me.

Owen shook his head. "But Mason gave Gin until midnight Saturday to find the ledger. This is Thursday night. It's not even close to the deadline yet."

Emery sneered at him. "I don't give a fuck what Mason wants. I only took this gig so I could have another crack at Blanco. I still owe her for killing Elliot and Madeline. Uncle Elliot took care of me growing up, and Madeline was like my sister." Her face hardened. "Blanco's going to pay for taking them away from me."

So Mason hadn't sent her after me. Good to know my uncle was going to keep his word and honor the deadline. Then again, he seemed to want the missing ledger more than anything else, even my death.

Still, I should have realized that Emery might go rogue and try to take me out. Sure, Elliot Slater and Madeline Monroe had hurt my friends and tried to murder me first, but I could understand Emery's rage at losing them, and I would have done the same thing if I'd been in her shoes. Oh, yes, I could appreciate the giant's anger, but it wasn't going to stop me from killing her. The bitch had tried to barbecue me alive inside the Pork Pit.

Emery cracked her knuckles a few more times, and then her hands stilled, and a cruel smile spread across her face, brightening her hazel eyes. "You know what? It doesn't matter if Blanco is here."

"And why is that?" Silvio asked.

Her smile widened. "Because I'll be quite happy to beat you both to death and leave your bodies lying on the side of the road."

Owen and Silvio both tensed, while a chill slithered down my spine.

"Maybe I'll even stick around and hide in the woods," she purred. "Wait for her to show up and find you. I would *love* to hear Blanco's screams when she realizes the two of you are dead."

Owen and Silvio didn't respond, but their hands curled into fists. They were both ready to fight.

Emery snapped her fingers. Owen and Silvio both flinched at the sound. So did I.

"Actually, I have a better idea," she said. "Boys, get our two new friends to head on out into the middle of the road."

She waved her hand, and the two giants moved over to where Owen and Silvio were standing. The giants gestured with their guns, and my friends had no choice but to step away from Owen's car. The two of them stopped on the double yellow lines in the center of the road.

"Let's play a game of chicken," Emery said, looking up and down the road. "That's a pretty sharp curve up ahead. Someone could easily come flying around it in their car and not even see you two idiots standing there. And then *smack*!" She slammed her right fist into her left palm. "The two of you would literally be roadkill."

Owen and Silvio both blanched. So did I.

Emery smiled again. "Oh, yeah, I like that idea *much* better than beating you boys to death. Besides, if I can't torture Blanco, I might as well have some fun with the two of you."

I looked up and down the road, just like Emery had done. She was right. The way the pavement curved, someone could come barreling around that corner at any second, plow into Owen and Silvio, and kill them where they stood.

I tightened my grip on my knife. Emery was right about something else too. Fuck Mason and his détente. I was taking her out now.

The two male giants stepped over to the edge of the road and kept their guns trained on Owen and Silvio. The giants were far enough away that my friends couldn't charge forward and tackle them without getting shot. Owen and Silvio glanced at each other again, clearly trying to figure a way out of this. Well, they didn't have to worry, because the Spider was here.

The two giants were so focused on Owen and Silvio that they didn't bother looking around to make sure I wasn't really here. Emery was smarter than that, though. She moved so that she was standing close to the road, then crossed her arms over her chest and leaned her hip against the side of the SUV. Every few seconds, though, she would glance around, still clearly searching for me.

I needed to take out Emery and the other two giants before a car barreled around the curve and slammed into Owen and Silvio, but how could I do that? The giants were so spread out that I couldn't plow into all three of them at once, and I wasn't fast enough to sprint out of the woods, move past the cars, and tackle the two men with guns before they shot Owen and Silvio. I needed to do something to distract all three giants at the same time. But what?

A breeze whistled through the woods, ruffling the white trash bag stuck in Owen's car window. My eyes narrowed, and an idea popped into my mind.

I waited until Emery turned her head in the opposite direction, then slithered out of the woods. Keeping low, I hurried forward and darted over to a clump of bushes near the rear of Owen's car. I waited a few seconds, but no one screamed or shouted a warning, so I peered around the branches. Everyone was in the same places as before. Emery by the SUV, the giants a few feet away from her, Owen and Silvio out in the road.

When Emery turned her head again, I skirted around the bushes and crept forward, plastering my body up against the side of Owen's car. Then I raised my head so that I could peer through the windows at the three giants.

I waited for Emery to look away again, then sidled forward, reached up, and grabbed hold of the white trash bag in the driver's window. It rustled a bit, but Owen hadn't closed the glass all the way, and the bag easily slid out of the crack. The second I had a good grip on it, I hunkered back down beside the car.

I waited a few seconds, but no shouts sounded. Emery and the giants hadn't heard the bag rustling. Good.

I searched the area around me until I found a heavy, fist-sized stone smooshed into the dirt. I pried the rock out of the ground and coated it with my Stone magic, the same way Mason's magic coated the sapphire paperweight I'd experimented with in Fletcher's office. Once that was done, I pried a smaller, gravel-sized stone out of the dirt. I coated it with my magic as well and slid it inside the trash bag. Then I set the bag down at the back end of the car and opened it up wide. The wind started ruffling the bag, just like I'd hoped it would.

I made sure the bag was in position, then sidled along the side of Owen's car and crouched down beside one of the front tires. Once again, I waited for Emery to turn her head, then darted across the open space between the two vehicles and kept going until I was all the way at the back of the SUV.

I leaned down and peered underneath the vehicle, staring at everyone's feet, but they were all in the same positions as before. Emery by the SUV, the giants a few feet away from her, Owen and Silvio out in the road. No one seemed to have noticed my skulking around. Excellent.

I stood up and looked over at the trash bag, which was still sitting at the back of Owen's car. I reached out with my Stone magic and focused on the gravel inside the plastic, imagining that I was shoving the small stone away from me, as though the gravel was a tiny punching bag that I was pummeling with my power.

I wasn't sure if it would work—but it did.

My magic moved the gravel, and then the wind picked up the plastic bag and sent it tumbling end over end down the asphalt. The two giants spun toward the snapping, rustling bag, pointing their guns at it instead of at Owen and Silvio. Emery jerked upright, although she relaxed again when she caught sight of the bag.

"Don't tell me you two are afraid of a little piece of plastic," she said, sneering.

The giants gave her sheepish looks. Emery sighed and shook her head. Owen and Silvio both tensed again. They knew it was far more than just a little piece of plastic.

Still hidden behind the SUV, I focused on the bag again. I sent out another wave of magic, and the gravel exploded like a firecracker, tearing the bag to pieces.

Emery jerked upright again. "What was that?"

I darted around the back of the SUV so that I was standing next to the road, close to everyone else. Then I reared back my hand and threw the fist-sized rock straight at the two giants with guns. As the rock arched through the air, I blasted it with my Stone magic, and the rock exploded like a grenade right between the two men, who both yelped and stumbled away in surprise.

The second the rock exploded, Owen and Silvio rushed forward, each tackling one of the giants. All four men tumbled down to the ground on the side of the road.

My knife still in my hand, I reached for my Stone

magic, hardening my skin, and sprinted forward, heading straight at Emery. The giant saw me coming, snarled, and stepped up to meet me. She raised her forearm and blocked my first attack with my knife, so I snapped up my free hand and flung a spray of Ice daggers out at her.

Emery wasn't expecting the quick secondary attack, and several needles of Ice stuck in her face and neck, making her look like an oversize porcupine. She screamed in pain and staggered away. I palmed a second knife and hurried after her, but Emery lurched around the side of the SUV, snapped open the passenger's-side door, and slammed it into my chest.

The move surprised me, and Emery put her considerable giant strength behind the blow, making the door break away from the frame. The impact threw me back five feet and knocked me on my ass. Even worse, the door landed on top of me, punching the air out of my lungs. If not for the protective shell of my Stone magic, the blow probably would have shattered my ribs.

I grunted with pain, but I managed to wiggle out from underneath the heavy metal door. I expected Emery to surge forward and kick me while I was down, but she threw herself into the passenger's side of the SUV and slithered over into the driver's seat. The key must have still been in the ignition, because the engine rumbled to life.

Emery threw the vehicle into drive, hit the gas, and yanked the steering wheel. She cranked the SUV in my direction, and I barely managed to roll out of the way of the churning tires. The second the vehicle zoomed past me, I staggered up and onto my feet, my knives still in my hands, even though they wouldn't do me any good against the SUV.

But Emery had other ideas. Instead of stopping and trying to back into me, she stomped on the gas again. The

SUV fishtailed wildly through the dirt and grass, but she regained control and steered it back onto the road. She floored it, and the SUV disappeared around the curve.

A curse tumbled out of my lips, but Emery was gone, so I focused on my friends.

Silvio let out a low, angry snarl and positioned himself on top of the giant he was fighting on the side of the road. The vampire's fangs glinted like razors in his mouth, and he snapped his head down and punched them into the giant's neck. The other man screamed and started beating at Silvio with his fists, but the vampire must have hit an artery, because blood spewed everywhere, and the giant's struggles quickly grew weaker and weaker.

Silvio was taking care of business, so I looked over at Owen, who was still battling the other giant. The two of them had rolled back out to the middle of the road and were fighting for control of the giant's gun. Owen punched the other man in the face, stunning him, and grabbed the weapon. Then he flipped the gun around and shot the giant twice in the chest. That man screamed and crumpled forward.

Owen tossed the gun aside and shoved the other man off him. Then he slowly stood up and leaned forward, putting his hands on his knees to try to get his breath back.

"You okay?" I called out.

"Yeah," he rasped. "You?"

"I'm good. Silvio?"

The vampire rolled off the other dead giant. He sat up and spat out a mouthful of blood. A disgusted look twisted his face, and Silvio swiped his hand across his lips, trying to scrub off the blood, although all he really did was smear it across his face. "I'm okay."

I went over, held out my hand, and helped Silvio to his feet. "Let's get out of here—"

An engine rumbled in the distance, cutting me off and getting closer and louder with each passing second. I whirled around. Through the trees, in the curve up ahead, I saw the gleam of headlights barreling this way. Emery must have turned around somewhere out of sight, and now she was headed back in this direction.

I spun around to Owen, who was still standing in the middle of the road. "Owen! Move!"

I surged forward to try to tackle and knock him out of the way, but I wasn't watching where I was going, and I tripped over the giant Silvio had killed. I stumbled and rammed straight into Silvio, making him fall back down. My own body pitched forward, my knives tumbled out of my hands, and I landed hard on my knees on the side of the road.

"Owen!" I screamed again.

But I was moving way too slowly, as was Owen. Even as he lurched to the side, I could tell he wasn't going to be fast enough to get out of the way. Emery was going to mow him down and win her game of chicken after all.

Owen was going to die right in front of me, and there was nothing I could do to save him.

I tried to scramble to my feet, but one of my boots got tangled in the dead giant's overcoat, and I couldn't yank it free. So I reached for my Ice magic and snapped up my hand. Maybe I could fling some Ice daggers out at the SUV and knock it off course. I doubted it would work, but I had to try. I would do *anything* to save Owen—

Crack!

A shot rang out, and a hole appeared in the SUV's windshield. I couldn't tell if Emery had been wounded, but the vehicle careened to the right. Owen threw himself in the opposite direction, and the SUV whizzed by less than two feet away from his body.

I expected Emery to slam on the brakes, whip the SUV around, and try again, but she hit the gas instead, and the vehicle zoomed out of sight. I waited, but the sound of the engine faded away, and it seemed as though she had left for good this time.

"Owen!" I finally yanked my foot free, got up, and rushed over to him. "Are you okay?"

"Yeah," he said. "I'm all right. Just a little banged up."

I helped him to his feet, and we hobbled off the road and over to Silvio. I looked Owen over from head to toe. His clothes were torn and dirty, and cuts and scrapes dotted his hands and knees, but he was in one piece. A sob rose in my throat, but I choked it down, threw my arms around him, and hugged him tight.

I had almost lost Owen. I *would* have lost him, if that shot hadn't rung out.

If someone hadn't saved him for me.

A flash of movement in the woods across the road caught my eye. My head snapped in that direction.

Hugh Tucker stepped out of the trees.

He was dressed in a gray overcoat and a matching suit, and a spiffy black fedora topped his head. My gaze locked on the rifle glinting in his hands. Of course. Only a few people in Ashland could make a high-pressure shot like that—Finn, Liam Carter, and Tucker.

The vampire tipped his fedora to me, then vanished back into the trees.

Hugh Tucker had shown up from out of nowhere and saved Owen from Emery the same way he had saved me from Alanna Eaton's men a few weeks ago. And once again, I couldn't help but wonder at the vampire's motives.

Had he followed Emery here? Had he hidden in the woods, hoping I would kill the giant like I had killed Alanna? And why save Owen? To guilt or leverage me into doing something for him in the future?

More and more questions filled my mind, but I had no idea what game Tucker was playing. And right now, I didn't care. The only thing that mattered was that Owen was alive.

I hugged Owen again, then drew back. "Are you sure you're okay?"

He nodded. "I'm fine. Thanks to you."

"What do you mean?"

He gestured at the road. "Emery would have run me over if you hadn't exploded that rock against her windshield and made her veer off course."

Silvio frowned at me. We both knew I'd done no such thing, but before I could tell Owen that, he leaned down and kissed me. I wrapped my arms around his neck and kissed him back, drinking in his feel, taste, touch, and smell. Several seconds later, the kiss ended, although Owen pulled me closer and buried his face in my neck.

I hugged him again, so grateful he was still alive. But in the back of my mind, I couldn't help but think about Tucker—and worry about what the vampire's latest favor would cost me.

16

Owen, Silvio, and I left the two dead giants where they had fallen, got into Owen's car, and drove back to my house. We sat in the vehicle while I reached out with my magic and scanned the yard and the woods, but Emery must have decided to lick her wounds, because the stones were quiet, and no one was lurking around the house.

The three of us went inside and got cleaned up. I checked in with Finn, Bria, and the rest of our friends, telling them what had happened and to be on guard. But everyone was okay, and Owen, Silvio, and I were the only ones who'd been targeted.

Silvio disappeared into the guest bedroom, while Owen and I crawled into bed together in my room. I was exhausted, and I quickly fell asleep, although sometime later, I started to dream, to remember…

I was hiding in the woods, waiting for Fletcher to show up and kill someone.

After I'd closed the Pork Pit, I'd gotten into my car and driven to Wade Brockton's house, which was located at the end of a road. The accountant's closest neighbor was around a curve, more than a half mile away, and his house butted up against some woods, offering an easy escape route out the back. The isolated location was an assassin's dream, and Fletcher could have done this job blindfolded, which was why I was standing in the woods, waiting for the old man to show up.

I had to talk him out of this.

I didn't know who the client was or why Fletcher had agreed to do the job, but he couldn't kill the accountant, not when the man had only been embezzling money to save his sick daughter. This kind of job went against everything *Fletcher had ever taught me about being an assassin. We helped people get* justice*—we didn't execute them for desperately trying to save their loved ones.*

I checked my watch. Ten minutes had passed since I'd arrived. I had been worried that Fletcher was going to beat me here, but I hadn't seen any sign of him so far, and everything was quiet. Lights burned in the house, and I could see a shadow moving around inside through the windows and curtains. Looked like the accountant had already settled into his nightly routine.

Headlights appeared in the distance, and a vehicle rolled into view. At first, I thought someone was visiting the accountant, but Fletcher's old white van rattled down the road. Even more surprising was the fact that Fletcher steered the van into the driveway and parked behind the accountant's sedan. That was brazen, even for the old man. Maybe he was pretending to be a delivery guy dropping off some barbecue.

Fletcher got out of the van and shut the door, but his hands were curiously empty. No Pork Pit delivery bag, no take-out containers, no weapons. He also walked toward the house with quick, easy familiarity, as though he'd been here before.

Did Fletcher know *the accountant?*

I frowned. But if that was the case, then why would he agree to kill the other man?

Fletcher had just stepped onto the porch when the front door opened. "Wade?" he called out.

But it wasn't Wade Brockton who stepped into the glow cast by the porch light—it was Billings, the redheaded giant who had been at the Pork Pit earlier.

This wasn't an assignment—it was a trap.

Fletcher cursed and stepped back, but it was too late to run. Three more giants clutching guns sprinted around the side of the house and flanked him.

Fletcher cursed again and raised his hands. "Where's Wade?"

Billings shrugged. "I killed him already. Don't worry, though. His daughter was with her mother tonight, so I spared her the horror of watching me beat her father to death."

Fletcher's lips pressed into a tight, grim line. "So your boss sends you to tell me to kill Wade, but you come here and do it yourself. Then you just wait for me to show up to warn him. Smart. Your boss isn't usually this much of a planner, a thinker.."

Billings shrugged again. "I guess he finally got tired of you fighting him at every turn. You had a good thing going, Lane. You should have just put your head down and done your job."

Fletcher shot him a disgusted look. "While the rest of you hurt, tortured, intimidated, and killed whomever you wanted? Even kids? I couldn't ignore that. No one with even half a heart could."

Billings's face remained impassive. Fletcher's insults didn't bother him.

I frowned again. Who were *these people? And how long had Fletcher been working for them? He had never mentioned being on someone's payroll, and I couldn't help but wonder why he'd kept it from me. Whatever his reason, it sounded like he'd been trying to get out from under these people's thumbs for quite some time.*

"Well, go ahead. Shoot me, and be done with it. I can't stop you." Fletcher held his arms out wide.

Panic punched me in the throat. I palmed a knife and stepped forward, ready to charge out of the woods, even though I knew I wouldn't be able to reach Fletcher before the giants killed him.

Billings shook his head. "Nah. You're not getting off that easy. We still haven't found the object in question."

I froze and held my position in the woods, although I wondered at the giant's words. What object? *What were these people looking for?*

"I thought the accountant might have it, but he swore up one side and down the other that he didn't. I questioned him very *thoroughly, and I believe he was telling the truth. That means* you *have to have it, Lane. And I'm going to get it from you—one way or another."*

Fletcher didn't respond, and Billings jerked his head at the other giants. "Get him inside."

Two of the giants holstered their guns, latched onto Fletcher's arms, and dragged him inside the house. Billings and the third giant followed them. The door slammed shut behind them, sounding as loud as the lid being dropped on a coffin.

Fletcher's coffin—unless I found some way to save him.

I held my position for another minute, just to make sure no more giants were lurking around, but they'd all gone inside, and they hadn't bothered to post a guard outside.

Still clutching my knife, I left the trees behind and hopscotched my way from one bush to another across the lawn until I reached the accountant's sedan in the driveway. I had started to move past the vehicle when I spotted a tire iron lying on the pavement. I grabbed the metal and gave it an experimental swing. The tire iron was definitely strong and heavy enough to crack a giant's skull. I tightened my grip on the impromptu weapon and moved on.

Instead of heading for the front porch, I plastered myself up against the side of the house, hugged the wall, and went around to the back. I peered around the corner. This side of the house also featured a large open-air porch, and two giants were smoking out here, although they were turned away from me and standing on the opposite end of the porch.

I hunkered down at my end of the porch, and for once, I actually got lucky. One of the giants flicked his cigarette into the grass.

"They should have the assassin tied down by now," he said. "I'm going back inside to watch Billings work him over. You coming, Stan?"

"In a minute, Mike," the other giant rumbled. "Let me finish this."

Mike nodded, opened the back door, and stepped inside. He shut the door behind him, and his footsteps creaked across a few floorboards before fading away. He must have gone into some room closer to the center of the house.

That left Stan standing alone. The giant was still sucking on his cigarette with his back to me, so I hooked my knee up onto the porch, then slithered forward onto the wooden boards. They didn't creak at my weight, so I slowly stood up, still clutching my knife in one hand and the tire iron in the other. I glanced in through one of the windows, but no one was in the kitchen, so I kept going. Besides, if I killed the giant quietly enough, maybe no one in the house would realize I was here.

Stan shifted on his feet, making the boards moan and groan under his heavy weight. He kept smoking, so I crossed the porch, creeping closer and closer. The giant was completely absorbed in his cigarette, and he never noticed my shadow slowly growing bigger and darker next to his.

When I got close enough, I deliberately put all of my weight down on one of the boards he was standing on.

Creak.

The soft sound finally caught Stan's attention. The giant dropped his cigarette onto the porch, crushed it under the toe of his wing tip, and turned toward me. "Hey, Mike, did you need another smoke—"

I lunged forward and buried my knife in his throat. Stan let out a choked gurgle and sucked in a breath, like he was going to try to scream, so I ripped my knife out of his throat, then bashed the tire iron against the side of his head. The metal cracked against his temple, and the giant swayed ominously on his feet, like a tree about to fall. I lashed out with my boot and kicked him off the side of the porch.

The giant's body hit the ground with an audible thud, *but it was still much quieter than if he had crashed onto the wooden floorboards.*

I hurried across the porch and plastered myself up against the side of the house. Then I waited, counting off the seconds in my head.

Five…ten…fifteen…twenty…thirty…

A minute passed, but no footsteps thumped in this direction. No one seemed to have heard me kill the giant, so I tucked my bloody knife up my sleeve, then reached out and tried the knob. It turned easily and quietly in my hand, and I cracked the door open and stepped into the kitchen.

Appliances hugging the walls, a table in the center, dirty dishes in the sink. The kitchen looked like any other, and I moved through the area and peered into the hallway beyond.

Thwack.

Thwack-thwack.

Thwack.

I grimaced, recognizing the sounds of fists hitting flesh, followed by a low, pain-filled groan. Billings was already beating Fletcher. My heart squeezed tight, but I resisted the urge to charge forward. It wouldn't do the old man any good if I got captured too. No, right now, I had to be cold and ruthless and set aside my worry. So I tightened my grip on the tire iron and tiptoed down the hallway.

The corridor turned and opened up into a large common area that was part living room and part office. Fletcher was tied down to a chair in front of a fireplace. Spattered blood stained the fireplace stones and the wall behind him, and more red drops and smears covered the floor around his chair. Billings must have beaten Wade Brockton to death in here, although I didn't see the accountant's body. Maybe the giants had already dumped him in the woods outside.

Mike and another giant were in the room with Billings and Fletcher, although they were both near the back. Mike was pawing through a desk drawer, while the other man was plucking books off a shelf, flipping through them, and then tossing them onto the floor. What were the giants looking for? And why did they think Fletcher could help them find it?

Truth be told, it didn't really shock me that Fletcher had something the giants wanted. The old man loved *digging up dirt on people, and it was almost inevitable that he'd finally gotten caught with his hand in the cookie jar, so to speak. Part of me was surprised it had taken this long for someone to target him.*

While the other two giants kept searching, Billings stepped up in front of Fletcher. He cracked his knuckles a few times, then bent down so that he was at eye level with the old man.

"Make it easy on yourself, and tell me what I want to know," Billings said. "Otherwise, I'm going to have to drag this out for as long as possible."

"You make it sound like you're just doing your job, like you're just another employee punching the clock and dutifully following your boss's orders." Fletcher shook his head. "Don't you ever get tired of following orders? Of swallowing down your own ideas and wants and needs and pride in favor of someone else's desires?"

Billings chuckled. "Look at you, getting all philosophical. But no, I don't think about any of that. The money is good, which is all that matters to me. I'll leave the deep thinking to fools like you."

Fletcher didn't respond, so Billings casually reached out and slapped him across the face. The old man's head snapped to the side, and he let out another low grunt of pain. My heart squeezed tight again, but I didn't charge into the room. Billings could easily snap Fletcher's neck before I reached them.

I had to do something to get Billings to move away from Fletcher, but what? I glanced down at the tire iron still in my hand, and an idea popped into my mind.

The two giants were still searching for the mystery

object, and Billings's back was to me, so they didn't see me creep into the room and hunker down behind the couch—but Fletcher did.

My furtive movements caught his eye, and he blinked a few times, as if he wasn't sure I was really here. He must have realized that he wasn't imagining things, because he winked at me. I grinned back at him, despite the grim situation. Fletcher trusted me to get us out of here alive, and that meant so much to me—far more than he would ever know.

"What are you smirking at?" Billings growled.

That was all the warning I had before the giant glanced over his shoulder. I ducked down behind the couch and huddled against the fabric, wondering if Billings had seen me. I forced myself to take slow, steady breaths, even as I listened for the slap of the giant's shoes on the floor.

Silence. A few more seconds passed. Then the bastard hit Fletcher again.

Thud.

Thud-thud.

Thud-thud-thud.

The sound of Billings punching Fletcher rang out, along with the old man's coughs and groans. After about thirty seconds, the beating stopped. Fletcher let out two more coughs, then fell quiet. I peered around the edge of the couch again.

Billings had only hit Fletcher a few times, but he'd made them count. The old man's nose was broken, his lips were split, and blood gushed down his face. His eyes had already started to blacken, and his rapidly bruising skin was puffing up and stretching tight over his cheekbones.

"Well?" Billings demanded. "Do you feel like talking yet? I'm really hoping you say no. I barely had to touch the

accountant before he started screaming. I always like a challenge."

My hand tightened around the tire iron. He wanted a challenge? Well, I was going to give him one. But first, I had to get him away from Fletcher. Then I could focus on freeing my mentor and killing the giants.

"Hey," Mike called out. "Shouldn't Stan be back by now? Unless he decided to smoke that whole pack of cigarettes."

Billings's eyes narrowed in thought. It would only be a few seconds before he realized that Fletcher had backup. I had to act now, *so I surged to my feet, drew my arm back, and hurled the tire iron at Billings as hard as I could.*

Crack!

My aim was true, and the metal spun through the air and beaned the giant in the side of his head, making him growl and stagger away from Fletcher. I ran around the couch, charged past the coffee table, and plowed my shoulder into the giant, knocking him even farther away from Fletcher.

Billings growled again and stumbled back against the desk. He hit the wooden surface, bounced off, and fell to his knees. He tried to get up, but he slipped on the piles of books the other giant had tossed onto the floor.

"Get her, you idiots!" Billings yelled.

The other two giants scrambled to follow his orders, but Mike had to step over his boss, while the other man had to wade through the piles of books. That gave me a few precious seconds of space and freedom to sprint over to Fletcher. I palmed a knife, leaned down, and sliced through the ropes that bound his arms to the chair.

He flashed me a grateful smile and shot to his feet. His green gaze flicked past me, and his eyes widened. "Watch out!"

Fletcher grabbed me by the arms and spun me around, shielding me. A second later, Billings punched a letter opener he'd swiped off the desk into Fletcher's back. The old man yelped, and Billings shoved him away. Fletcher hit the floor hard, and he didn't move after that.

For one horrible, heart-stopping moment, I thought Billings had killed Fletcher, that he was dead.

Then Fletcher let out a low groan, reached around, and yanked the letter opener out of his back. He was down but not out.

Billings advanced on me, along with the other two giants. I darted to my left, heading for the man who was still wading through books. He stopped, cursed, and fumbled for the gun under his suit jacket.

I leaped over the books, braced my free hand on the edge of the desk, and kicked out, catching the giant square in the chest. My kick was hard enough to throw him backward into the glass doors in the rear of the office. The glass and wood exploded with a thunderous roar, showering debris everywhere. The giant screamed and tumbled to the ground.

I hurried over to finish him off with my knife, but I didn't have to. Several shards of glass had punched into the giant's back, and a long, thin piece of wood was sticking out of his throat like a kebab skewer. Blood gushed down the giant's neck, and he was already gasping for breath. It wouldn't be long before he bled out, so I turned my attention back to the other two men.

Mike was quicker than the first giant, and he grabbed his gun, snapped it up, and started firing at me.

Crack!

Crack! Crack!

Crack!

I hardened my skin with my Stone magic an instant before the bullets slammed into my chest, although the force of the projectiles still made me stagger into a bookcase along the wall. My body rocked the entire case from top to bottom, and the remaining volumes slipped off their shelves and joined the other books littering the floor.

Click.

Click-click.

Click.

Mike kept firing until his gun was empty, then cursed and stopped to reload. I sucked down a breath, ran forward, and threw myself feet first onto the desk. I easily slid across the top of the slick wood and plowed into him.

The giant cursed again and tried to lurch away, but his feet got tangled up in the books covering the floor, and his legs flew out from under him. I raised my knife high and threw myself forward again.

Mike hit the floor, and I landed on top of him. I put the full force of my body weight behind my blade, which punched into his chest all the way up to the hilt. Mike screamed and lashed out, slamming his fist into my face.

The blow knocked me off him, and my head clipped the side of the desk. The one-two punch of the giant hitting me and then me plowing into the furniture made my head spin and white stars explode in my eyes. I lost my grip on my Stone magic, and my skin reverted back to its normal, vulnerable texture. I also hit the floor hard, making even more pain explode in my back to go with what was pounding through my face and skull.

I groaned, but I forced myself to roll over onto my hands and knees. There was one giant left, and I needed to finish off Billings before he came at me again—

A hand dug into my hair and yanked me upright, making

me yelp. Billings spun me around, grabbed my shoulder, and drew back his fist to punch me. Through the white stars filling my vision, I spotted a blur of movement behind the giant. Suddenly, Billings screamed.

Fletcher ripped the letter opener out of Billings's back, then snapped it up and stabbed it deep into the giant's neck. Billings screamed again and staggered forward. He hit me, and the two of us tumbled down to the floor.

The giant coughed and coughed, and his blood splattered all over my face, neck, and hands, coating me in its wet, sticky, coppery warmth. Billings coughed a final time, and then his head dropped, and his body went slack and still on top of mine.

"Gin!" Fletcher dropped to his knees, grabbed Billings's shoulder, and shoved the dead giant off me. Then he leaned forward, a concerned look on his face. "Are you okay?"

I blinked the last of the white stars out of my eyes and nodded. At least, I started to nod, but that made even more pain ripple through my face and skull, so I stopped.

"Yeah," I rasped. "I'm okay. Just a little banged up."

Fletcher offered me his hand and helped me to my feet, and we stood there, wobbling and holding on to each other for support. I wasn't the only one who was banged up. Billings had really done a number on Fletcher's face, and he looked as bruised and battered as I felt—

A phone rang. At first, I thought it was the house landline, but then I realized that the sound was coming from Billings's pants pocket. Fletcher leaned down, pulled out the phone, and stared at the number on the screen. A disgusted sneer twisted his bruised, bloody face, and his fingers curled around the phone like he wanted to hurl it across the room.

"Who is it?" I rasped again. "Their boss?"

"Yeah."

"The man you're working for too," I said, an accusing note in my voice.

Fletcher grimaced, but he didn't deny it. "Yeah."

His index finger hovered over the phone, as though he was tempted to answer the call, but he threw the device down onto Billings's body instead. Fletcher opened his mouth to say something, but he froze and cocked his head to the side, as though a noise had caught his ear.

The rumble of a car engine sounded outside. And not just one engine—multiple engines, as though a whole convoy of vehicles had pulled up to the front of the house.

Fletcher grimaced again. "We need to leave. Now."

He staggered out of the office and hurried into the back of the house. I yanked my knife out of the giant I'd killed, then followed him. Fletcher cracked open the back door and looked around, but the coast was clear, and he stepped outside and crossed the porch. I was right behind him.

The second we were off the old weathered boards, Fletcher picked up the pace, running across the grass and heading toward the woods. He rarely moved so quickly, especially when he was injured, which told me just how worried he was.

We reached the edge of the woods. I expected Fletcher to keep going, but instead, he slid behind a large maple and peered around the trunk. I stopped beside him.

"What are we waiting for?" I whispered. "I thought you wanted to get out of here. My car is parked on the far side of the woods."

"I do want to get out of here," Fletcher whispered back. "But I need to see him *first."*

He must be talking about Billings's boss. I had no idea

why Fletcher wanted to see the man who'd set him up to die, but I wasn't leaving my mentor.

The two of us fell silent. It was full-on dark now, but thanks to the moonlight, I could easily make out the three black SUVs parked in front of the house. The vehicles' headlights were still on, and the bright, steady glows illuminated the lawn. I didn't see anyone sitting in the SUVs. Those people must have gone into the front of the house while Fletcher and I had been sneaking out the back.

A few more lights clicked on inside the house, then several shouts and curses drifted outside. The giants' bodies must have been discovered.

"Gin," Fletcher asked in a low, urgent voice. "Did you bring your usual supplies?"

"Yeah. I left the bag out here in the woods."

"Bring me your rifle," he said.

I hurried over and grabbed the bag. Then I unzipped the top, reached inside, and handed him the weapon. Fletcher hefted the rifle, checking to make sure it was loaded and getting a feel for it, even though it belonged to him, and he'd used it countless times before. When he was satisfied, he stood up, raised the rifle to his shoulder, and pointed it at the back door.

"Come on, you bastard," Fletcher muttered. "Step outside and show yourself so I can finally put a bullet between your eyes."

I stayed still and silent by his side. I didn't know who he was talking about, but I wholeheartedly agreed with his sentiment. Billings's boss had tried to have Fletcher tortured and killed. The mystery man deserved to die for that, as far as I was concerned.

So we stood there and waited—and waited and waited.

Fletcher never moved, never faltered, never wavered,

even though he was injured and his arms had to be aching from holding the rifle for so long.

A minute passed. Then two, then three, then five.

More shouts and curses rang out from inside the house, but no one stepped out onto the back porch.

"Maybe he won't come back here," I whispered.

"Oh, he'll come," Fletcher muttered again. "He'll want to know if I escaped."

We kept standing there, still waiting for this mystery man to appear. A dozen questions crowded into my mind, mainly who this man was and why Fletcher hated him so much, but I didn't want to ruin the old man's concentration, so I kept quiet.

Finally, after about five more minutes, shadows started moving past the windows, heading toward the back of the house.

"That's it," Fletcher murmured. "Open the door and step outside. You know you want to check and see if I'm lying dead in the yard."

The back door eased open, almost in answer to his whispered words. Fletcher shifted on his feet and took more careful aim with his rifle. I stood beside him, not moving a muscle and scarcely daring to breathe for fear of ruining his shot.

The door opened, and a man stepped out onto the back porch.

Crack!

Fletcher fired, and the man dropped to the porch, dead from the bullet that had punched into his skull.

The echoes of the shot faded away, replaced by eerie, utter silence. For several long, tense seconds, nothing happened. No shouts, no screams, no people moving around inside the house. Nothing.

Then the back porch light snapped on, clearly illuminating the dead man—another giant.

"Dammit!" Fletcher snarled. "He used one of his men as bait. We need to move. Follow me. Hurry, Gin, hurry!"

Still clutching the rifle, he whirled around and rushed deeper into the woods. I kept staring at the house, but no one else stepped out onto the back porch, and the lone light burned like a single golden eye smugly mocking us both.

"Come on, Gin!" Fletcher hissed. "Before he sends the rest of his men after us!"

He wasn't one to run from a fight, which made me even more curious about who was inside the house. Billings's boss must be truly powerful to make Fletcher retreat. I stared at the house a moment longer, then turned and followed the old man into the shadows...

My eyes fluttered open. For a second, I thought I was back there in the woods, darting around trees, skirting past boulders, and jumping over fallen logs with Fletcher. Then I blinked a few times, and I realized that I was safe in bed with Owen.

As far as my nightmares went, that one had been pretty mild, so I snuggled closer to Owen, shut my eyes, and tried to go back to sleep. But after about ten minutes, I gave up. I just couldn't sleep right now, so I slipped out of bed, threw on a robe and some slippers, and left my bedroom.

I tiptoed down the hallway and stopped outside Silvio's room. Light spilled out from underneath the crack at the bottom of the door, and the faint murmur of conversation drifted through the wood.

"I don't know why I'm calling you," Silvio said.

A pause, as though he was listening to someone.

Then a snort from Silvio. "Do you flirt with every man you meet this way?"

Another pause.

Then a low, surprised laugh from my assistant. "You have a horrible sense of humor."

I smiled. It seemed as though Silvio had finally given in and called Liam Carter. Good for him. Silvio deserved someone special in his life. I didn't know if Liam would make Silvio happy in the long run, but at least the vampire was getting back out into the dating world. I just hoped Liam was the true, trustworthy ally I needed him to be—for everyone's sake.

I didn't want to disturb Silvio's call, so I crept past his door and headed downstairs. I ended up in Fletcher's office and flipped on the lights. The broken glasses and bottle of gin were still lying on the floor, along with the folders, papers, and photos I'd shoved off the desk last night. I sighed, but I went into the kitchen, got a broom, a dustpan, and a trash can, and returned to the office.

I quickly swept up the glass, although it took me a few minutes to peel the folders, papers, and photos off the floor, since they had gotten drenched in gin and were stuck to the wood. After I got a few photos loose, the others peeled up much more easily, and a minute later, I grabbed the last one—the picture of Fletcher and Mason standing in the woods.

I started to set the photo aside with the others, but the grim set of Fletcher's mouth and the absolute blankness in his eyes made me take another look at the image. The old man seemed...*exhausted*, as though Mason had used his Stone magic to grind all the fight out of Fletcher's bones, and it was all he could do to remain upright.

My gaze lingered on Fletcher's suit, and I wondered if the photo had been taken at someone's funeral—maybe even my father's funeral. If so, that would certainly explain why Mason looked so smug and Fletcher so miserable.

Once again, I started to set the photo aside, but I found myself plopping down in the desk chair, grabbing the magnifying glass, and examining the image. Mason's smile. Fletcher's anguish. The two men and their expressions were as different as they could be, right down to the way Mason had his arm slung around Fletcher's shoulders, while the old man was clutching his tie as though it was strangling him.

For the third time, I started to set the photo aside, but once again, I peered a little more closely at it. My gaze snagged on the pin in the center of Fletcher's tie. When I'd looked at it last night, I'd thought it was a spider rune, but the ends seemed a little too sharp and pointed for that. A thought occurred to me, and I started counting the slightly blurry rays. One, two, three…

Nine. The pin featured nine rays, not eight. Fletcher wasn't wearing my spider rune—he was sporting the Circle's ring of swords.

I rocked back in the chair, my mind churning. Then I dug my phone out of the pocket of my robe and pulled up the pictures I'd taken at Blue Ridge Cemetery earlier tonight. I laid my phone on the desktop, next to the photo of Fletcher, and compared the various pictures.

I wasn't imagining things. The symbol Fletcher had scratched into Tristan's tombstone was the same Circle ring-of-swords rune he was wearing in the photo with Mason. My mind kept churning. Mason had probably given Fletcher the tie pin, maybe even ordered Fletcher to wear the symbol he hated so very much. But why would Fletcher carve the rune into my father's tombstone? What kind of message was he trying to send me?

And it *was* a message. I was certain of it. Everything else Fletcher had left behind about the Circle had been a message, and this was no different. I just had to figure out what it meant.

The longer I stared at the photo of Fletcher and Mason, the less I focused on the tie pin and the more I examined Fletcher's suit. He'd only had a couple of them, and I recognized this one as his funeral suit.

My mind kept churning. Mason, Fletcher, the old man's funeral suit. They all got me to thinking about where else I had seen the ring-of-swords rune recently…

The answer hit me like, well, a sword through the gut.

Fletcher hadn't been toying with me by carving the Circle rune onto my father's tombstone—he'd been telling me where to look. Suddenly, I realized where he had hidden the missing ledger.

"You sly fox," I whispered, a grin spreading across my face.

I picked up the photo and kissed the old man's gin-soaked face. Maybe it was my imagination, but the anguish in Fletcher's features seemed to ease a bit, as if his ghost was happy I'd solved the mystery.

Now all that was left to do was figure out how exactly I could get my hands on Mason's precious ledger.

✲ 17 ✲

I stayed in the office another hour, planning the best way to get the ledger. When I was finished, I turned off the lights and went to bed, happier than I'd been in days.

Plotting against my enemies always invigorated me.

At breakfast the next morning, Friday, I didn't say anything to Owen and Silvio about my plan, since they probably would have tried to talk me out of it. Besides, they couldn't help with it, and the fewer people who were involved, the less dangerous it would be.

"You're in a good mood," Silvio said.

I slid a plate with a stack of blueberry pancakes, a mound of scrambled eggs, and several strips of bacon onto the table in front of him. "Am I?"

His gray eyes narrowed. "Yes, a *much* better mood. What are you up to, Gin?"

I shrugged off his suspicious question. "I've decided that instead of moping around and wondering where Fletcher might have hidden the ledger, I'm going to fully enjoy today, especially Mallory's bridal shower at Northern Aggression."

Owen dug into his pancakes, eggs, and bacon and sighed with happiness. "Are you sure you don't want me or Silvio to go with you?" he mumbled through a mouthful of food. "Or Liam Carter?"

I shook my head. "Nope, this is a bridal shower, so ladies only. Besides, Mallory, Roslyn, Bria, and Lorelei will be there. We'll be fine."

A concerned looked creased Silvio's face. "The last time you, Mallory, Roslyn, Bria, and Lorelei went somewhere, Emery Slater kidnapped three of you from the Posh boutique."

I sat down at the table with my own breakfast plate. "That was before I knew Emery was back in town. Now that I know she's lurking around, I can take precautions. Besides, not even Emery is stupid enough to attack all of us at once, especially not when Mallory has invited so many people to her shower—very rich and important people who will have their own bodyguards cooling their heels in the parking lot."

Owen swallowed some orange juice. "What about the ledger?"

"We'll start looking for it again after the bridal shower," I said.

He nodded and drank some more juice. Silvio kept eyeing me with suspicion, so I steered the conversation to other topics, mainly Mallory and Mosley's wedding.

We finished breakfast, and Silvio drove us into the city. Silvio and I dropped off Owen at his office building, then headed over to the Pork Pit. I got started on the day's cooking, while Silvio pulled out his phone and used it to check his reflection and make sure his tie was perfectly in place, along with his gray hair.

"Got a hot lunch date?" I teased.

"No," he said in a defensive tone. "Can't I just want to look my best?"

"Sure," I drawled. "But Liam won't be in today. Mason's already threatened me here, so there was no reason for Liam to come to the restaurant, especially since I'll be gone most of the afternoon. I texted and told him to focus on security for the wedding, so I'm afraid the next chapter in your epic love story will have to wait until tomorrow."

"It's not a love story," Silvio grumbled.

"Not yet." I grinned. "But soon, I imagine, given how you were flirting with him on the phone last night."

A faint pink blush streaked across Silvio's cheekbones, and he shifted on his stool. "I will neither confirm nor deny that."

I laughed, but I'd teased him enough, so I returned to my prep work.

Sophia, Catalina, and the rest of the waitstaff came in, and I opened the restaurant. I worked through the lunch rush, and then Silvio drove me over to Northern Aggression, Roslyn's nightclub.

Despite its Northtown location, the outside of the club was largely plain and featureless, except for the neon sign over the front door—a heart with an arrow running through it. At night, the neon sign would burn red, yellow, and orange, but it was dark now, since it was only two in the afternoon. Someone, Roslyn most likely, had wrapped blue and silver streamers around the sign and had taped white paper wedding bells and hearts around the club's entrance to mark it as the bridal shower location.

Silvio peered through the windshield at the steady stream of women heading inside. "Are you sure you don't want me to wait for you?"

"Nope," I said, pointing out Bria's sedan. "See? Bria's already here, and she's going to give me a ride back to the Pork Pit or back home, depending on how long the shower runs. I know you're worried about Mason and Emery, but I'll be fine, Silvio."

Worry creased his face, and he gave me a disbelieving look.

"Trust me. The only danger here is what will happen once the debutantes, society ladies, and grand dames get liquored up." I paused. "I wouldn't want to be the stripper who has to deal with them."

Silvio blanched. "Lorelei hired a stripper for her grandmother's bridal shower?"

"Nope." I grinned. "Mallory hired the stripper. Picked him out herself from the nightclub staff, according to Roslyn."

He shook his head. "Try not to get too wild in there."

"I make no such promises."

I grinned at him again, then grabbed a gift bag from the backseat, got out of the car, and headed toward the nightclub.

During the evening, a long line of people would have been waiting to get into Northern Aggression, but since this was a private daytime event, I gave my name and showed my driver's license to the giant bouncers guarding the entrance. Once they cleared me, I went into the club. Two more giants were waiting at a podium inside, and they checked my name and ID a second time before letting me pass. After what had happened at the Posh boutique, Mallory and Roslyn weren't taking any chances with their guests' safety.

I stepped inside the large room that served as the heart of Northern Aggression. A dance floor surrounded by tables and chairs, booths along the back wall, a long bar made of glittering elemental Ice with shelves full of liquor bottles and glasses gleaming behind it. The inside of the club looked the same as always, but Roslyn had dressed it up for the shower.

White, blue, and silver streamers were hanging from the ceiling, along with matching paper wedding bells and enormous banners boasting the words *Mallory + Stuey = True Love*. White cloths covered the tables, along with centerpieces of white, blue, and purple orchids and blue candles burning inside glass jars. Silver heart-shaped confetti had been sprinkled down the length of the elemental Ice bar, adding even more sparkle to the festivities.

More than a hundred women in pretty dresses and power pantsuits were milling around, and tuxedo-clad waiters were already circulating through the crowd, offering everything from tiny cucumber sandwiches and bite-size almond-flavored wedding cakes to glasses of champagne and shots of whiskey. High society meets hard liquor.

Mallory was holding court on a stool near the center of the bar. A large blue-crystal tiara was perched on her snow-white hair, while a blue sash adorned with the words *Here Comes the Bride* in glittery silver letters was slung across her chest.

Lorelei was sitting beside her grandmother, along with Roslyn. Bria was standing nearby and chatting with another group of women.

I headed over to Mallory, Roslyn, and Lorelei. "And how is the blushing bride-to-be?"

Mallory airily waved her glass of champagne at me. "I'm far too old to blush, Gin. Although this champagne is making me giggle. Just a little, though."

I started to tell her that champagne always made me

want to sneeze, but Mallory let out one of those little giggles, then turned to Roslyn and hugged her tight.

"Roslyn!" she squealed. "You planned such a lovely party! Ladies, let's give Roslyn a big round of applause!"

The polite applause quickly turned into a round of loud, enthusiastic *woo-hoos!* Some of the ladies had already had a little too much champagne and whiskey. I grinned, left Mallory to her friends, and put my blue gift bag on the table reserved for presents at the far end of the bar.

Lorelei trailed after me. "What did you get her?"

"A couple's spa weekend in Cypress Mountain. I figured Mallory and Mosley could use a nice, relaxing getaway after everything that's happened over the last few months."

"You mean my evil brother Raymond Pike coming to Ashland and trying to murder me? Or Alanna Eaton trying to kill Mosley? Or you, me, and Bria getting kidnapped from the Posh boutique the other day?" Lorelei ticked off our recent greatest hits one by one on her fingers.

I shrugged. "Take your pick."

She snorted, flagged down a passing waiter, and grabbed a napkin and a couple of cakes off his tray. I checked my watch.

Lorelei caught the motion. "What are you up to, Gin?"

"What do you mean?" I asked in my lightest, brightest, most innocent I'm-not-doing-shit voice.

Her blue eyes narrowed, and she moved her finger through the air, as though she was drawing a circle over my face. "We've known each other long enough for me to realize when you're up to something. Besides, you actually came to the shower."

"So? I wanted to help celebrate Mallory's big day."

"So you *should* be looking for Mason Mitchell's ledger.

Not wasting time here watching Mallory and her society friends get sauced. Ergo, you're up to something."

"Did you just use *ergo* in a sentence?"

Lorelei sniffed. "Of course. I have mad vocabulary skills." She speared me with a sharp, knowing gaze. "Now, what are you up to, Gin?"

Bria walked over to us, saving me from answering, and deposited her own gift bag on the table.

"It's a silver heart locket for Mallory and a set of matching cuff links for Mosley," Bria said, seeing Lorelei's curious look. "I bought them online from a shop in Cloudburst Falls and had them engraved with their names and the wedding date."

Lorelei smiled. "How thoughtful. Grandma will love that. And your spa weekend, Gin."

"What did you get them?" Bria asked.

Lorelei waved her hand at another gift bag. "A ski trip to Snowline Ridge."

Someone called Lorelei's name, and she went over to talk to the other woman. I jerked my head, and Bria and I sidled away from them.

"Are you ready?" Bria whispered.

Last night, after I had decoded Fletcher's message, I had texted Bria and told her my plan for finding the ledger. The first step was sneaking out of Mallory's bridal shower.

"I'm ready. Follow my lead, and look casual."

I meandered over toward the bar, smiling and nodding at the folks I passed, as though I was on my way to get a drink so I could start boozing it up with everyone else. Bria trailed along in my wake, as though she too were going to get a drink. Eventually, the two of us wandered down the length of the bar, crossed the dance floor, and reached the club's back wall. I opened a door there, and Bria and I slipped through to the other side.

I quickly shut it behind us and waited, but no one knocked or opened the door. It didn't seem like anyone had spotted us, so I led Bria through the hallways until we reached the club's rear exit. We slipped through that door and stepped out into a parking lot littered with potholes. I glanced around, but no one was sneaking a smoke by the trash cans, so I crept over to the side of the building. Bria followed me.

I peered around the nightclub, staring into the main parking lot in front. A lone black SUV was sitting by itself at the far edge of the space, three hundred feet from the club entrance. The vehicle hadn't been there when Silvio dropped me off. The windows were tinted, so I couldn't see who was inside, but I was betting it was Emery Slater and some more giants. Mallory's shower had also been announced in the newspaper, and it seemed the giant had decided to stake it out, probably so she could try to kill me again when I left.

I wondered how Emery had explained the loss of her two giants last night to Mason. No doubt, she'd blamed me for their deaths, although I doubted she'd told Mason that she'd tried to murder me before I found his ledger.

"Emery?" Bria asked, also spotting the SUV.

"Probably. Let's go before she gets the bright idea to have someone watch the back of the building."

Bria and I slipped away from the nightclub, crossed the street, and headed into a nearby alley. I looked around the corner, but the black SUV didn't move from its position in the Northern Aggression parking lot. Emery must have thought we were still inside the club. Good.

I led Bria to the far end of that alley and through two more, until we reached an old white van parked on one of the side streets. The alley was deserted, so I cautiously approached the vehicle. I peered in through the driver's-side window, but the interior was empty, so I crouched down. No bombs or tracking devices had been attached to the undercarriage, and I didn't sense any elemental magic emanating from the vehicle. A relieved sigh escaped my lips.

Unbeknownst to Silvio and Owen, I had texted Liam Carter this morning, left him a set of van keys under the front-porch mat at Fletcher's house, and told him to bring the vehicle here. Liam had agreed without asking any questions. Then again, that was part of what I was paying him for.

"Are you sure you want to do this?" I asked, getting to my feet and pulling my own keys out of my pocket. "You don't have to come. You know how dangerous this is."

Bria shook her head. "And that's precisely why I'm coming. Someone needs to watch your back, and given where we're going, that someone should be me."

I flashed her a grateful smile. I was hoping she would say that, which was one of the reasons I'd filled her in on my plan.

We both got into the van, and a minute later, we were zooming toward our destination—and, I hoped, the missing ledger.

It didn't take me long to navigate through the Northtown streets. Fifteen minutes later, my van cruised past the closed iron gate that fronted the Ashland Historical Association. I drove past the grounds at a steady speed, as though I was just passing through, although I eyed the landscape the whole time.

According to the association's website, the mansion and grounds were closed to the public during the winter months, and I didn't see any guards loitering around the gate. But Emery had said she'd installed signal jammers and surveillance cameras in and around the mansion, and she would probably get an alert if anyone came near the structure who wasn't supposed to be there.

I kept driving until I came to another, much smaller mansion about a mile down the road. No iron gate fronted this property, and a *For Sale* sign adorned the lawn, so I pulled into the driveway and parked. Bria and I watched the house, but no one came outside to see who we were and what we wanted. I also reached out with my magic, but the stones' murmurs were soft and muted, as though no one had lived in this mansion in several months. The place was empty. Perfect.

Bria and I grabbed a couple of duffel bags of supplies, headed into the woods on the back side of the mansion, and hiked over to the historical association property. I looked for cameras mounted in the trees, but I didn't see any, and it didn't take us long to reach the edge of the woods. We both stopped and peered at the Mitchell family mansion in the distance.

A couple of black SUVs were parked in the front driveway. Looked like Mason and his men were here after all. My gaze lingered on the baby-blue sports car also sitting in the driveway. And they had company.

Worry swirled through me, but I pushed it down. My mission was out here, and I couldn't do anything about whatever was happening inside the mansion.

"Can you believe our father grew up here?" Bria asked. "After not knowing anything about him for so long, seeing his childhood home seems surreal, like something out of a dream. When Mason told us they lived here, I half expected Tristan to come striding through the door. Weird, I know."

I reached out and squeezed her hand. "I don't think it's weird. Every time I see Mason, I keep thinking that's exactly what Tristan would look like if he was still alive. It's like staring at a monster who's wearing our father's face. I *hate* it. And I especially hate Mason for taking Dad away from us, and Mom and Annabella too."

Bria squeezed my hand back. "Then let's find the ledger and use it to make the bastard pay."

I nodded, and we moved on. Instead of heading toward the mansion, we moved away from it toward our ultimate destination.

The Circle family cemetery.

Bria and I hunkered down at the edge of the woods and peered out into the cemetery. I didn't see any surveillance cameras or motion sensors mounted to the trees, but their absence didn't surprise me. Emery probably didn't think there was anything here worth stealing—but I knew better.

I reached out with my Stone magic again, listening to the rocks hidden in the grass, along with the tombstones, crosses, and other markers, but they only murmured of the wind, the weather, and the steady march of time that was slowly wearing them down.

"We're clear," I whispered.

Bria nodded, and we got to our feet and stepped into the cemetery.

I ignored the rows of graves and headed for the pavilion in the center. I glanced around again, making sure we were still alone, then walked up the steps, crossed the open space, and went over to my father's tomb. My soft footsteps seemed to boom as loud as cracks of thunder in the pavilion, but I pushed my unease aside. Bria stepped up beside me, and we both studied the tomb.

Up close, the gray slabs of stone were much plainer than I expected. A band of vines and flowers lined the base of the tomb, and the same pattern curled up all four corners before forming another band around the lid. A panel on the side featured the dates of my father's birth and death, along with his full name—*Tristan Horatio Mitchell*—carved in fancy cursive letters. There was no mention of him being a beloved husband, father, or brother. Not here.

"We haven't had a chance to talk much over the past few days," I said. "How are you handling things?"

"You mean the fact that our families, the Mitchells and the Snows, are responsible for decades of evil in Ashland, dating back to when the town was founded?" Bria shook her head, making her blond ponytail slap against her shoulders. "I don't know what to think about that, and I don't know how to feel, other than disappointed. Although I wonder…"

"What?"

She gestured out at the rest of the cemetery. "I wonder what would have happened if Eira had lived and Tristan too. If they had just gone along with Mason. I wonder if we would have grown up in that world, if *we* would have been part of the Circle. The next generation dutifully carrying on the family legacy, no matter how awful, twisted, and evil it is."

"I don't know, but I hope not. Maybe that's why Mom and Dad tried to destroy the Circle. Maybe that's why they tried to expose Mason. So that you, me, and Annabella wouldn't have to carry on that legacy."

"That's what I hope too," Bria said in a low, sad voice. "It's the only thing that's kept me going, but I guess we'll never know for sure."

No, we wouldn't, thanks to Mason. Anger and sorrow bubbled up inside me, but I pushed the emotions down. The longer we stood here, the more danger we were in, so I jerked my head.

"Come on. Let's get started."

Bria crouched down and unzipped her black duffel bag, pulling out a small, collapsible shovel. I grabbed the same sort of shovel out of my own bag, then leaned down in front of my father's tomb. I traced my fingers over Tristan's name, then dropped my gaze lower, searching for the same sort of crudely carved telltale ring-of-swords rune that Fletcher had scratched into my father's tombstone at Blue Ridge Cemetery.

But I didn't find one.

No runes or other symbols had been scratched into my father's tomb, and the gray stone was smooth, shiny, and untouched, as if it had just been erected a moment ago. My heart sank. I had been so *certain* that Fletcher had been pointing me in this direction, that he'd carved the ring-of-swords rune into my father's marker to tell me to look *here*, at Tristan's tomb. Plus, it would have been just like Fletcher to hide the ledger right under Mason's nose. But it seemed I was wrong and that I had put Bria and myself in danger for nothing.

"Gin?" Bria asked. "Did you find the rune?"

I shook my head and moved around the tombstone, but I saw the same nothing as before. No runes or symbols were carved into the marble that shouldn't be here. But if Fletcher hadn't buried the ledger with my father, then where was it?

"Gin?" Bria asked. "Are we prying open the tomb or not?"

Frustrated, I surged to my feet, spun away from the tomb, and stared out over the rest of the cemetery. My gaze moved from one marker to the next, and my eyes slowly narrowed. Just because the ledger wasn't in my father's tomb didn't mean that Fletcher hadn't stashed the book in *another* grave. There were plenty to choose from.

I yanked my phone out of my pocket, pulled up one of the photos I'd taken in Blue Ridge Cemetery last night, and showed it to Bria. "See if you can find this symbol carved into any of the markers. It will be small and faint, probably right above the grass, someplace most people wouldn't notice it."

Bria took one side of the cemetery, while I searched the other, both of us moving from one tombstone, cross, or marker to the next. While we worked, I kept an eye on the surrounding trees and the path that led to the mansion. Just because there were no cameras or sensors here didn't mean that some giants wouldn't patrol through this area. But no one appeared, and we continued our search.

The more markers we looked at and eliminated, the more desperate I became. Mason's deadline to find and turn over the ledger was midnight tomorrow. If it wasn't here, then I didn't know where else to look. If Fletcher had hidden the ledger in the woods around his house or stashed it in some safety-deposit box under a fake name, then I would probably never find it.

Especially since Mason would kill me for failing—and my friends along with me.

Fifteen minutes later, I had finished with the markers on my side of the cemetery, although Bria was still looking at the ones on hers. I was about to double back through the rows and see if I'd missed anything when I spotted a final tombstone standing off by itself at the far edge of the cemetery. I hurried in that direction. The marker itself was nothing fancy, but the name carved into it made me blink in surprise.

Hugh Tucker.

The date of Tucker's birth was listed but not his death, since that hadn't happened yet. Curious. Most people only had tombstones erected if their spouses died before them. I wondered if Tucker had ordered this one to be put up—or if Mason had done it as a warning.

Either way, I crouched down and examined the tombstone from top to bottom. Unlike the other markers, which were grand, hulking monstrosities covered with flowery poems and platitudes, Tucker's stone was plain and simple, with no extra adornments.

I was about to turn away from it when I noticed a slightly darker spot near the bottom. My heart started pounding, but I forced myself to lean forward and carefully peer at the stone. I had been wrong. Tucker's marker did have one adornment, a ring-of-swords rune carved into the lower right-hand corner, the same place it had been on my father's tombstone in Blue Ridge Cemetery.

My heart pounded a little harder and faster. "Bria! Over here!"

My sister rushed over. She blanched when she saw it was Tucker's tombstone, but the two of us went to work with our shovels. We hadn't dug down all that deep, maybe a foot, when the point of my shovel *thunked* against something.

I froze, as did Bria. Then I stabbed out with my shovel again. *Thunk.* Something was definitely buried in this grave, which should have been completely empty, since Tucker wasn't dead yet.

I dropped to my hands and knees, as did Bria, and we both frantically scraped our shovels down into the dirt. A minute later, we uncovered a silverstone box about the size of a large laptop. I yanked the box out of the dirt, ignoring the grime that covered my hands, and set it on the ground.

"Open it," Bria said in an eager voice.

The smart thing to do would have been to fill in the dirt as quickly as possible, then grab the box and leave. But I was as eager and curious as Bria was, so I wrapped my hand around the small padlock, coated it with my Ice magic, and then shattered the Ice and the lock along with it. The instant the lock was out of the way, I cracked open the top of the box, holding my breath, and hoping, hoping, hoping I would find the mysterious ledger inside.

And I did.

A black book like the one Mason had shown us was wrapped in plastic and nestled inside the box.

"This is it," I whispered.

"Open it," Bria whispered back. "Open the plastic, and see what the ledger says."

I reached out to do that very thing, but then I thought of what Fletcher would do in this situation. I'd confirmed the box contained the ledger. Ripping off the plastic to see what information might be inside would definitely be pushing my lousy luck.

So I shook my head and closed the box. "No. Let's put the grave back together as best we can, then leave. We can look at the ledger later, when we're someplace safe."

Bria didn't like it, but she nodded, and we filled in the hole. It wasn't the best or neatest job, but I grabbed some dead branches and several handfuls of dried leaves from the woods and scattered them across the dirt, as though the wind had blown them into the cemetery. Maybe the forest debris would keep anyone from looking too closely at the grave and realizing that someone had been digging here.

The second that was done, I collapsed my shovel and stuffed it into my duffel bag. Bria did the same with hers, and we both slung our bags onto our shoulders. I leaned down and grabbed the silverstone box from the ground, then looked at my sister.

"Let's get out of here," I said.

She nodded, and we both headed toward the edge of the cemetery. We were almost to the tree line when I saw a shadow move out of the corner of my eye. I whirled in that direction. A familiar figure was standing on the stone path to my right.

Hugh Tucker—and he was pointing a gun at me.

✲ 18 ✲

Bria and I both froze. Tucker sidled along the path, moving a little closer to us. He eyed Bria, as if making sure she wasn't going to draw her own gun, then focused on me.

His black gaze lingered on the box in my hand. "I see you found the ledger. How nice of you to retrieve it for me, Gin."

I tightened my grip on the box. "I didn't find it for you. I found it for *me*. So I can destroy Mason."

Tucker shook his head. "The ledger won't help you do that, and it won't get you anything but dead."

I frowned. The vampire's face was its usual blank, inscrutable mask, but something in his tone bothered me. It almost seemed like he knew *exactly* where the ledger had been all along. But how could he know that? Fletcher had hidden the ledger here for me to find…hadn't he?

I pushed away my questions and self-doubt. *No*. I was just imagining things. Tucker *always* had his own agenda, and I wasn't going to fall for another one of his tricks.

He took another step closer and held out his hand. "Give me the box, Gin. Trust me. It's for the best."

"Why?" I snarled. "So you can give it to Mason and get back into his good graces? So he will fire Emery and restore you as his right-hand man? Forget it."

"Give me the ledger." He aimed his gun at Bria. "Or I will shoot your sister."

Bria let out a soft curse, and anger shimmered in her blue eyes, along with her Ice magic. The fingers of her left hand curled into a fist, as though she was debating whether to sling a spray of Ice daggers at Tucker. I was thinking of doing the same thing. But the vampire was extremely fast, and he could probably dodge any attack Bria and I might make and still manage to fire at her.

"You want to shoot someone, then shoot me," I growled. "Point the gun at *me*, not Bria."

An amused grin curved the corners of Tucker's mouth. "So you can use your Stone magic to harden your skin and simply let my bullets bounce off you? No thanks."

I growled in frustration. That was exactly what I'd been planning on doing, along with tackling the vampire and making him eat that gun barrel-first.

Tucker took another step closer to Bria, still pointing his weapon at her. He held out his free hand. "Give me the box. Now. Or Bria isn't going to like what happens next."

My eyes narrowed. He was pointing the gun at Bria but not at her head or heart. No, he was aiming at her shoulder, as though he only planned on winging her if I didn't cooperate.

Tucker had tried to kill me or have me killed several times over the past few months, but he had never done the same to Bria. Oh, he had ordered some kidnappings, but as far as I knew, he had never truly threatened my sister with permanent, grievous bodily harm, and I had a suspicion he wouldn't pull the trigger now.

"You're bluffing," I said. "You're not going to kill Bria. You *can't*. She reminds you too much of Eira."

Bria blanched at the reminder that he had been in love with our mother. Tucker's lips pressed into a tight, thin, unhappy line, but he didn't deny my accusation.

"Just give me the ledger," he snapped. "And let me save you from yourself, Genevieve. For once in your life, *listen* to me."

I frowned. That bothersome tone rippled through his voice again, the one that made me think he knew far more about the ledger than he was letting on. In that moment, I felt Hugh Tucker was trying to tell me something important without actually saying the words, just like Fletcher had done with this whole Circle treasure hunt.

"What are you up to, Tuck?" I asked.

"Just give me the damn ledger," he snapped again. "Now. Or I *will* shoot Bria."

Shooting Bria wasn't the same thing as killing her, but I didn't want my sister to get hurt, so I held out the box. I could always surge forward, tackle the vampire, and wrest his gun away—

Click.

For a sickening moment, I thought Tucker had shot Bria after all, but then a familiar figure stepped out of the woods, a gun in her hand.

Lorelei Parker.

Tucker had been so focused on Bria and me that he hadn't noticed Lorelei creeping up on his blind side. Neither had I. One second, it was just the three of us. The next, Lorelei had appeared in the cemetery like some vengeful ghost.

"You're not going to shoot anyone," Lorelei said. "Throw down your gun. Now. Or I'll put a bullet in your skull, Mr. Tucker."

He tipped his head to her. “Ms. Parker. Always a pleasure.”

Lorelei snorted. “I doubt that. But I left my grandmother’s bridal shower for this, and you’re going to do *exactly* what I say. So toss your gun away. Gently.”

Tucker hesitated, but he did as she commanded.

The vampire’s gun hit the ground at Lorelei’s feet. Her gaze dropped to it for just a split second, but that was all the opportunity Tucker needed. Before I could shout a warning, he lunged forward and grabbed Lorelei’s wrist. The two of them struggled, but Tucker managed to knock her gun away. Lorelei cursed, and Tucker spun her around and hooked his arm around her neck.

Bria and I both froze again. My sister had pulled her own gun, while I had palmed one of my knives, but Tucker could easily snap Lorelei’s neck before Bria and I could attack him.

“So sorry to disappoint you, Ms. Parker,” Tucker purred. “But I don’t particularly like getting shot. I prefer to avoid such unpleasantness.”

Instead of being frightened, Lorelei let out a low laugh. “Me too. So keep your fangs to yourself.”

Tucker’s black gaze dropped to her throat, and I could have sworn a spark of hungry interest flickered across his face, although it vanished in an instant. “Please. I’m a gentleman. I would never bite a lady without her permission.”

“Too bad I can’t say the same,” Lorelei replied.

He frowned. “What do you mean?”

She turned her head so that she could see his face out of the corner of her eye. Then she smiled. “I don’t ask permission before I stab people who are manhandling me.”

Magic flashed in Lorelei’s blue eyes. A long Ice dagger

popped into her right hand, and she plunged the weapon deep into Tucker's thigh.

Tucker hissed with pain and loosened his grip. Lorelei spun away, then whirled right back around, surged forward, and punched him in the face. Tucker hissed again and staggered back, his nose bloody and that Ice dagger still stuck in his thigh.

Bria snapped up her gun, and I raised my knife, and we both rushed forward to flank Lorelei.

"Let's go," I said.

Bria, Lorelei, and I backed away from Tucker and stepped into the woods. He watched us go, but he didn't try to follow us. The second he was out of sight, I jerked my head at my friends.

"Run. Now."

So we ran. And ran and ran. Ten feet, fifteen, twenty, fifty.

When we were a hundred feet away from the cemetery, I held up my hand, and we all slowed down. I glanced back over my shoulder, but I didn't hear Tucker crashing through the woods after us, and he wasn't shouting for anyone to help him.

Had he actually come here alone? Why? And why wasn't he chasing after us? Or at least yelling for help? The quiet troubled me far more than if he'd been screaming at the top of his lungs.

Whatever Tucker's motives, it seemed as though he was going to suffer in silence. So I plunged deeper into the woods, with Bria and Lorelei following along.

It didn't take us long to hike through the woods and reach the neighboring mansion where I'd parked my van. The property was still empty and deserted, although Lorelei's car was now sitting in the driveway.

"How did you find us?" I asked.

Lorelei shrugged. "I could tell you were up to something, so I left the bridal shower, got into my car, and started driving up and down the streets, looking for you. I spotted you and Bria getting into your van a few blocks away from Northern Aggression. I hung way back so you guys wouldn't see me, but after a few turns, it wasn't hard to tell you were coming here."

Well, at least she had followed us the old-fashioned way, instead of hijacking my phone like Silvio sometimes did. I'd turned off the device before I'd gone into Northern Aggression to keep my assistant from tracking me.

"Thank you for coming," I said. "I don't know what would have happened with Tucker if you hadn't shown up."

Something flickered in Lorelei's eyes at the mention of the vampire, although the emotion quickly vanished. "You should have just told me what you guys were planning. I would have been happy to help."

"I know, but I didn't want to put anyone else in danger. It's bad enough Bria and I came here, especially with Mason and his men inside the mansion."

Lorelei nodded, accepting my explanation and apology, then gestured at the dirt-covered box in my hand. "The missing ledger, I presume?"

"Yeah."

"Now what?" Bria asked.

Lorelei checked her watch and sighed. "Unfortunately, I need to go back to the nightclub. There are still two more hours of party games and drunken debauchery, not to mention the stripper."

Her lips curled, and her nose crinkled with disgust. Yeah, I wouldn't have wanted to watch my grandmother hoot and holler and stuff dollar bills down a guy's G-string either.

"Well, be careful when you and Mallory leave the club. It's only a matter of time before Mason realizes that I have the ledger, and he might try to grab you, Mallory, or Mosley for leverage," I said. "Bria and I will loop in everyone else about what's going on."

Lorelei nodded. "Where are you guys going?"

"Fletcher's house. We'll regroup there and see if we can figure out what's in this ledger that is so important to Mason. I'll keep you posted."

Lorelei promised to do the same, then got into her car and left. Bria and I slid into my van. My sister drove while I called our friends.

"I *knew* you were up to something at breakfast this morning. I knew it!" Silvio exclaimed. "You should have let me come with you, Gin."

"I needed you to keep an eye on the Pork Pit," I replied. "Besides, it was just a hunch. I didn't know for sure the ledger was buried in the Circle cemetery. Did anything unusual happen at the restaurant this afternoon?"

He huffed, still annoyed with me. "Well, I know you weren't expecting him, but Liam showed up, although he left as soon as I told him that you weren't here. He said he would text you later."

Hmm. Liam hadn't texted me this afternoon. I wondered what he was doing, but he wasn't my top priority right now.

"That's fine. Tell Sophia to stop cooking, send the waitstaff home, cash out the current customers, and close down the restaurant as fast as she can. Then you go pick up Owen and meet me at Fletcher's house. I'll call Finn."

Silvio agreed. We hung up, and I dialed Finn. My brother also wasn't happy about being left out of my scheme, but he agreed to finish his work at the bank and come to Fletcher's house. I also texted Jo-Jo, Xavier, and the rest of our friends, telling them what had happened and to keep a watch out for Emery Slater and her men.

By the time I finished my calls and texts, Bria was parking in the gravel driveway in front of Fletcher's house. I reached out with my Stone magic and did my usual checks, but no one was lurking around.

Bria and I got out of the van and hustled inside the house. We went to the den, and I set the silverstone box on the coffee table. I was too curious to wait for everyone else, so I opened the box, grabbed the ledger, and used one of my knives to slice through the plastic. Then I sat down on the couch and studied the book.

It was a simple black ledger, just like the one Mason had shown us the other day. No letters, runes, or other marks adorned the cover or spine, although the pages had yellowed with age.

Bria sat down on the couch beside me. I looked at her, and she nodded back. I drew in a breath and let it out. Then I slowly cracked open the ledger to find…

Numbers—rows and rows of numbers.

I frowned. Not what I'd been expecting. I flipped through the pages, but each one was the same—long sequences of numbers handwritten in neat rows.

"What do you think this means?" I asked.

Bria tapped her finger on the open page. "Those look like account numbers."

My frown deepened. "Accounts for what?"

A sharp knock sounded on the front door, and a key scraped in the lock. "Gin! Bria!"

Familiar voices sounded, floorboards creaked in the hallway, and Silvio, Owen, and Finn hurried into the den. Finn checked on Bria, and Owen came over to me. Silvio stood in the doorway with his arms crossed over his chest, still annoyed with me.

Owen hugged me tight, then pulled back. "Why didn't you tell us what you were planning?"

"Because Mason has spies everywhere, and Bria and me slipping away from the bridal shower seemed like the quickest, easiest, and safest thing to do. Besides, I didn't know for sure the ledger was buried in the cemetery. But it was, and now we just have to figure out what it means."

I opened the ledger again, and everyone gathered around as I turned the pages.

Finn's eyes narrowed. "Let me see that."

I handed over the ledger. He sat down on the couch and flipped through several pages, running his index finger down the rows of numbers. A minute later, he stopped and lifted his green gaze to mine.

"These are bank accounts," Finn said.

I reared back in surprise. "Are you sure?"

He shrugged. "Well, I can't be absolutely *sure* without taking the ledger to First Trust, logging into our system, and comparing the account numbers. But at first glance, yeah, I'd say these were bank accounts. See these numbers?" He pointed to one of the rows. "Every account at First Trust starts with that same sequence. And some of the other starting sequences belong to different banks."

Bria frowned. "Why would Mason care so much about a ledger filled with bank accounts? Unless…"

"Unless the accounts have money in them." Silvio finished her thought. "Serious amounts of money."

A harsh, bitter laugh tumbled out of my lips. So this was

all about *money*. Of course. I should have known. Most things were, especially in Ashland, and especially when it came to the Circle.

"Why are you laughing?" Owen asked.

I gestured at the ledger. "Because this is Fletcher's *leverage*. This is how he got Mason to let him leave the Circle. Somehow Fletcher got his hands on this ledger, which means he probably had access to these accounts."

"Dad must have held Mason's money hostage," Finn said, thinking out loud. "Dad probably set it up so that *he* was the only one who could access the accounts. He probably returned a little bit of the money each month so long as the Circle left him alone. Sort of like a reverse blackmail scheme. Only instead of demanding money from someone to keep a secret, Dad *gave* money to Mason to keep from having to work for the Circle."

It was another Reverse Trojan Horse, just like the move Fletcher had used so we could assassinate Liam Carter's client all those years ago. I'd always known that Fletcher was clever, but in this case, his sheer audacity impressed me. You had to be stone-cold to pull off a scheme like this, especially against someone as powerful as Mason, someone who kept trying to capture and torture the information out of you.

I thought about the dreams, the memories I'd been having of Wade Brockton, the accountant Fletcher had been sent to kill. Brockton must have been the one who actually embezzled the money from the Circle. That was why Billings had tortured the accountant and Fletcher—the giant had wanted to know where the ledger and the money were.

I wondered if Fletcher had encouraged Brockton to steal from the Circle, if he'd seen the accountant as a way to finally get out from under Mason's thumb. And Mason must have been the person Fletcher had wanted to kill that night, although it hadn't happened.

The more I turned my theories over in my mind, the more sense they made, but something about this whole situation still didn't add up. I tried to put my finger on what it was, but the answer eluded me.

"But the Circle has millions of dollars at its disposal," Bria said. "Why would Mason suddenly care so much about a ledger that's been missing for years?"

"You're forgetting that Deirdre lost a good chunk of the Circle's money with her outlandish spending and risky investments. Plus, Tucker wasn't able to get his hands on those jewels Deirdre stashed at the Bullet Pointe theme park. And Damian Rivera's estate will be tied up for years with lawsuits by the families of the victims of Bruce Porter, aka the Dollmaker serial killer." Finn ticked off the Circle's recent misfortunes on his fingers. "So Mason probably needs the missing ledger and the money it contains."

He was right. The Circle's coffers had been severely depleted in recent months. Still, I wondered how much money Fletcher had stolen from Mason—and what my uncle was planning to do with the funds. He must desperately need the money for *something*. Otherwise, Mason never would have revealed himself, much less told me about the stolen ledger.

"So now what?" Silvio asked.

I looked at Bria, Finn, Owen, and Silvio. They all stared back at me, patiently waiting for me to reveal our next move. My heart squeezed tight. We might have found the ledger, but that didn't change the fact that Mason had more elemental magic than I did and could still kill everyone I loved.

I drew in a breath and let it out, knowing there was only one thing we could do. "We're going to give the ledger to Mason."

"What?" Finn asked in an incredulous voice.

"No, Gin," Bria shook her head. "No."

"Are you sure you want to do that?" Owen asked.

"There has to be another way," Silvio chimed in.

My friends kept chattering, but I held up my hands, and they slowly quieted. "Mason Mitchell is the strongest elemental any of us has ever seen. Even if I could get past Emery and her giants, I still don't know how to actually *kill* Mason, since he can use his Stone magic to block any attack I make. So I have to turn over the ledger. That's the best way to keep you guys safe."

"But what about what *Dad* wanted?" Finn asked in a harsh, accusing voice. "He left that ledger in the Circle cemetery for you to find, Gin. Not me or Bria or anyone else. He wanted *you* to have it."

My heart twisted at his words, but I ignored the sensation. "I know that Fletcher wanted me to use the ledger against Mason. And that's exactly what I'm going to do."

"How?" Bria asked. "It's the end of the business day. There's no way we can get to First Trust and check the accounts before the bank closes for the weekend."

"We don't have to check the accounts today," I said, grinning. "All we have to do is make a copy of the info."

✲ 19 ✲

Finn and Silvio got busy copying the ledger. Finn took photos of each and every page with his phone, then texted the pictures to Silvio so the vampire could upload them to his cloud storage. Owen went along behind them and double-checked to make sure they didn't miss any pages or pictures.

While the guys worked, Bria and I showered and changed. Thirty minutes later, I walked back into the den to find Bria and Owen looking over Finn's and Silvio's shoulders. Finn put down his phone, while Silvio tapped a final few keys on his laptop.

"It's done," Owen said, looking over at me. "We copied all the pages and account numbers, so we'll still have access to the information even after you give the ledger to Mason."

"Good," I replied. "Even if we can't access all the accounts before he does, I still want to get an idea of how much money is left in them and how much Fletcher was paying out to Mason every month."

My phone rang. I pulled the device out of the back pocket of my jeans and checked the number on the screen.

Unknown. But I had a funny feeling I knew exactly who was calling.

"Hello?"

"Hello, Gin." Mason's voice snaked into my ear. "Hugh says you have something that belongs to me. I want it. Now."

My fingers curled around the phone. So Tucker had ratted me out after all. Of course he had. He hadn't gotten the ledger for himself, so he'd tattled to my uncle that I had it. The vampire was once again playing both sides against the middle.

Bria, Owen, Finn, and Silvio looked at me, and I mouthed my uncle's name. They all tensed, worry filling their faces.

"Bring the ledger to the Pork Pit," Mason said. "You have thirty minutes."

"Or else?"

"Or else I'll crush your restaurant—with Sophia inside."

My fingers curled even tighter around the phone. "You're bluffing. Sophia's not there. I sent everyone home early."

"I never bluff, Genevieve."

Several sharp sounds rang out, like Mason was snapping his fingers over and over again. After that, silence. And then…

"Sorry, Gin," Sophia's voice rasped through the phone. "I was waiting for some customers to finish eating when Emery and her men came inside. They made me keep the restaurant open. There are more people eating now."

An icy fist of dread clutched my heart, but I forced myself to stay calm. "It's okay. I'm coming to get you. Just hang tight."

Sophia didn't answer, but Mason came back on the line.

"Ledger. Pork Pit. Thirty minutes. Or Sophia dies, along with everyone else unlucky enough to want barbecue tonight."

The bastard didn't wait for a response. He hung up on me.

The thought that Sophia was in danger, that she might already be hurt, made me sick to my stomach, but there was nothing I could do but give Mason what he wanted. I couldn't let her die, and I couldn't let him execute the innocent people eating in the restaurant. My friends and I made a hasty plan, and we left Fletcher's house five minutes later.

Silvio drove as fast as he dared on the curvy mountain roads. Owen was in the car with us, while Finn and Bria were following in another vehicle, taking the curves just as quickly. Eventually, Finn turned his car down another road and headed off toward the salon, since I'd asked him and Bria to watch over Jo-Jo.

I also texted Jo-Jo and told her what was going on, but she didn't respond. She was probably still busy with her last few salon clients of the day.

I also texted Liam Carter, but he didn't respond either. Worry rippled through me about where he was and what he might be doing, but I forced myself to push the emotion aside. Liam was probably busy overseeing the last-minute details for Mallory and Mosley's wedding tomorrow. Either way, neither he nor Jo-Jo could help us right now, so I silenced my phone and put it away.

Fifteen minutes later, Silvio steered his car through the downtown loop and stopped at the other end of the block from the Pork Pit. The restaurant's neon sign was lit up, illuminating the two giants guarding the front door and the three black SUVs sitting at the curb.

"Why does Mason want to meet here?" Silvio asked. "Why didn't he insist you go back to the historical association mansion?"

"Mason probably came here so that Emery and the giants could grab someone to use against me, and they got lucky and nabbed Sophia. Besides, it would have taken more time for them to drive back to the mansion, and Mason doesn't want me to have the ledger a second longer than necessary. That's probably why he decided to stay here." I paused. "And because he's a petty son of a bitch."

"What do you mean?" Owen asked.

I gestured at the sign of the pig holding a platter of food over the front door. "Making me hand over the ledger in Fletcher's restaurant is the perfect way for Mason to thumb his nose at the old man one last time."

I looked past the two giants and the three SUVs and studied the flow of traffic on the street and the sidewalks. It was just after six o'clock, and most folks were heading home. A steady stream of cars cruised by, and dozens of people strolled along the sidewalks. I eyed the vehicles and the faces, but no one paid any attention to Silvio's car. It didn't seem like Mason had planted anyone in the crowd to keep an eye out for us. Then again, he didn't need to. He had Sophia, which was all the leverage he needed to get me here.

"Let's get this over with," I muttered.

Owen and Silvio nodded, and the three of us got out of the car and slowly approached the restaurant. I went first, clutching the ledger, while Owen and Silvio watched my back. The two giants stationed outside snapped to attention when they caught sight of me, and one of them knocked on the window, signaling the other guards inside—and Mason, of course.

The giants moved out of my way. I ignored them, yanked open the front door, and stepped inside the Pork Pit.

At first glance, everything seemed normal. Several folks were sitting at the tables, chowing down on barbecue sandwiches, baked beans, fries, and onion rings, completely oblivious to the danger lurking around them. My gaze roamed over the six giants in black suits who were positioned around the restaurant. Two in a booth by the front door, two more in a booth next to the restrooms, and the final two at a table close to the double doors that led into the back of the restaurant.

Emery Slater was perched on Silvio's usual stool at the counter, watching Sophia, who was plating up thick wedges of freshly baked cornbread. A murderous expression filled the Goth dwarf's face, and she kept glancing at a cast-iron skillet on the counter like she wanted to snatch it up and slam it into Emery's face. I knew the feeling, but neither one of us could attack the giant. Not with all the innocent people in here.

"What do you want us to do, Gin?" Owen asked in a low voice.

"Help Sophia fix food and wait on the tables, and make sure that everyone pays up and leaves as soon as possible," I murmured. "I don't want people to panic, but the sooner they get out of here, the better off they'll be."

Owen crossed the storefront, stepped behind the counter, and tied on a blue work apron. Silvio joined him, and the two of them started helping Sophia fix sandwiches, spoon up baked beans, and pour drinks.

That left me to face Mason.

My uncle was lounging in the same booth by the

storefront windows where he'd sat yesterday. Hugh Tucker was at a nearby table, and he seemed to have completely recovered from Lorelei stabbing and punching him in the Circle cemetery. Pity.

I slid into the booth and set the ledger on the tabletop. Mason stared at it a moment, then focused on me.

"Hugh said you found the ledger buried in my cemetery," he said. "Where was it, exactly?"

Surprise surged through me, but I kept my face blank. It seemed Tucker hadn't told Mason the ledger had been buried in the vampire's grave. Why wouldn't Tucker reveal that? It seemed like such a trivial thing to hide. Still, if he wasn't going to admit to it, then neither was I.

"It was in Mab's grave. Buried in a silverstone box about a foot down."

The lie slipped easily off my tongue. Not a flicker of emotion crossed Tucker's face, and I held my breath, wondering if he was playing a game and would call me out on the lie to further ingratiate himself with Mason. But Tucker didn't say anything, and the moment passed.

Mason shook his head and let out a low, amused laugh. "Clever Fletcher. He put it in the one place I never thought to look."

He laughed again, then reached out and took hold of the ledger. I also reached out, wrapping my hand around the opposite end.

Mason's amusement instantly died. Tucker tensed, as did Emery and the other giants, along with Sophia, Owen, and Silvio.

"What's in here that's so important?" I asked.

Mason tilted his head to the side and studied me with narrowed eyes. "Don't play dumb, Gin. You were too curious not to look inside."

I shrugged. "Of course I looked inside, but all I saw were nonsense numbers."

Mason studied me even more closely, but I stared right back at him, my face absolutely calm and blank. He tugged on the ledger, and I let him yank it away. Mason set the book off to his side of the table, out of my reach.

"Despite all this unpleasantness, my earlier offer still stands," he said. "Come work for me, Gin."

I jerked back in surprise. Now that he had the ledger, I'd expected him to leave as quickly as possible. Maybe even try to kill me on his way out the door. Not offer me a job again. "Why on earth would you want that? You could never, ever trust me. Not after all the horrible things you've done to my family."

"*Our* family," Mason corrected, then shrugged. "You have some unique talents, Gin. Talents that are being utterly wasted slinging barbecue. If you worked for me, we could change Ashland for the better. Just think of all we could accomplish—together. No one would be able to stand against us. Not the underworld bosses, not the other members of the Circle, no one."

It was my turn to laugh. "I'll give you this. You certainly paint a pretty picture." My chuckles faded away. "But my answer is the same as before—*I* will *never* work for *you*."

"Then you're as foolish and shortsighted as Fletcher was."

"For seeing through your lies and bullshit?" I snorted. "Well, then, you can call me foolish and shortsighted any day of the week and twice on Sundays."

Another amused look filled Mason's face. Once again, my insults didn't bother him.

"Where are my manners?" he drawled. "Thank you ever so much for retrieving the ledger, Gin. You don't know what this means to me. Or what I'll be able to do now, thanks to your doggedness and ingenuity."

The thought of Mason using the money in those accounts to hurt people turned my stomach, but I couldn't stop that right now any more than I could stop him from using his Stone magic to reduce the restaurant to rubble and kill everyone inside.

Mason plucked the ledger off the tabletop and got to his feet. Tucker pushed back from his table, Emery slid off her stool, and the other giants scattered around the restaurant also stood up. This plague of locusts was finally leaving.

"And so our business is concluded." Mason loomed over me, a pleasant smile fixed on his face. "And I won, the way I always do. Fletcher never quite learned that lesson. Don't make the same mistake he did, Gin. I'm giving you a reprieve, and you should make the most of it."

Mason braced his hand on the tabletop and leaned down, his face inches away and his cold gray eyes level with mine. "Our business might be concluded, but my terms remain the same."

"What terms?" I asked.

He leaned a little closer, his warm breath brushing my face. "From this moment forward, if you interfere with Circle business, with *my* business, in any way, shape, or form, I *will* kill you," Mason purred in his smooth, silky voice. "But only *after* I've made you watch while Bria and the rest of your friends meet the same grisly fate as Tristan. So think on that, Gin. Think what the price will be before you start shouting revenge and plotting against me."

His threat delivered, Mason straightened up, tucked the ledger under his arm, and strolled out of the Pork Pit.

✲ 20 ✲

I made sure Sophia was okay, helped her with the last of the food and the customers, and closed the restaurant.

Silvio, Owen, and I followed Sophia back to Jo-Jo's house. Finn and Bria were waiting on the front porch with Jo-Jo, who was pacing back and forth. The Deveraux sisters had a tearful reunion, and Jo-Jo thanked me for keeping Sophia safe. I smiled and nodded and said all the right things, but I was angry, bitter, and seething inside.

Mason fucking Mitchell had gotten the better of me.

I didn't know what to do about that. I didn't know what I *could* do without putting us all in even more danger. He had the ledger, and he could still reach out, kidnap, and kill us anytime he wanted.

My uncle was right—he had *won*.

"What do you want to do now, Gin?" Finn asked, interrupting my dark thoughts. "Start digging into the ledger accounts?"

Despite the cold, we were still standing on the front porch. I looked at everyone. Finn, Bria, Owen, Silvio, Jo-Jo, Sophia. Once again, my friends were waiting for me to give them some direction—but I didn't have any.

Not now, not tonight. Not after I'd worked so hard to find the ledger, only to end up turning it over to Mason. Even though I had kept my friends safe and we had the account numbers, I still felt I had let Fletcher down. He had kept that ledger safe and hidden for years, and Mason had pried it away from me after only a few hours. I hadn't just let Fletcher down. I had completely *failed* him—and myself too.

"Gin?" Owen asked.

I forced myself to smile at everyone. "No more work and bad guys tonight. It's late, and we have a big day tomorrow. Let's concentrate on Mallory and Mosley's wedding. I want everything to be perfect for them. Once the wedding is over, then we'll plan our next move."

Everyone nodded, accepting my decision. I smiled again, but their trust made me feel like an even bigger failure—and worse, a fraud who was going to get them all killed.

The night passed by quietly, and the next morning, Saturday, Valentine's Day, dawned clear and bright. It was still bitterly cold, but the cheery sunshine made it the perfect day for a winter wedding.

Just before noon, Owen pulled his car up to the front of the Five Oaks Country Club. He handed his keys off to one of the valets, while Silvio and I grabbed garment bags and more out of the trunk. Owen retrieved his own bags, and we headed for the entrance.

Five Oaks was made up of five circular buildings, and the main center structure had been decked out with white, blue, and silver ribbons, along with white paper wedding bells and hearts, just like all the other wedding venues I'd been to this week. An enormous royal-blue banner, bigger than any of the others I'd seen, was hanging over the club's main entrance, and its shiny silver letters screamed out *Congratulations, Mallory and Stuey!*

A couple of giants were stationed by the entrance, checking people's invitations and IDs and ticking off the names on their clipboards. Their navy suits, light blue shirts, and silver ties marked them as Liam Carter's men. According to a text Liam had sent me last night, Mallory had decided to color-coordinate the security guards with the rest of the wedding, and she'd even found white orchids for each guard to pin to their suit jacket.

Owen, Silvio, and I showed our invitations, stepped inside the country club, and walked down a long hallway that was also decked out with ribbons, bells, hearts, and banners. At the far end of the corridor, Roslyn Phillips was standing behind a podium, a clipboard in her hand, directing several giants and dwarves who were carrying tables and chairs into the grand ballroom behind her. A couple of Liam's guards were standing nearby, keeping an eye on things.

Roslyn checked something off on her clipboard, then looked up and smiled as we approached her. My friend was wearing a lovely royal-blue cocktail dress, along with sapphire chandelier earrings.

"What do you think?" I drawled. "Are you going to branch out and make wedding planning part of your business?"

She let out a rueful laugh. "I don't think so. I was happy to help Mallory since her original planner got the flu, but I'll stick to handling Northern Aggression. C'mon. Everyone else is already here."

Roslyn led us through a couple of hallways and over to a

wing that featured several private rooms. She knocked on a door, and we stepped into a large suite to find Mosley standing in front of a full-length mirror. The elderly dwarf looked quite handsome in his classic black tuxedo, although he seemed to be having a bit of trouble with his black bow tie.

"I can never fix these stupid things," Mosley growled.

"Here," Finn said, going over to him. "Let me."

My brother was already dressed to impress in his own tuxedo, complete with a perfect bow tie. The black suit jacket and white shirt brought out his walnut-colored hair and green eyes, and he looked so much like Fletcher it made me want to cry. I always missed the old man a little more on special occasions, and he would have loved being here to watch his friend Mosley get married.

"My, my, my," I drawled, trying to mask my sudden sadness. "Don't you two gents look handsome?"

Finn finished with Mosley's tie, then preened at his own reflection in the mirror. "You're absolutely right. We *do* look handsome."

Mosley rolled his eyes at Finn, then came over, grabbed my hands, and gently squeezed my fingers. "Gin," he rumbled, his hazel eyes bright and happy. "I'm so glad you and everyone else could be here for our special day."

I smiled at him. "I wouldn't have missed it for anything."

I left Owen and Silvio with Finn and Mosley, so the two of them could don their own tuxedos. Roslyn led me to another suite down the hallway, then headed back to her post to make sure the ballroom was set up for the reception.

"There you are," a low voice called out.

I turned to find Liam Carter striding down the hallway toward me. Like the rest of his security staff, Liam was sporting a navy suit, light blue shirt, and silver tie, although a blue orchid was pinned to his lapel, marking him as the boss.

Liam stopped in front of me, his face full of concern. “How are you? And Sophia?”

I’d left him a voice mail last night, telling him what had happened at the Pork Pit. Liam had texted back and apologized for not being at the restaurant.

“I’m fine, and so is Sophia. How are you? We haven’t had a chance to talk much in person the past few days.”

“I know. You hired me to protect you, and I wasn’t there when you needed me.” He shook his head. “I’m sorry, Gin.”

No, Liam Carter hadn’t been around when I’d needed him. Not at the Posh boutique and not when Mason had come to the Pork Pit last night. Some of that was my fault, for keeping Liam at arm’s length, for not letting him get physically close enough to do his job, and for trying to handle things on my own like I always did.

Still, the paranoid part of me wondered how much of Liam not being around was *his* fault. So far, Liam had done everything I’d asked, and I had no real reason to be suspicious of his motives or loyalty. But try as I might, I couldn’t ignore those sharks swimming around and around in my watery tank of worry, just waiting to tear me to pieces.

But I forced myself to plaster a smile on my face. “Don’t worry about it. You couldn’t have done anything to change the situation. How are things here? I saw your men out front and at the ballroom. Everything seems to be going smoothly.”

“It is—so far.” Liam glanced up and down the hallway, as if making sure we were still alone. “My people have this place locked down tight, but I’m still concerned. Especially given what happened between you and Mason last night.”

"I gave Mason what he wanted, so he should be busy with his precious ledger today. But I appreciate you looking out for Mallory and Mosley. I'm sure everything will be fine."

I gave him another fake smile. I would be *ecstatic* if things went merely fine today, since that would be a marked improvement over everything else that had happened this past week.

A shadow flickered across Liam's face, but he nodded. "I'm sure you're right. Anyway, I need to make my rounds. See you later."

He spun around and strode back down the hallway.

I watched Liam until he vanished from view, but he seemed to be going about his job, just like he said. So I knocked on the door, opened it, and stepped inside.

The luxury suite was twice the size of Mosley's and decked out with everything a bride-to-be could want, from champagne chilling in a bucket in the corner, to a tray of chocolate-covered strawberries, to still more trays of drinks and snacks on a long table by the windows.

Mallory was sitting at a vanity table in the living room while Jo-Jo fluttered around and teased the older dwarf's white hair into a fluffy cloud. Jo-Jo was wearing a royal-blue dress, along with a string of pale gray pearls, but Mallory was clad in a blue silk robe.

Jo-Jo had already finished with Lorelei, and she'd made my friend look even more stunning than usual. Lorelei's black hair hung in loose, pretty waves around her shoulders, while smoky shadow enhanced her blue eyes and plum gloss highlighted her lips. Her royal-blue maid-of-honor dress brought out her beautiful skin and strong, toned body, and silver stilettos glittered on her feet.

Bria and Sophia were also here. Bria was in her royal-blue bridesmaid dress and silver stilettos. Her blond hair also hung in loose, pretty waves around her shoulders, and Jo-Jo had given her smoky eyes and plum lips to match Lorelei's look. In a nod to her Goth style, Sophia was sporting a royal-blue pantsuit with chunky black heels, and a blue crystal heart dangled from a black velvet ribbon around her neck.

"Gin! There you are!" Mallory waved me over.

I put my bags on a chair, then bent down and took her hands in mine. "Thank you for letting me be a part of your special day."

Mallory blinked a few times, tears gleaming in her eyes. "No, darling. Thank *you*. If it wasn't for you, I wouldn't be here, and neither would Stuey. We owe you so much."

Now I had to blink back tears. "No more than I owe you," I rasped, my throat tight.

Jo-Jo finished with Mallory's hair and doused it with roughly half a can of hairspray. While Mallory's hair set, she snacked on some champagne and strawberries along with Lorelei, Bria, and Sophia.

I took a seat in front of another vanity table. Jo-Jo stepped up and rested her hands on my shoulders.

"How are you doing, darling?" she asked in a soft, sympathetic voice. "I know handing over the ledger to Mason was hard for you."

More tears stung my eyes, betraying my frustration and disappointment, but I ruthlessly blinked them back. "I'm fine. I'm just glad Sophia is okay."

"Me too." Jo-Jo smiled at me. "Now, let's get you gussied up."

She gave me the same look as Lorelei and Bria—smoky eyes, plum lips, loose hair curled into soft waves. I studied my reflection. Jo-Jo had done an excellent job, as always, but no amount of makeup could hide the worry flickering in my eyes and creasing my pale face, and no pretty hairstyle could cover up the high, tense set of my shoulders.

Mallory, Lorelei, Bria, and Sophia were still laughing, talking, and gulping down champagne and strawberries on the other side of the suite, but Jo-Jo stayed next to me.

"You look like your mind is a thousand miles away. What are you thinking about?" she asked. "Fletcher?"

I let out a breath. There was no use denying it. Not to her. "Yeah. I can't help but wonder why Fletcher hid the ledger in Tucker's grave. It just doesn't make sense. Mason might not have thought to look there, but Tucker would have sooner or later."

Jo-Jo patted my arm. "Well, I'm sure you'll figure it out. But for now, everyone's safe, and you gave Mason what he wanted, so maybe he'll leave you alone. This is Mallory and Mosley's day. We should enjoy it as much as possible."

She was right. Today was about Mallory and Mosley and their love. Not me and my incessant worry and paranoia.

I squeezed her hand. "Thank you for talking some sense into me."

Jo-Jo squeezed my hand back. "Anytime, darling. Now, I need to do the bride's makeup."

She winked at me in the mirror, then went back over to Mallory.

Bria helped me zip up my bridesmaid dress, and I checked in the mirror to make sure the long skirt hid the two knives strapped to my thighs. I might have given Mason the ledger, but I was still wearing my weapons, along with my spider-rune pendant and matching ring, both of which were filled with my Ice magic. I wanted to be prepared in case something unexpected happened.

The mood in the suite grew more and more jovial. Soon I was drinking champagne, and we were taking selfies. I snapped more photos than Lorelei, Bria, and Sophia combined. Jo-Jo was right. This *was* a good day, and I wanted to always remember it.

"And here comes the bride," Jo-Jo called out several minutes later.

Mallory stepped out from behind a dressing screen in the corner of the suite. "Well? What do you girls think?"

She was wearing the silver-blue sheath dress with cap sleeves and silver sequined waistband from the Posh boutique, along with matching kitten heels. Silver shadow made her eyes seem bluer than normal, while a soft pink gloss covered her lips. A pearl-and-diamond choker sparkled around her neck, while a matching pearl-and-diamond tiara glinted in her fluffy white hair.

"You look stunning." I grinned. "I should have known you had a diamond tiara."

Mallory preened, reached up, and patted the tiara. "A girl can't possibly get married without one, now, can she?"

I laughed. "No, she certainly can't."

We hung out in the suite for another half hour, laughing, talking, and sipping champagne, before Roslyn knocked on the door.

"It's time," she said.

Mallory nodded and threaded her arm through Lorelei's, and we all grabbed our bouquets of white, blue, and purple orchids and left the suite. We followed Roslyn through the country club and over to a long hallway. A set of closed double doors stood at the far end.

"All right, ladies," Roslyn said. "It's go time. The groom, his best man, and everyone else are waiting inside. Are you ready to get married?"

Mallory gave a firm nod. "I was ready the moment Stuey asked me."

Roslyn smiled. "Good. You guys know what to do. Just wait for the music, and follow the cues. Gin, you're up first. Then Bria. And finally, Lorelei will escort Mallory."

We took our positions. A few minutes later, classical music started drifting through the closed doors. The music got a little louder, and the doors opened. I clutched my bouquet even tighter and strode forward.

I had attended weddings at the country club before, but Roslyn and the staff had really outdone themselves. The ceremony was being held in a glassed-in ballroom that overlooked the club's gardens. White, blue, and silver ribbons had been strung up around the room, along with paper wedding bells and hearts, and dozens of white and blue candles bathed the area in golden light. Guests dressed in tuxedos and ballgowns relaxed in comfy white wicker chairs on either side of the center aisle. White, blue, and purple orchid petals had been strewn over the pale blue carpet, adding a sweet vanilla note to the air.

The carpet stretched for about fifty feet before ending at a raised dais that featured a white trellis covered with white and blue orchids and tiny white fairy lights. Mosley was standing on the dais, along with the minister who was going to perform the ceremony.

Finn, Owen, and Silvio were also on the platform. They all looked quite handsome, but my gaze locked on Owen, who was truly stunning in his tuxedo. His black hair gleamed under the lights, and his violet gaze was soft and warm on mine.

I slowly walked the length of the carpet to the dais, and Owen moved forward, bent down, and held out his hand. I took it, and he helped me step up and onto the dais.

"You look beautiful," he murmured in a low, husky voice.

I winked at him. "So do you."

Owen grinned, then stepped back.

Bria walked down the aisle next, and Finn helped her up. He murmured something in my sister's ear that made her blush and give him an adoring gaze. Finn winked at her, then returned to his side of the dais.

The classical music trailed off, and an expectant hush fell over the ballroom. The opening strains of the traditional wedding march sounded, everyone stood, and Lorelei and Mallory stepped into view. A chorus of appreciative *oohs* and *aahs* rang out. Lorelei escorted her grandmother down the aisle, and Mallory smiled and nodded at everyone.

I looked across the dais at Mosley, who was smiling widely. Finn clapped his boss on the shoulder, and Mosley smiled even wider.

Lorelei and Mallory reached the dais. Silvio helped Lorelei step up, while Mosley did the same for Mallory. Mosley kissed Lorelei on the cheek, then took Mallory's arm. She grinned at him, and the two shared a quick kiss.

"Hey, now," Lorelei drawled. "You have to get married first before you start the honeymoon."

Laughter rang out. Mallory and Mosley grinned at Lorelei, then shared another quick kiss that made everyone laugh again.

The amused chuckles faded away, and the guests took their seats. Mallory and Mosley faced the minister, who cleared his throat and began the traditional speech.

"Dearly beloved, we are gathered here today…"

Mallory and Mosley's wedding went off without a hitch, and several minutes later, they kissed yet again—this time as husband and wife. The happy couple walked down the aisle, smiling, waving, and soaking up the hearty applause of their friends and family.

Mallory and Mosley left the ballroom, as did the rest of the wedding party. For the next thirty minutes, Bria, Lorelei, and I posed with Mallory and Mosley, along with Finn, Owen, and Silvio as the photographers took shot after shot.

Once that was done, we went to the grand ballroom in the center of the country club for the reception. White, blue, and silver ribbons hung from the ceiling, along with those ever-present wedding bells and hearts, while tiny white fairy lights adorned orchid-covered trellises all around the room. Crystal vases full of white and blue orchids perched on the tables, which were covered with pale blue linens. An impressive buffet had been set up along one of the walls, and the tantalizing scent of freshly baked bread curled through the air, along with other delicious aromas.

The wedding guests had already dug into the buffet, and everyone was eating, laughing, talking, and drinking. Mallory and Mosley moved forward and were immediately swarmed by well-wishers. A few minutes later, a swing band started playing, adding even more buoyant cheer to the occasion.

Finn spun Bria around on the dance floor, while Lorelei boogied with Silvio. Owen and I danced for a while too, and then he danced with Sophia while Jo-Jo whirled around with Cooper Stills, her gentleman friend. Roslyn and Xavier also grooved to the music.

Eva Grayson, Violet Fox, and Catalina Vasquez were giggling with Elissa Daniels, another college student, while Jade Jamison, Elissa's older sister, was talking with Dr. Ryan Colson, her significant other, along with Phillip

Kincaid and Warren T. Fox. All our friends were here.

The only thing that dimmed my enjoyment was the bodyguards wandering around the perimeter and Liam Carter, who was standing at the end of the bar, surveying the crowd, a worried frown on his face. Then again, it was his job to be worried, even when everything was going well. I watched him for a few minutes, but nothing changed, so I put my own concerns about Liam out of my mind and focused on the festivities again.

The reception continued into the afternoon, although the crowd and the party finally started to wind down around six o'clock. After eating my fill from the delicious buffet, I slow-danced with Owen.

I sighed with contentment. "This has been one of the best, happiest, most relaxing days I've had in…well, I don't know how long."

"You mean because you haven't been in one cemetery or another, digging up graves?" Owen teased.

"For starters. Seeing you looking so debonair in your tuxedo didn't hurt matters either. Neither did those delicious desserts on the buffet."

Owen arched an eyebrow. "Well, it's good to know I rank higher than desserts on your list of likes and priorities."

I tapped my index finger on my lips, pretending to think about it. "I don't know. Those mini chocolate lava cakes were awfully good. What are you going to do to top that, Grayson?"

Owen spun me around and gave me a wicked grin. "Oh, I can think of a few things. They mostly involve getting you out of that gorgeous dress."

I wrapped my arms around his neck. "Tell me more—"

My words died on my lips, and I stopped dancing right there in the middle of the floor. For a moment, I didn't understand what was wrong. Then I realized that all the stones of the country club were muttering, as though they had been violently startled awake. Even worse, I could feel the impending violence rushing through each and every one of the stones, like a hurricane about to blow us all away.

"Gin?" Owen asked, still holding on to me. "What's wrong?"

I opened my mouth to answer him, maybe even shout out a warning, but I never got the chance.

Gunshots rang out, and people screamed and ducked behind tables and chairs. I whirled out of Owen's arms, reached through the slit in my skirt, and grabbed the knife holstered to my right thigh.

Emery Slater stormed into the ballroom, along with several giants.

✲ 21 ✲

Emery raised her gun and fired more shots into the air, as did the other giants. Most people screamed again and hunkered even farther down behind the tables and chairs. A few frightened folks ran over to the glass doors on the far side of the ballroom and tried to wrench them open, but the doors were locked.

People rushed by Owen and me, the panicked force of them almost pushing us both down to the dance floor. I tightened my grip on my knife, kicked off my silver stilettos, and headed toward Emery.

Owen grabbed my arm. "No! You can't fight them all, Gin!"

"I have to try! Get everyone out of here!" I yelled back at him over the continued screams, shrieks, and shouts.

Someone bumped into us, tearing Owen away from me. He tried to move forward, but the rushing crowd pushed him farther and farther back.

"Gin!" he yelled again. "Gin!"

The panicked guests swept Owen all the way off the

dance floor, and he ended up close to where Lorelei, Mallory, and Mosley were standing.

My head snapped back and forth, and I scanned the ballroom, searching for my other friends. Finn and Bria were over by the bar. Like me, they were trying to head toward the danger instead of away from it. So was Silvio, who was coming up on my right side. Sophia and Jo-Jo were also trying to fight their way through the crowd toward me.

Finally, my gaze landed on Liam Carter, who was standing beside the open ballroom doors, along with several of his bodyguards. Liam was clutching his phone in one hand and his gun in the other, but instead of engaging the wedding crashers, he and his people were clearly standing down.

Anger sizzled in my chest. This time, Liam was here, in the midst of the danger, but he wasn't lifting a finger to help me or anyone else. No matter whose side he was truly on, I had thought him a good enough person not to stand by while others were needlessly hurt. Apparently, I had been wrong. Bitterness washed through my body, churning alongside my anger.

Liam must have sensed my disgusted gaze, because he looked in my direction. He shrugged, as if to say there was nothing he could do.

Well, he might not be willing to do anything, but I sure was.

The giants moved forward, still firing their guns into the air. By this point, everyone had fled from the dance floor, leaving me a clear and open path, and I raced toward the closest giant. He saw me coming and aimed his gun at me, but I snapped up my hand and flung a spray of Ice daggers out at him. The daggers *punch-punch-punched* into his throat and chest, and he toppled to the floor without making a sound.

Crack!

Crack! Crack!

Crack!

The giants kept firing their guns, so I focused on the next-closest one. That man also aimed his weapon at me, but his gun *click-click-clicked* empty, and he had to stop and reload. I closed the distance between us and sliced my knife across his throat. He too dropped to the floor.

I whirled around, searching for the next target, but more giants with guns poured into the ballroom. Emery let out a loud, ear-splitting whistle. The giants stopped shooting, but every single one of them pointed their gun at the crowd. Across the ballroom, Emery stared me down, her meaning crystal clear. Surrender, or watch people die.

I had no choice but to jerk to a stop, my bloody knife still clutched in my hand.

The giants quickly spread out, taking control of the ballroom. People huddled on their hands and knees, their faces shocked and pale, their eyes wide with fear. No one moved, although a few whimpers and soft, muffled sobs rang out.

Mallory, Mosley, and Lorelei were still standing together. Lorelei had positioned herself in front of the dwarven couple, and her fingers were twitching, as though she wanted to unleash her Ice and metal magic against the giants. She looked at me, and I shook my head. Lorelei's lips pressed together, but she could see how badly the odds were stacked against us. We couldn't attack—not without getting a whole lot of innocent people killed.

I glanced around the rest of the ballroom. Owen was close to Lorelei, while Finn was standing by himself, his hand against the small of his back, ready to draw the gun he had hidden there. Bria was next to the bar, her eyes narrowed, her hands curled into tight fists. Just like Lorelei, my sister looked like she wanted to blast the giants with her Ice magic. Anger filled Sophia's and Jo-Jo's faces as well, and they seemed ready to unleash their Air power on the intruders.

Phillip Kincaid was hovering over Eva Grayson, who was huddled on the ground, while Xavier was doing the same thing to Roslyn, and Ryan Colson was shielding Jade Jamison and Elissa Daniels. Warren Fox and Cooper Stills were watching over Violet Fox and Catalina Vasquez, who were crouching behind a table.

A couple of giants stepped forward and aimed their guns at me. I tossed my bloody knife down onto the dance floor, then grabbed the second weapon holstered to my left thigh and threw it down as well.

Once Emery was sure the ballroom was under her control, she moved forward and stopped in front of me. She glanced at the two dead giants on the dance floor, then focused her hazel gaze on me.

"You really should have given Mason what he wanted. Now he's going to kill you in the most painful manner possible." Emery paused, a sly grin spreading across her face. "Actually, forget I said that. I'm going to be quite happy to watch while he crushes your bones and then twists you into more pieces than a bag of pretzels."

I frowned. "What are you talking about? I gave Mason the ledger. What more does he want?"

The giant shook her head. "Don't play dumb with me, Blanco. I don't like it, and neither does your uncle."

For a moment, I thought she was mocking me, but her tone was cold and matter-of-fact. I'd done something to piss off Mason, although I had no idea what.

But it was going to cost me—maybe everything.

Emery waved her gun at me. "Come along quietly, and I'll tell my men to stand down. Otherwise, they'll start shooting, and they won't care who they hit or how many times."

Several horrified gasps rang out, along with more whimpers of fear and choked, muffled sobs. The sounds made my heart squeeze and icy worry shoot through my veins. I didn't care what happened to me, but I couldn't let all these innocent people suffer because of my mistakes.

I glanced around the ballroom at my friends again, but their faces were as grim as mine. Owen, Lorelei, Finn, Bria, Sophia, Jo-Jo. They all knew I didn't have a choice—and exactly what would happen once Mason got his hands on me.

Behind Emery, several more giants streamed into the ballroom, although these men were wearing the blue suits and white-orchid lapel pins that marked them as working for Liam Carter. They too had their guns out and ready.

One of the men whispered something in Liam's ear. He nodded, then walked over to stand beside Emery. Liam's blue gaze locked with mine. Something flickered in his eyes. It almost looked like regret, but the emotion vanished in an instant, replaced by cool, calm confidence. He had made his choice, and now we all had to live—and perhaps die—because of it.

Liam turned to face his new employer. "The perimeter is secure. You're clear to move out with Blanco. No one's going to stop you, and I have your vehicle ready and waiting at the curb."

"You bastard," a low voice hissed.

I glanced to my right. Silvio was the one who'd spoken. The vampire's hands were clenched into fists, and he was glaring at Liam like he wanted to punch the other man in the face—repeatedly.

"You bastard," Silvio hissed again. "You traitor. You're supposed to be on *our* side. Gin *paid* you to be on our side."

Liam shrugged. "And Mason Mitchell offered me a far more lucrative contract. It's just business, Silvy. Nothing more, nothing less."

Silvy? Seemed like Mosley wasn't the only one with a nickname.

An angry flush stained the vampire's cheeks. "Don't you *dare* call me that."

Emery rolled her eyes. "A lover's spat? Now? Really?"

Liam shrugged again. "Unfortunately, things didn't get that far, although not for lack of trying on my part."

He grinned at Silvio, who gave him another murderous glare. The vampire shifted on his feet, and his eyes narrowed, as if he was calculating the distance between the two of them and wondering if he could bury his fangs in Liam's neck before Emery and the other giants shot him.

Liam realized it too. Silvio snarled and charged forward, but Liam coolly snapped up his gun and pulled the trigger.

Crack!

A single shot rang out, and a bullet whizzed by Silvio's ear and blasted into one of the doors on the far side of the ballroom. The glass shattered, making people scream again, although the panicked cries quickly faded away, swallowed up by a tense, uneasy silence.

Silvio flinched and stopped short, although his gray eyes narrowed with even more fury.

Liam smirked at the other man. Then he spun toward me, snapped up his gun again, and pulled the trigger.

Crack!

Another shot rang out. Liam took me by surprise, and I didn't have time to reach for my Stone magic to protect myself. The bullet punched into my upper left arm, making me scream and stagger back. Still, the hot, throbbing sting of the wound was nothing compared to Liam's betrayal. I should have known better than to trust him. Now all those hungry sharks were breaking through the glass walls of the watery tank of worry in my stomach and coming to take a bite out of me, just like Mason would in real life.

"Gin!" Silvio yelled.

He started to rush over to me, but Emery waggled her gun at him.

"Ah-ah-ah. You stay right where you are," she purred.

Murderous rage filled Silvio's face, but he once again stopped short.

I grimaced and looked down at my wound. The bullet had blasted through my arm, a through-and-through, and blood was running down my skin. More blood had spattered onto my bridesmaid dress, and the drops looked like purplish-brown sequins dotting the blue fabric. Still, it could have been worse—so much worse.

My mind whirled, thinking about that, and I raised my gaze to Liam. "You traitor," I snarled. "You're going to pay for that."

Liam kept his gun trained on me. "Shall I shoot her again?" he asked Emery in a bored voice. "Perhaps in the leg?"

"No," Emery replied. "Mason wants her in one piece—more or less. He wants to be the one to punish her."

She gave me a smug grin, then swept out her hand to the side. "Move, Blanco. Now. Or my men start shooting."

Once again, I looked at my friends. Owen, Finn, Silvio, Sophia, Jo-Jo. Mallory, Mosley, Lorelei. Everyone else.

Finally, I focused on Bria. Her lips trembled, and tears gleamed in her blue eyes. My baby sister knew better than anyone what sort of gruesome fate awaited me at Uncle Mason's hands.

I shook my head, silently telling her not to risk coming after me, but her nostrils flared, and her mouth flattened out into a hard, thin line. She wasn't going to listen. Owen and Finn also had similar mulish expressions. Like it or not, they were going to try to track me down. My heart squeezed tight with worry, but all I could do was hope that Bria and the others could somehow survive whatever confrontation they might have with Mason.

Because I probably wasn't going to.

"Move," Emery commanded.

Even though it broke my heart, I turned away from my friends and shuffled out of the ballroom.

✲ 22 ✲

A couple of giants led the way, with Emery behind me and the rest of her men flanking us, their guns up and ready to shoot. In the distance, I heard Liam Carter's voice drift out of the ballroom.

"We're going to lock the doors. If anyone attempts to come after us, a couple of very nasty rune bombs will explode," he called out. "Trust me when I say that you don't want to be the one who tries to open these doors."

More shocked gasps and soft sobs rang out, but I pushed them out of my mind and focused on what I needed to do. I might have a couple of holes in my left arm, but now that we were away from everyone else, maybe I could at least kill Emery before the rest of her men either shot or beat me to death. I'd much rather go down fighting here than let Mason torture me.

We were quickly approaching the front entrance, and I reached for my Ice magic. As soon as we walked through the doors, I was going to shatter the glass with my Ice power, then turn around and blast my enemies with every bit of magic I had—

We passed a mirror on the wall. Out of the corner of my eye, I noticed Emery flexing her fingers. I reached for my Stone magic and whirled around, but I was too slow. I didn't harden my skin in time, and the giant's fist plowed straight into my face, just as it had done that day outside the Posh boutique.

White stars exploded in my eyes, my head snapped back, and I hit the floor. I tried to grab hold of my Stone magic to protect myself from further assault, but my face and head were pounding, and I couldn't quite get a grip on it.

Emery loomed over me. "I've been wanting to squash you for a long time now, Spider. Looks like I'm finally getting my chance."

She drew back her foot and kicked me in the face. More white stars exploded in my eyes, but they almost instantly turned to black.

Lights out.

"I didn't realize y'all were going out tonight," a soft feminine voice drawled.

Fletcher shrugged. "It was a last-minute thing."

I snorted. That was an understatement.

Jo-Jo heard the derisive sound and glanced over at me, her eyebrows raised in curiosity, but I shrugged back.

An hour ago, Fletcher and I had been running for our lives through the woods behind Wade Brockton's house, but we had escaped, gotten into my car, and driven over to Jo-Jo's house.

The dwarf had already healed my cuts, bumps, and bruises, and she was now sitting next to Fletcher, who was lying in one of the cherry-red salon chairs. Jo-Jo reached for her Air magic and moved her hand back and forth over Fletcher's face, using her power to stitch the Tin Man back together again. The sharp, pricking feel of her Air magic made me shift in my chair, but it didn't bother me as much as usual. Maybe that was because everything seemed small and insignificant compared to how close I'd come to losing Fletcher.

A few minutes later, Jo-Jo healed the last of Fletcher's injuries. She dropped her hand and released her magic. "There you go, darling. Good as new."

He nodded. "Thanks, Jo-Jo."

She smiled at him, then looked over at me. She must have seen the worry in my grim face and the questions in my eyes, because her eyebrows rose again. I didn't say anything. Neither did Fletcher.

Jo-Jo cleared her throat and got to her feet. "I'm going to get cleaned up. Then I'll make some chicory coffee for you, Fletcher, and some hot chocolate for Gin."

She left the salon, and the wooden steps creaked as she headed upstairs. A few seconds later, a door shut, and water started running in one of the bathrooms.

"That was a close call tonight, eh?" Fletcher finally said.

I crossed my arms over my chest. "Are you going to tell me who those giants work for? And why their boss wanted you dead? After he had you tortured for information?"

Fletcher shook his head. "You're better off not knowing. Trust me on that."

"Trust you?" I gave him a disgusted look. "I did *trust you. Right up until you left the Pork Pit to assassinate a man who was just trying to save his sick daughter. A man who is now* dead, *apparently due to you and your machinations."*

I gave him another disgusted look, then stormed out of the salon. I thought about stomping upstairs, but Sophia was asleep in her bedroom, and I didn't want to wake her. So I settled for striding down the hallway and going out onto the front porch. I really, really, really *wanted to slam the front door behind me to let out some of my anger, but I closed it softly instead. Just because I was pissed off was no reason to damage Jo-Jo's door.*

She wasn't the one who had lied to me.

It was a bitterly cold night, but I was still so angry that the chill didn't bother me. I paced back and forth, my boots snapping against the wooden boards—

Creak.

The loud screech made me grimace. I'd forgotten about the old creaky board at the top of the porch steps. If my quick, steady pacing hadn't woken Sophia, then that probably had. But there was nothing I could do about it now, so I sighed, sat down on the steps, and leaned my shoulder against the railing.

A few seconds later, the front door eased open, and Fletcher crossed the porch. He too stepped on that creaky board and grimaced at the loud noise it made.

"I keep meaning to fix that," he said, sitting down across from me on the steps.

I didn't respond. Fletcher sighed and leaned his shoulder against the opposite side of the porch railing.

"It's a long, sad story, but here's the gist of it. I got involved with some folks who weren't who I thought they were," he said in a low, tired voice. "I did a lot of jobs for this one guy over the years. Some of them were good jobs, and I took out a lot of nasty folks who had hurt other people."

Despite my anger, I couldn't help but ask the obvious question. "But?"

Fletcher sighed again, and his entire body sagged. "But I slowly realized the man I was working for was the worst of the worst. He manipulated me for a long time. Telling me all the lies I wanted to hear."

I frowned, wondering who could have hoodwinked Fletcher so thoroughly, but I didn't have any room to judge. Not too long ago, I had killed an innocent man named Cesar Vaughn because his son, Sebastian, had tricked me into believing that Cesar had been abusing his daughter, Charlotte.

"You made a mistake," I said in a calmer, kinder voice. "It happens."

Fletcher nodded, but his mouth still twisted with disgust. "Yeah. But I was hurt and angry and arrogant, and I never thought this sort of thing could happen to me*. That* I *could be so completely, utterly* fooled*."*

His head dropped, and he tucked his chin to his chest, like a turtle trying to pull the vulnerable part of itself back into its shell.

"So you worked for this horrible mystery man," I said. "How does the accountant fit in?"

"I told you the truth. Wade Brockton needed money for his daughter's medical care, so he started embezzling from this man we both worked for. A few months ago, I caught wind of what Wade was doing. I should have told him right then and there to knock it off, to return as much of the money as he could, leave town, and never come back."

"But?"

Fletcher sighed again. "But I didn't. Instead, I saw Wade's stealing as an opportunity to finally free myself from this other man, to make him leave me alone once and for all."

"What happened?"

He let out a breath, as if he was steeling himself for his next confession. "I asked Wade to embezzle more money—a whole lot more money. I wanted to take away as much of it as I could from my enemy. But I got greedy, other people noticed the theft, and it ended up costing Wade his life. Now his daughter has to grow up without her father. I'll never *forgive myself for that."*

Sympathy filled me, and I reached over and grabbed his hand. "You made a mistake, just like I did with Sebastian Vaughn."

"I know." Fletcher fell silent for a moment, then fixed his green gaze on me. "But we're the kind of people who can't afford to make mistakes, Gin. If nothing else good comes from this, then remember that. We might not be richer or stronger than our enemies, so we have to be smarter, *and we have to fight smarter. Otherwise, good people get* hurt, *good people* die."

He kept his gaze steady on mine and squeezed my hand, his wrinkled fingers warming my own.

I nodded, telling him that I understood and would take his words, his warning, to heart. "But what about the mystery man? The one you tried to kill tonight?"

Fletcher shook his head. "Don't worry about him, Gin. Thanks to Wade, I have a plan that will finally get rid of this man. He's never going to bother me again." The old man's mouth twisted. "It will cost the bastard too much if he does."

His cryptic words puzzled me, but I didn't ask Fletcher about his plan. I doubted he would tell me, since he hadn't even said the mystery man's name. Once again, I wondered exactly who this man was, but that seemed to be a secret Fletcher was determined to keep.

The old man gently tugged his hand out of mine. He

chewed on his lip, thinking, then plucked a silverstone knife out of his boot. Fletcher stabbed the point of the knife into the wood in the corner of the creaky board we were still sitting on.

"What are you doing?" I asked.

"Leaving you a reminder," he murmured, dragging the knife through the wood.

He quickly finished with the blade, then brushed away the wood chips. I leaned forward and squinted at the symbol he'd carved into the board—a small circle surrounded by eight thin rays.

My spider rune.

I traced my fingers over the symbol, the rough edges of the wood pricking my skin. "Why my spider rune?"

Fletcher looked at me, his face serious. "So you'll never forget what we talked about. So if you're ever feeling unsure of yourself or something you're about to do, you can sit down, look at this rune, and remember this night." He hesitated. "And if something ever happens to me, then you can come here and remember old Fletcher."

*"*Nothing *is going to happen to you," I said in a fierce voice. "Not even if I have to kill this mystery man myself."*

Fletcher smiled a little at my poison promise, then shook his head. "Don't worry about me, Gin. I have a nasty habit of surviving. Besides, someone is helping me. Someone who hates this man just as much as I do."

Fletcher was working with someone else? Who? And why did they hate the mystery man?

He stared at me, his green gaze steady on mine. "Promise me that you'll remember what we talked about. Promise me that you won't make the same mistakes I did. That you'll always try to fight smarter than your enemies."

"I promise," I whispered.

The winter wind whistled across the porch, tearing my words away, although I could still hear their faint echoes in my mind.

Fletcher nodded. "Good. Now, let's go inside and get some of Jo-Jo's chicory coffee and hot chocolate. My old bones could really use it tonight."

We both got to our feet. I went over to the front door, then stopped and glanced back over my shoulder. Fletcher was still standing by the porch steps, staring down at my spider rune carved into the wood.

"Something wrong?" I asked.

He looked up at me and smiled again. "Nah."

Fletcher stepped away from the creaky board, and we headed into the house together...

For a moment, I could have sworn that I heard the old man's footsteps on the porch. Then the sound came again, and again, and again. I was definitely hearing footsteps, only they weren't Fletcher's quick, light tread. No, these footsteps were much louder and heavier...like they belonged to Emery Slater and her men.

I jerked the rest of the way awake. Two giants were clutching my arms and carrying me between them like a sack of potatoes. Emery was walking in front of us, with more giants plodding along behind us.

The constant shifting of my body between the two giants made my head ache and more white stars explode in my eyes. My wounded arm also throbbed at the motions, but I pushed the pain away, ignored the stars, and glanced around, trying to figure out where we were.

Wide, spacious rooms, antique furniture, pretty plaster lining the ceilings. My stomach twisted. We were in the Mitchell family mansion.

We approached a staircase. I expected the giants to haul

me up to Mason's study, but they walked by the steps. My stomach twisted a little more. I knew where we were headed.

Eventually, Emery stepped through a door, and we trooped outside onto the large stone terrace at the back of the mansion. She held up her fist, calling a halt.

The giants set me down on my feet, and I yanked out of their grasp. Those two men stepped back and drew their guns, as did all the others. I looked from one face to another, but I didn't recognize any of the men, and every giant wore a black suit. These were Emery's goons. None of Liam Carter's people were here.

"Your uncle wants to see you," Emery purred, drawing her own gun. "Now, come along, and don't do anything stupid, or my men will shoot you."

I didn't have a choice, so I shuffled forward. Emery led me across the lawn, through the woods, and over to the Circle family cemetery. My stomach twisted for a third time. Of course, Mason would bring me here so he could kill me, just like he had killed my father.

I wasn't sure how long I'd been unconscious or what time it was, but the sun had set, and the cold night had already taken hold of the landscape. Darkness cloaked the surrounding woods, but the wrought-iron torches planted at the corners of the pavilion were all lit, like fireflies suspended in glass globes. The soft golden glows made the tops of the tombstones and crosses glimmer, even as they cast the rest of the markers in deep shadows.

More giants with guns ringed the front half of the cemetery. Liam Carter was also here, with Hugh Tucker standing next to him. My gaze flicked past them. Mason was deeper in the cemetery, standing in front of the pavilion, his back turned to me.

Emery waved her hand, telling me to walk over to Mason, so I did. She followed me, as did Liam and Tucker and several of the giants. Emery and Liam moved so they were standing off to the side, but Tucker strode up and stopped right next to my uncle.

My face, head, and arm were still pounding, but I ruthlessly pushed the pain away again and reached for my Stone magic, making sure I had a good, solid grip on it.

Mason stared at his sick shrine a moment longer, then faced me. "I was just admiring your father's tomb. I've always loved how the gray stone glows at night, almost like a moon."

"Why did you bring me here?" I growled. "What do you want now?"

He shrugged. "I want what I've always wanted, Gin. The ledger."

I frowned. "But I gave you the ledger yesterday at the Pork Pit."

Mason sighed and shook his head. "You're even more like your father than I thought. Nothing but lies ever comes out of your lips."

My frown deepened. I truly had no idea what he was talking about. Mason snapped his fingers, and Tucker stepped a little closer to him. I hadn't noticed it before, but Tucker was holding the black ledger. He handed the book to Mason, who waggled it at me.

"This is the ledger you gave me, the one you claim to have found in this cemetery."

I opened my mouth, but he didn't let me speak. Instead, he gave me a disgusted look and tossed the book onto the ground at my feet.

"What a clever little liar you are, Gin," Mason said. "You really had me going. For a few hours last night, I truly believed that you had found the ledger here, that Fletcher had hidden it right under my nose all these years. But of course, I know that's a lie now."

I opened my mouth to ask what he was talking about, but once again, he didn't let me speak.

"But that's not the worst mistake you made," Mason snarled. "That's not the error that's going to cost you your life. No, the worst mistake you made was giving me a *fake*."

✲ 23 ✲

For a moment, I didn't understand what Mason was saying, but then his words hit my mind like the proverbial ton of bricks. I rocked back on my heels.

A fake? The ledger was a *fake*?

For another moment, I thought Mason was playing some weird game, but his dark, murderous expression told me that he wasn't lying. A sick, sick feeling flooded my stomach, and I couldn't help but think about all the time and effort I had spent worrying about the ledger over the past few days. All of that had been for *nothing*.

No wonder my uncle wanted me dead. I would have gleefully murdered me too.

And I couldn't help but curse myself as well. Given the two fake blue ledgers that had been floating around the Eaton Estate a few weeks ago, I should have considered the possibility that this black book might also be a phony, a decoy. But my own oversight and Mason's wrath didn't stop the inevitable question from popping into my mind: if this ledger was a fake, then where was the real one?

I shook my head. "I'm telling you the truth. Fletcher hid

that ledger in *this* cemetery. If it's a fake, then I don't know anything about it. I barely even had a chance to look at it, remember? You made me give you the ledger almost immediately after I found it."

"Oh, stop lying, Gin," Mason snapped. "Somehow you found out what was in the ledger, and you had one of your friends, probably Mr. Lane, concoct a clever fake. It almost fooled me. You should congratulate yourself on that."

"I didn't give you a fake. At least, not on purpose." I stabbed my finger at Tucker. "He was here. He saw me take the ledger from the cemetery. He tried to stop me."

Mason looked at Tucker, who shrugged. The vampire wasn't going to speak up, not even to confirm my story, not now when it really mattered. I shot him a disgusted look. Tucker's lips pinched together, but he kept quiet. Still, the longer I looked at him, the more I thought about what had happened between us here yesterday.

Tucker had tried to stop me from taking the ledger. I had expected that. But he had claimed that I was making a mistake and that he was trying to save me from myself. Why would he say those things unless…

He had *known* the ledger was a fake.

My mind spun around, but more and more thoughts sprang up next to that first one, like weeds growing in a field. The only way Tucker could have realized the ledger was a fake was if he had known *exactly* what it contained. But how could he? He hadn't looked in the ledger yesterday, so he must have seen the volume sometime in the past.

And the only way—*the only way*—for Tucker to have looked at the ledger before it was buried in his grave was if Fletcher had shown it to him.

Fletcher had been working with Hugh Tucker.

The idea boggled my already thoroughly boggled mind, but the more I thought about it, the more sense it made. During our talk on Jo-Jo's porch, Fletcher had said he was working with someone who hated Mason just as much as he did. He *had* to have been talking about Hugh Tucker.

After all, the vampire had loved my mother and tried to save her from Mab, and he'd told me more than once that everyone in the Circle saw him as nothing more than a guard dog that carried out Mason's orders. Sure, Tucker had tried to kill me, but he'd spent far more time helping than hindering me over the past few months.

I'd always thought Tucker had been playing his own game with both me and my uncle, and now I knew exactly what it was. He'd tried to help Fletcher take down Mason, but the two of them had only managed to get some of Mason's money, instead of killing him outright. Then, for whatever reason, Fletcher and Tucker had made a fake ledger and buried it here in the Circle cemetery.

I wondered why Fletcher had drawn the ring-of-swords rune on Tristan's tombstone pointing me to the fake ledger's location. Maybe he'd thought I could use the book to somehow trick Mason.

Either way, Tucker had been too much of a coward to help me finish the job he and Fletcher had started all those years ago. Instead of telling me the truth, Tucker had let me flounder around for *months*, as well as search high and low for a ledger that was probably lost forever. Now Mallory and Mosley's reception had been ruined, my friends had been put in danger again, and I was going to face my uncle's wrath. All because of Tucker's lies.

Anger sizzled through me with the heat of a thousand suns. I had never wanted to murder the vampire more than at this moment.

Tucker must have seen the realization and the rage dawn in my eyes, because he shifted on his feet, suddenly uncomfortable. He probably expected me to start shouting accusations, but I kept my mouth shut. If Mason knew the true depths of Tucker's betrayal, he would kill the vampire in an instant. Tucker wasn't getting off that easy. Oh, no. Let the duplicitous bastard live with the guilt of my death just like he had lived with my mother's death all this time. Maybe that would finally prompt him to act against Mason, although I doubted it. Fucking coward.

I glared at Tucker a moment longer, then focused on Mason again. "I didn't know the ledger was a fake. I thought it was the real deal and that Fletcher was being clever by burying it in your own backyard, so to speak."

"You actually seem to be telling the truth for a change. Good for you, Gin." Mason paused. "But it's not going to save you."

"If you think I gave you a fake because I know where the real ledger is, then you're wrong." I gestured out at the cemetery. "This was my last option, the last place I thought it might be. If that ledger is a fake, then the real one is gone for good, because I don't know where else to look."

He tilted his head to the side, staring at me as though I were, well, a spider he was contemplating crushing under the toe of his shiny black wing tip. "I really do think you're telling the truth." His face hardened. "But it's still not going to save you."

Magic erupted in his eyes, making them burn a bright, eerie gray. Mason snapped up his hand, and the tombstone closest to me exploded into a hundred pieces.

✲

Even though I had been expecting the attack, even though I used my own Stone magic to harden my skin, Mason's power still cut right through mine like a knife tearing through a tissue. He didn't just shatter the marker—he also grabbed hold of the broken bits and chunks of stone and hurled them at me.

The shards and shrapnel slammed into my body one after another. I grunted with pain and tried to push back with my own magic, tried to stop—or at least redirect—the bits and chunks of stone, but it was no use. Mason was so strong in his power that the busted rocks *punch-punch-punched* into my body one after another.

Finally, it stopped.

I swayed on my bare feet, my dress torn, my skin cut, bruised, and bleeding. Sweat poured down my face, and pain radiated out through every single part of my body. Mason had only used a small fraction of his power, but I felt like he'd just dropped a house on me.

And it was only going to get worse—so much *worse*.

Mason tilted his head to the side again, studying me even more dispassionately than before. "And to think that Mab was actually *afraid* of you. That *you* actually managed to kill *her*." He shook his head. "I always suspected she was a weak, silly fool."

He waved his hand again, and the next tombstone over—Mab's, ironically enough—exploded. Once again, he pummeled me with the resulting chunks and shards, despite my protecting myself with my Stone magic.

And that was just the beginning.

Mason shattered tombstone after tombstone, then used his power to throw the resulting rubble at me. One by one, all those sharp corners and broken edges plowed into my body, opening up deep cuts and making bruises bloom. In less than a minute, I was a bloody, tattered mess, and my Stone magic was the only thing keeping the rocky rubble from completely crushing my bones.

It wasn't just that Mason was stronger than me—he was also incredibly skilled in his power. He waved his hands up and down and back and forth, directing the bits of stone through the air like a maestro conducting an orchestra. Only instead of music, the resulting notes were the sharp shrieks of pain that spewed out of my lips.

I'd suspected this would happen, had been dreading, fearing, and worrying about it for days, ever since I'd seen my father's autopsy photos. But now that the moment was finally here, the sharp, certain realization shredded my heart just like the stones were shredding my body.

My uncle *was* going to kill me—and there was nothing I could do to stop him.

Through the hazy clouds of granite and marble dust that filled the air, I looked at the people gathered around to witness my slow execution. The giants wore bored expressions, as though they had seen their boss do this sort of thing many times before. They probably had. Emery was grinning widely with smug glee, as though she was watching a football game and her favorite team was absolutely destroying its hated archrivals. Liam was chewing on his lip, and he kept glancing back and forth between Mason and me.

And then there was Hugh Tucker.

The vampire looked from me to Mason and back again. A muscle ticked in his jaw, and his hands were clenched into fists. Even though he had tried to kill me himself, Tucker didn't like watching Mason literally stoning me to death. It must have reminded him of what Mason had done to Tristan. Or maybe Tucker was thinking about how Mab had burned my mother to death. Whatever thoughts were running through his mind, for once, the vampire's blank mask had fallen away, and he actually looked sick to his stomach, as though he might vomit.

The latest onslaught of stone stopped, and the cemetery was utterly, eerily quiet.

Somehow I was still standing, but just barely, and I'd pretty much exhausted my Stone magic. All I had left was my own natural Ice power, including the reserves stored in my spider-rune pendant and the matching ring on my finger. But I didn't know what good my Ice magic would do me. Mason wasn't going to let me get close enough to stab him with an Ice knife. Even if I did, he could simply harden his skin and block the attack.

Mason stared at me, his lips puckered in thought. "Perhaps you are a bit tougher than I gave you credit for, Gin. Tristan was already screaming and blubbering by this point. You could start begging me for your life like he did. I might be a little more lenient to you, since you didn't betray me nearly as badly as your father did."

It took me a moment to get my breath back enough to answer him. "You might…make me…scream. You might…pummel me…to dust. But I…will…*never*…beg for anything…from you…you blackhearted son of a bitch."

Mason shrugged, then lifted his hand again. "Suit yourself. Either way, you'll still be dead, Genevieve—"

"Enough," a harsh voice snarled. "*That's enough.*"

For a moment, I thought I'd only imagined the voice, but then Mason turned to his right, and I realized who had spoken.

Hugh Tucker.

Mason regarded the other man with a cold expression. "It's only enough when *I* say it's enough. Remember your place, Hugh."

Instead of being frightened, Tucker let out a low, ugly laugh, with years of pent-up anger rippling through that one harsh note. "Remember my place? You never let me *forget* my fucking place. Not for one moment ever since we were kids. It's one of the reasons I despise you so much."

Mason returned Tucker's laugh with an equally harsh one of his own. "Do you really think I'm an idiot? That I don't know how much you hate me? I *enjoy* your scorn. It's as sad, pathetic, and impotent as you are. You're like a whipped dog, Hugh. No matter what I do, you always come back to me."

Tucker shook his head. "You might have been right about that in the past but not now. I'm sick of you and your games and especially your cruelty. You could have banished Tristan from Ashland all those years ago, but you didn't. Instead, you killed your own brother. And not because he betrayed you, not because he tried to oust you from the Circle, but because you're a weak, insecure, jealous son of a bitch. A sadistic bastard who enjoys making people fear him."

Mason didn't respond, but a muscle ticked in his jaw. Tucker's sharp words were hitting him as hard as those stones had punched into me.

"Tristan might have been your twin, but everyone knew *he* was the better man, the stronger man in every way that really matters," Tucker continued. "People actually *liked* Tristan and *wanted* to follow his leadership. Not because he made them afraid like you did but simply because he respected them. And that infuriated you to no end."

Mason's eyes glittered with a cold light. "You are dangerously close to making me forget how useful you can be, Hugh. And how much I enjoy torturing you."

Tucker stared the other man down, his black eyes just as

cold as Mason's. Tension filled the cemetery, and everyone looked back and forth between them. Liam and the giants stayed frozen in place, but Emery sidled forward, putting herself in the open space between the two men, ready to defend Mason if it came down to that.

But it didn't.

After several long seconds, Tucker bowed his head, capitulating once again to Mason. Disappointment washed through me, along with more than a little bitterness. For one brief, fleeting moment, I'd thought that Tucker might actually do the right thing and try to make up for some of the wrongs he'd done to me and my family. That he might break away from Mason and finally be his own man. But once again, the vampire had chosen his own survival above everything else, even his own dignity. Fucking coward.

Tucker must have seen the disgust on my face, because he flinched and looked away from me.

"And now, Gin, it's time for you to join your parents," Mason purred. "Don't worry. I'm sure there's enough space in my pavilion for your tomb. I'll put it right next to Tristan's. That way, you and your traitorous father can finally be reunited."

He waved his hands again, and more and more tombstones exploded, the shrapnel flying through the air, punching into my body, and slowly shredding me to pieces. I staggered back and forth like a ship listing in a storm, trying to avoid the worst of the flying rubble, but I couldn't. I also couldn't push away the pain any longer, and more hoarse screams spewed out of my lips.

Through the clouds of dust, I could see Mason smiling, Emery too, but Tucker had a different reaction. He dropped his head and turned around as though he couldn't bear to watch my death. Emery smirked at him, then stepped forward so she would have a better view of my execution.

And that's when Tucker finally struck.

Quick as a blink, he closed the distance between himself and Emery, wrested the gun out of her hand, whipped around, and shot Mason in the back with it.

Crack!

The sound of the shot booming out was even louder than the rubble still pummeling me, but Mason didn't fall. My uncle had more than enough Stone magic to harden his skin and pummel me at the same time.

Mason turned to the side and let out a low laugh. "Please. I always watch my back whenever you're around, Hugh. Now that you've finally shown your true insolence, I'm going to make you watch Gin die before I kill you."

Tucker's shot might not have killed Mason, but it had distracted him, and some of the rubble landed at my feet instead of punching into my body. I staggered to the side, once again trying to catch my breath.

We might not be richer or stronger than our enemies, so we have to be smarter, *and we have to fight smarter.*

Fletcher's voice whispered in my mind. I wasn't sure why the thought popped into my head. Maybe because he had been talking about Mason that night on Jo-Jo's porch, and Mason was slowly stoning me to death. Despite the pain pounding through my body, I forced myself to think about Fletcher's words. My Stone magic hadn't worked against Mason, hadn't fazed him at all, but I still had my Ice power. But how could I use it to save myself?

Another bit of rubble flew at me, propelled by the last lingering traces of Mason's magic. Instead of trying to deflect it with my Stone power like I had the other pieces, I coated this chunk with my Ice magic instead. The second the cold crystals covered the rock, it dropped harmlessly to the ground.

My eyes widened, wondering if it was a fluke, but I covered another incoming bit of shrapnel with my Ice, and it too dropped harmlessly to the ground. And I realized something important, something I should have known all along.

Mason had to be able to actually *feel* the tombstones in order to use them against me.

An idea took root in my mind, and my gaze darted around, searching for a place where I could test out my theory and make my last stand. The cemetery was far too open. I needed someplace more secure, more enclosed, more like…

The pavilion.

Everyone was still staring at Tucker, who had his stolen gun aimed at Mason's head. No one was paying attention to me, so I gritted my teeth, ignored the pain shooting through my body, and sprinted toward the pavilion. Out of the corner of my eye, I saw two giants snap up their guns.

"No! Don't shoot!" Mason yelled. "She's mine!"

I kept running. Behind me, I could feel Mason reaching for even more of his magic, more power than he had used so far. He was going to toss another tombstone at me—or worse.

Someone—Tucker, I think—let out a vicious curse, and several more gunshots rang out. I cringed, but no bullets slammed into my back, so I kept going, my gaze focused on the pavilion. I was thirty feet away.

Twenty feet. Ten. Five, four, three, two, one…

Even though every single muscle in my body protested, I leaped up the steps. Behind me, I could sense the cold, hard strength of Mason's power rolling this way. I stepped under the pavilion roof, then whirled around and reached for my Ice magic, hoping that my desperate gambit would work.

Yes, the pavilion was made of stone, but maybe I could crouch down behind my father's tomb, cover it with my Ice magic, and use it to block and shield myself from Mason's power long enough for me to run out the far side of the pavilion and escape into the woods beyond.

I started backing toward the tomb even as I kept an eye on my enemies. I didn't know if I could save myself, but I might delay my death—at least until my Ice magic ran out.

Liam, Emery, and the giants were hunkered down behind a couple of intact tombstones, as was Tucker. The vampire rose up to fire off another shot at Emery, but his stolen gun made a small, empty *click.* Tucker cursed and tossed the weapon away.

Mason didn't care about the battle raging off to the side. He stalked through the grass toward the pavilion, his magic crackling through his eyes like streaks of gray lightning. "You're not getting away that easily," he hissed.

Tucker's head snapped around, and his mouth set into a hard, determined line. He surged to his feet and started running toward Mason, moving faster than I had ever seen him move before.

In the distance, Emery cursed. "Mason! Behind you!"

But my uncle was completely focused on killing me. He waved his hand again, and the tombstone closest to the pavilion exploded, the pieces zipping through the air toward me. This stone was larger and heavier than the others, and if it hit me, it would almost certainly kill me outright. I reached for even more of my Ice magic to try to block the attack.

Tucker reached Mason. But instead of tackling the other man, the vampire ran right past my uncle, his black gaze locked on me.

"Gin! Watch out!" Tucker yelled.

Then, at the last possible moment, right before the shattered stones would have hit me, Tucker leaped into the pavilion, darted in front of the projectiles, and wrapped his arms around me, shielding me with his body.

Thwack-thwack-thwack.

The stone shrapnel hit his back and tore into his body with loud, wet, sickening sounds.

Tucker screamed with pain, but he churned his legs, shoving us both deeper into the pavilion. I hit the ground hard and slid back a few feet, with Tucker sprawled on top of me.

"Use your…Ice magic," he rasped in a weak voice. "Don't try to fight…his power. Block it instead…"

Tucker's voice trailed off, and his body went slack and still on top of mine. I hesitated, torn about what to do, but I slapped my hands down onto the vampire's back and sent out a blast of Ice magic, freezing his gruesome wounds. Tucker didn't even scream at the brutal assault, telling me what bad shape he was in. But I'd done all I could for him right now, so I craned my neck to the side.

In the distance, outside the pavilion, Mason raised his hand again. My uncle grinned at me, and another wave of Stone magic started to roll off him—

Crack!

Another shot rang out. For a second, I thought Emery, Liam, or one of the giants was firing at Tucker and me, but Mason grunted and spun away from me.

Crack!

Crack! Crack!

Crack! Crack! Crack!

More and more shots rang out, this time targeting Emery and the giants. My friends were here. They had found me, and they were trying to take down Mason.

My uncle raised his hand, probably to shatter more tombstones and send the shards shooting out at my friends, but Liam darted forward and grabbed his arm.

"There are too many of them! We need to get out of here!" Liam screamed.

He yanked Mason back while Emery and the giants hunkered down behind the remaining tombstones and fired at my friends. Mason wrenched away from Liam and whirled back around to me. His gray eyes burned with hate, and his magic swirled around him like an invisible storm.

Mason snapped up his hands and unleashed his power. This time, instead of targeting another tombstone, he focused his magic on the pavilion, and once again, there was nothing I could do to stop him.

With a thunderous roar, the stone roof over my head shattered into a thousand pieces.

☼ 24 ☼

The pavilion roof started to fall, but my gaze darted back to Mason. A satisfied sneer twisted his face, and he lifted his hand again, probably to turn the chunky rubble into stone daggers raining down on me. But Liam grabbed my uncle's arm again, spoiling his aim, and the invisible wave of his magic shot harmlessly through the center of the pavilion.

Liam yanked Mason out of my line of sight, but Bria, Finn, and Owen appeared in the cemetery in the distance. With one hand, Bria unloaded her gun at Emery and the other giants. With her other hand, she flung out spray after spray of Ice daggers at them. Finn was clutching guns in both hands, coolly dropping giant after giant, while Owen was swinging his blacksmith hammer at anyone who got in his way, slowly but surely moving closer to me.

But they weren't going to reach me in time.

"Gin!" Bria screamed. "Get out of there!"

But there was no time for that either, not with Tucker still lying on top of me, his back and most of his body stiff and frozen from my Ice magic. So I raised my arms straight up, with my palms facing the collapsing ceiling, and reached for my Ice magic, pulling every last scrap of it out of my body, along with the reserves stored in my spider-rune jewelry. I sent all that cold power spewing up and out of my hands and then down to the floor, creating a lopsided dome that arched over me and Tucker.

The first chunk of rubble hit my Ice dome and almost punched it to pieces, but I gritted my teeth and shoved even more magic into the shape, making it as thick and hard as possible. But the rubble was too large and heavy, and my Ice wasn't strong enough to hold it all back. It was just a matter of time before I ran out of power and the stones smashed through the Ice and flattened me and Tucker like pancakes.

Smack!

Smack! Smack!

Smack! Smack! Smack!

Chunk after chunk of rubble dropped down from the shattered ceiling and slammed into my barrier. Through the silvery sheen of Ice, I could see the dark pieces of stone hammering at my protective dome like broken fists. But I couldn't stop the rubble. I could barely protect myself right now.

I could already feel myself weakening as I used up the natural magic in my body, and soon I would exhaust the reserves in my spider-rune pendant and ring too. Once that happened, the rubble would quickly punch through my Ice and crash down into my body.

And then I would die.

I sent out another wave of Ice magic, using up what was left in my body. A second wave drained the power out of my ring. And a third and final wave exhausted what was left in my spider-rune pendant.

Smack!

Smack! Smack!

Smack! Smack! Smack!

The rubble kept hitting my dome, and a tiny crack appeared in the Ice above my head. Then a second crack. Then a third. Then a dozen, all at once. The dome dipped, and I held my breath, knowing that I was about to be crushed to death—

At the last instant, right before the dome would have collapsed under the force and weight of the falling rubble, another wave of magic zipped through the elemental Ice, filling in all the jagged cracks. The magic kept coming and coming, and the Ice kept growing and growing, becoming thicker and harder, turning my pitiful dome into a much larger, stronger barrier.

"Bria," I rasped in relief, although she couldn't hear me.

My sister kept feeding her magic into the Ice dome. I was out of power, so all I could do was lie there and watch.

I don't know how much time passed. A minute, maybe two. But the last of the ruined roof fell, and the final bits and chunks of rubble slammed into the top of the Ice dome.

By this point, so many broken stones covered the dome that they blocked the light, leaving me in complete darkness. All I could do was lie there, with Tucker's body still draped over mine. My arms and legs trembled from exertion, exhaustion, and adrenaline, and sweat dripped off my face. The salty moisture added to the sharp sting of the dozens and dozens of cuts that crisscrossed my body.

I must have blacked out for a minute. The next thing I knew, light had returned to my world, and a man was peering at me through the Ice. His features were distorted, as though I was staring at him in some weird fun-house mirror, but my heart still lifted at the sight.

"Owen," I croaked.

I didn't think he heard me, but I could have sworn his eyes widened.

"She's alive!" Owen yelled. "Finn! Silvio! Sophia! Help me!"

More voices sounded, and everyone started yelling and shouting, although the Ice dome muffled their words, and I couldn't tell what they were saying. Several *scrape-scrape-scrapes* rang out, as though my friends were dragging chunks of rubble off the dome. Then, a few seconds later, Owen's face appeared on the other side of the Ice again.

"Gin!" he yelled. "Cover your head! I'm going to use my hammer to get you out!"

Somehow, despite my exhausted muscles and still-trembling body, I found the strength to cross my arms over my face.

Crack!

Crack! Crack!

Crack!

Owen hit the Ice over and over again with his blacksmith hammer, and cold chunks of the dome started to rain down on me, just like the roof rubble had.

CRACK!

The dome shattered with a loud roar. In an instant, I was covered in elemental Ice, as though I were taking a bath in the crystallized chunks. The cold was another shock to my system, and the heavy weight made it hard to breathe. I kept my arms over my face, trying to suck down as much air as I could.

More shouts rang out, and I could feel pieces of Ice being lifted up and off my body. My breathing became easier, although the cold had seeped into my bones, making me shiver. A few seconds later, the Ice was removed from around my head. I let my arms fall to my sides and sucked down breath after breath, not quite believing I was still alive.

Owen's face appeared above mine again. "Gin!"

I tried to tell him that I was okay, but it just felt so good to breathe that I couldn't manage it.

Owen dropped to his knees in the rubble, clawing through the Ice and shoving it off me as fast as he could. Beside him, Finn, Silvio, and Sophia did the same.

My friends made quick work of the Ice, and Owen leaned over and cupped my face in his hands. His skin was cold, and his fingers were bleeding from where the Ice and stones had cut his skin.

"Gin?" he whispered. "Are you okay?"

"Still alive," I rasped. "Tucker?"

To my surprise, Lorelei appeared on my other side. The vampire was still sprawled on top of me, and she leaned down and put her fingers up against his neck. After a moment, something flickered in her eyes. Relief, maybe.

"Still alive," she said. "Although his heartbeat seems very faint, weak, and slow."

"Forget about Tucker," Owen growled. "Jo-Jo! Jo-Jo! Where are you?"

"Coming, darling!" Jo-Jo's voice drifted over to me.

Owen started to shove Tucker off me, but I reached out and grabbed his hand.

"No," I rasped. "Tucker saved me. Tell Jo-Jo to work on him first."

Owen frowned. "Are you sure?"

"Yes. Save Tucker. Promise me."

I could tell that he didn't want to do it. That he wanted to grab his blacksmith hammer, raise it up, and cave in Tucker's skull for everything the vampire had done to me, to us. Part of me wanted that too—but I wanted Mason dead more.

Owen gave me a reluctant nod. "Okay. We'll try to save the bastard—if only so that you can kill him yourself later."

I smiled and squeezed his hand. "Thank you." I drew in a breath. "And thank you for coming for me."

Owen squeezed my hand back, tears gleaming in his violet eyes. "I will always come for you, Gin," he growled in a fierce voice. "*Always*."

I opened my mouth to say how much I loved him and that I would always come for him too, but the pain and exhaustion swept over me, and I couldn't hold them back any longer. In an instant, they had sucked me under, drowning me in the darkness.

Sometime later, I was aware of this pricking sensation working its way up and down my body, like a thousand tiny electric needles were relentlessly stabbing their way deeper and deeper into my skin. I grunted with pain, and a warm, soothing hand landed on my forehead.

I opened my eyes to find Jo-Jo leaning over me. She was still wearing her blue dress and gray pearls from the wedding, but her white-blond curls were flying every which way around her head, and her pink lipstick was smeared across her face, along with the rest of her makeup. Jo-Jo looked tired, but another wave of her Air magic surged into my body, and those electric needles returned, healing my many cuts and bruises. This time, I managed to swallow down the snarl in my throat.

I looked around. My friends had moved me out of the pavilion, and I was lying on a rubble-free patch of grass in the cemetery—with Hugh Tucker right next to me. The vampire's eyes were closed, and his face was deathly pale, but his chest rose and fell in slow, steady rhythm.

"Tucker?" I rasped.

"Still alive—for now," Jo-Jo said. "I did my best, but his wounds were bad. Real bad. I fixed his body as best I could, but he wasn't breathing for a few minutes. We'll just have to wait and see if he wakes up."

Worry rippled through her voice. I could hear what she wasn't saying—that my wounds were bad too, and we'd just have to wait and see.

"I don't have any magic left to feed you," Bria said, a sob rising in her voice. "I don't have any way to help you heal her."

"It's okay, Bria." Lorelei spoke up. "I still have magic left. I can help Jo-Jo."

"Me too," Owen chimed in.

"And me," Sophia rasped.

I blinked, and I realized that my friends were gathered around, forming a circle around me. Owen, Finn, Silvio, Bria, Lorelei, Sophia. They'd all come to rescue me. Tears gathered in my eyes, and I opened my mouth to tell them how much their love and friendship meant, but I didn't get the chance.

"All right," Jo-Jo said in a low, tired voice. "Let's see what we can do."

She leaned down and looked into my eyes. "I'm sorry, darling, but this is going to hurt. A lot."

I tried to nod, but another wave of her Air magic washed over me, stronger than before. Then Lorelei's Ice and metal. Then Sophia's Air. And finally, Owen's metal. All mixing and mingling together in my body.

I screamed once, but the pain was too much to bear, and the blackness swept me away again.

Sometime later, the pain finally faded away, and I drifted in and out of consciousness, seeing little snapshots of what was happening. Owen carrying me out of the cemetery. Finn and Silvio laying me on a bed in one of Jo-Jo's guest rooms. Jo-Jo and Sophia approaching me with bowls full of warm water and washcloths. Bria gripping my hand in hers.

"Sweet dreams, Gin," my sister whispered, and kissed my forehead.

I didn't have sweet dreams, but I didn't have any more nightmarish memories. There was just more blackness, but I welcomed the void.

Sunlight streaming in through the windows woke me the next morning. The rest of the house was quiet, so I lay in bed, thinking about everything that had happened and how close Mason had come to killing me. He *would* have killed me, if not for Hugh Tucker. I didn't know how I felt about the vampire saving my life again. I just hoped Tucker was still breathing so I could figure it out.

Eventually, I started hearing people moving around downstairs. Time to get up and face the new day and all the new problems it would bring along with it.

I threw back the covers and got out of bed. Despite Jo-Jo healing me, every single part of my body still felt stiff and sore from Mason's pummeling, but I put on a fresh set of clothes, trudged downstairs, and headed into the salon.

Owen, Finn, and Bria were sprawled on couches around the room, checking their phones, while Silvio was standing at the long counter, typing away on his laptop.

Jo-Jo was perched in a seat next to Hugh Tucker, who was lying back in a salon chair. Like me, the vampire had also been cleaned up and was now wearing a black fleece robe patterned with white pirate skulls. I made a mental note to buy Sophia a new robe to replace this one. Tucker's eyes were still closed, but his face wasn't quite as deathly pale as it had been last night, and his breathing seemed easier.

"So I take it the bastard's going to live?" I drawled.

Everyone snapped around to me.

"Gin!" They all shouted in unison.

In an instant, I was swarmed, and Owen, Finn, and Bria tackled me for a group hug that almost sent me tumbling to the floor. Even Silvio joined in, giving me a very firm pat on the shoulder.

"All right, guys, all right," I said with a laugh. "I'm okay. Really."

Finn, Bria, and Silvio retreated, but Owen threaded his fingers through mine and sat down next to me on one of the couches.

"What happened?" I asked. "After Emery Slater marched me out of the wedding?"

Finn gestured at my sister. "Bria and Lorelei used their Ice magic to disable the rune bombs that Liam Carter and his men left behind at the country club."

Bria snorted. "Those weren't bombs. They were more like weak firecrackers. All Lorelei and I had to do was Ice them over, and they fizzled right out. Even if the bombs had gone off, they wouldn't have hurt anyone."

"Either way, you were magnificent." Finn winked at her, and Bria grinned back at him.

Finn looked at me again. "As soon as we escaped the ballroom, we jumped into our cars and went over to the historical association mansion, since that seemed like the most logical place for Emery to take you. We heard the noise of the fight, and we had just reached the cemetery when Tucker played hero and Mason collapsed that roof on top of you both."

My brother shivered, telling me how worried he'd been.

"We managed to drive off Emery and the giants and make it over to the pavilion," Bria said. "I could feel how you were using your Ice magic to protect yourself against the falling stones, so I got as close to the pavilion as I could and tried to feed you my power."

"Well, it worked. I could sense your magic mixing with mine. You saved me, Bria."

My sister smiled, but, like Finn, she still looked troubled.

"Of course, the only problem with the Ice dome was that it cut off your air," Bria continued. "I thought you were going to suffocate before we got you out of it, but Owen smashed through it with his blacksmith hammer."

I leaned over and kissed his cheek. "My hero."

Owen grinned and hugged me close, but he couldn't quite hide the concern in his eyes. He too realized just how close Mason had come to killing me.

"What happened in the cemetery?" Owen asked. "Why was Mason so angry with you?"

I told the others about the fake ledger. When I finished, they looked even more worried than before.

"Now what, darling?" Jo-Jo asked. "Do you have any idea where the real ledger is?"

I shrugged, not really answering her question. "Now we regroup. Where are the others?"

"Sophia is at the Pork Pit, keeping an eye on things there," Finn said. "Most everyone else is hunkered down in their respective homes, although Phillip Kincaid took Eva, Violet, and Catalina over to the *Delta Queen*."

The *Delta Queen* was Phillip's riverboat casino and full of giant guards who were loyal to him. The girls would be safe there.

Then another thought occurred to me, and I grimaced. "What about Mallory and Mosley? And their guests?" I sighed. "I totally ruined their wedding."

"You didn't ruin anything, Gin," a voice called out.

Mallory stepped into the salon, followed by Mosley and Lorelei. I let out a quiet sigh of relief that the dwarves were in one piece, then got to my feet and went over to them.

"Can you ever forgive me?" I asked.

Mallory hugged me tight, cracking my back in the process. "There's nothing to forgive. Stuey and I got married, and everyone was okay, except for a few cuts and bruises. That's the most important thing."

Tears stung my eyes at her easy forgiveness, and I hugged her back.

"So now what?" Finn asked. "Because I don't know about you, but I've run out of ideas where to look for this stupid ledger."

"Forget the ledger. What are you going to do with *him*?" Bria jerked her thumb over her shoulder at Tucker, who was still unconscious on the salon chair.

I eyed the vampire. Part of me wanted to grab a pair of Jo-Jo's scissors, march over, and stab him through the heart. But I couldn't do that. Not now, after he had saved my life—again. Not when he had been willing to sacrifice himself for me. Like it or not, Hugh Tucker and I were in this thing together.

I turned to Lorelei. "If we take him to my shipping container, will you keep an eye on him?"

The container was my secret hideout, the place where I had stashed much of the information I had on the Circle. It was currently located in Lorelei's shipping yard on the bank of the Aneirin River.

Surprise filled Lorelei's face, along with something else I couldn't quite put a name to. After a few seconds, she nodded. "Yeah, I can watch him. But why do you want to take him to your shipping container?"

"Because I want him out of sight while he heals."

Understanding flashed in her eyes. "You want Mason to think Tucker is dead."

I shot my thumb and forefinger at her. "Bingo. Bria's right. Forget the missing ledger for right now. We have something even better—*Tucker*. He has worked for Mason and the Circle practically his entire life, so he knows all about how Mason and the other members operate."

Silvio's eyes narrowed. "You're going to use him for information. That's why you had Jo-Jo save him."

I stared down at the unconscious vampire. "Absolutely. As soon as he's better, Hugh Tucker is going to tell me everything he knows about the Circle."

✲ 25 ✲

After that, we all got busy. Well, my friends got busy. I lounged on a salon chair beside Tucker, resting and getting my strength back while we hashed out our next moves.

Crisis or not, everyone had jobs, friends, and family members that needed attention. Everyone agreed to be careful and to keep up the buddy system we'd employed so far.

I thought my friends would be safe enough for the time being. According to Silvio and Finn, none of their sources had seen Mason, Emery, or the giants since they had fled from the Circle cemetery. My uncle and his minions were out there somewhere, regrouping, just like we were. It would probably be a while before our next clash, but I still warned everyone to be vigilant in the meantime.

Owen, Finn, and Bria all needed to swing by their respective offices and check on various things, so they left together. Mallory and Mosley stepped outside to pull Mosley's car closer to the house, so that Tucker could be transported over to my shipping container. Jo-Jo and Silvio went to help the two dwarves, but Lorelei stayed in the salon, staring down at Tucker, an unreadable expression on her face. I went over and stood beside her.

"It's okay to like him," I said. "He is nothing if not interesting."

She jerked back, as though I had slapped her across the face. "*Me*? Like *him*? Hugh Tucker, your hated nemesis?" She let out a bitter laugh, then shook her head, making her black braid flap against her shoulders. "I wouldn't be a very good friend if I did that."

"You've been an *amazing* friend," I said in a firm voice. "You came to rescue me, and you helped Jo-Jo save me. I wouldn't be here if it wasn't for you and everyone else. Including him."

I jerked my head at the unconscious vampire. "He saved me too, and I can't forget that, no matter how much I might want to. So you have my blessing. No matter what happens between the two of you."

Lorelei's face softened. She nodded at me, and I returned the gesture.

Jo-Jo and Silvio came inside, scooped up Tucker, and carried him out to the car. Then Jo-Jo went with Lorelei, Mallory, and Mosley to get the vampire settled in his new accommodations. That left Silvio and me in the salon.

Silvio was still standing at the counter and typing away on his laptop, and I was on one of the couches, trying to take a little catnap, although the staccato *stab-stab-stab-stab* of his fingers on the keyboard was making it difficult. A phone chirped, and Silvio glared at the device, which was lying on the counter next to his elbow.

"Why don't you answer that?" I asked.

"Because it's not my phone. It's *your* phone," he replied in an annoyed voice. "Roslyn brought it over while you were sleeping this morning. She found it in Mallory's suite with the rest of your things."

He gestured at a large brown paper bag sitting on the counter, and I went over and looked inside. Roslyn had packed up my regular clothes, shoes, and everything else I'd taken to the country club yesterday, along with the two knives I'd thrown down onto the ballroom dance floor when the giants captured me. I tucked the weapons up my sleeves and made a mental note to thank Roslyn for retrieving them.

My phone chirped again, and Silvio eyed the device like he wanted to break it apart with his bare hands.

"Problems?" I drawled.

"Your phone has been beeping every fifteen minutes or so. Someone keeps texting you, although I can't see who because your phone is locked."

I grinned. "Ah. You're upset because I changed my password, and you can't snoop on my device anymore."

Silvio sniffed. "It's not *snooping*, per se. I consider it part of my duties as your assistant to check your messages."

My phone chirped again. Silvio rolled his eyes, grabbed the device, and shoved it into my hand.

"Answer it, and tell whoever that is to knock off their incessant messaging," he growled. "It's driving me crazy."

He returned to his laptop, and I unlocked the phone with my new password—*BarbecueIsForever*. I scrolled through the text messages, but they were all variations on the same theme.

You still alive?

A relieved breath escaped my lips, and a tight knot of tension loosened in my chest. Even better, those relentless, paranoid sharks finally stopped swimming around in the watery tank of worry in my stomach.

I texted back. ***Still alive. Need to meet. Salon.***

I sent the message and waited for the reply. My phone beeped less than a minute later.

On my way.

I put my phone away and looked at Silvio. "Come on. Let's make some hot chocolate and sit on the porch."

He frowned, wondering what I was up to, but he headed into the kitchen. I rifled through the things Roslyn had brought to the salon, plucked something out of my purse, and slid it into my pocket. Then I went into the kitchen to make the hot chocolate.

Thirty minutes later, Silvio and I were out on the front porch. My assistant settled himself in one of the rocking chairs, with a blanket over his lap to ward off the chill, but I sat down on the steps where I'd had that long-ago conversation with Fletcher.

Being in this spot made me feel close to him again. Fletcher had given me some good advice back then, maybe the most important advice he'd ever shared, and I was going to follow it to the letter from here on out. Because being smarter than Mason was the only way I was going to beat my uncle at his own game.

Silvio and I hadn't been outside long, maybe five minutes, when a baby-blue sports car cruised up the hill and parked in Jo-Jo's driveway. The driver got out and walked over to the front porch.

Liam Carter.

Sometime since the cemetery fight, Liam had showered and changed into a fresh navy suit. Curiously enough, he was holding a box of gourmet chocolates under his arm.

Silvio snarled, shot to his feet, and started across the porch. I stood up and grabbed his arm, stopping the vampire from launching himself at the other man.

"You bastard!" Silvio hissed. "How dare you show your face here!"

"Hey! Hey!" I said. "It's okay. I asked Liam to come."

My words sank in, and Silvio frowned at me. "What? Why would you do that? He changed sides. He sold you out. He helped Emery Slater kidnap you!"

"Yes, he did," I replied. "But Liam isn't working for Emery or Mason. Not really. He works for *me*."

Silvio blinked and blinked, glancing from me to Liam and back again. "But…but he *shot* you. And he shot at *me*. And his men planted those rune bombs on the ballroom doors to keep us from going after you."

Liam shrugged. "Sorry about that. I had to make it look good." He cleared his throat, stepped forward, and held out the box in his hand to the vampire. "But I brought you some apology chocolates. Your favorite kind. The ones you mentioned on the phone the other night."

Silvio stared at the box, then whirled around and stabbed his finger at me. "Explain yourself, Gin. Right now."

"When we first saw Mason at the Eaton Estate a few weeks ago, I could feel how strong he was in his magic, and I knew I couldn't beat him elemental-to-elemental. Not only that, but I realized I needed more information about Mason, his magic, and how the Circle works. So I decided to try to plant someone in Mason's organization, someone inside the Circle who could give me that information."

"Reverse Trojan Horse," Liam said in a helpful voice. "Well, maybe just Regular Trojan Horse in this case."

I nodded. "Something like that."

Silvio frowned again. "What are you two talking about?"

"I'll explain it later," I said. "Once I killed those two giants at Blue Ridge Cemetery, I knew it was just a matter of time before Mason realized that I'd offed his men and came after me and everyone I care about. So I decided to hire Liam for protection."

Understanding dawned in Silvio's eyes. "But not for protection. Not really. You *wanted* Mason to steal Liam away, so you could finally have your inside man."

"Yep. I knew Mason had taken the bait when I saw Liam's car at the historical association mansion when Bria and I dug up the ledger in the Circle cemetery."

"I just pretended to let Mason woo me over to the dark side," Liam added. "I met with him that afternoon, hemmed and hawed a bit, and then took the bribe he offered me to betray Gin."

I looked at Liam. "Although I have to confess that you had me going at the wedding. I didn't know whose side you were really on. At least, not until after you shot me. Even then, I still had some doubts."

Silvio threw up his hands. "And how did that prove Liam was on *your* side?"

"Because Liam is an expert marksman," I replied. "He could have easily incapacitated me with that shot, but it was only a through-and-through. The damage was minimal. Besides, I told Liam, if he had to shoot someone, to make sure it was me."

My assistant sighed and shook his head. "If anyone else said that, I would say they were crazy. But that sort of warped logic makes perfect sense for you, Gin."

I shrugged. We both knew I would rather take a bullet, literally, than let any of my friends do it.

Silvio turned back to the other man. "But you shot at me too," he accused.

"I had to make it look good," Liam repeated. "The reception was a test. Mason didn't trust me then, and I knew that firing at you and wounding Gin would help sell the illusion that I was on his side."

"That bullet whizzing by my head didn't feel like an *illusion*," Silvio growled. "And I'm certain the one punching into Gin's arm didn't either."

"I know, but it couldn't be helped. That's why I brought apology chocolates." Liam glanced at me. "Sorry, Gin. They only had one box at the store."

I shrugged again. Liam's loyalty was far more valuable than a box of sweets.

"I really am sorry about the wedding," he continued. "I didn't know Emery and her men were going to kidnap you until they showed up. Given the time crunch, it was all I could do to figure out how to mostly defuse the rune bombs she brought along."

I'd figured as much, and Liam had made the right choice, trying to protect the innocent guests.

He held the box of chocolates out to Silvio again. After a few seconds, the vampire grudgingly took it.

"Just because I'm accepting these doesn't mean I forgive you," Silvio snapped. "One lousy box of chocolates doesn't even *begin* to make up for what you did."

Liam grinned. "Well, then, I look forward to making it up to you the rest of the way."

Silvio snorted at his flirting, then looked at me. "Nor does it make up for keeping me in the dark and all your other reckless, stupid actions. Mason almost killed you, Gin."

Yes, he almost did, which was something I didn't want to dwell on right now. I'd have plenty of nightmares to remind me.

"But Mason didn't kill me, and we all live to fight another day." I turned to Liam. "Does he trust you now?"

Liam nodded. "I think so. I put him up in one of my safe houses last night, although Emery moved him this morning. She definitely doesn't trust me, and she doesn't like me bending her boss's ear, but I've got my foot in the door."

"Good. Why don't you go inside and have some hot chocolate? You and Silvio can talk about how to set up a secure communication method and a regular meeting schedule. I want to know everything Mason does."

Liam turned to Silvio, and a grin slowly spread across his face. "What do you say, Silvy? Coffee date?"

The vampire shuddered a little, as though those words had a bad connotation, but he sighed. "Fine. Although you do realize that we're only going to be even when *I* get to shoot at *you*."

Liam's grin widened. "You say the sweetest things."

Silvio huffed, but they went inside the house. I waited until their footsteps had faded away, then sat back down on the top step again. Now that I was alone, I scooted over to the side where my spider rune was. When Fletcher had first carved the symbol, it had been rough, raw, and jagged, but the passage of time had smoothed it out until it was little more than a faint mark in the wood.

I traced my fingers over the rune and smiled, thinking of the old man. Then I glanced around, making sure I was still alone. When I was sure no one was going to stick their head outside to see what I was doing, I palmed a knife and crouched down in front of the porch. I studied the steps a moment, then stabbed my knife into the seam at the end of the top step.

I wiggled the blade back and forth, making the wood creak and groan and slowly peeling up that floorboard. Ever since I'd had that dream, that memory, of sitting here with Fletcher, I had been thinking about this place, and it had finally occurred to me that I'd never seen the old man actually *fix* this step, although I knew he had, since it had stopped squeaking soon after our talk.

The plank finally popped up. I set it aside, then leaned forward, my heart picking up speed as I peered down into the hollow space beneath, hoping, hoping, hoping I would finally find what I was looking for.

And I did.

Something gleamed in the shadows, and I reached down, grabbed the item, and pulled it up into the light. It was a silverstone box just like the one I'd found in Tucker's grave. My heart pounded even faster, and my hands shook as I shattered the padlock with my Ice magic, tossed it aside, and cracked open the box to find…

A black ledger wrapped in plastic.

This was it. This was the *real* ledger. I knew it in my bones.

My hands were still shaking, but I peeled away the plastic, grabbed the ledger, and opened it. To my surprise, it was blank, except for a single series of numbers written in the center of the first page in Fletcher's spidery handwriting.

It was another bank account number.

I once again wondered how much money Fletcher had stolen from Mason, but I quickly pushed that thought aside. The dollar amount didn't really matter, although it must be substantial for Mason to go to so much trouble to try to retrieve the funds.

No, the thing that really mattered was that Mason needed the money for something *right now*. Thanks to my mother's blue ledger, I had plenty of information on the Circle's past misdeeds, but I had no idea what the group's current plans were. Tucker could help with that, though, when—*if*—he woke up.

Even if the vampire remained comatose, I was going to recover Mason's money from the account Fletcher had stashed it in. I might not have more elemental magic than my uncle, but money was another form of power and could be wielded just as viciously as one of my silverstone knives. Cutting Mason off at his financial knees just might be the first step to actually killing him.

I started to close the ledger, but then I realized that something else had been tucked into the front—an envelope with my name written on it.

I set the ledger aside. My hands were still shaking, but I managed to open the envelope and pull out the letter inside.

Dearest Gin,

If you are reading this, then I am dead. You probably know why I am writing this and the awful thing I have to confess.

I worked for Mason Mitchell.

Mason is your uncle and the head of the Circle. I hurt people for him. I killed people for him. There are no words to describe how much pain and guilt this causes me, even to this day, or how much I wish I could go back in time and undo all the damage I did on Mason's behalf.

I could take the easy way out and blame it all on Mason. On how he lied to me and manipulated me. On how he promised to help me find and kill Deirdre for threatening Finn when my boy was a baby.

But that's not the whole truth.

No, the whole truth is that I was heartbroken after Deirdre's betrayal. She was gone, but I wanted to hurt her, even though she wasn't here anymore. So I settled for hurting other people instead. Unbeknownst to me at the time, one of those people would eventually be you, when Mason killed Tristan, your father.

This is my deepest regret and my greatest shame.

Eventually, I learned the truth about Mason, but that didn't change all the horrible things I'd already done for him.

Still, I tried to atone for it the best I could. I'm sure you remember Wade Brockton, the accountant who died, and our conversation on this very porch that night so long ago. Wade didn't embezzle money just to help his sick daughter—he stole money for me too.

I promised to protect Wade, but I failed in that, just like I failed you.

But I still have the money. In the ledger, you will find the number to a bank account. Show it to Finn. He can help you access the funds.

Mason only cares about three things: his magic, his money, and the power those things give him. I couldn't do anything about his magic, but I took away his money. It's up to you to finish doing what I couldn't, to destroy Mason and the Circle.

We might not always be richer or stronger than our enemies, but we can always fight smarter.

With all of my love,
Now and always,
Fletcher

By the time I finished reading the letter, tears were streaming down my cheeks, and that sharpest sting of Fletcher's betrayal throbbed in my heart again. I wished he had trusted me with the truth, but I could understand why he had kept it to himself.

Fletcher had been ashamed, and he hadn't wanted me to

view him in a different light or think less of him. And I probably would have if he had told me the truth that night on the porch. I'd been young then. I might have seen how ugly the world could be, but I hadn't fully realized how easily people could get turned around and twisted up in the muck until they didn't even recognize themselves anymore.

Fletcher was right. Nothing could change what he'd done. All the people he'd hurt and killed for Mason, all the times he'd lied to me, all the ways Mason had hurt me and my family. But the old man had tried to make up for his mistakes, and he'd left the ledger for me to find. In the end, Fletcher had tried to do the right thing, and I couldn't ignore that.

Back at the Circle cemetery, Tucker said that Mason had killed my father because he had been jealous of Tristan. Maybe that had been part of it, but I thought that Tristan's betrayal was the thing that had truly driven Mason over the edge, much like Fletcher's deception had wrecked me over the past few days.

Being betrayed so thoroughly by a loved one brought a whole host of emotions along with it—anger, disbelief, embarrassment, and, most of all, a dark, seething bitterness.

Mason had embraced that bitterness, reveled in it, and so many people were dead as a result, including most of my family.

I didn't want to be like my uncle. I didn't want Fletcher's betrayal to linger, to fester, to warp me like Tristan's betrayal had warped Mason. If it did, I would *never* be able to trust anyone ever again, not even my closest loved ones. The uncertainty, worry, and paranoia would slowly eat away at my relationships and would be far worse than any physical torture Mason could ever inflict on me. I needed my friends, my family, now more than ever, and there was only one way to make peace with everything that had happened.

"I forgive you, Fletcher," I said in a soft voice.

As soon as the words left my lips, I felt lighter, freer, and that sharpest sting in my heart faded to a slightly more manageable throb. Oh, the wound would ache for quite some time, but the hard part was done, and now I could work on moving past the hurt Fletcher had caused me. It might take me a while—it might take me a long, long while—but I'd get there eventually.

I traced my fingers over my spider rune that the old man had carved into the wood so long ago. Then I grabbed the ledger, got to my feet, and headed inside the house to tell Silvio and Liam what I'd found.

A weapon to utterly destroy Mason fucking Mitchell.

✲ GIN BLANCO WILL RETURN ✲

About the Author

Jennifer Estep is a *New York Times*, *USA Today*, and international bestselling author, prowling the streets of her imagination in search of her next fantasy idea. She is the author of the following series:

The Elemental Assassin series: The books focus on Gin Blanco, an assassin codenamed the Spider who can control the elements of Ice and Stone. When she's not busy battling bad guys and righting wrongs, Gin runs a barbecue restaurant called the Pork Pit in the fictional Southern metropolis of Ashland. The city is also home to giants, dwarves, vampires, and elementals—Air, Fire, Ice, and Stone.

The Crown of Shards series: The books focus on Everleigh Blair, who is 17th in line for the throne of Bellona, a kingdom steeped in gladiator tradition. But when the unthinkable happens, Evie finds herself fighting for her life—both inside and outside the gladiator arena.

The Mythos Academy spinoff series: The books focus on Rory Forseti, a 17-year-old Spartan girl who attends the Colorado branch of Mythos Academy. Rory's parents were Reapers, which makes her the most hated girl at school. But with a new group of Reapers and mythological monsters on the rise, Rory is the only one who can save her academy.

The Mythos Academy original series: The books focus on Gwen Frost, a 17-year-old Gypsy girl who has the gift of psychometry, or the ability to know an object's history just by touching it. After a serious freak-out with her magic, Gwen is shipped off to Mythos Academy, a school for the descendants of ancient warriors like Spartans, Valkyries, Amazons, and more.

The Black Blade series: The books focus on Lila Merriweather, a 17-year-old thief who lives in Cloudburst Falls, West Virginia, a town dubbed "the most magical place in America." Lila does her best to stay off the grid and avoid the Families—or mobs—who control much of the town. But when she saves a member of the Sinclair Family during an attack, Lila finds herself caught in the middle of a brewing war between the Sinclairs and the Draconis, the two most powerful Families in town.

The Bigtime series: The books take place in Bigtime, New York, a city that's full of heroic superheroes, evil ubervillains, and other fun, zany, larger-than-life characters. Each book focuses on a different heroine as she navigates through the city's heroes and villains and their various battles.

For more information on Jennifer and her books, visit her website at www.JenniferEstep.com. You can also follow her on Facebook, Goodreads, BookBub, and Twitter, and sign up for her newsletter on her website.

Happy reading, everyone! ☺

Other Books by Jennifer Estep

THE CROWN OF SHARDS SERIES

Kill the Queen
Protect the Prince
Crush the King

THE MYTHOS ACADEMY SPINOFF SERIES
FEATURING RORY FORSETI

Spartan Heart
Spartan Promise
Spartan Destiny

THE MYTHOS ACADEMY SERIES
FEATURING GWEN FROST

Books

Touch of Frost
Kiss of Frost
Dark Frost
Crimson Frost
Midnight Frost
Killer Frost

E-novellas and short stories

First Frost
Halloween Frost
Spartan Frost

The Black Blade series

Cold Burn of Magic
Dark Heart of Magic
Bright Blaze of Magic

The Bigtime series

Karma Girl
Hot Mama
Jinx
A Karma Girl Christmas (holiday story)
Nightingale
Fandemic

CPSIA information can be obtained
at www.ICGtesting.com
Printed in the USA
LVHW111541090720
660247LV00002B/171